# BROWN'S REQUIEM

James Ellroy

First published in Arrow in 1995

15

Copyright © 1981 James Ellroy

First published in the United Kingdom in 1984 by
Alison & Busby Ltd

Arrow Books Limited
The Random House Group Limited
20 Vauxhall Bridge Road, London SW1V 2SA

www.rbooks.co.uk

Addresses for companies within
The Random House Group Limited can be found at:
www.randomhouse.co.uk/offices.htm

The Random House Group Limited Reg. No. 954009

A CIP catalogue record for this book
is available from the British Library

ISBN 9780099649014

The Random House Group Limited supports The Forest Stewardship
Council (FSC), the leading international forest certification organisation.
All our titles that are printed on Greenpeace approved FSC certified paper
carry the FSC logo. Our paper procurement policy can be found at:
www.rbooks.co.uk/environment

Printed and bound in Great Britain by
CPI Antony Rowe, Chippenham, Wiltshire

**To Randy Rice**

# New Author Introduction

I wrote this novel sixteen years ago. I was a thirty-one-year-old geek working as a caddy at Bel-Air Country Club in Los Angeles. I had recently quit drinking and using drugs – and I was determined to write an autobiographical epic second to none.

I quickly realized that my life, though more colourful than most, was essentially an inward journey that would not lend itself all that well to fiction. I then ladled a big load of violent intrigue into my already simmering, tres personal plot – and the result is the novel you are about to read.

*Brown's Requiem* is heavily beholden to Raymond Chandler – an icon I've come to dislike quite a bit. Big Ray was a true original who created a truly original style that lazy-assed writers have been imitating with some success for many years. I owe Ray a two-fold debt: he got me going, and he showed me that imitating him was a dead-end street on GenreHack Boulevard.

This is a righteous *private eye* novel: fast, profane, densely plotted for a first work. It's got that discursive philosophical tone that all good, bad and indifferent private eye novels have. I dig this book because its a summation of my life up to that point when I picked up a pen to write it.

I hope *you* dig *Brown's Requiem*. I hope you read all my books in succession and come to believe that each one is better than the previous.

*James Ellroy, Kansas, 7th April 1995*

# 1

# I, PRIVATE EYE

# 1

Business was good. It was the same thing every summer. The smog and heat rolled in, blanketing the basin; people succumbed to torpor and malaise; old resolves died; old commitments went unheeded. And I profited: my desk was covered with repo orders, ranging in make and model from Datsun Sedan to Eldorado Ragtop, and in territory from Watts to Pacoima. Sitting at my desk, listening to the Beethoven Violin Concerto and drinking my third cup of coffee, I calculated my fees, less expenses. I sighed and blessed Cal Myers and his paranoia and greed. Our association dates back to my days with Hollywood Vice, when we were both in trouble and I did him a big favor. Now, years later, his guilty *noblesse oblige* supports me in something like middle-class splendor, tax free.

Our arrangement is simple, and a splendid hedge against inflation: Cal's down payments are the lowest in L.A., and his monthly payments the highest. My fee for a repossession is the sum of the owner's monthly whip-out. For this Cal gets the dubious satisfaction of having a licensed private investigator do his ripoffs, and implicit silence on my part regarding all his past activities. He shouldn't worry. I would never rat on him for anything, under any circumstances. Still, he does. We never talk about these things; our relationship is largely elliptical. When I was on the sauce, he felt he had the upper hand, but now that I'm sober he accords me more intelligence and cunningness than I possess.

I surveyed the figures on my scratch pad: 11 cars, a total of $1,881.00 in monthlies, less 20 percent or $376.20 for my driver. $1,504.80 for me. Things looked good. I took the record off the turntable, dusted it carefully, and replaced it in its sleeve. I looked at the Joseph Karl Stieler print on

my living room wall: Beethoven, the greatest musician of all
time, scowling, pen in hand, composing the *Missa Sol-
emnis,* his face alight with inward heroism.

I called Irwin, my driver, and told him to meet me at my
place in an hour and to bring coffee—there was work on
the line. He was grumpy until I mentioned money. I hung
up and looked out my window. It was getting light. Hollywood, below me, was filling up with hazy sunshine. I felt a
slight tremor: part caffeine, part Beethoven, part a last
passage of night air. I felt my life was going to change.

It took Irwin forty minutes to make the run from
Kosher Canyon. Irwin is Jewish, I'm a second generation
German-American, and we get along splendidly; we agree
on all important matters: Christianity is vulgar, capitalism
is here to stay, rock and roll is evil, and Germany and
Judaica, as antithetical as they may be, have produced
history's greatest musicians. He beeped the horn, and I
clipped on my holster and went outside.

Irwin handed me a large cup of Winchell's black and a
bag of donuts as I got in the car beside him. I thanked him,
and dug in. "Business first," I said. "We've got eleven delinquents. Mostly in South Central L.A. and the East Valley. I've got credit reports on all of them and the people all
have jobs. I think we can hit one a day, early mornings at
the home addresses. That will get you to work on time.
What we don't snatch there, I'll work on myself. Your cut
comes to three hundred seventy-six dollars and twenty cents,
payable next time I see Cal. Today we visit Leotis McCarver
at 6318 South Mariposa."

As Irwin swung his old Buick onto the Hollywood Freeway southbound, I caught him looking at me out of the
corner of his eye and I knew he was going to say something serious. I was right. "Have you been all right, Fritz?"
he asked. "Can you sleep? Are you eating properly?"

I answered, somewhat curtly, "I feel better in general,
the sleep comes and goes, and I eat like a horse or not at
all."

"How long's it been, now? Eight, nine months?"

"It's been exactly nine months and six days, and I feel
terrific. Now let's change the subject." I hated to cut Irwin
off, but I feel more comfortable with people who talk
obliquely.

We got off the freeway around Vermont and Manchester and headed west to the Mariposa address. I checked the repo order: a 1978 Chrysler Cordoba, loaded. $185 a month. License number CTL 412. Irwin turned north on Mariposa, and in a few minutes we were at the 6300 block. I fished out my master keys and detached the '78 Chrysler's. 6318 was a two-story pink stucco multi-unit dump, ultra-modern twenty years ago, with side entrances and an ugly schematic flamingo in black metal on the wall facing the street. The garage was subterranean, running back the whole length of the building.

Irwin parked in front. I handed him the original of the repo order and tucked the carbon into my back pocket. "You know the drill, Irwin. Stand by your car, whistle once if anyone enters the garage, twice if the fuzz show up. Be prepared to explain what I'm doing. Hold on to the repo order." Irwin knows the procedure as well as I do, but even after five years of legalized ripoffs, the whole deal still makes me nervous, and I repeat the instructions for luck. Strange things can happen, have happened, and the L.A.P.D. is notoriously trigger-happy. Having been one of them, I know.

I dropped down into the garage. I expected it to be dark, but the morning sunshine reflecting off the windows of the adjacent apartments provided plenty of light. When I spotted CTL 412, the third car from the end, I started to laugh. Cal Myers was going to shit. Leotis McCarver was undoubtedly black, but his car was a full dress taco wagon: chopped, channeled, lowered, with a candy apple, lime-green paint job with orange and yellow flames covering the hood and sweeping halfway back over the sides of the vehicle. Black enamel script over the rear wheel wells announced that this was the "Dragon Wagon." I got out my master key and opened it. The interior was just as esoteric: fuzzy black and white zebra-striped upholstery, pink velveteen dice hanging from the rear-view mirror, and a furry orange accelerator pedal in the shape of a naked foot. The customizing must have cost old Leotis a fortune.

I was still laughing when I heard the scrape of a footstep off to my left near the backend of the garage. I turned and saw a black man almost as big as I am striding toward me. There was no time to avoid a confrontation. When he was ten feet away, he screamed "Motherfucker" and charged me. I was in the walkway, now, and just before he made contact I sidestepped and tripped him with a kick at his knee. As he struggled to get to his feet I kicked him once in the face, once in the neck, and once in the groin. He was moaning and spitting out teeth.

I dragged him over between two cars near the back of the garage and patted him down for weapons. Nothing. I left him there, got into his chariot, and pulled out onto Mariposa. Irwin was still standing there by his car, as if nothing had happened. "He tried to jump me, and I waxed him. Get out of here. Tomorrow, same time, my place." Irwin turned pale. This was the first time anything like this had happened. "Didn't you hear anything?" I yelled. I jammed on the gas, peeling rubber.

I looked in the fur-bordered, rear-view mirror. Irwin was just starting to get into his car. He looked like he was trembling. I hoped he wouldn't quit me.

I turned left on Slauson and right on Western, half a mile later. I had been driving for five minutes or so when I discovered that *I* was trembling. It got worse, so bad that I could hardly hold the wheel steady. Then I felt my stomach start to churn and turn over. I pulled into the parking lot of a liquor store, got out, and vomited on the pavement until my stomach and lungs ached. My vomit tasted like coffee and sugar and fear. After a few minutes I started to calm down. A group of gangly black youths lounging against the liquor store wall and passing around a bottle of cheap wine had watched the whole scene, laughing at me like I was some rare breed of alien from outer space. I took several deep breaths, got back into the car and headed out to the Valley to see Cal Myers.

By the time I hit the freeway, my adrenalin rush had subsided. In five years as a repo-man I had had a dozen or so such encounters, been shot at twice, and beat up badly once. But this was my first confrontation since getting sober, and I was pleased that the old instincts and tricks were still there. I don't like hurting people, no sane man does, but there had been no alternative this time. My six years with the fuzz had taught me to read people for signs of violence, and that man had meant to fuck me up.

I recalled another repo from about three years back: a memo had come in from the bank stating that a woman had stiffed Cal with a rubber check for two months' delinquent payments and three months in advance. I checked out her home address and learned from her neighbors that she was a honcho at the local Scientology Center, a lesbian, and a Welfare recipient. No one at the Scientology joint or her apartment building had seen her for several days, so I broke in late that night and discovered she had moved out completely. When I told Cal what had happened and described the woman's lifestyle, he went nuts. Cal is a big right-winger and took the ditch-out as a personal affront. He told me to find the woman and repo the VW bus regardless of the time and expense involved, promising me a fat bonus if I succeeded.

Through coercion and bribery I got the Scientologists to relinquish the woman's new address in Berkeley. I flew up there, getting drunk on the plane. After sleeping off the booze in a rented room, I took a cab to the address I had been given. No VW bus, no one at home. I had the cabbie run me by the Scientology Celebrity Center. XLB841 was not in the lot, or on any of the surrounding blocks. I told him that we had some waiting to do, promising him fifty dollars plus the meter if he kept me company. He agreed.

Berkeley gave me the creeps: the people passing by looked aesthetic and angry, driven inward by forces they couldn't comprehend and rendered sickly by their refusal to eat meat. A lot of people passed through the center, but I didn't notice any celebrities.

Finally the VW bus pulled in. Suddenly I was pissed. I had tickets for the L.A. Philharmonic that night, and here I was, four hundred miles away, putting the arm on some counter-culture bimbo for her sleazy bus. Rather than waiting until she entered the building and pulling a simple ripoff, I ran across the street and intercepted her. Flashing my repo order in her face, I yelled, "I'm a private investigator and I have a repossession order for this vehicle. You have five minutes to remove your things, then she goes."

The pretty young woman nodded along with me, but when I went for the driver's side, she attacked. I had the key in the door when I felt a sharp kick in my leg. I turned around, the door half open, and caught her purse full in the face. I had never hit a woman, but I swung around and cocked my right arm. Then I hesitated. The heavy leather purse was arcing toward me again, and I grabbed it with both hands, wrenched it free, and hurled it across the parking lot. She was at me now, shrieking and clawing at my face. Her shrieks alerted the Scientologists within the building and I could see them goggling through the plate glass window. I grabbed the woman and flung her to the ground.

Luckily, the bus started easily. People were pouring into the parking lot. I swung out into the alley behind the lot. The woman was on her knees hurling invectives. Her best shot was "urban barracuda." The cabbie was nowhere to be seen. I found the address of the cab company in the phone book, drove over, and left the dispatcher with an envelope containing fifty scoots. He told me Manny, the hackie, would get it when he clocked out.

I went back to Berkeley to move out my things. I sorted out my observations of the woman, her lifestyle, and her reaction when I presented her with the price of her culpability. I came to one conclusion: if life was to be a game of give and take, with a rational morality deciding who gives and who takes, I would have to watch my personal morality, but stay on the side of the takers. I drove over the Bay Bridge and got a room at the Fairmont, a magnum of Mumms and a call girl. L.A. looked good the next afternoon.

I left the freeway and turned onto Ventura Boulevard, where you can buy anything you want, and anything you don't want. The storefronts on this smoggy expressway feature manifestations of every scheme, dream, and hustle the jaded American mind can conceive. It is beyond tragedy, beyond vulgarity, beyond satire. It is supreme guilelessness. There are approximately eight billion of these storefronts—and three billion new and used car lots. Cal Myers has three: Cal's Casa de Carro, Myers' Ford, and Cal's Imports. He makes big bucks. He could sign a contract with a credit agency for his repossessions and save money, but we go back a long time, and he likes as well as fears me.

I ditched the bean-mobile at the Ford lot and dropped the keys and repo order with the sales manager. He told me Cal was across the street at Casa de Carro filming a commercial.

Cal comes from the same ethnic background I do and we both have blunt, ruddy faces, dark hair, and brown eyes. Black German. There the resemblance ends: he's much smaller and far more dynamic-looking. The TV cameras were panning as Cal walked down a line of parked cars, stopping in front of each one and extolling its merits. When he got to the last one, he introduced his dog Barko, a senile German Shepherd, to the TV audience. Barko is a nice enough dog, although he smells. He's been with Cal since before he hit it big. When he was younger, Barko would make on-camera running leaps onto the hoods of cars, turn around, and bark repeatedly at the camera while subtitles were run across the bottom of the TV screen detailing all the wonderful facts about the car he was sitting on. Ingenious. Now that he's decrepit, Barko has been kicked upstairs to a supporting role: a three-second introduction and a pat on the head from Cal.

Rather than stand around watching dreary retakes of Cal's spiel, I walked over to his office and let myself in. The large room was out of another era, and I liked it: knotty pine walls with lush, dark-green Persian carpets over an oak floor, bookshelves crammed with texts and picture books on World War II, knotty pine beams studded with ornamental horseshoes. The largest beam, directly over Cal's giant oak desk, held the Myers Coat of Arms; a vulgar configuration of crosses, flowers, and trumpets around a wounded boar's head. The walls were festooned with framed photographs of Cal in the embrace of various politicians who had welcomed his campaign contributions. There was Cal with Ronnie Reagan, Cal with Sam Yorty, Cal solemnly shaking hands with Tricky Dick Nixon before his fall.

Cal came in, grinning. "Jesus, Fritz," he said, "what a work of fucking art! That guy, what's-his-name? McCoover? We should hire that fucker to redo all our waiting rooms, sales managers' offices, even redesign our magazine ads. Dragon Wagon! Ha! Ha! Ha! You know what it is, don't you, Fritz? It's those goddamned Ricardo Montalban Cordoba ads, 'I am a man, and I know what I want. I want Cordoba!' Old Ricardo is a Mexican, this guy McCoover has gotta be a nigger, he sees the ad on TV, decides he wants to be a Mexican, and fucks up a beautiful car designed for white people! Jesus! Fucking Madison Avenue will fuck you every time." Cal shook his head. "Two good things came out of the deal, though. One, we got old

Dragon Baby back, and two, Larry found a bag of weed in the glove compartment. I told him to take it to Reuben and the guys at the car wash. Sparkle up their day."

I forgot to mention that Cal is also the owner of Cal's Car Wash, a tax dodge that he operates at a loss to "give my customers the best of . . . *total* service for their cars." He hires nothing but wetbacks, and pays them the minimum wage, naturally. Little goodies, such as the weed and the occasional cases of beer he sends over, keep them from seeking more profitable work, like dishwashing. I decided not to tell him about my fight with McCarver. It would only prompt another racist tirade, undoubtedly not as amusing.

"We've got one down, ten to go. I'll get them all provided they haven't skipped town with no leads," I said. "One a day, something like that. All the people are working."

"Good, good. I have faith in you. You'll do your usual superb job." Cal looked at me seriously. "Any plans for your future? It's been a while now; I think you'll make it."

"No real plans, as yet. Europe this fall, though. Work will slack off here, and I can catch the great orchestras of Germany and Austria at the beginning of their concert seasons."

"You speak the language, too."

"Enough to get by. I want to hear great music in its birthplace. That's the main thing. Check out Beethoven House in Bonn, the Vienna Opera, Salzburg. Take a boat ride up the Rhine. I have a feeling that there are all kinds of hot chamber ensembles, unsung, playing in little country inns all over Germany. I've got the money, the weather is good in the fall, and I'm going."

"Before you leave, we'll talk. I'll give you a list of good hotels and restaurants. The food can be great over there—or lousy. Right now, though, I have to split. I'm due on the tee in half an hour. Do you need any money?"

"Not for myself, but I need three hundred seventy-six dollars and twenty cents for my driver." Cal went to the wall safe, extracted the amount, and handed it to me.

"You take care, Fritz," he said, leading me outside, grabbing a twenty-pound bag of dried dog food as he locked the door behind him. He called to his secretary,

"Feed Barko, will you, honey? I think he's hungry." The attractive, bespectacled blonde smiled and went for Barko's dish.

I looked at Cal and shook my head. "All the money that dog has made for you, you cheap fuck, and you still feed him that dried shit?"

"He likes it. It's good for his teeth."

"He doesn't have any teeth."

"Then I must be a cheap fuck. I'll see you, Fritz."

"Take care, Cal."

Larry, the sales manager at Casa, fixed me up with an old Cutlass demo, loaded. I told him I'd hang onto it for a week or so and return it gassed up. Rather than check out the places where my repo'ee's worked, I decided to take the day off, maybe see my friend Walter. I headed down Ventura toward Coldwater. It was ten-thirty, and hot and smoggy already. Driving over the hill I felt good; relaxed and even a little hungry. Coming down into Beverly Hills, I felt again that my life was going to change.

## 2

I've got my own tax shelter, the Brown Detective Agency. It's a detective agency in name only. As far as the IRS knows, I'm a starving gumshoe, declaring nine grand in total income and paying $275 in income tax. I save about eighty bucks a year by claiming myself as a deduction. I used to advertise in the Yellow Pages, before the repo racket got lucrative, and actually handled a few cases, mostly runaway kids who had dropped into the drug culture; but that was years ago, when I had more illusions about myself as an urban manipulator. I still retain my office, an $85 write-off, in a crummy office building on Pico in Rancho Park. I keep my library there and go there when I want to read. It's a dump, but it's air-conditioned.

I decided to head for the office now, since Walter was probably still passed out from last night's bout with T-Bird and TV. I parked in the lot, crossed the alley to the Apple Pan, and returned with three cheeseburgers and two coffees to go. I had wolfed down two of the burgers by the time I opened my office door. It was musty inside. I hit the air-conditioning immediately and settled into my chair.

It's not much of an office; just a small, square room with venetian blinds over a rear window facing an alley, a big, imitation-walnut desk with a naugahyde swivel recliner behind it for myself, a cheesy Bentwood rattan chair for clients, and an official-looking file cabinet that contains no files. There are two photographs of me on the wall, both designed to inspire confidence: Fritz Brown, circa 1968, my Police Academy graduation picture; and one of me in uniform taken three years later. I was drunk when that one was taken and, if you look closely, you can tell.

I scarfed my last burger, flipped on KUSC and sat back. The music was early baroque, a harpsichord trio; nice, but without passion. I listened anyway. Baroque can send you off on a nice little cloud, conducive to quiet thoughts, and I was off on one of them when the doorbell rang. It couldn't be the landlord, since I paid by the year. Probably a salesman. I got up and opened the door. The man standing there didn't look like a salesman, he looked like a refugee from the Lincoln Heights drunk tank. "May I help you" I said.

"Probably," the man replied, "if you're a private detective and this is your office."

"I am, and it is." I pointed to the visitor's chair. "Why don't you have a seat and tell me how I can help you."

He sat, grudgingly, after checking out the furnishings. He was close to forty, and fat, maybe 5'6" or 7" and about 220. He was wearing ridiculous soiled madras slacks three inches too short in the leg, a tight alligator golf shirt that encased his blubbery torso like a sausage skin, and black and white saddle golfshoes with the cleats removed. He looked like a wino golfer out of hell.

"I thought private eyes was older guys, retired from the police force," he said.

"I retired early," I said. "They wouldn't make me chief of police at twenty-five, so I told them to kiss my ass." He got a bang out of that and started to laugh, kind of hysterically. "My name is Fritz Brown, by the way. What's yours?"

"I'm Freddy Baker. You got the same initials as me. You can call me Fat Dog. It ain't no insult, everybody calls me that. I like it."

Fat Dog. Jesus. "Okay, Fat Dog. You can call me Fritz, or Mr. Brown, or Daddy-O. Now, why do you need a private investigator? Incidentally, the fee for my services is one hundred twenty-five dollars a day, plus expenses. Can you afford that?"

"I can afford that, and more. I may not look like no millionaire, but I'm holding heavy. I'll whip some bread on you today, after I tell you what I want." Fat Dog Baker bored into me with wild blue eyes, and said "It's like this. I got this sister, my kid sister, Jane. She's the only family I got. Our folks is dead. For a long time now she's been staying with this rich guy. A Jewish guy. He's old; he don't try no sex stuff with her—it ain't like that—he just supports her and I never see her no more. This guy, he don't want her to have nothing to do with me. He pays for her music lessons, and Janey, my own sister, shines me on like I'm a piece of shit!" His voice had risen to a shout. He was sweating in the air-conditioned room and had clamped his hands around his thighs until his knuckles were white.

"What do you want me to do? Is your sister over eighteen?"

"Yeah, she's twenty-eight. I wasn't thinking about hanging no morals rap on him, I just know he's not right somehow! Somewhere, somehow, he's using my sister for something. She won't believe me, she won't even talk to me! You could follow her, couldn't you? Follow him, tail him around town, check out what he's into? He's fucking her around somehow, and I want to know what's happening."

I decided not to pass it up. I could work it in on my offtime from the repo's. I liked the idea of a surveillance job. It sounded like an interesting change of pace.

"Okay, Fat Dog, I'll do it. I'll tail your sister and this nameless bad guy. We'll give it a week. I'll dig up all I can. But first, I need some more information." I got out a pen and a notebook. "Your sister's name is Jane Baker and she's twenty-eight years old, right?"

"Right."

"Have you got a photograph of her?" Fat Dog got out an old hand-tooled wallet and handed me a snapshot. Jane Baker was a good-looking woman. There was humor in her mouth and intelligence in her eyes. She looked like the antithesis of her fat brother. When I put the photo in my desk drawer, Fat Dog looked at me suspiciously, like he had just handed me an ikon and was afraid I would break it. "Don't worry," I said, "I'll take good care of the picture and get it back to you."

"You do that. It's the only one I got."

"Now tell me about this guy. Anything and everything you know."

"His name's Sol Kupferman. He owns Solly K's Furriers. His address is 8914 Elevado. That's in Beverly Hills up north of Sunset, near the Beverly Hills Hotel."

"Describe him."

"He's about sixty-five, skinny, curly gray hair. Big nose. A typical Hebe."

I wrote down the information, such as it was. "What can

you tell me about Kupferman? I take it your plan is to confront your sister with whatever dirt I can dig up on him."

"You got the picture. That's my plan. I heard lots of things about Solly K. All bad, but all rumors. Caddy yard stuff, you got to consider the source. It's *feelings* I got about him. Like *intuition*, you know what I mean?"

"Yeah. How did your sister meet Kupferman?"

"I was loopin' Hillcrest, maybe ten, twelve years ago. That's right down the street where all the Hebes play golf. She used to visit me in the caddy shack; sometimes she worked the lunchcounter there. But I didn't like her to. Loopers got dirty mouths. Anyway, that's where she met Solly K. He's a member there. He met her out on the golf course. She used to take walks out there. He got her interested in music, got her to start taking music lessons. She's been living with him ever since. She says he's her best friend and her benefactor. She hates me now. That Jew bastard made her hate me!"

Fat Dog was close to losing control, close to tears or some sort of outburst. His anti-Semitism was repulsive, but I wanted to know more about him. Somehow his insane rage grabbed and held me.

I tried to calm him down. "I'll give this my best shot, Fat Dog. I'm going to stick close to both of them and find out everything I can on Kupferman. You hang loose and don't worry."

"Okay. You want some bread now?"

The iconoclast in me trusted there was some kind of logic in his lunacy. "No, if you're holding as heavy as you say you are, I've got nothing to worry about. I'm going to give this thing a week or so. You can pay me then."

Fat Dog whipped out the fat old Mexican wallet again, and this time pulled out his roll. He fanned it in front of me. There must have been sixty or seventy C-notes. I wasn't surprised. A lifetime in Los Angeles had taught me never to take anything at face value, except money. Fat Dog wanted me to be impressed. I hated to disappoint him, so I tossed him a bone. After all, he was tossing me a big one. "Woo! Woo!" I said. "I'm ditching this racket and becoming a caddy! Get me a hot-looking mama with a nice swing who likes to fuck. I'll give her the old nine-iron on the course and off. Woo! Woo!" Fat Dog was laughing like a hyena, threatening to fall off his chair. I had delivered. I hoped he didn't want more. Acting like a buffoon tires me quickly.

After a minute or so, he regained his composure and got serious again. "I know you'll do me good, man. The Fat Dog can judge people, and you're okay."

"Thanks. What's your phone number and address? I'll be needing to get in touch with you."

"I move around a lot, and in the summertime I sleep outside. I'm hard to find. L.A.'s full of fucking psychos, and you never know if one of 'em has your number. You can leave messages for me at the Tap and Cap—that's a beer bar at Santa Monica and Sawtelle. I'll get them."

"Okay, one last thing. You said your sister is a musician. What instrument does she play?"

"One of those big wooden things that stand up on a pole."

The cello. That was interesting. As Fat Dog waved and walked out my office door, I found myself wondering if she could be any good.

I called an old friend who worked L.A.P.D. Records and Information and gave him three names, descriptions, and approximate years of birth: Solomon "Solly K" Kupferman, Frederick "Fat Dog" Baker, and Jane Baker. I told him I would call later for whatever info he had dredged up.

I got my Cutlass demo out of the lot. It looked prosperous enough for surveillance in Beverly Hills. I drove east on Pico and turned left on Beverly Drive, traveling up through the heart of the Beverly Hills business district, passing by shops catering to every taste in fashion, trinketry, and affluent boredom. North of Santa Monica the ritzy business facades gave way to ritzy personal ones: large, beautifully-tended lawns fronting Tudor mansions, Spanish villas, and pseudo-modern chateaus. When I crossed Sunset, the homes became larger still. This was the "pheasant under glass" district.

Sol Kupferman's house was two blocks north of Sunset, off of Coldwater. It was some pad: a Moorish estate, immaculate white with twin turrets flying the California Bear flag. The house was set back at least forty yards from the street. A family of stone bears foraged on the broad front lawn, and there were two Cadillacs parked in the circular driveway: a one-year-old Eldorado convertible and a four- or five-year-old Coupe de Ville.

I parked directly across the street and decided to wait only one hour, not wanting to risk a confrontation with the ubiquitous Beverly Hills fuzz. I got out my binoculars and checked the license numbers on the two Cadillacs. The Eldorado bore a personalized plate: SOL K. The Coupe de Ville had one, too: CELLO-1. So far, my case was working out. I switched on the radio just in time to catch *Luncheon At The Music Center* on KFAC. Thomas Cassidy was interviewing some French bimbo on the state of current French opera. The guy had lousy manners. You could hear him dropping his fork.

I turned off the radio and reached again for my binoculars. I was training them on Kupferman's front door when it opened and a man in a business suit came down the steps carrying a briefcase. I had seen him before, I knew that immediately, but it took a few seconds for my formidable memory to supply the time and place: the Club Utopia, late 1968, just before the place burned itself into immortality. The man—who fit Fat Dog's description of Kupferman perfectly—got into the Eldorado and backed out of the driveway and onto the street, passing me in the opposite direction.

I pulled into his driveway, and backed out to follow him. I caught him at the corner just before he turned right on Coldwater. I let a car get between us as Coldwater turned into Beverly Drive, and we headed south into Beverly Hills. It was a short trip. He turned right on Little Santa Monica and parked on the street half-a-block down. I drove on. He had parked in front of Solly K's Furriers. From my rear-view mirror I could see him enter the building. He had to be Kupferman.

In December of 1968, the Club Utopia, a sleazy neighborhood cocktail lounge located on Normandie near Slauson, was fire-bombed. Six patrons of the bar fried to death. Surviving eyewitnesses described how three men who had been ejected from the bar earlier that evening had returned just before closing and tossed a Molotov cocktail into the crowded one-room lounge, turning it into an inferno. The three men were apprehended by L.A.P.D. detectives a few hours later. They admitted their culpability, but denied it was "their idea." They claimed the existence of a "fourth man" who met them outside the bar after they were thrown out and who "instigated the whole thing." No one believed them. The men, who worked as painters and possessed long criminal records, were tried and convicted of murder. They were among the last people to be executed in the gas chamber at San Quentin.

I remember the case well, although I had nothing to do with it. At the time I was a twenty-two-year-old rookie working Wilshire Patrol. To unwind after work, I would go with patrolmen friends to bars to booze and trade war stories. One night after Thanksgiving '68 I was riding around with another rookie named Milner. Somehow, we ended up at the soon-to-be-famous Club Utopia. We were sitting at the bar, and the man sitting next to me got up suddenly and spilled whiskey all over my expensive, newly-purchased white cashmere sweater. He was a thin, Semitic-looking man in his fifties, and he apologized effusively, even offering to buy me a new sweater. I good-naturedly shrugged it off, although I was pissed. The man left after several more apologies.

I have something close to total recall. I never forget a face. It had been over a decade, but I was certain: the man at the bar that night was Sol Kupferman. He had barely aged. A strange coincidence that probably meant nothing. If I ever got to speak to Solly K, I would ask him "What were you doing in a crummy bar on the south side in the fall of '68?" And he would very rightfully look at me like I was insane and say, "I don't know" or "Was I?" or "I don't remember."

I considered my options. I could wait around and tail Kupferman after he left his office, or I could take off and resume my surveillance the next day. I decided to head toward the old neighborhood to see my friend Walter.

## 3

Western Avenue between Beverly and Wilshire and the blocks surrounding it constitute the old neighborhood. Situated two miles west of downtown L.A. and a mile south of Hollywood, there is nothing exceptional about it. The prosaic thrust of the ordinary lives lived there produced nothing during my formative years but an inordinate amount of male children, a good portion of whom assumed roles emblematic of the tortured 60's: Vietnam veteran, drug addict, college activist, burned-out corpse. The neighborhood has changed slightly, topographically: Ralph's Market is now a Korean church, old gas stations and parking lots have been replaced by ugly pocket shopping centers. The human core of the neighborhood, the people who were in early middle-age when I was a child, are elderly now, with resentments and fears borne out of twenty years of incomprehensible history.

And that makes the difference. The library on Council and St. Andrews still has the same librarian, and the bars on Western still supply Wilshire Station with an extraordinary amount of drunk drivers. But it's different now; it's a middle-American graveyard inhabited by the malaise of my past, and I feel chills of doom whenever I drive through it, which I do frequently.

I got out shortly after my parents died, as did most of the guys I grew up with. But my friend Walter is still there, ensconced at the old house on 5th and Serrano, with his lunatic Christian Scientist mother, his TV set, his science-fiction books, his records, and his Thunderbird wine. He is thirty-two years old, and we have been friends for twenty-five. He is the one person in my life I have loved unequivocally. I do not judge his inertia, his self-destructiveness, his complex relationship with his mother, or his incipient psychoses. I accept his oblique love, his self-hatred, and anger. Our relationship is twenty-five years of shared experience: together and in our separate solitudes; books, music, films, women, my work, and his fantasy. Here Walter has the upper hand: he is far more intelligent than I, and in the fifteen years since high school his sedentary lifestyle has afforded him time to read thousands of books, from the profound to the trivial, to assimilate great music into the bedrock of his consciousness, and to see every movie ever to pass the way of the TV screen.

This is an extraordinary frame of reference for an agile mind, and Walter has taken fantasy into the dimension of genius. His is pure verbal fantasy: Walter has never written, filmed, or composed anything. Nonetheless, in his perpetual T-Bird haze he can transform his wino fantasies into insights and parables that touch at the quick of life. On his good days, that is. On his bad ones, he can sound like a high school kid wired up on bad speed. I hoped he was on today, for I was exhilarated myself, and felt the need of his stimulus: the power of a Walter epigram can clarify the most puzzling day.

I stopped at the Mayfair Market to pick up three chilled short dogs. Walter works best when inspired by the right amount of T-Bird. Too little invites peevishness, too much, incoherent rambling. T-Bird is Walter's drink of choice because it is cheap and easily obtained by threatening his mother, ripping off her purse, or mowing the lawn for a few bucks.

I went around to the back yard, where Walter's room jutted out from the house proper onto the dead brown grass. Walter is a lousy gardener. I could hear the TV going inside. I rapped on his window. "Yo, wino Walt," I said. "I'm here. I brought gifts. Come on out." I walked back into the yard, pulled up a lawn-chair, popped a can of ginger ale for myself, and arranged the three short dogs symmetrically on the old metal table beside me.

Walter shuffled out five minutes later, wearing cut-off jeans and a Mahler sweatshirt. He is about 5'11" with curly light-brown hair and extremely light-blue eyes. Though not fat, he tends to waddle.

"Welcome, Fritz. You did bear gifts. How thoughtful." He sat down beside me, grabbed a short dog, and drained it in one gulp. Color came into his face, his eyes seemed to expand and his whole body gave a slight twitch. He was on his way. He pulled out a pack of Marlboros, lit one, and inhaled deeply. I wondered what direction our conversation would take. "You look pensive, Fritz. Troubled also, somewhat. Thinking about your future again? You look like you could use a drink. I know you won't go for it though; only half of you wants it. Whether or not it's your better half, I can't say. I only know you better than anyone, including yourself."

"Fuck you. You're right, though, I have had my future on my mind. It's been a strange day so far. A crazy caddy is paying me a hundred twenty-five dollars a day plus to dig up dirt on some rich guy his sister is living with. He looks like a bum, but he carries a six-thousand dollar roll. Crazy, Daddy-O!"

"You'll do a good job. You're a born dirt-digger. You have no morality whatsoever. A boyish-looking shark. We are the same age, and you look twenty-five while I look forty. This I attribute to your refusal, even at your most desperate, to drink cheap wine. Fritz, who do you really think killed the Black Dahlia?"

I groaned at the mention of this mutual obsession from our boyhood drinking days. "I don't know. And you know what? I don't care. Change the subject, will you?"

"Okay, for now. Toss me another dog, will you? I'm thirsty." He downed this one in two gulps. His face was downright florid now. His eyes were getting maniacal, and I knew he was going to start talking either science-fiction or his mother. The two are more or less synonymous.

"The old girl has finally reached her zenith, Fritz. She's senile but cagey, and still a master game player. She intends to live forever and is on the lookout for new victims. My father, God rest his soul, and I were just the beginning. She's been prowling these senior citizens dances and she's picked up this fruit vendor, a dago, kind of semi-rich—he owns about a dozen produce stands out in the Valley. And I think the old girl is going to marry him! Seventy years old, hasn't fucked since I was conceived, and now this. I can't believe it. He can hardly talk, he just grunts. He's got emphysema, he carries around a little oxygen shooter—it looks like a raygun. Jesus! She's set financially; she doesn't need his dough. I've told her that within five years the antimatter credit card will be in operation, that all she'll have to do is walk up to any bank, lay her rap into the loudspeaker, insert her card and get all the bread she needs. Within eight years we'll all be transported to the sublunar void, where the controlled environment will enable us to live for centuries in perfect health. The dumb cunt can't see it coming, and she's going to throw it all away for some wop fruit vendor. She's afraid to be alone. You know that, don't you, Fritz? When she's got the wop sewed up, she'll give me the boot, like she did my old man, and I'll have to get a job. I *still* can't believe it." He reached for the last bottle, but I grabbed it first.

"Not yet. You'll be into your 'moon to earth, moon to earth' routine in a minute. I've got to split. I've got this case I'm working on and a big load of repo's, so I probably won't see you for a week or so. Right now, I want to go home and listen to some music. Remember the Hollywood Bowl Season starts next week, and I've got us a box. Don't worry about the dago—if he gives you any shit just rip off his oxygen gun. I've got to go."

"Okay. If anything drastic comes up, anything you think I can clarify for you, give me a call."

"Okay, Walter. You take care. I'll see you."

On the way home I tried not to worry about Walter. It had been a bad session today. I hadn't gotten what I needed from him, or imparted what I felt he needed. His ongoing suicide was painful to watch. I stopped at a pay phone and called Irwin at work.

He wasn't as upset by the violence yesterday as I had thought. He agreed to stay with me; and his loyalty was so touching that I offered him an extra 5 percent of my action for no extra work. Then I dropped my bomb: I told him that I had a case, and that the ten delinquents were all his. He didn't believe me at first, but finally it sank in. I told him to get his hot-headed Israeli nephew to do the actual ripping-off for him. After thanking me effusively, he hung up.

When I got home I put Schubert on the turntable to try to put Walter out of my mind. It worked for a while, until I remembered that Schubert was about Walter's age when he died.

## 4

I began my surveillance of Jane Baker the next day. Sol Kupferman was a more logical place to begin, since he was supposedly the villain of this triangle, but I had visions of tailing him to his office in the morning, to some swank Beverly Hills eatery for lunch, and back to his pad at the end of the day. A big drag. Jane Baker was probably more mobile. And she was certainly better looking.

I arrived at my post across the street from Kupferman's around 8:00 A.M. No one in Beverly Hills gets up before then, except butlers and maids. I had my own car, a '69 Camaro Ragtop, and I was all set for a day of sleuthing, wearing a sports jacket and tie, shined shoes, and carrying an assortment of official-looking badges, from "Special Deputy" to "International Invesigator." I had bought them at a novelty shop on Hollywood Boulevard. No repo-man should be without them.

Jane Baker walked out the door at nine forty-five. She more than did her photograph justice. Dressed in a russet cotton-linen pantsuit, her hair tied into a bun, she looked like the prototype of a confident young career woman. As she walked past Kupferman's Eldorado to the older de Ville, I trained my binoculars on her face. It was hard to picture this slender, efficient-looking woman as the sister of the grubby Fat Dog, yet the resemblance was there: the full cheeks, the widely-spaced eyes, and a certain determined set to the mouth that was sensual on Jane and ugly on her brother.

There was a fair amount of traffic heading south toward the Beverly Hills shopping district—women in Cadillacs and Mercedes on their morning shopping pilgrimages to the boutiques of Fat City—but Jane was easy to follow. We went south on Beverly Drive to Big Santa Monica, then east all the way into Hollywood. It was a pleasant drive. The sky was smogless and the Hollywood Hills were alive with greenery. Jane Baker turned left on Highland and pulled into the parking lot of a Bank of America branch.

I parked three spaces away, gave her two minutes and then followed her into the bank. It was busy, the height of the early morning rush, so it was a few minutes before she got to see a teller. I passed by her on the opposite side of the velveteen waiting ropes and observed the transaction. The teller was counting out a large number of fifties. There appeared to be close to a grand on the counter. Jane stuffed the bills into her purse.

I hotfooted it outside and back to my car, wondering why a Beverly Hills woman would travel all the way to Hollywood to do her banking. And where would Jane Baker be going with a grand in her purse?

She didn't leave me hanging for long. A minute later she was behind the wheel and gunning it north on Highland. She was harder to tail this time, deftly weaving in and around the morning traffic. North of the Hollywood Bowl she turned onto the Hollywood Freeway. Soon we were spinning over the Valley, its northern horizon freighted with smog.

I almost lost her a couple of times, but when she hit the Victory Boulevard offramp, I was right behind her. She led me into the poorer residential areas of Van Nuys. No sidewalks. Ugly eight- and ten-unit apartment buildings and small houses painted in depressing pastel shades. I had done a lot of repo-ing around here; people trapped with deadend jobs often neglect their car payments. Jane pulled over abruptly against the dirt shoulder of a particularly seedy street. I passed on by her and stopped at the corner. Out of my rear-view mirror I watched her walk up a gravel driveway and enter a tiny yellow wood frame house.

Jane showed five minutes later and within a few minutes we were back on the Ventura Freeway, this time south-bound. She was driving smoothly now, and I stayed several cars back, my eyes half-glued to the road, and half-glued to her long car aerial. I followed her onto Hollywood Freeway, headed east. Ten minutes later Jane signalled her departure from Freeway Land and I followed her north on Vermont and East on Normal Avenue, a rundown street of apartment buildings which house students from nearby L.A. City College. When she parked I was right behind her.

My stomach was growling and I was losing patience. It hit me that Fat Dog might try to duck me for my bill. He was riding high now, but he had the air of a horseplayer who hit it big and was flashing the roll he was certain to lose. The idea of being stiffed by a golf course flunky pissed me off.

Jane had trotted across the street and into an old four flat. This time I could see that it was an elderly man who admitted her. I wrote down the address. She returned just seconds later, practically running to her Cadillac. She tore out, and I was all set for hot pursuit, but my car wouldn't turn over. Shit! It was the capper to a frustrating morning. I watched Jane Baker turn right and zoom out of sight.

I got out of the car, my stomach turning over like a hungry dog's, and opened the hood. I'm no mechanic, but I spotted the trouble immediately. A distributor wire had come loose. The repair job took one second, but of course, Jane Baker was long gone. I walked around the corner to Vermont and found a Mom and Pop market crowded with students on lunch break. I bought a quart of milk and two refrigerated pastrami sandwiches. I found an alley around the corner and took a long overdue leak behind some trashcans. A black couple strolled by hand in hand as I was doing this and snickered at me. I was getting a bad play from blacks lately, probably karmic revenge for my years with the L.A.P.D.

I ate my lunch outside my car and reviewed my options. I decided to concentrate on Sol Kupferman. He was probably just a nice old fart with a hard-on for a beautiful young cellist, but it was Fat Dog's C-note-and-a-quarter a day.

Driving away, I remembered yesterday's phone call to R&I. I found a pay phone on 3rd and Vermont and buzzed my old buddy Jensen. It took him a few minutes to get to the phone, "Yo, Jensen," I said, "this is Fritz Brown. You got that information for me?"

"Hold on, Brownie. You got a pencil?"

"Yeah, shoot it."

"Okay, on Jane Baker, no criminal record. We got a whole shitload of Jane Bakers here, but none of them

could possibly be her, according to the age and description
you gave me. I checked D.M.V. and they gave me this:
Jane Margaret Baker, D.O.B. 3–11–52, L.A., brown and
blue, 5'9", 130. The usual numbers of the usual citations,
except for two reckless-driving citations, no booze or dope
involved. Does that sound like her?"

"That's her. Shoot me the other two."

"Okay. On Frederick 'Fat Dog' Baker, we got some interesting shit. Three vandalism beefs as a juvie, all three
times the judge recommended counseling. That figures.
Two weinie wagger convictions as an adult: 8–14–59 and
2–9–64. Not registered as a sex offender, probably drunk,
just got the urge to whip out his cock and take a piss.
Under employment, we got him down as a caddy, and
believe me, for a caddy that's par for the course, no pun
intended. They're the low-lifers of the world. Give the asshole his due, though, he ain't been in no trouble for sixteen
years. He . . ."

I butted in. Jensen was a loudmouth and this could go
on all day. "We have to speed this up, Daddy-O, I'm
parked in the red and there's a metermaid checking out my
Doctor On Call sign suspiciously. I don't want a ticket, I've
got no way to fix them anymore."

"You're still a crazy fucker. Okay, Sol Kupferman.
D.O.B. 5–13–15. No criminal record, per se. Twice a
material witness for the grand jury. Both times they were
investigating bookmaking. This was in '52 and '55. That's
it."

That was enough. I thanked Jensen and hung up. Nothing surprised me, except the dope on Kupferman. Jane
Baker's two reckless driving convictions indicated nothing
but youthful verve. That Fat Dog was an exhibitionist
was no shocking revelation. He was a disturbed man. But
Solly K existing on the edge of, or in, the vice game twenty
years ago was interesting, doubly so when coupled with my
knowledge of his presence at the Club Utopia in '68. Small
bars like that were often fronts for bookie operations.

It was time to go and talk to the one person I know who
is profoundly knowledgeable of the dark secrets of Los
Angeles. I headed toward the Sunset Strip to see Jack
Skolnick. In honor of Jane Baker I played the Dvorak
"Cello Concerto" on the way.

Jack Skolnick has had a checkered past. For over forty

years he has maneuvered on the fringes of L.A.'s high society, entertainment monolith, and underworld with the finesse and discernment of some sort of rare animal. Like a pig snorting truffles, he knows just where to look, and dig. Under his euphemistic title of "agent" he has pimped, supplied rigged game shows with "contestants," served as a tour guide for visiting dignitaries (showing them the "real" L.A.), sold information to the cops, run mail order scams, solicited funds for political candidates of all persuasions, pushed gourmet marijuana brownies, and operated a canine obedience school. His knowledge of Los Angeles and the eccentricities of its moneyed people is astounding. I had a feeling he could tell me something about Sol Kupferman.

Jack's office was on the sixth floor of a big apartment building on Sunset, a block east of Fairfax. His home was the apartment next door. The place wasn't zoned for business, but "Jack Skolnick Enterprises" was so vague he got away with it.

I gave his foxy young secretary my name and she sent me directly in to Jack's office. Jack was sitting behind his desk, reading the newspaper. He looked good. I told him so.

He was surprised to see me. He put down his paper and stood up to shake my hand. "Fritz, baby, so do you! You've put on some weight. Sit down. How's tricks, Fritzie? Still got the repo gig? Hatchet man for Cal Myers?"

It wasn't quite a jibe, so I let it pass. "More or less. I've still got my P.I.'s license though, and the agency going on the side. Right now I'm on a case. What about you? What's your latest scam?"

"Currently, I'm in the escort business. I provide businessmen with an attractive, intelligent woman to be seen with at various functions."

"In other words, you're pimping."

Jack shook his head in mock dismay. "Fritz, baby! Would I do a thing like that?"

"Only if it made money."

"I protest, Fritzie! My girls are all in college!"

"Yeah, majoring in fucking. Enough bullshit. I've got a client who's interested in a man you may know something about. Sol Kupferman. You heard of him?"

Jack gave me a cagey look and nodded his head. "I

knew him slightly, maybe twenty years ago when I had my chauffeur gig. I used to fix him up with a limo and a driver. We used to talk sometimes."

"About what?"

"Just rebop. The weather, that kind of shit. Nothing too heavy. But I heard talk about him."

"Such as?"

"Such as he was a money man, tax advisor to organized crime in the 40's. Such as he was a noncombatant, some kind of tax wizard. He made the mob a bundle."

"That's it?"

"What are you fishing for, Fritzie?"

"Kupferman was subpoenaed as a material witness to the grand jury, back in the 50's. They were investigating bookmaking. What do you know about that?"

"I know that back in the 50's the grand jury was convened every time someone laid a fart. It was the McCarthy era. If the grand jury called up Kupferman, it was probably because he knew somebody who knew somebody. That kind of thing."

"What else can you tell me about him?"

Jack smiled again. "That he had a lot of heart and a lot of class. A real mensch. I bought my daughter a mink stole from him a few years ago. He remembered me and gave me a good deal. He's a mensch."

"You remember the Club Utopia firebombing?"

"Yeah. A bunch of people got fried, then the State fried the fryers. What about it?"

"I heard Kupferman used to frequent the place. I thought it was a funny coincidence. Can you put a handle on that?"

"Yeah, I can. Life is filled with funny coincidences." I was digging for more questions when the phone on Jack's desk rang. He picked it up and bellowed into it: "Liz, baby! How did it go?!" I got up and we shook hands across his desk. He placed his free hand over the receiver. "Let's get together soon, Fritz. Dinner, what say?"

"Sounds good, Jack. I'll call you."

He nodded goodbye. As I walked out his door I could hear him exclaiming gleefully, "A congressman? And he wanted to do that with you?"

When I got down to street level, the city was cooling off. I decided to drive home, and then go looking for Fat Dog.

The case was turning into an exercise in futility, and I would feel better about it with some of Fat Dog's money in my pocket. I put the top on my car down and cruised east on Sunset. Knots of young hookers were starting to appear, sitting on bus benches and giving male motorists the eye. I toyed with the idea of picking one up, but only briefly; they looked too sad.

At home, I watched the sunset from my balcony. The nicest thing about nighttime is the clarity, and in L.A. that means shadows and neon. The night was alive now. I went looking for my client.

Santa Monica Boulevard and Sawtelle Avenue, one-half mile south of the Veteran's Administration complex, is the nadir of West Los Angeles. It's a strange bottom, not too dangerous unless you're waxing profane about the masses of wetbacks who live in the fleabag hotels there. Chilled short dogs dominate the refrigerated sections of the half dozen liquor stores on this compact skid row, and the doomed old men from the V.A. who scarf them up are the saddest things I've ever seen. But "Graveyard West" has its positive side: the Nuart Theatre is a great revival house and the Papa Back Bookstore is a mecca for counter-culture literati. All in all, despair wins out by a nod, and the neighborhood is the ideal place for a thirty-five-year-old hippie on the sauce.

I parked my car at a gas station across the street from the Nuart and went looking for the Tap & Cap. I found it around the corner from the theater on Sawtelle. It was a dumpy beer bar with a neon sign advertising its hours: 6 A.M. to 2 A.M., the maximum the law allows. When I entered I was struck with a thousand deja vu's. This place had been described by Fat Dog as a caddy hangout, and the two dozen or so men sitting at the bar and hanging around the pool tables had to be caddies. They were dressed more or less alike: beat up golf-type slacks that had originally cost good money, knit shirts—most of them bearing mascots or symbols on the pockets—and hats—a wide variety of them, from sunvisors to baseball caps to Tyrolean pork pies. I had seen scores of men dressed like this over the years, sunburned and middle-aged, dressed too distinctly to be bums, yet not quite looking like normal citizens. Caddies.

I took a stool at the end of the bar. Behind the bar, above the shelves of beer glasses, was a giant photographic collage of blown-up photos of leading jockeys and their mounts interspersed with Polaroids of bar regulars playing softball and guzzling brew. I couldn't pick out Fat Dog. I got the bartender's attention. "I'm looking for Fat Dog Baker," I said. "He told me I could get a line on him here."

"I ain't seen Fat Dog for a week or so," the bartender said. "But if you wanna leave a message, I'll see he gets it when he comes in."

"No, I have to see him tonight." I took a five spot out of my wallet and laid it on the bar in front of him. I gestured at the men behind me playing pool. "Do any of these guys know Fat Dog? Know where I could find him?"

He deftly snapped up the fiver and pointed to a scarecrow-like older guy playing around with the jukebox. "That's Augie Dougall," he said. "He loops with Fat Dog kind of semiregular. Ask him, he might know. Buy him a pitcher. He likes Coors."

I thanked the bartender, awarding him one of my rare winks, and carried the chilled pitcher and a glass over to the jukebox. I tapped the scarecrow on the shoulder. He turned around and almost knocked the beer out of my hands. "This is for you," I said and pointed to a small table a few feet away. "I'm a friend of Fat Dog Baker. I'd like to talk to you for a minute."

We sat down and he dove into his suds. He was about 55, and very tall, maybe 6'6". He couldn't have weighed more than 140. He looked guileless and gentle, so I played it straight with him. "I'm doing a job for Fat Dog," I said. "I know you're an old looping buddy of his, so I thought maybe you could tell me where he's staying."

"Okay. You're not a cop, are you?"

"No."

"You kind of look like one."

"I traded in my badge for a set of golf clubs. Fat Dog is going to teach me the game." Augie didn't laugh or change his expression. His eyes remained locked into mine. He slopped up some more beer. It struck me that he must be closed to retarded, with an idiot savant's antenna for the heat.

"You picked a good teacher, buddy. Nobody knows golf like the Fat Dog. Nobody can read greens like him neither. You put that putt where he tells you, and whammo, it's in the cup."

"Fascinating, but what I'm interested in is where I can find him, tonight."

Augie Dougall went on, "Fat Dog don't like to sleep indoors. He says it's bad for him. He has bad dreams. He's been loopin' Bel-Air lately and sleepin' on the course on this little hill off of the eighth hole near this little lake they got. He . . ."

I interrupted, "You mean he sleeps on the grounds at Bel-Air Country Club?"

"Yeah. They got this gate off of Sunset near this girl's school. There's this big statue of Jesus there. Fat Dog hops the fence. He's got a nice little place all set up for his-self . . ."

I didn't let him finish. I tossed him a hurried thank you and left the bar. I could hear the beginning of an argument as I walked out the door. It had to do with the merits of Arnold Palmer's swing versus Ben Hogan's. It was picking up tempo as I strode up Sawtelle toward my car, looper voices trailing hero worship and anger into the night.

I knew the entrance Augie Dougall was talking about. Jesus stood guard over the student parking lot at Marymount Girl's School. I parked beside the gate Fat Dog would have to climb over to get to his retreat and put on some music conducive to forming plans on a warm summer night: Mozart's Fortieth Symphony, light and graceful, the antithesis of the nervous boredom my case was turning into.

When the music ended I waited in silence for an hour or so, then heard Fat Dog's loud footsteps coming toward me on the driveway. He was muttering something unintelligible. I called out softly so as not to frighten him. "Yo, Fat Dog. You've got a visitor."

"Who's that?" he called back nervously. "Friend or foe?"

"It's Fritz Brown, Fat Dog. I've got to talk to you."

"Fritz baby! My buddy! The private-eye man! You got some good shit for the Fat Dog?"

I opened my passenger door. "I've got some information for you. I don't know how good it is."

He sat down beside me on the front seat, and gave me a warm handshake. His hand was greasy and he smelled of dry leaves and sweat, the price of outdoor living. "Shoot it to me, Jack," he said.

"It's like this," I said, "I've been tailing your sister and Kupferman. Not long enough to establish any routine, but long enough to tell you there's no hanky-panky going on." It was a lie, but a kind one. "More importantly, I've talked to a former associate of Kupferman's and checked him out with the fuzz. I can tell you this: a long time ago, Kupferman was a money man for organized crime. An accountant, actually, He was a material witness to the grand jury twice, when they were investigating bookmaking. That was back in the 50's. I get the distinct impression that he's been clean for a long time."

"So where do you go from here? What else are you gonna do?"

"That's up to you. I can subpoena the grand jury records. That takes time, plus money for an attorney. I can continue my surveillance, which will probably yield no dirt. I can talk to other people who know Kupferman and see what they have to say. That's about it."

"You go to it, man. This is important to me."

"There's the question of money, if you want me to continue. I'll give you a flat rate. One week of my time, an even grand. That includes expenses. It's a good deal. I'll submit you a written report on all the shit I've dug up. One thing, though, I need the money tonight. And another, I'm going on vacation at the end of the week. No business, okay? You got the bread?"

"Yeah, but I'm not holding it. I never do at night. Too many psychos around. You ain't safe, even sleeping outside. We got to take a ride for the moolah. Okay?"

"Okay. You've got it in cash, right?"

"Right."

"Where do we go?"

"Venice."

Venice, where the debris meets the sea. It figured my canine friend would do his banking there.

I took surface streets to give me time to converse with my client. He was far more interesting than either of the people I was investigating. Mob minions gone legit and

amateur musicians were commonplace, but caddies who
slept on golf courses and carried around six or seven thousand dollars were rare, and probably indigenous to only
L.A. I decided to do some polite digging in the guise of
small talk. "How's the looping business, Fat Dog? You
making any money?"

"I'm doing all right. I've got my regulars," he said.

"When I was a kid, my dad used to drive us by Wilshire
Country Club every Saturday on the way to the movies. I
used to see these guys carrying golf bags on their shoulders. It looked like a lot of work. Don't those bags get
heavy?"

"Not really. You get used to it. You work Hillcrest or
Brentwood though and you break your balls. Them kikes
got cement in their bags. And none of 'em can play golf.
They just like to torture their caddy. They pay you a few
bucks more, but it's just so they can feel superior while
they torture you."

"That's an interesting concept, Fat Dog. Sadism on the
golf course. Jewish golfers as sadists. Why do you dislike
Jews so much?"

"Dislike ain't the word. I never met one who kept his
word, or could play golf. They rule the country and then
complain how they can't get into good clubs like L.A. or
Bel-Air. When I'm rich though, I'm gonna have me a
whole caddy shack full of Jewish goats. I'm gonna get me a
big fat Spaulding trunk and load it down with umbrellas,
golf balls, and extra clubs. The bastard's gonna weigh
about seventy-five pounds. I'm gonna have a nigger caddy
pack it on the front nine, and a Hebe on the back. I've got
a friend, a rich guy who feels like me. He's gonna have a
bag just like mine. We're gonna make these fuckin' Jews
and niggers pack us double. Ha-ha-ha!" Fat Dog's laughter
rose, then dissolved into a coughing attack. Tears were
streaming down his cheeks. He stuck his head out the
window to catch some air.

I prodded him a little. "You ever caddy for Kupferman?"

Regaining his breath, Fat Dog gave me a quizzical look.
"Are you kidding? He had a coon pack his bag. Jews and
niggers are soul brothers."

We were on Lincoln now, heading south. On Venice
Boulevard we turned west, toward the beach. Within a few
minutes we were on the edge of the Venice ghetto, known

to Venetians as "Ghost Town." Fat Dog told me to stop on a street named Horizon. It wasn't much of a horizon, just dirty wood-framed four and eight flats with no front yards. It was trash night and garbage cans lined the sidewalk. Spanish voices and television battled for audial supremacy. There was no place to park, so Fat Dog told me to let him out and come back in ten minutes. I had other ideas.

He hopped out. Through my rear-view mirror, I watched him trot around the corner to my left. As soon as he was out of sight, I jumped out and tore after him, leaving the car double-parked. I slowed to a walk as I reached the corner. Fat Dog was nowhere in sight. I walked to the end of the block, looking in windows and checking out drive-ways. Nothing. I got back into my car and circled the streets surrounding Horizon at random. When I returned to the spot where I had dropped Fat Dog, he was standing there. He handed me a roll of bills as he got in.

I counted the money. There were twenty fifty-dollar bills. Nice new crisp U.S. Grants. "One week, Fat Dog. No more, no less. After that, it's farewell."

"It's a deal. Fritz is a German name, right?"

"Right."

"Are you German? Brown ain't no German name."

"I'm of German descent. My grandparents were born there. Their name was Brownmuller. When they came to America they shortened it to Brown. It was good they did. There was a lot of discrimination against Germans here during the First World War."

"Fucking A!" Fat Dog said. I could feel him getting keyed up. "It was the Jews, you know that. The Germans wouldn't take none of their shit. They owned all the pawn-shops in America and Germany, and bled the white Christians dry! They—"

·I started the car and pulled away, trying not to listen. I turned right on Main Street and headed north. It was get-ting to be too much; I was getting a headache. I turned to Fat Dog. "Why don't you can that shit, and right now," I said, trying to keep my voice down. "You hired me to get information for you, not to listen to your racist rebop. I like Jews. They're great violinists and they make a mean pastrami sandwich. I like blacks, too. They sure can dance. I watch *Soul Train* every week. So please shut the fuck up." Fat Dog was staring out his window. When he spoke he was surprisingly calm. "I'm sorry, man. You're my buddy. My friend is always telling me not to sound off on politics so much, that not everybody feels like we do. He's right. You go around shooting off your mouth and everybody knows your plans. You got no surprises left for nobody. I'm the man with the plan, but I got to cool it for now."

I was curious about his "plan," maybe a Utopian vision of unionized caddy fleets, blacks and Jews excluded, but I decided not to ask. My headache was just abating; "Tell me about yourself, Fat Dog. I was a cop for six years and I never met anyone like you."

"There ain't much to tell. I'm the king of the caddies, the greatest fucking looper who ever packed a bag. I'm strictly a club caddy, and proud of it. Those tour baggies ain't nothin'. Carrying single bags for a good player ain't jack shit. Two on your back and two more on a cart, that's the real test of a goat. I know every golf course in this city like the back of my hand. I'm a legend in my own time."

"I believe you. That was a pretty hefty roll you whipped out on me yesterday. With that kind of dough, how come you sleep outside?"

"That's personal, man, but I'll tell you if you tell me something. Okay?"

"Okay."

"How come you quit the police force?"

"They were about to can me. I was drinking heavily, and my fitness reports were shot to hell. I was too sensitive to be a cop." It was approximately a third of the truth, but my remark about my "sensitivity" was an outright lie.

"I believe you, man," Fat Dog said. "You got that look, nervous like, of a juicehead on the wagon. I could tell you was by all the coffee you was drinking the other day. Juicers on the wagon are all big coffee fiends."

"Back to you, Fat Dog," I said. "Why the outdoor living?"

He was silent for a minute or so. He seemed to be formulating his thoughts. We had made our way up to Sunset, and I was maneuvering eastbound in heavy traffic, around wide curves and abrupt turns. When he spoke his voice was tighter, less boisterous, like someone trying to explain something intrinsic and holy. "Do you dig pussy?" he asked.

"Sure," I said.

"Have you ever wanted to have a broad that could give you everything you've ever wanted? That you never had to worry about? I mean, you never had to worry about her fucking no other guys, you just *knew* she was loyal? And this broad, she's *perfect*. Her body is exactly like the one you've always dreamed of. And she's even nice to be around after you've fucked her? That's how I feel about golf courses. They're beautiful and mysterious. I don't sleep good inside. Nightmares. Sometimes when it·rains, I sleep underneath this overhang next to the caddy shack at Bel-Air. It's dry, but it's outside. It's peaceful on golf courses. Most of the ones in L.A. got nice homes next to them. Big old-fashioned ones. The people leave their lights on sometimes 'cause they think no one's looking at them. I seen all kinds of strange shit that way. Once when I was camped out on Wilshire South, I saw some dame beat up her dog, just a little puppy, then get it on with another dame, right there on the floor. These rich cocksuckers who belong to these clubs, they think they own their golf courses, but they just play golf on them, and I live on them, all of them! The courses around here are the primo land in L.A., worth billions of bucks, and I've got them all for my personal crash pad. So I pack bags and I'm the best, and I know things that none of these rich assholes will never know."

"What kind of nightmares do you have?"

Fat Dog hesitated before he answered. "Just scary shit," he said. "Monsters, dragons, and animals out to get me. Never getting to see my sister again."

"I tailed your sister today. She withdrew some money from a bank, then visited some people in the Valley and around Vermont and Melrose. Do you have any idea of who these people are?"

"No!" Fat Dog screamed. "You're the private eye, you find out! I'm paying you a grand to find out! You find out about that Jew bloodsucker Kupferman, too! I'm paying you! You find out!"

I turned on to the golf course access road, stopped the car, and looked at Fat Dog. He was red-faced and shaking, his eyes pinpoints of fear and hatred. My client was insane. I started to speak, something consoling, but he started screaming again. "You find out, you cocksucker! You're

working for the Fat Dog, don't you forget that!" He got
out of the car and walked up to the fence. He started to
scale it, then turned around to give me a parting salvo.
"You ain't no German, you fuck. Nigger lover! Jew lover!
You couldn't even keep a job with the fuzz, you . . ."

My headache came back, full force, and I got out of the
car. I ran to the fence and pulled Fat Dog off by his belt.
As he landed, I spun him around and hit him in the stomach, hard. He doubled over, gasping, and I whispered to
him, "Listen, you fucking low-life. Nobody talks to me
that way, ever. I took a look at your rapsheet today, and I
know you're a weenie-wagger. You've got two choices as of
now. You can apologize to me for what you said, and I'll
continue to work for you. If you don't apologize, I'll throw
a citizen's arrest on you for indecent exposure. With your
two priors it means registration as a sex offender, which is
not pleasant. What's it going to be?"

Fat Dog recovered his breath and muttered, "I apologize."

"Good," I said. "You've got one week of my time. I'll
leave a message at the bar if I need to get in touch with
you. You'll get my best job. At the end of the week I'll
submit a written report." I gave him a boost and he managed to make it over the fence. I watched him walk into
the darkness of his sanctuary, then drove away, my revul-
sion cut through with the strangest, sickest sense of fasci-
nation.

There was no place to go but Walter's. I drove out
Wilshire feeling numbed physically and caught on the
horns of a moral dilemma: I had been hired by a vindictive
lunatic to disrupt the lives of two decent people. I had the
chance to bail out of my case but I didn't. I *couldn't*; I was
spellbound by a madman. It seemed an insoluble problem,
so I willed myself not to think, which only compounded
my numbness.

I couldn't find a parking space on Walter's block, so I
parked on his front lawn. If his mother saw my tire marks,
she would resign me to Christian Science hell, but I decided to risk it. I walked into the back yard. The light in
Walter's bedroom was on, and through it I could see him
passed out in his chair in front of the T.V. On the screen a
giant reptile was attacking a Japanese metropolis, knocking

over skyscrapers with his tail. I toyed with the idea of shooting Godzilla and watching the T.V. implode, but Walter would never forgive me. There were two empty pint bottles of Scotch on the floor beside his chair. That was ominous. Walter was a winehead, and when he couldn't threaten or cajole his mother into wine money, he would rip off flat pint bottles from the Thrifty Drug Store on Wilshire and Western. Hard liquor was an oblivion trip for my beloved friend, and he was an inept shoplifter. I was afraid that if he were busted, the arresting officers would recognize his lunacy and railroad him to Department 95 and Camarillo.

I pried off the windowscreen and climbed into his room. I lifted Walter onto his bed and stuffed two fifties into his shirt pocket. As I shut off the T.V., Godzilla was getting blasted by some sort of atomic death-ray. "I love you, you crazy bastard, but you break my heart," I said, turning off the lights, and going out the window. It was getting chilly. I drove home and fell asleep on the couch with my clothes on.

# II

## LOOPERS AND CELLISTS

## 5

The moral imperative of my case hit me when I woke up the next morning. Was Fat Dog Baker dangerous? Was he a physical threat to Sol Kupferman and Jane Baker? Exhibitionists are the most docile of sex deviates, but Fat Dog had shown a volatile streak. If he were planning to harm either his sister or Kupferman, it was my duty to stop him. Investigating Fat Dog with his own money struck me as wildly ironic, absurdist theater in L.A. I decided to start in Venice.

I drove down LaBrea and caught the Santa Monica Freeway westbound. It was ten o'clock and the smog was starting to roll in. Maybe soon the environmentalists would outlaw cars, and I would have to find work repossessing horses. Fortunately for me, Cal Myers would see it coming and corner the market on beasts of burden. I could see it now: Cal's Casa De Caballo, Cal's Imports (Arabian horses, naturally) and Cal's Palomino. Cal would be cutting his T.V. commercials knee deep in horseshit.

When I arrived in Venice, I parked in the exact spot where Fat Dog had got out last night. I had a simple plan: Check out every vacant house, lot, and garage for four blocks south, and question whomever I ran into. Fat Dog was hard to miss, and someone in the area might be able to give me a lead. I walked. It was getting hot, and the coat and tie I was wearing didn't help. I was getting wary looks from people sitting on their porches, taking the air. I looked like a cop. In Venice, no one but the fuzz wears a coat and tie.

The first two blocks were fruitless. On the third block I saw a wino wandering down the street, drinking from a brown paper bag. He had a wily, lucid look about him, so I gave him a toss. Whipping out my phony badge, I committed a misdemeanor: "Police officer," I said. "Maybe you can help me."

The wino gave me a frightened nod. When I finished describing Fat Dog, he practically screamed at me: "I seen that shitbird! Does he wear a shirt with a little crocodile on it? And a baseball cap?"

"That's the guy."

"What are you after him for?"

I made it good: "Molesting little boys."

"I knew it! Once I was sittin' on this driveway and the shitbird tells me to move my ass. He said it was his property. He looked like a crazy, so I moved. Shitbird."

"Do you remember where you were?" I asked.

"Sure. The place is around the corner."

"Take me there. Now." We turned the corner and the wino led me to a small wood frame house. There was a dirt driveway that ran back into a yard overrun with weeds and high grass. In the rear of the yard was a tar-papered shack with no windows, standing awry atop a weed patch. It was a perfect visual representation of Fat Dog's paranoia. I thanked the wino and told him to take off. He trotted away, giving me a funny look over his shoulder.

I decided to do a little breaking and entering. I checked out the front house first, knocking at the front door, then the back. No one home. I walked into the back yard. Broken toys lay strewn among the weeds. Luckily, the door to the shack was hidden from the street, and the lock was a joke: a simple hinge with two screws bolted into the door jamb and a carry over metal strip attached to a cheap padlock. I found a curtain rod in the yard among the broken toys. It had bent edges that looked thin enough to use as a screwdriver. I tried it. No go. My impatience got the best of me, and I wedged the rod inside the metal strip and snapped the whole mechanism off. The wood splintered, leaving craters where the screws had gone in. There was no way to cover my tracks.

I opened the door and fumbled for a light switch. I flipped it on, and an overhead bulb on a cord illuminated the dark corners of a man's mind. It took minutes for the full import of the room to hit me, the photographs that covered the four walls were too staggering: women, mostly Mexican, in every conceivable posture of debasement with donkeys, horses, dogs, and pigs. Interspersed with them were photos of Hitler and his henchmen in various stern poses. Goering, Goebbels, Eichmann, Himmler, the whole sick crew. There was a workbench running along the back wall and above it was a collage of concentration camp atrocity photos: mounds of corpses hanging out of ovens and piles of skeletons lying in a mass grave.

When I checked out the contents of the workbench, I started to tremble. There were a half-dozen gallon cans of gasoline, empty bottles, stacks of asbestos padding, and a pile of safety gloves, all neatly stacked. In a cardboard box underneath the bench were dozens of celluloid strips and cord fuses arranged according to size. It was an arsonist's workshop, and when the full implication of that hit me I started to tremble even harder: Kupferman. The Utopia. Fat Dog's insane hatred of Solly K. Jesus. My head was pounding, beginning to ache, so I ransacked the place. Expecting to find money, I found nothing but porno books, cans of white paint, and historical tomes on Nazi Germany. I banged all along the rough wood walls, looking for places to hide small objects. Nothing. I got down on my hands and knees and checked the flooring all around. Nothing. I checked the photos on the wall a second time. The horror pictures were ripped out of the history books stored under the bench. The porno pics I judged to be recent and shot in Mexico: the actresses were Latina's and were sporting 70's style hairdos and the furnishings of the apartment used as a shooting stage were up to date. In over half of the photographs a black naugahyde couch was in evidence, and it was covered with cheap bordertown souvenirs: bull banks, piñatas, handbags, and blankets.

The women in the photographs were uniformly ugly and pathetic looking, except one. She was an Anglo, about 17 or 18, with high firm breasts and a red natural. She was performing with men, not animals, indicating a higher status.

I tore half a dozen of the pictures from the walls and stuffed them into my jacket pocket. It was broiling in the room, and I suddenly realized I was drenched in sweat. Before I left I tried a con job. Since there was no way to cover my tracks, I tried to put the blame on some local punks. Maybe Fat Dog would fall for it. I pried open a can of paint, found a brush and painted "Death to honkys," "Crips Rule," and "Criplets Venice" on the outside wall near the door. Then I ripped more photos off the walls, threw them on the floor and dumped the can of paint on top of them. I left the door open and split for the car, hoping no one would see me. I had myself a real case now.

I went looking for a telephone. In Venice that takes some doing. Pay phones are easy prey for Venetian junkies and the first three I checked out had been gutted. I finally found one that worked and called Mark Swirkal's office. Swirkal runs an attorney service, delivering writs and summonses and filing court papers. He knows the L.A. court system from every angle and can locate any official paper within a matter of hours. He had hired me a few times to serve summonses to hardcase types, and now I was shooting him some business in return.

I told him what I wanted. The Club Utopia firebombing case: the names of the victims, the name of the owner and his last known address, the names of the cops who made the arrests, the name of the insurance company and agent who serviced the claim, and, most importantly, notes on all testimony pertaining to the alleged "fourth man." I promised him a C-note and told him I would call back in four hours. He hung up, chomping at the bit.

I walked across the street to a burrito joint, and scarfed up an enchilada plate and coffee. My head was reeling with the implications of what I had just learned. It gave me a headache, so I got some Excedrin out of the glove compartment and chased four of them with coffee. Somehow my mind quieted. My speculations would be futile until I talked to Mark Swirkal. But one theme emerged: I wanted it to be Fat Dog, for the sake of my own revenge. The L.A.P.D. with its overblown reputation blows a big time, highly publicized murder case only to have it solved years later by a former flunky cop they forced to resign. Almost reflexively I sized myself up in the full-length mirror at the back of the restaurant. My appearance was inconclusive: an outsized thirty-three-year-old man, neither handsome nor ugly. Personal qualities and morality open to interpretation.

I had three and a half hours to kill before calling Swirkal, so I got the car and went cruising. I drove by Kupferman's fur showroom, and saw his car parked in front. Relieved, I drove by his big house north of Sunset. CELLO-

1 was parked in the driveway and faint cello chords drifted toward me across the broad front lawn. I stopped my car to listen and threw Jane Baker my silent resolve: that as long as I was around, no one would hurt her or her benefactor. I decided to go see Mark Swirkal in person.

Mark's office was in a dingy turn of the century building on 6th and Union, just outside downtown L.A. proper and close to all the midtown courts. The building had been ruled unsafe after the big '71 earthquake, but never condemned. Mark loved to save a buck and the attorneys he worked for didn't care where he hung his hat; he was the fastest process server and courthouse bulldog in L.A.

I took a rickety elevator to the third floor. His waiting room was open and sparsely furnished—two folding metal chairs with Harbor General Hospital stenciled on the back and a stack of *Playboys* and *Good Housekeepings* on the floor. I opted for a *Playboy*.

Swirkal showed a few minutes later and led me into his office, which was smaller and more cluttered than mine, and not air-conditioned. We shook hands, then he opened his window and his mouth. Mark talks very fast. "I got what you wanted, Fritz. More or less. The trial was short so the transcript was short, first off . . ." Mark waited while I got out my notepad and pen. "First off," he continued, "the Club Utopia was insured. The agent who sold the policy also investigated it for the company, Prudential. His name is James McNamara. The victims' names were Philip Crenshaw, Henry Hadwell, Jacqueline Gaffany, Anthony Gonzalez, William Eastero, and Margot Jackson. You got that, Brownie?"

I caught up with him. "Keep going," I said.

"Okay. The arresting officer was Detective Lieutenant Haywood Cathcart, 77th Street Division. Now regarding the so-called fourth man. He was described as 'a short fat guy, kind of grubby . . . a red-faced man in his late twenties . . . fat and mean looking . . . but no wimp. He had on one of those little tennis shirts with the crocodile on the pocket.'" Fat Dog. Eureka. Salvation. Mark went on talking, but I didn't hear a word he was saying. Finally, he stopped. "What's the matter, Brownie? I got lots more testimony on the fourth man."

"Skip it. I've got enough."

"Are you okay? You look pale."

"I'm fine. Tell me about the owner of the Utopia."

"Okay. His name is Wilson Edwards. There was no mention of his address in the transcript."

I gave Mark Swirkal a big nervous smile and handed him two of Fat Dog's fifties. "Good work, Daddy-O," I said.

Mark stuck the money into his pocket. "You want to tell me what this is about?" he asked. "The Utopia bombing is a dead issue."

"I can't now. Someday I will, though. Right now, I'd like to use your phone."

"You go right ahead. I've got to split. Lock the door behind you."

"I will."

We shook hands again, then Mark thanked me and gave me a puzzled look as he headed out the door. When I heard him get into the elevator I let out a giant whoop of joy and reached for the telephone.

I called Prudential Insurance at their main office on Wilshire. Yes, James McNamara still worked for them. No, he was not in at the moment. I convinced his secretary to relinquish his home phone number. He answered on the second ring. I told him I was a writer doing a book on famous Los Angeles crimes. Would he consent to an interview on the Utopia case? He would indeed. He sounded almost eager. We agreed to meet at a restaurant near his home in Westchester at eight-thirty tonight. When I hung up I let out another whoop of joy, this one even louder.

I pulled into the parking lot of the steakhouse on Sepulveda at exactly eight twenty-five. I inquired after McNamara with the maitre d', and he pointed out a large man drinking alone at the bar. I walked up and introduced myself. McNamara grasped my hand warmly. He had the lonely, desperate look of a brother juicehead hungry for company. I judged him to be in his late forties, and about a quarter of the way drunk. We adjourned to a table, where I laid out a spiel about the book I was writing. When our waitress came, he ordered a double martini and opened up.

"The Club Utopia firebombing was the ugliest thing I've ever seen," McNamara said. "I went all through Korea with an infantry company and saw nothing to compare to it. The fire itself was no big deal. It was out by the time I got there. It was the bodies that were so terrifying. They were roasted beyond recognition and swollen up like pork sausages. There was a liquor store that was still open down the street, and there was a big crowd of rubber-neckers hanging around, guzzling out of paper bags. When the stiffs got carted out and the smell hit, there was a regular epidemic of puking. Booze puke all over the street and the smell of those bodies. Jesus."

"How did you get there so fast?" I asked.

"It was funny," he said, "I was a claims investigator in those days, but I was selling policies on the side. I sold a full coverage policy to Edwards, the owner: damage, vandalism, fire, theft, comprehensive—strange for a cheapshit little bar like that, but what the hell? I was watching T.V. when the news bulletin came on. 'Bar bombed! Six dead!' Naturally, I hotfooted it down there fast since I knew it would be on my caseload."

"And Edwards survived the bombing and collected a settlement, right?"

"Right. He wasn't there that night. He got the thirty-five-thousand total coverage payment. Since it was an open and shut case, the cops nabbing the bombers so quick, we paid off fast."

"What happened to Edwards?" I asked.

"Beats me," McNamara said. "He took the money and ran. Wouldn't you? He was a character, in and out of trouble all his life. When I sold him the policy, I attached a note to the file recommending thorough investigation of all claims he submitted. Of course, the bombing was the *only* claim he submitted, and it was legit."

My steak arrived and I dug in. McNamara ordered another double martini. He was on his way.

"Can you give me a full description of Edwards?" I asked. "Full name, D.O.B., last known address?"

"Can do," he said. "After you called, I stopped by the office and picked up the file. What I don't remember, this baby does." He rummaged through some papers on his lap. "Here it is. Wilson Edwards. Born Lincoln, Nebraska, 12–29–33. White male, brown and blue, 5'11", 180. A couple dozen arrests, through 1960. Minor stuff: trespassing, second degree burglary, possession of marijuana, shop-

lifting. When I sold him the policy in '66 his address was
341 S. Bonnie Brae, Los Angeles."

I wrote it all down. "Were you satisfied with the police
investigation?" I asked. "What about the 'fourth man?' "

" 'The fourth man' was bullshit. The killers, Magruder,
Smith, and Sanchez, were buddies—painters. They were in
the Utopia earlier that night. Drunk. They got fresh with
some women and were bounced by the bartender. They
came back just before midnight. Magruder opened the
door and threw a three-gallon pail of gasoline into the bar.
Sanchez followed it with a lighted book of matches. Six
people fried to death. Smith was out in the car sleeping.
Several survivors of the fire saw Magruder and Sanchez do
it. Two men who survived had worked with Magruder and
knew his address. He and Sanchez were arrested later
that night in the driveway of his apartment building. They
were both passed out from their drunk. They got Smith at
his house later that morning. The 'fourth man' routine was
just a dodge to beat the death penalty. It didn't work. They
all went to the gas chamber."

I pressed on. "The arresting officer was named Cathcart,
right?"

"Right. Haywood Cathcart. A choice asshole. When I
got to the scene, right in the middle of the whole commo-
tion, fire trucks, police cars, reporters, I saw a group of
plainclothes cops talking. I tell them I represent Prudential
as an investigator, and would they mind talking to me.
Cathcart won't even let me finish. He yells at me that this
is police business, that he doesn't want any insurance
bimbo fucking things up. Then he has a harness bull escort
me to my car. A choice shithead."

"Let's talk about the victims," I said. "Did you pay out
any money to their next of kin?" I was fishing now, hoping
to luck onto something that would start my wheels turning.
McNamara consulted his memory and his martini.

"Yeah, we did," he said. "Ten thou apiece to the next of
kin of four of the victims. The other two victims were
elderly transients with no known next of kin."

"Did any relative or friend of the victims sue? Either
your company or Edwards? Or make any trouble?"

McNamara laughed. "No one sued, but one loco made a
lot of trouble. Anthony Gonzalez's kid brother, Omar.
Tony Gonzalez was a Golden Glover back in the 50's.

Omar worshipped him. He was about sixteen when his brother got French fried, and to say that he took it hard would be an understatement. He was probably the only one in L.A. who believed the fourth man existed, and Jesus Christ, did he make a stink about it. He pestered the cops, found out I was investigating the case for the insurance company, and then pestered me. He bugged the newspapers. It was insane. You remember the *Joe Pyne Show?* Every week he'd be in the audience. They had this thing called the Beef Box, where people from the audience could get up and air their gripes. Every fucking week Omar would be up there, running off at the mouth about the Utopia case and how the fuzz let the mastermind get away. He said the mastermind, that was what he called him, had a grudge against one of the victims and so he bombed the bar just to kill that one person. That way the cops wouldn't check that one person's enemies out. Kill six to get one. He said that Sanchez, Magruder, and Smith were just dupes. When they were executed, he took out a black-bordered ad in the L.A. *Times.* A full page. 'When will the mastermind responsible for the death of my brother be brought to justice?' etc. He used to hang out at 77th Street and buttonhole Cathcart, give him a hard time, expound on his latest theory. He bugged me a lot too, but I never resented it. Omar was a very bright kid, but his brother was strictly a punk. A barfly reliving his days of fistic glory. You remember a book—they made a movie out of it—*Magnificent Obsession?* That's what it was for Omar." McNamara's eyes were clouding over with booze and nostalgia.

"What happened to him?" I asked.

"Oh, he's still around. He liked me. I was patient with him. He used to come by my office and talk about his obsession and what he wanted to do with his life. He hated Cathcart and used to say he was going to join the L.A.P.D. so he could run all the assholes like Cathcart out. He sends me a card every Christmas. He's had the same job, off and on, for years. Mechanic at a gas station in Hollywood. He's also some kind of counselor at a drug recovery program in the Barrio. A great kid. Lotta heart."

"Where's the gas station where Omar works?" I asked.

"It's a Texaco on Franklin and Argyle. If you talk to him, give him my best. Wish him good luck from me."

I said I would and grabbed the check. I thanked Mc-Namara and left him to his memories. I was glad to be sober.

Leaving the restaurant, I felt a strange surge of affection for Fat Dog Baker. He was growing in my eyes, from misanthropic buffoon to brilliant and daring killer. Stranger still, I felt that he had some secret knowledge that was important to me, some new epigram on urban wonder. I had beat up on a killer, and now it was time to make amends and win back his confidence before lowering the boom.

I checked my watch. Nine-thirty. Fat Dog should be asleep on the grounds at Bel-Air Country Club by now. But a golf course is a big place, and I might stumble around half the night looking for him, and scare him off in the process. It wouldn't do to upset my gravy train, so I drove to the Tap & Cap to look for an escort.

The escort I had in mind was Augie Dougall, but he wasn't there. The noise in the bar was deafening, country and western mawkishness coupled with loud voices. The Tap & Cap was bustling tonight, and the golf attire and sunburned faces told me it was packed with caddies. The same bartender I had talked to the previous night was on duty, so I went to him for a referral. He told me that every looper in the joint knew Fat Dog, and that no one could stand him. When I asked him who disliked him the least and might be willing to help me locate him, he pointed out a blond guy in his early forties named Stan The Man.

Stan The Man was the perpetrator of the country-western ear-splitting, standing by the jukebox, feeding it coins. Of all the caddies in the place, he looked like the only one capable of giving me a hard time. He had the wary eyes and angry mien of someone who had done time, so I decided on the phony badge ploy.

After ten minutes of cowboy laments, I got my chance. Stan The Man moved from his perch at the jukebox and walked back to the can. I waited a minute, then followed him. He was walking away from the urinal, zipping his fly, when I braced him. I whipped out my badge. "Police officer," I said. "I'd like to talk to you."

Stan The Man flinched, then said "Okay."

"We'll go outside," I said, "the bar's too noisy."

He muttered "Okay" again. I started to feel sorry for him. He obviously had a long history of being hassled by fuzz in odd places.

I tried to quash his fears. "You're in no trouble. I just want to talk to you about a caddy you know." Stan The Man just nodded. We moved out onto the street. The night air was welcome after the smoky din of the bar. "Let's take a walk," I said, "my car's just up the street."

As we walked I learned that Stan The Man was one Stanley Gaither, late of Brentwood Country Club, Los Angeles Country Club, Bel-Air Country Club, and the L.A. County Jail system. His thing was auto theft. He said it was compulsive, that he was on probation, hoeing the straight and narrow and seeing a psychiatrist. This came out in a torrent of words, unsolicited. He was lonely and I started to like him. I introduced myself as Sergeant Brown. Once we were in the car, I said, "It's like this, Stan. I'm interested in Fat Dog Baker, and I heard you got along with him as well as anyone. Is that true?"

"Kind of. We've known each other for years. Looped a lot of the same clubs. I don't hate him like a lot of guys do. Is he in big trouble?"

"No, I just want to talk to him. Tonight."

"Are you with vice?"

"No. Why do you ask?"

"I don't know. A crazy fucker like Fat Dog sleeps outside, never changes his clothes. I've always had this feeling Fat Dog was some kind of pervert. I mean, shit, he used to be the golf-ball king of L.A. He had three hotel rooms filled with nothing but golf balls, fifty thousand of 'em. He was keeping every driving range in the city supplied and keeping a fifty thousand ball reserve. Fifty thousand golf balls at ten cents a ball is five grand! Fat Dog paid rent on three hotel rooms to keep 'em safe, while he slept on the fifth tee at Wilshire. A guy who'd do something like that has got to be a pervert. Don't you think so?"

"Maybe. What does Fat Dog do with his money? I heard he still carries a heavy roll."

Stan considered this. "I don't know," he said. "I think he just likes to look at it. That, and go to Tijuana. He loves T.J. He goes down there all the time. He's crazy about the dog races. He loves that scumbag town. The mule act, the

Chicago Club, the whole scene. He's always saying he's gonna retire down there and race dogs. He hates Jews and niggers, but he loves Mexicans. He's got to be a pervert."

Stan The Man looked at me expectantly, hoping his information would be enough and that he could go. It wasn't, and tonight I needed a tour guide. "You've caddied at most of the clubs in L.A., haven't you, Stan?"

"All of 'em. I'm a loopin' motherfucker."

"Good. I need you to take me around tonight. I want to talk to Fat Dog. We'll start with Bel-Air. Okay?"

Stan The Man's "okay" was resigned and sorrowful, the lament of a man used to carrying freight and complying with orders. I started the car and we took off.

The Bel-Air course yielded nothing, but it was beautiful. Armed with flashlights, the reluctant Stan The Man and I searched for an hour and a half. We hopped the fence by the statue of Jesus and made our way north. Stan claimed that he knew all of Fat Dog's campsites and that it wouldn't be necessary to check out the whole golf course. He explained to me that Bel-Air was a tight urban course built in and around little canyons. That was why the big houses that loomed off to our right looked so close: they *were* close.

We walked up a steep hill that led to the first tee. It was pitch black, and the grass smelled wonderful. The view when we reached the top was so beautiful that for a minute I completely forgot the purpose of my mission. The golf course spread out before me, deep black hills that seemed to promise peace and friendship. It was very still and chilly —a good ten degrees cooler than the city proper—and clear, the lights of Los Angeles etched sharply in pastel shades. I was here to talk to a murderer, a psychotic whose lifestyle was incomprehensible to me, and yet for a split second I envied him the solitude of his urban hideaway. If he lived here he had superb taste and the very best of two worlds; nestled in the arms of a great city, yet free, during the night hours, from all her strife.

We crossed the "Swinging Bridge," a suspension bridge over a deep canyon that carried golfers from the tenth tee to the tenth green. It was aptly named, for a night breeze and the weight of two men sent it swaying gently. Stan broke the silence and told me that on a clear day you could see all the way to downtown L.A. and the San Bernardino Mountains.

Shining our flashlights into sand traps, we walked up from the green into a tunnel. Stan said that this was the end of the line, that no way would Fat Dog camp out on the back nine. He hated it too much, calling it the toughest nine holes he had ever packed. I believed Stan. The still night beauty of this place seemed to have informed us with a wordless rapport. We made our way back the way we had come.

Once back in the car, Stan The Man sighed. "Well," he said, "we got a choice to make. There's four more country clubs on the West Side: Riviera, Brentwood, Hillcrest, and L.A. You can forget Riviera. They don't have caddies, and Fat Dog sleeps out only on courses where he knows the caddy master. Brentwood and Hillcrest are Jewish clubs, and Fat Dog ain't camped out on them courses in years. That leaves L.A. and it's huge. Two courses, thirty-six holes. If Fat Dog's in town, that's probably where he's at."

"Let's hit it, then," I said. We drove south, along the periphery of the U.C.L.A. campus, to Wilshire, then east. It was shortly past midnight, and I was getting tired.

"Your best bet is the south course," Stan was saying. "There's a gate on Wilshire that's open twenty-four hours. There's a bunch of wetback maintenance guys who live there. They got their own barracks. We can park in their lot. There's the gate coming up. Slow down." I did. The gate led down to a woodsy nothingness. I could hardly see. Stan was giving explicit directions. "Real slow now, hang a right now and stop."

I stopped and Mexican music hit me. Then I heard laughter. As my eyes became accustomed to the darkness, I could see a large, one-story bunkhouse off to my left. There were men sitting on the doorway steps drinking beer. They stopped talking as they heard us approach. I grabbed my flashlight and thermos of coffee and beckoned to Stan The Man to follow me. We walked up to the beer drinkers. "Hola," I said, "we're looking for El Perro, Perro grande y blanco?"

It broke the ice. The five or six voices that answered my query were friendly. As best I could understand them, they all said the same thing: they hadn't seen any big, white dog. I should have told them I was looking for a fat dog, but I didn't know the Spanish word for fat. "Gracias, amigos," I said.

"De nada," they returned. As Stan and I moved into the darkness, they turned their mariachi music back on. Silently I wished them a good life in America.

The L.A. south course was flatter than Bel-Air, and more urbanbound. The lights of the Century City business monoliths about a half mile away cast an eerie glow on the trees and hills. Stan was directing me to the spot where he thought Fat Dog was most likely to be: the eleventh tee. Our flashlights played over the terrain, picking out scurrying rodents. In the distance I could hear the hiss of a sprinkler.

Fat Dog was not residing on the eleventh tee. Somehow I didn't care. I was astounded that I had lived in Los Angeles for over thirty years, had prided myself on my knowledge of my city, and had missed out on all this. This was more than the play domain of the very rich, it was quite simply another world, and such diverse types as caddies, wetbacks, and burned-out ex-cops had access to it, on whatever level of reality they chose to seek. Golf courses: a whole solar system of alternate realities in the middle of a smogbound city.

I decided to explore all the city's courses, with my cassette recorder, on future sleepless nights. After Fat Dog Baker was safely locked up in the pen or the loony bin, of course.

I trained my light on a pair of wooden benches next to the tee. "Let's sit down," I said. I opened the thermos of coffee and poured Stan a cup, drinking mine directly from the container.

"You like it here, don't you?" Stan asked.

"Yeah," I said, "I'm surprised it took me this long to discover it."

We sipped coffee and stared into the darkness. We were facing north. Wilshire was a narrow strip of light in the distance. Cars glided silently along it.

"There's something I have to tell you," I said. "I'm not a cop. I'm a private investigator. I shanghaied you out here illegally. You can take off, or I'll drive you wherever you want to go."

I could feel Stan The Man staring at me in the dark. After a few moments, he laughed. "I knew there was something funny about you, I knew it, but I just couldn't put my finger on it. How come you're looking for Fat Dog?"

"I'm working for him. He hired me to do a little work for him."

"What kind of work?"

"It's confidential. Do you want to split? I'll drive you home."

"Naw, I like it here too. What kind of cases do you handle?"

"Mostly I repossess cars."

Stan laughed, wildly. "Now that's really funny," he said. "I used to steal cars and you repo them. That's a fucking scream!"

"Tell me about looping," I said.

"What about it?"

"Everything."

Stan The Man thought for a minute. What he had to say surprised me: "It's kind of sad. You show up and sign the list in the morning. If there's play, you work. Basically you carry two bags, one on each shoulder. You usually get twenty bucks for eighteen holes. The ladies stiff you about half the time. Some of the men do, too. Some members pay real good, but the caddy master's buddies get those loops. The way you make money in the looping racket is by getting regulars who take good care of you, and by pressing thirty-six holes, which is a lot of fucking work. Or you get foursomes, two on your back and two on a cart, and you make up to forty scoots. Or you get high-class putter jobs with gamblers and high rollers who know how to pay. But it's the guys who suck ass with the caddy master who get that action. Me, I just push thirty-six four days a week and spend the rest of my time fucking off. That's the great thing about looping. You can take off all the time you want, as long as you show up on weekends and for tournaments. It's also why you get so many bums as caddies, there's always cash on hand for booze or dope or the horses.

"We get some young college kids out at Bel-Air now. They got that young golfer image. The members eat it up and whip out heavy for those snotnose cocksuckers. None of 'em know shit about golf, they just know how to hand out a good snow job. They snort cocaine and blow weed out on the course. There's also the horseplayer clique. The caddy master is a bookie, and the guys who bet with him get primo loops. But caddies never save their dough. They either blow it on booze or pussy or gambling or dope. They're always broke. Always coming out to the club to make a measly twenty bucks to get drunk on. Loopers is always hobnobbing with big money, and they never have jackshit themselves.

"For instance, there's this Brentwood goat named Whitey Haines. He's an epileptic and a big boozehound. He used to loop Bel-Air, but he got fired 'cause he kept having seizures out on the course. It shook up the members. Anyway, the Bel-Air pro, he felt real guilty about eighty-sixing Whitey. Whitey ain't doing too good over at Brentwood; them hebes like their goats healthy.

"You see, Whitey is always going on two-week drunks. Them seizures scare the shit out of him, and the booze fixes him up, temporarily. Right before he goes on a drunk, he comes back to Bel-Air and cries the blues to the pro. Tells him he's got to see his dying aunt, or go to the hospital for some tests, or have hemorrhoid surgery, some line of horseshit like that. He puts the bite on the pro for two and a half C's and then splits. After he gets back from his drunk, he starts paying him back: ten here, fifteen there, twenty there. As soon as he gets his debt all paid off, Whitey comes back and pulls the same routine all over again: 'I got cancer of the armpits, pro, lend me two-fifty so I can get it cured.' The pro whips it out on him, and they're off and running again.

"Now the pro knows that Whitey is lying, and Whitey knows that he knows, but they play that charade over and over, 'cause the pro is a caddy who made good, who was good at playing golf and sucking up to money, and guys like Whitey Haines eat him up. He thinks, 'Jesus, if I didn't have such a sweet smile and a sweet swing, I might have ended up like this asshole, packing duck loops and on the dole.' So what's two hundred and fifty scoots on permanent vacation from your pocket if it makes you feel like a humanitarian?

"Looping continues to fucking amaze me. If you think Whitey Haines is a sad case, you ain't heard nothing yet. Take Bicycle Pete. He's dead now. He got fired from Wilshire for never taking a bath. He stunk like a skunk. Rode a girl's bicycle all over town and wore a Dodger cap with a propeller on top. Lived on Skid Row. Everybody thought he was retarded. He kicked off of a heart attack in his room. When the ambulance guys came to take his stiff away, they found over two hundred grand in diamonds in his closet.

"Then there's Dirt Road Dave. The ugliest guy I ever seen. Got this lantern jaw that sticks out about two feet. Used to hit all the invitationals. No caddy master would let him loop regular. He couldn't even work Wilshire, and that's the bottom of the line. So he'd loop invitationals to supplement his welfare check. He had a regular routine: at the end of the day, when all the loopers were hanging around the caddy shack, he'd chug-a-lug a half pint of bourbon, get up on a card table and suck his own dick. We used to throw quarters at him while he did it. He was one of the most famous caddies on the West Coast. Then he made his big mistake. He started doing it in public. The public didn't understand. Only caddies and perverts could dig his act. Old Dave's in Camarillo now.

"It's the loneliness, that's what gets me about looping. All these sad motherfuckers with no families, no responsibility, don't pay no income tax, nothing to look forward to but the World Series pool at the Tap and Cap, the Christmas party in the caddy shack, the next drunk, or the big horse that never hits. We got this college kid, a real smart kid, who loops weekends, and he says that caddies is 'the last vestige of the Colonial South. Golf course cotton pickers lapping at the fringes of a strained noblesse oblige.' He said that we were a holdover from another era, that we were a status symbol, and it was worth it for clubs to keep us around, to uphold their image.

"Caddies on the pro tour is absolutely necessary, of course, but that's another story. The club caddy is on his way out. Carts is coming in. Riviera went cart three years ago. Caddies is gonna blow it. They're too unreliable. Never showing up, or showing up drunk. I'm lucky. If worst comes to worst, I can always do reupholstering. That's my trade, but I hate it. I like looping for the freedom. I'm my own boss, except for the time I'm picking cotton. Besides, it ain't too late for me to change my life. I'm only thirty-nine, like Jack Benny. My probation officer and my shrink have been helping me out a lot. I ain't stolen no cars in over a year. Group therapy's been helping me. My shrink tells me I don't have to be a caddy if I don't want to. That I can be what I want.

"It ain't that way for Fat Dog, though. He's locked into it. He don't want to do nothing else. He hates niggers and he hates Jews, and that's all he's got. The shrink told me that people who hate other people real bad usually hate themselves. Maybe that's how it is with Fat Dog. He's got no friends, except maybe Augie Dougall, who's the only one in the world lame enough to put up with his shit. Fat Dog is always talking about this rich and powerful guy he knows, that he's gonna team up with someday, but that's bullshit. Fantasyland. If he wasn't such a cheap, nasty prick, I'd feel sorry for him.

"Looping wouldn't be such a bummer if it wasn't for the guys who loop. Golf's a great game, and golf courses is beautiful. It's just the poor sad fuckers who pack the bags for a bunch of poor sad fuckers who can't hit the ball that makes the whole thing so sad."

Stan The Man finished his soliloquy, and I sighed in the darkness. I said, "I feel for you. I know how it is to be trapped, watching your life hotfoot it away. If your up-holstering gig falls through, I can help you get started in the repossession racket. I know a lot of people. You could get paid for ripping-off cars. You'd have lots of free time to pursue whatever you wanted. Consider repo-ing, you might like it." I took one of my business cards out of my wallet and handed it to him. "You can reach me at one of these numbers. I'll do all I can to get you started."

Stan put the card into his pocket and stared at me for a long moment. "Thanks," he said. "I mean it. This has been one crazy night. I always figured that if someone offered me a break it would be some rich member at the club who liked the way I called putts, not some private eye repo-man. Let me think about it, okay? This is all happening real fast."

"Think it over. Kick it around with your shrink. He might think it's a bad extension of your disease, like me drinking all this fucking coffee to get a little wired. Let's get out of here. I'll look for Fat Dog later. Right now I'm cold and tired."

We walked back to the car. A heavy fog was rolling in, clinging to the greenery and creating deep oceans of mist. There was silence in the maintenance shack as we passed it. I drove Stan to his hotel in Culver City. We shook hands. He thanked me effusively, and promised to consider my offer. As I drove back to my pad all I could think of was one phrase: "Looping is sadness."

## 6

The following day it seemed like a good idea to let sleeping Fat Dogs lie, at least for the moment. There were other angles to check out. My case was turning into a splendid example of inductive logic: searching for evidence a decade old to convict a killer whose identity I already knew. Since I was seeking to link Sol Kupferman to the Club Utopia, it seemed logical to start with the owner, Wilson Edwards.

Remembering that McNamara told me Edwards had a criminal record, I called Jensen at R&I for an address. He came through: Edwards had been busted the year before for possession of heroin. His address at that time was the Hotel Rector on Western Avenue just south of Hollywood Boulevard. I put on my intimidation outfit; a checked cotton sportcoat, tie, and contrasting slacks, and drove there.

The Hotel Rector was a thousand years old, and bespoke a despair that was uniquely Hollywood: the lobby was crowded with elderly pensioners awaiting their monthly stipends, black prostitutes, and low riders drinking beer. It smelled of urine and liniment. The loneliness there was almost tangible.

The old man at the desk told me that Wilson Edwards was still at the Rector and staying in room 311. I took the stairs. The hallways didn't smell any better than the lobby and hadn't been swept recently.

I knocked on 311. No answer. I knocked again. This time I heard the rumbling of a voice aroused from sleep. I knocked again, louder. Footsteps approached the door. "Eddie?" a voice called tentatively. "Is that you?"

Not wanting to disappoint anyone, I answered, "Yeah, it's me. Open up."

The man who opened the door was truly horrific. He looked like one of the concentration camp victims on the walls of Fat Dog's shack: his gray skin hung slackly from prominent cheekbones, his eyes were sunken and filmy and the T-shirt and boxer shorts he was wearing encased his shrunken torso like a tent. He was shaking, and it took him several moments to realize I wasn't Eddie. "You're not Eddie," he said finally.

"You're right," I said. "I'm not. Are you Wilson Edwards?"

"Yeah, are you fuzz?"

"No, I'm a private investigator. May I come in? I'd like to talk to you."

His eyes turned shrewd, and as he sized me up he grabbed the door jambs with both hands for support. The veins in both arms were nearly obliterated. He was a long time junkie. I grabbed his left wrist. He tried to pull away, but I held on. Some of the tracks were recent.

"Is Eddie your connection?" I asked. "Are you sick now? You can tell me." I tried to soothe him. "I won't hurt you, I just want to ask you a few questions. It won't take long."

Seeing that he had no choice, Edwards motioned me inside. "I'm not sick yet, but I will be soon," he said as I shut the door behind us. Then he started to laugh. "Man, that's funny. I'm dying of cancer but I'm not sick yet. That's funny." He pointed to a beat-up armchair. "You have a seat. I'm gonna geez. I can't talk to you till I get over these shakes."

I sat down and Edwards went into the bathroom and shut the door. I checked out the room: it reeked of body odors, but was clean. Edwards was evidently something of a jazz buff. There were dozens of albums arranged neatly on a wall shelf, mostly be-bop and modern jazz. There was no phonograph in sight. Edwards returned to the room. He looked relieved, but no healthier. His eyes were dilated and his shakes had stopped.

His voice was somewhat calmer. "Dilaudid used to be delightful, but now I've got to be smacked-back for all the pain to go. Let's make this fast. I don't want you here when Eddie shows up."

"How long have you got?" I asked.

"Maybe four, five months."

"You should be in the hospital."

"No way, José. That chemotherapy shit is a bum trip. I want to go out walking with my Lucy." He made a gesture with his hand, indicating shooting up.

"Who supplies your stuff? It doesn't look like you've got much money."

"You didn't come here to ask me that, did you?"

"No, I didn't. I came here to talk to you about the Club Utopia."

For an instant surprise flashed into Edwards's eyes, then he recovered and gave me a death's head smile. "The Club Utopia burned down on December 10, 1968. The guys who did the job shuffled off this mortal coil two years later. The whole scene is a long-gone dead duck."

"Perhaps. You owned the place, didn't you?"

"Right."

"Where did you get the money to buy it?"

"I saved it."

"Where did you get the money for the liquor license?"

"I saved that, too."

"You need juice to get a liquor license. Who did you know at the licensing bureau?"

"I knew a guy. I forget his name. It was a long time ago."

"I don't buy it, Edwards. I've got you pegged. A smack addict jazz fiend, circa 1950. All those records and you don't even have a record player. A record player has got to be good for five or six spoons. You've never had a pot to piss in, except maybe while you were fronting for the real owner of the Utopia. Those tracks on your arms tell your whole life story."

"Things were different then. I had my shit together."

"Don't shit a shitter," I said, raising my voice. "I want the truth. It's important to me. We can do this either of two ways. One, we can wait until Eddie shows up, and I bust both of you for possession. That way you die in the jail ward of the County Hospital. Or, two, you can tell me what I want to know, and make a few bucks for your trouble. The choice is yours."

Edwards gave it some thought. Fear quashed his hipster act. "If I talk to you and it gets back to certain people, it would be bad for me. I just want to die in peace. You can dig that, can't you?"

"Sure. I'm a good liar. I can think fast. Wherever your information takes me, you can count on my not revealing my source. I live by the old code." The old code: never give up your informant unless it can give you access to more and better information.

It didn't take Edwards long. "What do you want to know?" he asked.

"Who really owned the Utopia, for starters," I said.

"It was a guy named Sol Kupferman. A rich guy. A furrier."

"Why was the joint in your name?"

"For tax purposes. Strictly a tax dodge. Kupferman owned half-a-dozen bars and liquor stores under phony names. He used to be in the rackets in the old days, and he couldn't get any liquor licenses."

"I heard that Kupferman was a big time bookie, back in the 50's. Was he running a book at the Utopia?"

"Nothing big. He had a wire going to help defray tax costs and overhead. He was running steady in the black because the wire took care of all that."

"Did Kupferman run the book himself?"

"No."

"Who did?"

"He had this guy Ralston, used to be a ballplayer, take care of his action at all his spots. Ralston worked at this country club where he was a member. Kupferman paid him good."

"How did he work it? Ralston, I mean."

"He used to come by at odd times to pick up his bets. The bettors would leave their bread with the bartender. Ralston sent a big spade around to pay off. Ralston used to send the bets out to the track with caddies from the club."

"What else do you know about the operation?"

"Nothing. I don't know what you're looking for, or why you're even interested in all this ancient history. That's all I know, but I can tell you this: it was just a small potatoes setup."

Edwards was getting nervous. He was remarkably lucid for a man so close to death, but now the strain was starting to show.

"I can tell you're starting to hurt. This might take a little longer. Why don't you go into the can and get straight?"

He took my advice. When he closed the bathroom door,

I hopped up from my chair and gave the room a quick toss. I opened drawers and cupboards and checked the contents of shelves. Nothing. Behind his record collection I found a County Disability check and a small prescription bottle of barbiturates. I let them lie. When Edwards came back, he looked no better. A corpse is a corpse. His voice was a little steadier though. He might have been able to handle himself twenty years ago.

"Shake it, daddy, what else do you want to know?" he said. Besides suffering from terminal cancer, he was suffering from terminal hipsterism.

"How did you know Kupferman? Why did he offer you this job?"

"Solly K knew my brother from his racket days. My brother was a punk, but he got around. My brother approached me, told me Solly needed someone to front a bar for him. I'd draw myself a cut each week, keep the books, and show up a couple of nights a week to make it look good. For a C-note a week. I took the job, it's that simple."

"What kind of man was Kupferman?"

"Solly K is a sweetheart, a truly gentle person. I know for a fact that he's been helping out a couple of old people whose kids got burned up in the torch. He felt real bad about the bombing. Like he was guilty himself."

"He's still taking care of you, isn't he?"

"What do you mean?"

"Dilaudid is not cheap and heroin is twenty-five dollars a spoon, and you get it delivered. Someone is keeping you from *really* hurting. You haven't got any money. Is Kupferman supplying you?"

Edwards began to tremble, and his voice rose to some otherworldly pitch of junkie indignation. "Solly K never hurt anyone! He keeps a lot of people from hurting! You never had a friend like that! Guys like you just know how to hurt people! That's how you get your rocks off. Guys . . ." His angry voice trailed off into a coughing attack. I had learned all I was going to. It was enough. I had Fat Dog's motive for the bombing down pat. I was anxious to be free of Edwards's death stench. I remembered the money I promised him, but decided against it. Edwards was still coughing as I went out the door. As I looked back at him, he feebly flipped me the finger.

The hot, smoggy air that hit me as I walked out onto the

street was a relief. Even the hookers and black pimps lounging in front of the All-American Burger looked good.

I walked back to the car, turned on the radio news and went into shock. A wail rose up in my throat as I listened: "A fire last night caused an estimated four million dollars' damage to the Solly K Fur Salon and warehouse in Beverly Hills. The fire broke out at one-thirty A.M., sweeping through the handsome structure on Santa Monica Boulevard and Bedford Drive. Beverly Hills firemen quelled the blaze before it could spread to other buildings, but not before the fashionable fur showplace burned to the ground. There were no injuries and the cause of the blaze is now being investigated. Meanwhile, on a happier note . . ."

I switched it off. My head was banging like cymbals gone mad, with guilt and fear racing for control of my mind. I fought them off, taking deep breaths and telling myself it was all to the good: Fat Dog's insanity was peaking and I was the only one who could stop him. I started the car and headed south on side streets, cutting corners and running stop signs.

I caught the Santa Monica Freeway westbound near Washington. There was a midmorning lull in traffic and I made good time. I got off the freeway at Lincoln and headed for the arson shack. The back yard looked the same: forgotten playthings and high grass. The door of the shack was open, and the place had been completely cleaned out: no arson supplies, tools, or pornography. The pseudo-gang graffiti I had painted on the walls had been crossed out with large brush strokes of the same color. Freshly painted obscenities covered the back wall near the workbench: "fuck," "cocksuck," "kill fuck," and "cocksuck bastard." I got down on my knees and looked around. Nothing.

Leaving the door ajar, I walked up to the front house and knocked on the door. A fat black woman in a muumuu answered. "Yes?" she said suspiciously.

I sized her up quickly as a T.V. watcher and took my act from there: "My name is Savage," I said, "I'm with the F.B.I. We have reason to believe that the man renting your back house is an escaped convict. We . . ." I never got the chance to finish. The woman threw open the screen door and almost threw herself on me, slamming her huge arms against her sides in frustration.

"You arrests that no good bum, officer!" she screamed. "That no good bum took off owing me two months' rent, and threw all kind of filthy pictures on the grounds for all the little childrens to see. You arrests him! He called me a nigger bitch!"

I placed an arm on her quaking shoulder. "Hold on, ma'am," I said. "Just let me ask a few questions, all right?"

"All right, Mr. Savage."

"First of all, is this man who rents from you about forty years old, short, fat, with dirty golf clothes?"

"That's the no-good bum!"

"Good. How long has he rented from you?"

"Goin' on four years. He don't live there, he just keep his Tijuana sin things there."

"What do you mean?"

"Dirty books! Dirty pictures! He tells me he the king of Tijuana. He tells me he gonna race dogs down there. He . . ."

I interrupted. "When did you see him last?"

"I sees him last night. He knocks on my door and says: 'Bye-bye, nigger bitch. I'm goin' to T.J. to claim my kingdom, but I'll be back to throw you in the gas chamber.' Then he points to the yard and says 'I left plenty of reading material for the kiddies.' Then he makes the devil's sign at me and runs down the street! You arrests him, officer!"

I didn't wait to find out what "the devil sign" was. I ran back to my car, leaving the woman standing on her porch, slamming her arms and demanding justice.

I took surface streets to Beverly Hills, to give me time to think. I put on KUSC. They were playing a symphonic piece that sounded like Haydn. I was exhilarated, so high that a cup of coffee might blow the top of my head off. I wondered what my elation stemmed from. My case had blown sky high, the two people I had vowed to protect were in grave danger, and Fat Dog Baker was almost certainly in Mexico.

Then it hit me. I was home. For the first time in my life I was on to something important, something vast and complex, and I was the sole arbiter of it. Before this, September 2, 1967 had been the pivotal date of my life. I was twenty-one. On that date I had heard, really heard, music for the first time. It was Beethoven's Third Symphony. Walter had been trying to get me to listen to classical music for years, to no avail. The First Movement of the *Eroica* went through me like a transfusion of hope and fortitude. I was off with German romanticism, listening to Beethoven, Brahms, Wagner, and Bruckner six, eight, ten hours a day. I had found truth, or so I thought, and a strange metamorphosis took place: infused with the romance of giants, I gave up my vague academic dream and became a cop. An uneasy, malcontented one at first, until the booze came along and made the low-level administration of power exciting beyond my wildest fantasies.

It worked for a while, but gradually I began fucking up. My performance on the streets deteriorated as my dependence on alcohol grew. I finally committed an irrevocable act, and my career was over. Fortunately I had done Cal Myers a big one during my days with the Vice Squad, and now I was the repo-prince of the new car king of the Valley.

I remembered what Stan The Man had said last night: that he didn't have to be a caddy. My feeling three days ago as I was waiting for Irwin had been prophetic: my life was changing, my vistas were endless in this charisma fixated society—if I didn't blow this case.

I parked and walked several blocks to the ruins of Solly K's fur empire. From a block away I could see a crowd of spectators looking interestedly into a roped-off area. Two patrolmen were watching the crowd. There was one patrol car and two red firemarshals' cars parked on the sidewalk.

When I got to the site of the leveled building I saw men in business suits poking in the rubble, carrying evidence kits and talking guardedly among themselves. I waited for them to finish. The site was one of total devastation: mountains of charred wood and insulation, piles of ashes, soot everywhere. It had settled on adjoining buildings and some storeowners had set workmen out to scrub down their walls.

I had had no idea how large Kupferman's warehouse had been. The facade was deceiving—the structure itself had extended back a quarter of a city block. From what I could see, no other buildings had been even singed by the fire. Fat Dog's arson skills had improved since his Molotov Cocktail days. I was impressed.

One of the detectives was walking out of the rubble,

brushing soot from his pants and looking worried. He was a burly cop, about fifty. I watched him move away from the crowd of onlookers toward an unmarked police car. I intercepted him as he unlocked the door. "Excuse me," I said, "my name is Brown. I'm a private investigator."

I handed him my photostat to prove it. He checked it out carefully and handed it back. "What is it, Mr. Brown? I'm very busy."

I ran off my hastily prepared cover story: "I won't keep you long. Sol Kupferman has hired me to look into the fire. He trusts the police and firemarshals to do a thorough investigation, but he wants this thing covered from all angles. Right now I only want to know one thing. Was it arson?"

The cop looked me over from head to toe. "You should know that police officers at crime scenes do not give out confidential information to civilians. We will be in touch with Mr. Kupferman. Good day."

I watched him get into his car and drive off. He had the drawn, abstracted look of a veteran cop just handed a tough one. His worried expression was more than enough confirmation. I walked back to my car, then headed for the gas station at Franklin and Argyle to see Omar Gonzalez, conspiracy buff.

Franklin and Argyle was a blast from my past; one of the big ones. In June of 1972, on information supplied by Jack Skolnick, I led a raid on the notorious Castle Argyle, methedrine capitol of the West Coast. An eight-story Moorish apartment house built in the 20's, the Castle Argyle was a hotbed of hippie intrigue in the early 70's. Skolnick had told me he had been approached by one "Cosmo," a UCLA chemistry major and resident of the castle, with an offer to sell him three gallons of liquid meth amphetamine for $5,000. The street value was close to half a million. I was hot for adventure and began staking the castle out, along with an obnoxious rookie patrolman named Snyder. We never told our superiors or the guys in Narcotics what we were doing. We were rogue cops, out for the big kill.

Cosmo lived on the sixth floor and had dozens of visitors nightly. Hiding behind some towering hibiscus plants, Snyder and I heard Cosmo's departing guests remark on the great quality of his stuff. After three nights of this, we decided we had enough to act on and scheduled our raid for the following evening. We could have pulled it off low-key, dressing in hippie disguises of beard, moustache, and love beads from Bert Wheeler's Magic Store on the Boulevard, and making a discreet buy before lowering the boom; but fueled by large quantities of Old Grand Dad, we decided to break the door down and go in with shotguns.

We did and it worked. Until Snyder got disappointed. Cosmo and his girlfriend submitted quietly, scared shitless by the two oversized short-hairs with badges pinned to their chests and wielding heavy firepower. They led us to their stash, let us handcuff them, and waited meekly as we phoned for a patrol car and a matron for the girl. But Snyder wasn't satisfied. He wanted to shoot off his shotgun. He was heartbroken that he had missed his opportunity. He said the bust was like getting laid without getting your dick sucked first.

He rumbled through the apartment opening drawers and knocking over chairs. Then he saw the Che Guevara poster, life-size, taped to a gilt-covered bedroom mirror. "Brownie," he called, "look at this." I came into the bedroom, leaving my handcuffed prisoners unguarded. Snyder, late of the U.S. Marine Corps was aghast with indignation. "I'm gonna kill him, I'm gonna kill that Commie cocksucker!" he cried, and blasted Che Guevara, the mirror, and a good part of the bedroom wall to kingdom come with his Remington pump. Before I could stop him, he blasted the other wall, sending Janis Joplin and Jimi Hendrix to hell. When the dust cleared, Snyder was grinning like a sated lover, our prisoners were screaming "Police brutality" and I quite literally shit in my pants.

A few minutes later we heard the sirens. I looked out the window and saw eight black-and-whites jamming up the streets. Knowing my trigger-happy colleagues craved excitement as much as my lunatic partner and I and might open fire at any moment, I ran down six flights of stairs, through the lobby and out the door of the building. When I hit the long walkway that led down to the street, I threw my hands above my head and yelled, "Police officer, don't shoot!"

Some of the cops standing by their patrol cars with hardware at the ready recognized me and motioned me to join them. My mind racing with stories to explain the shooting, I ran toward them. Just as I was about to reach the street my half-empty pint of Old Grand Dad slipped out of my waistband and broke on the sidewalk in front of me. At that moment a merciful death was all I wished for. Liquid feces were running down my legs and my career was ruined. I would have to get a job as a security guard for a buck fifty an hour and drink Gallo muscatel. It was all over. Until a tough-looking old patrol sergeant started to laugh. Others joined him as I stood there, mute, lest I increase my culpability. The laughter was getting louder as the old sergeant pulled me aside and whispered "Is there anyone hurt up there, son? Is your partner okay?"

I told him everything was okay, except for some property damage.

"We can handle that," he said. A group of officers went upstairs to rescue Cosmo and his girlfriend from Snyder, and Snyder from himself.

I was driven back to the station where I took a shower and changed clothes. In the report that was filed, no mention was made of the shotgun blasts (the suspects having been coerced into silence), my bottle, or the shit in my pants. Snyder and I received a commendation and by the perverse logic of the macho mentality my floundering police career was back in full stride.

The Mobil Station where Omar Gonzalez worked was catty-corner from the scene of my past triumph. The place was deserted when I pulled in, so I pulled up to the ethyl pump and served myself. I looked in vain for a Chicano in his late twenties. When my tank was full, I went searching for the attendant and found him under the lube rack working on a car. He turned around to face me, a stocky, affable-looking kid of about twenty. "I've got the exact change," I said, "I know you guys appreciate it." The kid gave me a pleasant smile as I handed him the money. "By the way," I said, "is Omar around? I'm a buddy of his."

The kid looked at me strangely. "Omar ain't been around for two weeks. He ain't at the recovery house, either. I don't know where the hell he is. He gets away with murder 'cause the customers like him. The boss would give me the axe quick if I pulled the shit Omar does."

"What kind of shit does Omar pull? I asked. "I haven't seem him in a while."

He screwed up his face into a parody of concentration. "Don't get me wrong, I like Omar. Everybody does. But he's always talking this Chicano Activist shit and taking off to hang out at the drug recovery crashpad, leaving me holding the fucking bag and leaving his goddamn car blocking up the station." The kid pointed to a ten-year-old yellow Plymouth. I was about to throw some more questions at him when a customer pulled in, a good-looking woman in a convertible. He forgot all about me and strode over to the pumps, his face contorted into a wolf grin.

I walked over to check out Omar's car. I wrote down the license number on my notepad, then looked in the front window. The seats were upholstered in white naugahyde and the brownish matter that was caked in splotches on the driver's side looked like dried blood. The back seat was covered with a green tarpaulin and underneath it were shapes resembling boxes. I didn't have to think twice. The doors of the car were locked and my master keys were back at my pad. I ran to my car and opened the trunk, digging out a blank repo order and my bumper jack.

The kid was finishing up with the woman in the convertible as I ran by him. I stopped and shoved the repo order in his face. "I'm a private investigator," I yelled, "This is a repossession order for that car. I'm taking it."

His jaw dropped and he just stood there while I went to work. I gave a quick look around for cops, then slammed the bumper jack full force into the front window of the Plymouth. The safety glass shattered inward and I reached through the hole and opened the door.

I scraped off some of the dried matter on the seat cover and smelled it. It was definitely blood. I swung the front seat forward, dug under the tarpaulin and pulled out two cardboard boxes. They were light and I slung them easily onto the trunk of the car to open.

The attendant was at my side now, looking nervous. "Hey man, are you sure this is legal?" he said, his voice breaking.

"Yeah, punk, this is legal. Now get the fuck out of my way," I said, almost screaming.

I watched him retreat toward the lube rack, then dug into the boxes. When I saw what I had I almost fainted. The first box contained bookies' ledgers, eight or nine of them, bound in brown leather. My Vice Squad experience was paying off: the bettors' names were in numbered code in one column, and in the succeeding columns were amounts of money, dates, and check marks probably indicating collections. I flipped through all the ledgers quickly. They were identical in their layout. The same margining, but with different codings, dates, and amounts of money. The dates went back twelve years. Wedged into the back of the bottom ledger were eight or ten blank Los Angeles County checks, the kind used for paying employees and disbursing Welfare money. I looked through all the ledgers for envelopes or something else to tie into the blank checks, but found nothing.

I ripped open the second carton and almost died on the spot. The box was filled with pornographic photos, identical in theme and backdrop to the ones I had seen on the walls of Fat Dog's arson shack: the same women, the same sleazy rooms, the same cheap bordertown souvenirs. Oh Omar, you crazy motherfucker, I kept thinking, what have you wrought! But I wasn't prepared for what came next: all the blood in my body jammed to my head and my lungs expanded and contracted like an accordion gone mad. I was looking at glossy color photos of Jane Baker, cellist, nude with her legs wide open, her mouth and eyes set in an attitude of sexual challenge: "Take me if you can. If you perform, I'll make it well worth your while." She had a beautiful, lithe body and her lust seemed genuine: her pubis was wet and her nipples were swollen.

My mind raced in a thousand different directions, and every variation of the Baker-Kupferman case that I came up with went haywire in the light of this new evidence. All I knew for certain was that I had two cases now.

I ran back to my car, got a crowbar out of my back seat and returned to the Plymouth and pried open the trunk. It was empty. I hauled the two boxes over to my car and locked them in my trunk.

The attendant was sitting in the office drinking a Coke, sullen and dejected. He looked up when I walked in, backing off like I was going to hit him. I controlled my excitement and spoke to him gently: "I'm sorry I yelled at you, but this is very important stuff I'm involved in. I've got to get in touch with Omar Gonzalez. It's urgent. I need his home address and the phone number of that drug rehab place where he hangs out."

He waited a moment, then flipped through a Rolodex next to the telephone. He called out a number and I grabbed the phone and dialed it. A woman answered on the third ring. I told her it was urgent that I speak to Omar Gonzalez. She said that Omar hadn't been at the center in over three weeks. She told me that he was an unpaid drug counselor who conducted group therapy sessions with Chicano youngsters, and that he came and went as he pleased. In a condescending voice she said that Omar was a passionate and mercurial young man, given to disappearing for weeks at a time, but a gifted counselor who had real rapport with young people. The woman started to embark on a discourse about the drug problem, but I cut her short and hung up.

The attendant was staring at me, slack-jawed and awe-inspired.

"What's Omar's address?" I asked.

He consulted the Rolodex again. "It's 1983 Vendome. That's in Silverlake. Tacoland."

I gave the kid one of my business cards. It had my home number as well as the office one on it. "If Omar shows up, you tell him to call me. Tell him it's very important. Tell him I know who killed his brother." I patted him on the shoulder and winked at him. He gave me a smile that tried hard to be conspiratorial. I got in my car and jammed for Silverlake.

Silverlake is a beautiful hilly enclave of middle and lower middle-class dwellings east of Hollywood. The hills are steep and the roads circuitous. Houses and apartment buildings are set back from the street and often hung with heavy shrubbery, so it's easy to get lost.

I turned off Sunset onto Silverlake Boulevard and went under the bridge that marks the informal border of the area. I expected it to take a while to find Vendome, but I blundered onto it, about half-a-mile north of Sunset. 1983 was a court of small bungalows separated by knee-high white picket fences. I parked half a block away and walked breezily into the courtyard. There was a bank of locked metal mailboxes next to the first bungalow on the left, where I learned that Omar Gonzalez lived in number 12. His box was crammed full of mail, so it was fair to assume Omar hadn't been around for awhile.

Bungalow 12 was at the backend of the court, on the

right. Like all the others, it was white clapboard, weather-beaten and musty. I rang the bell and got no answer, then tried the flimsy wooden door. It was locked. I walked around to the side of the bungalow and tried the windows. They were locked, and dust-covered venetian blinds kept me from peering in.

I went looking for the manager. The mailbox directed me to number 3. I rang the bell and an aging slattern in a housecoat opened the door suspiciously, keeping the screen door shut. When I told her I had a telegram for Omar Gonzalez in number 12, she jumped back as if buzzed by a swarm of bees. "Is something wrong, ma'am?" I asked.

"Omar ain't been around for weeks," she said, opening the door a crack and reaching for the nonexistent piece of paper with one hand.

"I can't do that, I have to give it to the addressee himself. Thank you, ma'am."

She gave me a frightened look and slammed the door. Something was wrong.

I walked to a liquor store at the end of the block and bought a ginger ale. Drinking it and eyeballing the pretty Chicanas passing by consumed twenty minutes. That seemed like a safe interval.

I walked back to the court. No one was around and the manager's door was closed and all the shutters drawn. On the porch of number 12, I gave a quick look in both directions, drew my gun and kicked the door open. Crouching in the combat stance, I went into the dark apartment, gently closing the door behind me.

It was dead quiet and I stood there a long moment until my eyes became accustomed to the dark. Gradually the outlines of a turned-over sofa, an upended bookshelf, and mound of books became visible. Several potted plants had been knocked off a windowsill, spreading broken plaster and dirt on the floor, and a large carpet had been pulled up and wadded ceiling-high into a corner. I moved cautiously, gun first, into the other rooms. The small kitchen off to the right was similarly devastated: the cupboards had been ransacked, dishes lay in heaps on the floor, and the refrigerator had been knocked over, its rancid contents fouling the air. The bathroom was a shambles, but the bedroom had been hit the worst: broken glass from wall mirrors was everywhere, the bed had been torn apart and the mattress ripped to shreds, clothes had been torn out of the closet and lay strewn on top of the other rubble. An old gas heater had been ripped out of the wall and now lay among the pile of mattress stuffing.

The trashers had done a good job: there was nothing *personal* to be found belonging to Omar Gonzalez. No papers, journals, or memorabilia of any sort, just the detritus of a young man's life. I poked about in the rubble some more, this time with the lights on. I was looking for bloodstains. There were none. I put my gun back in its holster, went into the bathroom, found a large towel and wiped every plane and surface I could have possibly touched.

The sunlight and hot summer air were jarring as I walked outside. I was troubled. For the first time since the onset of my case, I didn't know what to do.

Still troubled, I drove to the bank and withdrew two thousand in twenties for operating expenses, then went home and spent a long evening listening to Bruckner. Before I went to bed I laid out my light blue seersucker suit, yellow buttondown shirt, and navy blue print tie. I wanted to look good for Jane Baker.

At 7:45 A.M., I was stationed across the street from Kupferman's house. At eight-thirty Jane Baker walked out the front door, carrying her cello in a black leather case to her car and driving off down Elevado. I was close behind. She led me to the large park across the street from the Beverly Hills Hotel, where she parked and lugged her cello to a bench and set it up on its collapsible pod. I parked down the street. As I approached she was assembling her sheet music on its stand, and the first movement main theme of the Dvorak "Concerto" followed. I stepped into Jane Baker's life: "That concerto was Dvorak's best shot," I said. "Nothing else he did came close to it. Have you been playing long?"

Jane Baker gave me a long, slow look and a slow smile, tinged with the slightest bit of resentment. "I've been playing for ten years," she said.

I sat down on a bench facing her and she resumed her playing. I was uncertain as to whether to continue with small talk or drop my bomb. She took the decision out of my hands: "You were right about Dvorak," she said. "The cello concerto is his masterpiece. I wish I were equal to it."

"Maybe you will be someday."

"Maybe. You never know."

"Am I distracting you from your practice?"

"Not really, yet. Are you a musician? You don't look like one."

"I'm not. But I love great music more than anything in the world. I think it's the closest we'll ever get to pure truth."

Jane Baker was measuring my words with a hard-edged light in her eyes. "I agree, more or less," she said, "but I think maybe you are distracting me. This whole thing has the air of being rehearsed, on your part. I'm not afraid of you, but you're trying to manipulate me, and I don't like being manipulated through my music."

"Shall I cut the rebop, and get to the point?"

"Please do. I'll give you five minutes, then I have to practice."

"Fair enough. My name is Brown. I'm a private investigator. Your name is Jane Baker, cellist and nonconjugal roommate of Sol Kupferman, late of the fur business. Earlier this week I was hired to investigate you and Kupferman. I did. I didn't discover anything damaging or incriminating. About you two, that is. However, in the course of my investigation, I gathered a great deal of evidence that indicates that your brother Frederick, AKA Fat Dog, is a psychotic arsonist and is determined to wrest you away from Sol Kupferman, even if it means killing him. I'm sure he doesn't want to hurt you—you're his obsessive love object—but yesterday he burned Kupferman's warehouse to the ground. Tomorrow he might torch Kupferman's house and you may end up reduced to a pile of French fried guacamole in the process. I don't want that to happen. I want to find your brother and get him put away before he hurts anyone else. You can help me by getting Kupferman to talk to me, and by telling me everything you can about your brother."

During the course of my monologue Jane Baker had gone white. She put her cello and bow on the bench beside her and wrenched her hands. There was a vein in her forehead pulsing with tension. I stared at the ground to make it easier for her to regain her composure. When I looked up she was staring at me. "Freddy," she said, her voice quavering, "Jesus Christ. I always knew he was sick. But this. Oh, God! Can you prove what you've told me?"

"No."

"But you're certain?"

"Yes, I'm positive."

"How did you find all this out?"

"I can't tell you."

"You said someone hired you to investigate Sol and me. Who was it?"

"I can't tell you that, either. I'm sorry."

"Why can't you?! You make all kinds of accusations against my brother, say that my best friend and I are in danger, and you won't tell me a goddamn thing!"

I resisted an impulse to move to her bench and put my arm around her. "Do you believe what I've told you, Miss Baker?"

"Yes. Somehow I do."

"Good. Will you help me then?"

She hesitated a moment. "I think so. How?"

"Tell me about your brother."

"What about him?"

"A moment ago you said you always knew he was sick. You could start by elaborating on that."

Jane Baker was silent for a long moment. When she finally spoke her voice was steady. "Freddy and I were orphans. Our parents died when we were children. An auto wreck. I was four, which would have made Freddy twelve. There were no relatives to take us in, so we were shuffled around to various foster homes, always together. I was too young to really remember my parents, but Freddy remembered them and was convinced they had been killed by some sort of monster. He had terrible nightmares about this monster. We used to share the same bedroom in most of the foster homes, and Freddy was always waking up screaming about the monster. Once I asked him what it looked like, and he showed me a giant octopus in a horror comic book. Another time he showed me a photograph of a wolf and said it looked like that.

"He was a frightened and hateful boy, from the beginning. A sadist. We lived together for six years, until Freddy turned eighteen. I saw him torture animals many times, and it frightened me, but I shrugged it off. Burning ants

with a magnifying glass, things like that. He was a very
sullen boy and very fat, with terrible oily skin and acne.
None of the foster parents we had could get close to him.
His ugliness and meanness alienated the nicest of them,
until they wanted to get rid of him. The childcare people
wanted to keep us together, so I had to go where Freddy
did. When he turned eighteen, he went off and lived by
himself. He got worse. He used to come and visit me and
tell me ugly stories about killing dogs and cats. Once he
told me he shoved a whole litter of live kittens down a
garbage disposal. It was true, too; I found out later from
someone who saw it.

"When I was about fifteen, I went through a wild period
and ended up in a Catholic orphanage. As I got older,
Freddy started acting strange, sexually. Asking me all sorts
of intimate questions. He was caddying at Hillcrest then
and he would pester me to come out and look around,
telling me how beautiful it was. So I did. Freddy was right.
It was beautiful, especially after St. Vibiana's. So I started
hanging out there. Hiding out with a book in the trees
while the people played golf and taking long walks around
the course at sunset. I was kind of a crazy, lonely, searching young girl and I felt at peace there. I hated to have to
go back to the orphanage. I loved the golf course and the
dreams I dreamed there too much.

"So I ran away. Freddy got me a sleazy room in Culver
City and I spent all my spare time at Hillcrest, working in
the caddy shack and roaming the course. There I met Sol,
who is the kindest, most decent and compassionate person
I've ever met. Genuinely altruistic. He took an interest in
me. I had recently become interested in music—I would
take my little portable radio with me out on the course
for long concerts at night. I told Sol that I was an orphan,
that I lived in a crummy room and picked up a few dollars
cooking and cleaning out the caddy shack. I told him I
wanted to learn to play the cello more than anything in the
world. I remember his exact reply when I told him that. He
said, 'So be it.' So I went to live with Sol. He had a big
house and no family. I had my own room, my own tutor to
help me with my education, and the best cello lessons
money could buy. That was eleven years ago. I'm still
there. Sol has never asked anything of me except that I
seek beauty. This cello is a Stradivarius and almost price-

less. Sol bought it for me. In no way am I equal to it, but Sol thinks I will be someday. That's an example of how unqualified his love and respect for me is.

"But Freddy has hated Sol from the beginning, and it compounded the sickness that was already festering in him. While I was living in that crummy room in Culver City he used to come over and expose himself to me. Erect. It was sickening. I was frightened, but afraid to tell anyone for fear I'd get sent back to the orphanage. He was obsessed with me sexually then and I'm sure he still is. He writes me letters about how I'm his family and we should live together in Mexico and raise greyhounds, and about how Sol is an Israeli-Communist agent. I always read the letters out of hope that he's changed, somehow developed some degree of humanity; but there's no change, just hate and ugliness. I haven't seen my brother in four or five years. I want nothing to do with him, now or ever. And now you tell me he's an arsonist and he wants to kill Sol! Oh God, oh Christ."

I moved to Jane's bench and placed an arm around her shoulder. She didn't resist, just stared at the ground, her body clenched against an onslaught of tears. "Look," I said gently, "I understand. You've got a good life going for you, then this crazy non sequitur comes along. I'm a stranger, but I'm all right, really. You can check me out. I was a police officer for six years. I got involved in this thing against my will, but now that I'm involved I'm going to see it through. But I need your help. Will you help me?" I relinquished my arm from her shoulders.

Jane looked up at me and smiled, then fumbled in her purse for cigarettes and matches. Her hands were shaking, so I lit her cigarette for her. She inhaled deeply and her whole body seemed to crash in acceptance as she exhaled. "I take it that smile implied consent," I said. "Right?"

Jane stared at the ground and blew out another lungful of smoke. "Right," she replied.

"Good."

"Oh God, this is so fucking crazy! Look, I know you told me, but I've forgotten your name."

"Fritz Brown."

"Look, Mr. Brown—"

"Call me Fritz."

"Okay. Look, Fritz, I haven't seen my brother in five

years or so. Apparently this hatred for Sol that he's been harboring all these years has come to a head. Why now, I don't know—you can't expect a crazy man to act logically. The police were over at the house last night, talking to Sol. They told him the cause of the fire was arson. They asked him if he had any enemies, in business or otherwise. Sol said he didn't know of any. Sol told me the police always suspect the owner of the business when the place of business burns down. You know, setting fire to the place for the insurance money, which is ridiculous in Sol's case, because business was booming. But if you need help on this case and if you have circumstantial evidence pointing to Freddy, why don't you just go to the police and tell them? Get them to handle it."

"It won't work. All my evidence is related to another case that was solved *incorrectly* over a decade ago. My evidence would be disregarded because it makes too many police agencies look bad. I know the cop mentality. If I persisted in trying to convince them, I might jeopardize my license and I can't afford that. The only way to end this thing is for me to find your brother, arrest him, and secure a confession."

"I believe you. I hate bureaucrats, for good reason." Jane paused reflectively. "You said that you've investigated Sol. Then you probably know that a long, long time ago he was involved in the crime word. Big fucking deal. He told me about it. He never hurt anyone, but the cops and the district attorney hounded him, brought him up before the grand jury for nothing. Pure harassment. He almost got kicked out of Hillcrest because of it. So how can I help you?"

"First, some questions. Have there been any strange occurrences lately around your house? Strange phone calls? Someone calling, then hanging up when you answer? Any prowlers?"

"Nothing like that, but there has been something evil going on in the neighborhood, though I never connected it with Freddy. About a month ago there was a rash of animal poisonings. Someone was tossing poisoned hamburger into back yards. Four or five dogs and cats ate it and died. Our gardener's dog ate some and got very sick, but lived. We called the police but nothing came of it. Do you think it could have been Freddy?"

"Maybe. Did your brother ever mention specifically where in Mexico he wanted to settle down?"

"Yes. Somewhere near Tijuana or Ensenada. Baja California. Not the real Mexico."

"Did he ever mention a rich and powerful man that he was going to team up with? Maybe work for?"

"Yes. In his letters he was always mentioning a rich man who shared his anti-Semitic views. He was going to be this man's partner. I put it off as pure fantasy."

"Have you saved any of these letters?"

"I might be able to dig a few of them out of my wastebasket, if it hasn't been emptied."

"Will you try to find them for me?"

Jane put out her cigarette on the ground. "Yes," she said.

"Good. I have to see Kupferman as soon as possible. Will you arrange a meeting?"

Jane was already shaking her head "no" vehemently. "That's impossible, absolutely impossible, I can't have him worried about what you've told me, at least not yet. The loss of the warehouse has worried him terribly. He's not a young man, and he had a heart attack once. I'm afraid all of this will only . . ."

"It's for his own safety. I just want to see if he can tie a few things together for me."

"I'm sorry, I can't allow it. Please back off on this for now. Sol has a bodyguard with him now, keeping watch on him and the house. I'm sure we'll both be safe."

It was a big setback, but I decided not to press the issue. I changed the subject slightly. "Has the fire hurt Sol financially?"

"Not terribly. His insurance covers everything. He's still a very wealthy man. He has lots of other holdings, stocks and real estate. But the fire has hurt him emotionally. He loved his business and his customers and the people who worked for him. It will take at least a year to get it set up again. Sol is such a conscientious man. He cares so deeply. What a mess!"

We were silent for a few moments. Jane fingered the rich wood of her cello. "How do you feel, Jane?" I asked.

"I'm not sure. I believe what you've told me, but another part of me is standing outside of it all, saying it can't be happening. Do you think Freddy is in Los Angeles?"

"No, I think he's run to Mexico. I'm going down there in a day or so to bring him back."

"Be careful."

"I will be. Look, what are your plans for the next few days?"

"I don't know. Practice, of course. Keep an eye on Sol, see that he doesn't fret too much about the insurance negotiations. I know he'll be spending lots of time with the claims people. Why?"

"I don't know, I was just thinking aloud. Would you like to go to the Hollywood Bowl tonight? I've got a box of four seats, practically right on stage. It might help keep your mind off this. It's the Brahms First Symphony and Violin Concerto with Perlman. What do you think?"

"Are you asking me for a date?"

"Yeah."

"Well, I don't know."

I fished the photostat of my P.I.'s license out of my billfold and handed it to Jane. "See," I said, "the State Department of Vocational Standards says I'm a good guy, and if you want to check me out for a reference you can call Lieutenant Arthur Holland of the L.A.P.D. at the Wilshire Station. He'll tell you I'm a sterling character. What do you say?"

Jane Baker sighed and smiled. "All right, Fritz. You've convinced me."

"Great. We can get dinner, too. I know a great place. Shall I pick you up at seven?"

"That sounds fine."

"In the meantime, please be careful and try not to worry, okay?"

"I'll be careful."

"Good. Try to find those letters for me, will you? They might be important. I have to go now, I have errands to run. I know it sounds stupid, but everything is going to be all right. You can trust me." Jane looked at me, unsmiling. I stuck my hand out to her and we shook gently. "Tonight at seven," I said as I got up to leave.

Jane smiled. "I take it you already know the address," she said.

"Of course. I'm a big time detective."

*  *  *

When I got home I did some telephoning: I called the starters' desks at Bel-Air, Wilshire, Brentwood, Los Angeles, and Lakeside Country Clubs and inquired after Fat Dog Baker. I told the caddy masters that I was an insurance adjuster who had a juicy check for Fat Dog from a rich old man he had caddied for years ago. The old man had croaked and left Fat Dog a bundle for improving his putting stroke. Amazingly, they all believed me. Not amazingly, none of them had seen Fat Dog recently. That was good. I had my heart set on pursuit south of the border.

After my sojourn on the telephone, I ran my errands. At an electronics store in Hollywood I bought a high quality reel-to-reel tape recorder, a supply of blank tape, and a state of the arts condenser microphone. From Hollywood I drove to the Pico and Robertson area and leaned on Larry Willis. Larry Willis is a small-time black shoplifter, dope dealer, pimp, and food stamp recipient. He used to hang out at the Gold Cup on the Boulevard in the early '70s when I was working Hollywood Vice and I rousted him regularly. Once he called me a pig and I kicked his ass soundly. He fears me, for good reason, and thinks I still carry a badge. Fearing the worst when I came in his front door unannounced, he was only too happy to furnish me with what I needed: a dozen one-and-a-half-grain Seconal capsules.

My last stop was at a gun shop on La Brea, where I purchased a Browning 12-gauge pump shotgun and a box of shells. I had everything I needed for Mexico.

On the way to pick up Jane I reviewed the women in my life. There weren't many. There was Susan, a hard line San Francisco leftist eight years my senior, who I shacked up with when I was twenty-three. We met when I ticketed her for an illegal lefthand turn on Melrose and Wilton. I ran a warrant check on her and she came up dirty: a slew of unpaid traffic citations. But I couldn't bring myself to arrest her. She was too handsome and intelligent-looking. So I cited her and showed up at her apartment two days later with a bottle of Scotch, flowers, and a smile. She ditched the flowers in the toilet bowl and we killed the Scotch and became lovers. She could drink me under the table.

Our relationship lasted a hectic eight months. I met a lot

of interesting people—old time San Francisco unionists, superannuated beatniks, and dopers of all stripes. I was Susan's live-in curio: an outsized, crewcut cop who got drunk all the time and listened to Beethoven. Gradually, our cultural differences came to the fore and it was no go. Susan's idea of a lover's endearment was to call me her "sociopath with a gun."

Christine was my next inamorata: a car hop at Stan's Drive-In, catty-corner from Hollywood High. Christine wrote incomprehensible poetry and talked in riddles and metaphors. She was insane, a profound piece of passion pie one moment, a willful shrew the next. What a body! The last I heard she was a topless showgirl in Vegas.

It was a beautiful L.A. summer evening, ideal for the Bowl. Cruising west on Sunset with the top down my mind took flight with bits and fragments of the passing scene: the Strip gearing up for another go at nightlife, the giant lighted signs proclaiming rock groups and other coming attractions, the callow idolators of electric music cliquing up in front of the Whisky Au Go Go. And punk rock was out in force, well represented by skinny teenagers in '50s garb sporting green and blue hair and wrap-around sunglasses. One distaff punk rocker led another by a leash attached to a spiked dog collar. It was very naive, and I was feeling too good to be offended.

Stopped at the light at Sunset and Doheny, I checked my watch, then hitched myself up in my seat and gulped in the moment: 6:42 P.M., Friday, July 2. I committed the night air, the cloud formations, and the faces of the passersby to memory. It was my moment, spawned by my covenant and it would never be again. The light changed and I drove into Beverly Hills.

I parked my old Camaro in the long circular driveway behind Jane's Cadillac. Sol Kupferman's newer, darker one was gone. I rang the doorbell and first notes of the choral part of Beethoven's Ninth sounded off in chimes. A nice touch, no doubt added by Jane.

She threw open the door a moment later and bid me enter. I did. The living room was huge and lavishly appointed. Jane swept an arm toward the vast room, as though encouraging me to take it all in, but all I could look at was her. Her hair was down to her shoulders and she wore only the slightest touch of makeup. She looked demure yet sophisticated, a study in feminine charisma.

"Hi," I said. "You look good."

"Thanks," she said.

"Is Sol around? I want to sell him some fire insurance."

"Very amusing. No, Sol is not around. Run into any firebugs lately?"

"No, but I have run into a few caddies who might serve in that capacity. I prowl golf courses at night, hunting for golf balls and sleeping in sand traps. Take me to your wisest golfer."

Jane cracked up, doubled over in laughter and grabbed my arm for support. "Laughter in the face of adversity," she said, "what a scream. It's kind of decadent, but it feels good. Look, I've found two of those letters you wanted. But don't read them tonight, okay? I don't want to talk about the whole bum trip."

"Okay, I was going to suggest the same thing."

Jane squeezed my arm. "Good," she said. "Wait here and I'll get them. Then we can leave." She scurried off upstairs and I eyeballed the room. Interior decoration doesn't send me, but I can recognize superb design when I see it. The room had high ceilings; the walls were a rich mustard color. They were hung with oil paintings of sailing ships and landscapes from the last century. Large, tufted floral couches and easy chairs were arranged concentrically. Rich, dark wood was in abundance. The wide bay windows that fronted the street would provide gently reflected sunlight on bright days and a great muted view on darker ones. It seemed like a good place to live.

Jane returned with the letters and I stuck them into my back pocket without examining them. "Nice pad," I said, "out of the low-rent district."

Jane smiled. "I feel comfortable here."

"I'm glad. You deserve it. Now let's get out of here."

We drove east. Darkness had fallen and the stars shining in the clear sky competed with garish neon for primacy and won. They didn't usually, but the completeness of this night altered my perceptions of everything, including my city.

Jane and I talked comfortably.

"Why the cello, Jane?" I asked. "It seems an odd choice for a fledgling music lover. The piano or the violin seem more likely. Their virtuosity is overwhelming to a person just starting to appreciate music."

"Very true. I've asked myself the same question a million times. With me the cello was love at first hearing. It reflected all my deep, inchoate feelings. You know, the sadness, the weltshmerz that sensitive young girls feel. And it seemed so stable, so steeped in tradition! Anyway, I just flipped for it. And I started listening selectively, too. When I came to live with Sol, he bought me a stereo and hundreds of records. And I fell in love with string quartets. Someday I'll play with a good quartet, and that will be home."

"You're home now. Savor these years of practice and study. I know that when, years from now, you reflect on your life, you'll consider them among your finest."

"That's a lovely sentiment, Fritz. How did you become interested in music?"

I laughed. "It was sort of funny and totally unexpected. I was twenty-one and I didn't know what I wanted to do with my life. My parents had died recently and I was totally up in the air. They had wanted me to attend college and enter one of the professions. I went to Cal State for a year, to placate them, but I hated it. Their death let me off the hook. I was working for a gardener part time and living off the money from their insurance policy. One afternoon we were trimming shrubs in Pasadena and I heard thunderous, powerful music coming from the house of the people we were working for. It was the *Eroica*. It knocked me flat on my ass. I felt that I had come home, too."

"And you decided to become a musician? And it didn't work out?"

"Wrong. I decided to become a cop."

It was Jane's turn to laugh and she did, heartily. "That's so funny! What a non sequitur! Why did you quit the police force?"

"That's a long story. Maybe I'll tell you later tonight, if the music moves me to confession. I love Brahms and the L.A. Philharmonic isn't half bad, but I can't stand Mehta."

She could tell that I didn't want to talk about my police experiences, so she let it pass.

I turned north onto Highland. The Bowl traffic was already heavy. By the time we reached Franklin, we were crawling at a snail's pace. As we arrived at the vast expanse of parking area, I looked out with affection at the throngs of music lovers, nightlife lovers and just plain lovers all hurrying toward a summer rendezvous with Brahms.

Out of the corner of my eye I saw Jane dig into her purse for cigarettes and matches. She lit a cigarette nervously, inhaled, and threw it out the window. I pulled to the curb, my spirits sinking.

"What is it?" I asked.

"I don't know. Reality, I guess. I just know I can't take the goddamned Hollywood Bowl." I felt my spirits hit bottom.

"Shall I take you home?"

"No. I just don't want to be around people."

"A drive, then?"

Jane smiled. "All right."

We ended up in Ferndell Park, with its eucalyptus-shaded walkways and fish ponds. I was at a loss for small talk, so I impulsively took Jane's hand as we walked uphill toward the picnic grounds. Jane squeezed mine, and when I turned to look at her she gave a warm smile. "I love this place," she said. "You know L.A., don't you, Fritz?"

"I've lived here all my life. I think I know it. But it's changing. Every time I look around another landmark from my childhood is gone. Are you from L.A., Jane?"

"More or less. I was born here. My parents moved to Monterey when I was one. They died there, and the foster homes I lived in were here. Do you have a family?"

"No, my parents died within six months of each other when I was twenty. You know, it's funny. Most of the people I know are orphans or come from fragmented families—you and I, my friend Walter, the man I do a lot of work for. All strays awash in a sea of neon, all trying to survive and find a little more than survival."

Jane smiled at my half-hearted attempt at poetry. "You said earlier that you'd tell me why you quit the police force," she said.

"It's an ugly story, Jane. Are you sure you want to hear it?"

She squeezed my hand briefly. "Yes," she said. "I called Lieutenant Holland this afternoon, to check you out. I didn't tell him why I needed the information, just that we had met and you offered him as a reference. He said that you were a good man, but when I asked him if you were a good police officer, he was ambiguous. You can tell me, Fritz."

"All right. I was a shitty cop. I was drunk a good deal of the time, so I got shunted off to Hollywood Vice. A sympathetic sergeant told me I'd fit right in with the kind of people the Vice Squad dealt with: drunks, dopers, hookers, bookies, pimps, homosexuals, and perverts. The cream of Hollywood society. I did fit in and I enjoyed the job for a while. But gradually the despair of hassling people who should have been left alone got to me. I was depressed so I drank and popped uppers to kill the depression. Which brings us to Blow Job Anderson. He was a character out of my youth, from the old neighborhood, a legendary pervert who was seducing twelve-year-old boys when Walter and I were that age. He was six or seven years older than us. He was still living in the neighborhood and Walter told me he was seducing a new generation of kids. After I'd been working Hollywood Vice for eight or nine months, I found out that Blow Job Anderson was a big time informer to Narcotics Division. I went to the Commander of Narco and told him that Blow Job was a known pervert who had been seducing young boys since I was a kid. He told me not to worry, that he would take care of it. He didn't do a goddamned thing. I went to the guys in Narco themselves, and told them. They didn't care, either. They told me to cool it, that I had no proof, and that Anderson was a good snitch they couldn't afford to lose. Finally, word came down from the Commander of Hollywood Station: 'Shut your mouth about Blow Job Anderson.' I knew what I had to do. I got drunk one night and went looking for Anderson. I found him and broke both his legs with a lead filled baseball bat. I told him if I ever heard he was still bothering kids, I would kill him. While he was lying on the ground screaming, I poured a five pound bag of sugar into the gas tank of his Corvette. When I went to work the next day I was summoned to the Captain's office. He handed me a resignation form. 'I strongly suggest that you sign this,' he said. I did. Farewell, police career."

I had begun my story seeking absolution and had ended it on a note of intransigent pride. I wondered if Jane had noticed it. We stared at each other.

Finally, she spoke. "I don't care. I don't think any more or less of you for what you've told me. You just saw corruption that you couldn't take. You—"

"That wasn't it," I interrupted. "I wasn't an outraged moralist like most cops. I let plenty of perverts slide. I came down hard on others. It was arbitrary, dictated by mood. What I couldn't take was that Blow Job Anderson was more valuable to the L.A.P.D. than Fritz Brown. That was what ate me up."

"Did you abuse your power often when you were a policeman?"

"Yes, and terribly."

"I understand. You were a Dissension Center. You were drinking, but now you're sober. I was a Dissension Center, too. I loved power. Sexual power. I laid half the boys at St. Vibiana's. I loved having them want me, knowing that I could say 'no' and castrate them. Knowing that I could get what I wanted by offering my body in barter. But that was then. Now I have my cello. There's a good chance I'll be accepted at Juilliard in January. Now I'm a Unity Center. You are, too. You don't hurt people anymore, do you?"

"No," I lied.

"And you're not drinking. Do you have plans for the future?"

"Not really. I'm going to Europe this fall, though. A musical holiday. Germany and Austria."

"So am I! Sol has been pushing me toward a vacation for years. I'll probably leave in October."

"Maybe we can travel together," I blurted out.

"I wouldn't be surprised," Jane said, almost mockingly, "but right now what I'd like to do is listen to some good chamber music on a good stereo."

"I know just the place. I live there. Shall we go?"

"Yes, please."

So we went to my apartment, a few minutes' drive away. But we didn't listen to chamber music, we made our own. It was an urgent coupling, freighted with knowledge that tomorrow reality would come down hard. Afterward, I hooked up the bedroom speaker and put some Vivaldi on the turntable, with the volume down low. We lay in bed holding hands and not talking until I couldn't stand it any longer and burst out laughing. "Jane, Jane, Jane," I said. "Jane, a very traditional name. I like that."

She laughed along. "Fritz is a good ethnic name," she said, "I like that. You're scowling, dear. What is it?"

"I never know how I stand in situations like this."

"What do you mean?"

"I mean, will there be a next time?"

"Anytime. Including now."

I reached across the bed and pulled her toward me. We held each other tightly for several minutes, then made love again, this time more for reassurance than passion. Then we fell asleep.

I awoke at eight o'clock. I heard water running in the bathroom, and Jane came out a moment later, fully dressed. I knew from the look on her face that reality had hit. "Good morning," I said.

"Good morning. I have to go. I have my lesson at nine-thirty."

"What is it?"

"What the hell do you think it is?"

"Do you want to know?"

"Yes!"

I told her, omitting nothing. From Fat Dog's visit to my office, to the Utopia firebombing, to Sol Kupferman's past, to my assessment of her brother's psychoses, to the Omar Gonzalez angle. Jane's reactions ranged from head-shaking denials, to trembling, to sobbing. When she started to cry, I let her, making no move to provide comfort. I wanted her to be afraid. Finally, surprisingly, anger took over. Her wet face went red. I handed her a handkerchief and she wiped away tears. When she spoke, it was with heart-stopping resolution: "Get him, Fritz."

"I will."

"Do whatever you have to do. I don't want him hurting Sol or anyone else."

"I will."

"Would you take me home now, please?"

"Yes."

Jane rounded up her things while I pulled out the car. We drove to Beverly Hills in tense silence. A dozen funny, cheery remarks came into my mind, but I rejected them as fatuous. Finally, I spoke. "We have to talk about a few things, Jane."

"All right."

"I want you to tell Kupferman what I've told you. Tell him to be careful, to keep his bodyguard around at all times. Tell him that I want to talk to him when I get back from Mexico. Will you do that?"

"Yes."

"Tell him also that I don't give a damn about any of his past dealings. That includes the bookie operations at the Utopia. Tell him all I'm interested in is seeing Fat Dog put away."

A flash of anger came into Jane's eyes. "You're sure of what you've told me?" she said, her voice rising. "That Sol was bookmaking in the late '60s? Fifteen years after the grand jury? I won't have him slandered by anyone, including you!"

I looked over at her. "Easy, sweetheart. I'm sure. And it's hardly slander. Bookmaking should be legal."

Jane shook her head. Her whole manner was like a stifled scream. "I'm sorry. It's just that I know *I'm* strong enough to stand all this, but I'm not sure about Sol." I put my free hand on her knee and squeezed. She didn't respond. I pulled up across the street from the Kupferman mansion. Jane and I looked at each other. I didn't want a protracted goodbye and I sensed she didn't either. "Be careful in Mexico," she said.

"You be careful here. Practice well. You can give me a recital when I get back." We kissed hard and in an instant Jane was out of the car and running across the street toward the large house.

Driving away, I did a fairly good job of putting Jane out of my mind and concentrating on what I had to do next: find a quiet spot to read Fat Dog's letters. I pulled into the large parking lot at Hancock Park, and found a bench in the shade, surrounded by elderly Jews killing a summer midmorning, and a slew of plaster dinosaurs killing eternity. The letters were undated and barely legible. The postage stamps had been ripped off of all three when they were opened. Jane had said they were recent, though, within the past month. I plunged in:

"Deer Jane, my sister, I hope you are feeling good. I am too. I've been doing good at Bell-Air, lots of jucy loops. I'm the king there. They got nothing but winos looping there. I saw on T.V. this musical show, this big orchestra. They showed this woman playing that thing like you play. Only she don't play as good. I could tell. You dont need that scum Kupferman no more. I know. Jews got big money but they don't know the score. I do. I got a rich friend who does to. He likes me. I don't have to loop no more. I just do it cause I love golf. Soon I will be going to Mexico. To retire kind of. Live like I should, like a king. The king of caddies and king of dog racers. Why don't you come to? I've got lots of $!!!!!!! I know a feemale grayhound pup I can buy for 200!!!!! We can breed her and go big time at the track in T.J.!!!!!! Raise lots of pups, all champs!!! In Mexico they treat white people like kings!!!!! Tell that bastard Sol K to fuck off!!!! Come to Mexico and be with your family!! My friends got a big castle neer Ensinada. We can go fishing. You can play your thing in piece with nobody to bug you. My buddy can get you into a good band. All white. Listen to me!!!!! Jane!!!!! I'm your brother, your only kinn!!! A talented girl like you should stay with her family. We can have good times, like the old days before the Jew and the fiddle. Call me at the Tap & Cap 474-7296. Leave a messige and we can get together and go to Mexx. Don't dellay, call todday. Ha! Ha! I love you. Your brother, Freddy."

It was about what I had expected, grammatically and thematically, yet none of Fat Dog's surprising intelligence and cunning shone through. I quickly read the other two letters. They were simply repetitions of the first, but they reinforced my hunch that Fat Dog was now in Mexico, and that his rich friend might not be a figment of his imagination and might be a possible lead. I was itching to get started. But I had to see Walter first to check on his well-being and say *au revoir*. There was a fear on the back burner of my mind that I might never see him again. I quashed it and stuck Fat Dog's letters in my pocket and hotfooted it to the old neighborhood.

* * *

Walter didn't answer my ring and there was no response when I knocked loudly on the window of his room. This was surprising; maybe he was making the run to the liquor store. I walked back to the front steps to wait.

After five minutes his mother pulled up in her senile Mustang. She hates to spend money, unless it's on spiritual artifacts of the Christian Science Church, like her Wedgwood bone china plates inlaid with drawings of the Mother Church. Over the years Walter has sailed a number of them off the twelfth floor of the Franklin Life Building at Wilshire and Western, but she keeps replacing them. She'll withstand the greatest indignities with a stoic resolve to keep him under her thumb. Once Walter boiled her eighty-five dollar morocco-bound copy of "Science and Health—A Key To The Scriptures" in a pot that was equal parts water and Thunderbird. He presented it to her on a silver chafing dish embossed with the likeness of Mary Baker Eddy—in front of her Wednesday night Bible Study Class.

She saw me as she was locking her car and dredged up a smile from the dark recesses of the cold city that she lives in. "Well, Officer Brown, how nice to see you," she said.

"I quit the police department a long time ago, Mrs. Curran," I said, "you know that."

"Yes, and such a pity, too. You were so handsome in your uniform."

"No doubt. Where's Walter?"

"Chief Davis is such a fine man. I was hoping you would follow in his footsteps and make the police force your career."

"You would dig Davis. He's as crazy as you are. Where's Walter?"

"Walter? I think he's on hiatus somewhere. He left last night. He'd gone to one of those terrible A.A. meetings where everyone smokes cigarettes and takes the Lord's name in vain. You know how those meetings upset him. I'll give you your due, Officer Brown, you are not a nice man and you have an evil tongue, but you do know my boy. Although not as well as I do."

"Yeah, I do know old Walt pretty well. Do you know what I like most about him? His restraint."

"His restraint?"

"Yeah, his restraint at not having strangled you in your fucking bed a long time ago. Good day, Mrs. Curran."

I walked back to my car leaving Walter's madre to catalogue my indignity for future use against him. I was worried now. I had been unavailable to my friend for several days and he was in one of his periodic descents into reality, with all the terror that brings. When Walter takes off on what he terms his "periodicals," anything can happen. Once he bought two hundred tennis balls and hurled them at passing cars from the bus stop at Beverly and Van Ness. Another time he barricaded himself in a motel in Hollywood with a bag of weed and a supply of dexedrine and porno books, convinced he could kick booze that way. Both times I was able to effect some sort of reconciliation between Walter and the world before he was locked up.

But those were extreme examples of the "periodical." His standard operating procedure was simply to walk west on Wilshire until he hit the beach, with beer stops on the way to detox himself and prepare for what he considered the long but necessary nightmare of sober life. So I drove west on Wilshire myself, as slowly as possible in the middle lane. I got all the way to Brentwood before I spotted him sitting on a bus bench at Wilshire and Barrington, drinking out of a paper bag with a straw. I pulled up, opened the passenger door and called to my friend. He got in.

"You had me worried," I said. "I came by your place a few nights ago and you were passed out on the hard stuff." I turned around the corner and parked in the lot of a small market. I checked Walter out: the pudgy frame and brilliant light blue eyes looked normal, but the face had the gauntness and fear that sets in when he has been sober a few days. "What are you drinking?" I asked.

Walter pulled the brown bag off of his libation. To my surprise it was Vernor's Ginger Ale. "If you can do it, I can do it, you fascist motherfucker," he said, punching me in the arm jokingly. "Cold turkey, unless I get the shakes. Then it's the old tried-and-true twenty-four-hour beer detox."

"And then?"

"I don't know. Dope or A.A. There are advantages to both. The dope advantages are obvious: you fly. The disadvantages are the resultant paranoia of prolonged use and the illegality. I'm not cut out for jail. No science fiction, no T.V., and they make you work. The A.A. advantages are that you get healthy physically through abstinence, you meet people who might be potentially valuable business contacts, and you probably get laid." It was perhaps the fiftieth time I had heard this routine, but I didn't tell Walter that. He was close to the edge.

"There's another alternative," I said, "You can come and stay with me. We can fly up to San Francisco, go to the opera, hike in Golden Gate Park. I'll see that you eat and make fucking-A sure you don't drink."

"I'll consider it, but it probably won't work. Aesthetically, we are polar opposites. You cannot see the profundity of television, while I am mentally evaluating it and its effect for a magnum opus that will shake the conscience of the free world. I will be spoken of in the same breath as Kant and Nietzsche, guys who, of course, you have never read. You are the man of action and limited thought, the pragmatic diamond-in-the-rough intellect who rips off dumb niggers for their Cadillacs, sold to them by the fascist vampire. The karmic consequences will one day become obvious: you are going to get royally fucked in the ass. I, on the other hand, am the man of pure thought. A thinking machine. But I run on fuel, like any good machine. And that fuel is alcohol. It's Catch-22, my good friend. So what are we to do?"

"I don't know, in the long run. Right now though, we can make the Topanga run. Do you want to?"

"Let's do it. It's been a long time."

The Topanga run had been a mainstay of our relationship since the time I got my first car. It consists of Wilshire west to Pacific Coast Highway, P.C.H. north to the Topanga Canyon turn-in, Topanga Canyon Road through to the Valley, and the Ventura and Hollywood freeways back to L.A. It takes about an hour and a half, and during these rides Walter and I have enjoyed some of our finest conversations and closest rapport. So I pulled a U-turn on Barrington and turned right on Wilshire, headed for the beach. Out of the corner of my eye I watched Walter sip his ginger ale and peruse the passing scene.

When we were a few blocks from the ocean, he started to shout in frustration. "Shit fuck, rat's ass, motherfucker!! Shit fuck!!"

I looked over and his hands were shaking, tremors that

seemed to start in his fingertips and work all the way up to his shoulders, where he braced his back to contain them. "Five minutes, Walter," I said. "Hold on. Beer?"

"Fuck beer. Vodka. Kiddielands. I'm dehydrated."

Kiddielands meant a 7–11 Store. I remembered one on 15th and Santa Monica and jammed a left hand turn and punched the accelerator. I bought two large cherry Slurpees, gooey concoctions of sugar, red dye number 7, and ice. In the parking lot I dumped out half of each one and trotted down the street to a liquor store, where I bought two half pints of Smirnoff 100. I mixed the vodka and Slurpees— half pint to each container of red goo—while Walter watched hungrily, sitting on his hands to control his shaking. I handed him one of the large cups through the window. He held it between his knees and greedily sucked the dual poison into his system through a large straw.

I got into the car and waited. Walter sipped in silence for about ten minutes. When he spoke I knew he had been freshly restored to his old insanity. "Where have you been?" he said. "I've been calling you for days. I needed the dubious pleasure of your company." He held up his hands and placed them a few inches from the windshield. They were perfectly still.

"You wouldn't believe me if I told you," I said. "Do you still want to make the run?"

"Of course."

We rolled up the windows and I hit the airconditioning. Cold air flooded the car and we took off, awash in hazy sunshine that seemed to permeate everything from blacktop to billboards. As we drove north on P.C.H. the sun reflecting off the ocean was blinding.

"How did it start this time?" I asked Walter.

"It all happened at once," he said, throwing his straw and plastic lid out the window and drinking directly from the cup. "Dear is definitely going to marry the wop. It's all set. She's got him by the balls. She even got him to renounce his Catholicism, at least temporarily. A Christian Science Practitioner is going to perform the service. With his emphysema and Dear's claws into him, he probably won't last six months. He's been making friendly overtures toward me, no doubt to curry favor with Dear. He even offered to set me up in my own fruit stand. He looks like a gila monster and he smells like garlic. Dear treats him like shit.

It's depressing beyond belief. And I've been without T-bird. Dear ripped off that C-note you put in my pocket. It was you, wasn't it? Who else could it have been? She told me that I was in a blackout and offered her the money to pay for some of the damage I've done around the house. The usual threats ensued, on both sides, until she popped her final ace—'Walter, if you persist with this behavior, I shall have to call Judge Gray and have you committed.' You know the bitch will do it if I push her far enough, and Judge Gray has had it in for me ever since I poured wintergreen down his ugly daughter's bra in the eighth grade. He's Republican, Christian Science, and law-and-order militant: the trinity. So without funds, I have been ripping off Scotch from Thrifty's. And it hasn't been working. I drink and I drink and I'm not drunk, and then wham, I'm out like a light. And the music doesn't help either. I heard the Bruckner Third the other night on KUSC. Haitink and the Concertgebouw. Lonely Anton at his peak, and I didn't give a shit. Nothing's working anymore, everything's changing and it's driving me fucking batshit."

We entered Topanga Canyon with its green hills that resembled the Fjords. Knots of youthful hikers walked along a stream that runs parallel to the twisting blacktop, several of the women carrying babies papoose-style in specially rigged backpacks. Friendly dogs followed them, stopping frequently to explore interesting scents. Walter was staring out his window, where the edge of the roadside led to nothing but a steep drop.

"You want some advice, wino?" I asked.

"Sure."

"Don't lose the momentum you've got going. I know exactly how you feel. It's exactly how I felt ten months ago. The fear, the loss, the sense of slipping, the whole shot. Go with it. Don't let the old illusions take hold of you again."

"I think I'm really scared this time, Fritz."

"Good. Look, I have to go down to Mexico for a few days. I'm on a case, a real one. Try not to drink until I get back. Hit some A.A. meetings. It works for some people. Read. Stay away from Dear. Try to eat. When I get back you can move in with me. My life is just as up in the air as yours is, but for different reasons. I don't want to talk about it now. Things are looking up, for both of us. I've got a new friend that I'll introduce you to. She'll be your friend, too."

"A woman?"

"Yeah, a woman."

"Are you fucking her?"

"Shut up, Walter. I don't want to talk about it."

"Silence implies consent. You are fucking her. Big tits?"

I had to laugh. Walter is totally guileless and adoring when it comes to women.

"Average size. But beautiful. She's a cellist."

"No shit? Congratulations, Kraut. It's about time. You deserve a good woman."

"Thanks, wino. So do you. When was the last time you got laid?"

"The last time I dipped my wick was April 13, 1972. That cop groupie you fixed me up with. Small tits and pimples."

"Eight years is a long time. No wonder you're fucked up. If you want to get laid today, I can arrange it. In fact, it might be a good idea, help you keep your mind off the booze. I know a terrific-looking hooker, an ultra fox. She's got an apartment up from the Strip."

"Big tits?"

"Real melons. She loves intellectuals. I know you'll hit it off with her. Do you want to do it?"

Walter drained off the last of his first Kiddieland and threw the cup out the window. He pulled the lid off the second one and began sipping tentatively. "Fix me up when you get back," he said, "for the next few days I want to detox and rest." He gave me a smile that was equal parts love and fear of the unknown. Walter was in deep shit without a depth gauge.

When I dropped him off at his house an hour later, that smile still haunted me. But as I drove away, I wasn't thinking of my beloved friend. I was thinking of what might lie ahead in Mexico.

## 7

I could tell something was wrong from a half a block away. As I pulled onto Bowlcrest, I could see that the French windows leading to my balcony were pushed open and the living room lamp was on, casting an orange glow into the twilight.

I parked crossways in my driveway, blocking it, and grabbed my gun and handcuffs from the glove compartment. As I made for the stairway that led to my front door, I heard it slam and heard footsteps scurrying down to street level. Flattening myself against the stairwell, I counted the number of steps the intruder had taken and when he was five from the bottom I spun out from my hiding place and turned around to face him, my gun leveled at his head. He was a handsome Chicano in his late twenties, slender and athletic-looking. His black hair was fashionably long and styled. He didn't look like a Hollywood burglar. He looked more like a rock musician or a high-priced fruit hustler; sensitive in an arrogant way. He was wearing a yellow tank top and bellbottom cords. When he zeroed in on my gun barrel, he froze.

"Hold it right there, motherfucker," I said, "and give those eyes to me. Now put your hands on top of your head and lace your fingers." He complied. "Now walk toward me and when you get to the bottom of the stairs, turn around, bend forward and touch your elbows to the wall."

I patted him down thoroughly while keeping my gun aimed at his spine. Finishing my frisk, I pulled him into an upright position and had him place his hands behind his back, where I cuffed them. "Let's take a walk up to my pad," I said. I nudged him with my gun barrel and he moved up the stairs. I looked around for neighbors who might have viewed our confrontation; luckily, there were no telltale heads peeking out of windows.

I unlocked my front door and pushed him inside and over to an easy chair where I sat him down. I stuck my gun into my waistband and surveyed my living room. It was almost intact. Only my desk drawers had been gone through. Keeping an eye on my prisoner, I rummaged through my personal papers, work records, bank books, and memorabilia. Nothing seemed to be missing. I ducked a head into my bedroom and saw nothing amiss except a few open dresser drawers. Back in the living room I sat down on the couch directly across from the handsome young Chicano. He eyed me warily, stoically. He was no burglar. He didn't walk the part, talk it, or act it in any way. He had shown remarkable consideration in his search of my apartment. Burglars do not hit second-story apartments at dusk in the less affluent part of the Hollywood Hills.

"Hello, Omar," I said. "I was looking for you yesterday." There was no response, so I tried again. "You are Omar Gonzalez, aren't you? If you're not, it's the fuzz and the slammer. And maybe an ass-kicking, by me. I don't like the idea of people fucking around with my pad. You probably feel the same way, if you're Omar Gonzalez, that is. Somebody righteously thrashed old Omar's pad the other day. Really ripped it up. Looking for something. Bookie ledgers, maybe. Somebody righteously fried Omar's brother back in '68, too. I know who did it. Maybe you heard about the case, the Club Utopia firebombing? Three of the bombers were caught and executed, but the 'Mastermind' got away. You seen old Omar lately? I sure would like to talk to him." I gave the Chicano my widest, most innocent smile, the kind that won me First Place in a Beautiful Baby Contest in 1948.

"I'm Omar Gonzalez, motherfucker," he said.

"Good. I'm Fritz Brown. Don't call me 'motherfucker' again. It's not nice. Well, Omar, I think we need to exchange some information. What do you say?"

"I say you broke into my car and ripped me off for two boxes of stuff, that's what I say. The lock on my trunk is all fucked up. I had to tie it shut."

"Tough shit. You broke into my pad. I'd say we're even. Besides, we were both looking for the same thing, right?"

"You tell me."

"I know who instigated the Utopia torch. How I got involved isn't important. James McNamara told me about you, and how you've been obsessed with the 'fourth man' for years. I have my own reasons for wanting the bastard. I'm a licensed private investigator. I can arrest him and make it stick. You need me, for that reason. You've been messing with this case for years, in an amateur fashion, and you've obviously discovered something. The ledgers, the porno photos. Our investigations have been running along parallel lines. We need to compare notes. Together we may be able to find this scumbag." I watched Omar's macho-stoic reserve crumble. I went to him and unlocked his handcuffs.

He rubbed his wrists and smiled. "Okay, repo-man, let's do it." He reached over and we shook on it.

"Tell me about this investigation of yours," I said, "from the top."

"From the top, I just knew something was wrong with the way the cops handled the case. They caught the guys wham, blam, thank you ma'am. It made the cops look good. The three guys confessed, but when they said that a fourth guy was the ringleader, the cops thought it was a plea to beat the death penalty. I talked to Cathcart, the cop who headed the investigation, about it. 'What if it's true?' I asked. 'Do you honestly think these three drunks were crazy enough to knock off six people just because they got kicked out of a fucking bar?' I was a youngster then and Cathcart shined me on. I admit I was an imaginative kid. But at the trial I *knew* I was right. I mean, man, I *knew*. Those guys were telling the truth when they testified about the fourth man. The way they described him, it was just too real. The guy they described was just too fucking bizarre to be made up.

"I got a lot of publicity out of my crusade, even though everyone thought I was a crank. I was almost a regular on the old *Joe Pyne Show*. I developed a theory—that the mastermind was only after *one* of the victims—and that he torched the bar to hide his motive. I checked out the backgrounds of all the victims—except for my brother Tony, they were dull. Working stiffs, juiceheads, that type. The Gaffany dame was a semipro b-girl. I checked out Edwards, the owner of the joint—a dope fiend. I checked him out real good. Nothing on any of them.

"For a while I hung out with a guy who wrote for *True Detective* magazine. He found out that the Utopia had a bookie wire going—small-time. So I checked out some bookies who operated in the Normandie-Slauson area. They told me, yeah, there was a wire going, but it was amateur. They said Edwards ran it. So I checked out Edwards again. Nothing but a smacked-back junkie, all fucked-up on stuff. I got a lead on a big spade who used to make collections and payoffs—and he turned out to be doing five to life in Quentin for armed robbery with violence. Another dead end.

"Anyway, gradually I got into some other gigs—heavyweight scenes, the Chicano Movement, and this drug recovery program I work at—and I put my investigation on the back burner. I mean my hermano, Tony, was a righteous dude; I never loved anybody the way I loved him and I wanted to kill the puto who masterminded the torch, but I got my own life to think about, right? I'm twenty-seven years old. No fucking spring chicken. So anyway, I got involved in some other scenes and didn't think about revenging Tony so much.

"Then I get this phone call. What's the word? Anonymous. This dude asks me if I'm the Omar Gonzalez who used to be on the *Joe Pyne Show*. I say yes. Then he asks me if I'm still interested in the Utopia case. I say yes. Then he says 'I got some information.' And he tells me to get a pencil. So I do. He says: 'Richard Ralston, 8173 Hildebrand Street, in Encino. He was one of the bookies at the Utopia around the time of the bombing. Check out his house, maybe you'll find something to lead you to the fourth man.' Then he hangs up. Man, did that call shake me up!

"So I burglarize this guy Ralston's pad. At first, I find absolutely nothing suspicious. A bunch of old baseball souvenirs, photographs, T.V. set, records. A bag of weed. Nothing hot. Then I find this phony wall. I push it open and find these two boxes. I figure they got to be hot, so I rip them off. When I get home I check them out. Only the bookie ledgers make sense. The blank checks and the fuck pictures don't mean nothing. So I lock the boxes up in my trunk. Then I start checking this guy Ralston out—I tail him to work one day. He works at this fancy golf club. I start thinking, holy shit, one of the bombers described the fourth man as wearing one of those golf shirts with the alligator on it! Maybe he plays golf at this club.

"I was about to check it out when I got shot. I was in Echo Park one night and I had this feeling I was being followed. I was driving to a friend's place. All of a sudden this car pulls up. Blam! Blam! Blam! Blam! Three of the shots missed, but one grazed my shoulder. Somehow I knew it was coming, so I ducked and punched the gas. I lost them. I hid out at a friend's place. He drove my car to the station. I figured it would be safe there. But he forgot to take the boxes out of the trunk, like I told him to. Pinchey puto! The puto wouldn't go back for them! So I laid up at another friend's crib. My shoulder healed up good. I figured it was some punks I kicked out of the recovery house who shot at me, and that it was safe to come out of hiding, that they were probably fucked up on stuff somewhere.

"Then I went back to my apartment. It was destroyed. I went to get my car and the attendant tells me about this crazy repo-man who broke into my trunk. Then he gave me your card. I thought it was a trap. Somebody wants me dead. Maybe this cabron Ralston found out I'm onto him. That's why I broke into your place, to check you out. Now you talk, repo-man."

My mind was racing, divided between trying to place Ralston in the context of this new offshoot of the case and developing a cover story to keep Omar Gonzalez at bay while I nabbed Fat Dog. I gave Omar my most sincere look and lied big. Fuck him. He could read about the capture of his brother's killer in the papers.

"You were getting close, Omar," I said. "The fourth man *is* a member at Hillcrest. He had it in for Wilson Edwards, the owner of the Utopia. His wife ran away with Edwards. He masterminded the killing of six people for nothing. Edwards wasn't even at the bar that night. Ralston is blackmailing this guy. I've got an informant up near Santa Barbara who's got some evidence for me. Some tapes. I'm going there tonight to pick them up. Want to come along?"

Omar thought about it. He was eyeing me suspiciously. "How did you get into this thing, anyway?" he asked.

"Good question. A car dealer I worked for hired me to repo a car off a woman named Sanders. She's the fourth man's ex-wife. When I came around to get the car, she invited me into the house to talk. She told me she could put me onto a 'big scoop,' as she put it, if I didn't repo her car. She asked me if I had heard of the Club Utopia firebombing. I said yes. Then she told me how her ex-husband planned the whole thing. I believed her. This guy I'm going to see tonight was in on the blackmail scheme with Ralston." I could tell that he believed me. It was typical: members of minorities consider repossessors to be the scum of the earth—motivated by the basest of desires. The repo angle had convinced Gonzalez that I was telling the truth. He was no dummy, but he was easily manipulated through his prejudices.

"All right," he said, "it's crazy, but I believe you. All the fucking work I've done looking for this guy and you stumble onto him accidentally. Where do we go? Santa Barbara?"

"Right. South of there. Near Carpenteria, on the beach. There's a deserted motel where we're going to make the trade. He wants a thousand dollars, but he's not getting it. I'm ripping him off. You can come along as back up. We leave now. What do you say?"

"I say you're a nice guy. Repo ripoff in the night. You do much work in the Barrio?"

"Yeah. Taco wagons are my specialty. Also foxy Chicanas. Everytime I do a repo in Hollenbeck, I stop for a jumbo burrito and a piece of Mexican tail. It's charming talking to you, Omar, you're a lovely conversationalist, but our rapport is getting a little strained. So let's take care of business."

I tucked my .38 into my waistband and got my newly purchased shotgun and tape recorder from the bedroom and threw four days worth of clean shirts and pants into a suitcase. I handed it to Omar. He didn't say anything about it, his eyes were riveted to the shotgun. He was impressed. I was speaking his language now. As we walked out the door, he didn't notice me jam a blackjack and length of nylon cord into my windbreaker.

We drove north on 101. The suitcase, shotgun, and tape machine were nestled in the trunk, the other goodies on my person. Omar was quiet. I had been expecting a lot of militant jive talk and needling, but he was too sensitive for that; he was lost in contemplation, thinking he was approaching the culmination of a ten-year crusade. He was, but I would be the reaper of all glories to be had.

The Fourth of July weekend get-out-of-town traffic was heavy and we slowed to a crawl nearing Oxnard and Ventura. After that, it was smooth sailing and twenty minutes later I pulled off the highway near the Casitas Reservoir and took surface streets down to the long stretch of beach just south of Carpinteria. I was sure the Beach View Motel would still be there and would still be deserted. Walter and I had discovered the Beach View about five years ago. We were driving back from San Francisco, drunk, when a torrential rainstorm hit. Walter wanted to press on and catch *The War of the Worlds* on the Late Show, but I insisted we park on the beach and sleep it off. We found a beach access road, expecting to find a parking lot at the end of it, but we were wrong: what we found was the Beach View Motel, a squat, ugly, lime-green structure on a particularly barren stretch of oceanfront sand obscured from the highway. We spent the night there drinking and bullshitting. The dump had been born to lose and born for losers; but it would serve my purpose tonight.

The night was pitch black and it took me a while to find the sandy blacktop that led down to our destination. When I did locate it, Omar came out of his trance and started jabbering: "Are we here, man? Is this it?"

"This is it," I said, "we're a little early. The guy said ten-thirty. It's just after ten now. But that's good. I want to make sure we see him coming, in case he brought friends." Omar nodded staunchly. He was a courageous vato, but out of his league. To my chagrin, I was beginning to like him.

As we pulled up in front of the motel, my headlights caught litter-covered pavement, open doors, broken windows, and a profusion of empty beer cans. I killed the engine and said, "Take this flashlight and look around. I've got to get something out of the trunk."

I handed Omar the large five-cell, got out of the car, and walked around to open the trunk. Omar left the car and began flashing his light into the broken windows and battered doors. I counted to twenty, then walked over to him, and sapped him from behind with the blackjack. He crumpled in a heap, dropping the flashlight. I checked his pulse, which was steady, then bound his wrists and ankles with the nylon cord.

I dragged him into the room farthest from the access road and laid him down on a smelly sand-covered mattress. I wrapped my hand in my windbreaker and punched out the side and front windows. Omar would have plenty of air. Next I located half a dozen good-sized rocks and laid them outside of Omar's room. I went inside and checked his pulse again. It was still steady. I closed the door on Omar and barricaded it with my rock collection. Pleasant dreams, Omar. In the morning, I would call the Carpinteria fuzz and clue them into the overnight guest at the Beach View.

I pulled the car around, almost getting stuck in the sand, and drove away, the sea making eerie noises in the background. I took 101 southbound to its juncture with Interstate 5 near Nixon's pad at San Clemente. When I pulled into San Diego just after midnight I heard firecrackers going off all over the city. Happy birthday, America.

# III

## LOWER CALIFORNIA

## 8

The following morning, rested yet apprehensive, I crossed the border.

Tijuana is situated on a plain nestled among shallow brown foothills. Even with the ocean just a few miles to the north it swelters, and the sun reflecting off the iron roofs of the hundreds of shacks that cover those foothills gave my entrance to Mexico the surreal look of a bad hangover morning.

Coming into T.J. proper, past scores of giant liquor stores, auto upholstery dumps, and body shops, I ran through my itinerary: low-life bars, betting palaces, and the dog track. If they didn't pan out, I would try to run down a lead from the porno photos I had in my trunk: they were a more than coincidental link between Fat Dog and Richard Ralston.

Tijuana was teeming with activity as I turned onto Revalucion, its main drag. It was hot and noisy, the streets jammed with cars and the sidewalks packed with tourists and Mexican Nationals bartering in front of the profusion of curio stores that lined both sides of the street.

T.J. had changed since my first visit in 1962. I was still in high school then and had driven down with a group of buddies, bent on getting laid, getting drunk, and viewing the famous mule act. Except for our getting drunk, it was not to be. We did, however, get rolled by a Mexican tough who promised to fix us up with his sister, for free, because we were "cool dudes." My most overpowering impression of T.J. then was the poverty. There were endless streams of children hawking cheap blankets and religious medals by throwing them up at your face and screaming at you, hands outstretched, bodies planted firmly in front of you to block your progress, and hungry dogs, and comatose old beggars, too near starvation to give you a hard time. The poverty was still here—Tijuana eighteen years later was redolent of poverty—but it was poverty with hustle. The child beggars looked healthier and less desperate, and the streets looked like they were swept at least once a week.

I decided not to waste time and inquired after what used to be the heart of T.J. low-life, the Chicago Club. The on-leave marine I talked to leered at me and gave me directions. I walked south of Revalucion, where the sidewalks were slightly less crowded. It was broiling now and my shirt, which I wore out to conceal my gun, was soaked and stuck to my back. After about four blocks I hit the real poverty. Victim land. Streets populated by people—Mexican and turista—with the predator look. A skinny white youth brushed by me. "Reds, whites, three dollars a roll," he said. I told him to fuck off.

I hit my first in a long series of cheap bars. They were interchangeable; the people looked and smelled the same, the same fat Mexican girls danced nude on stage to bored catcalls. I described Fat Dog in detail to over fifty people, slipping out over two hundred dollars to bilingual Mexicans to translate for me. Nothing. Just a massive headache from over four hours of maudlin, saccharine Mexican music.

I walked back to Revalucion, deciding to hit a few nicer-looking joints before trying the dog track. I walked through three off-track betting palaces on my way over. No Fat Dog and no one willing to take time off from placing bets to talk to me.

I was getting hungry and decided to chance the food in the first halfway decent-looking juke joint I came to, which was La Carabelle. I knew right off the bat that this was a class place by T.J. standards: it was clean, the bar was well-stocked, the patrons looked a cut above the ones I had been questioning and the girls who danced on stage were pretty and slender and wore bikinis. I took a table near the edge of the dance runway. A waiter materialized and I ordered huevos rancheros and coffee.

The table adjoining mine was occupied by outsized, red-faced American men doing some hard drinking. From their short hair and the peremptory way they treated their waiter, I judged them to be Marine Corps brass, not likely to have information on my quarry. Still, they were talking loudly and when their conversation turned to golf, I listened.

"I was fucking surprised," one of them said, "a shit-ass town like this having a championship course. Par seventy-two! Greens like lightning. I was lucky to get away with an eighty-seven! Jesus, all those years at Pendleton and I didn't even know it existed!"

I leaned over and asked him where this golf course bonanza was.

The man started to get annoyed, then smiled broadly. His companions joined him and they all started jabbering drunkenly: "T.J. Country Club," "Are you from Pendleton, fella?" "Just south of town," "Near the dog track, greatest fucking Margaritas this side of La Paz," "Watch out for that trap on the fourth hole, it . . ."

I didn't wait for them to finish. I jammed out of the bar and maneuvered my way through the crowds on Revalucion to the lot where my car was parked. I couldn't believe it: the Tijuana Country Club? But the parking attendant told me it was true and gave me specific instructions on how to get there.

I drove south to the edge of town. The T.J. Country Club course was hard to miss: it was a giant patch of light green in an otherwise brown landscape. Signs directed me to the clubhouse, which looked like a miniature of the Alamo, with a poorly printed, peeling sign announcing "Club Social Y Deportivo De Tijuana."

I pushed my way through knots of golfers drinking beer and hoisting golf bags, looking for someone in charge. The room was dingy, the walls the same sandblasted adobe as outside. And the golfers looked crazed, not unlike some junkies I had seen, lining up in queues to buy golf provisions, pushing and shoving in their anxiousness to get to the first hole. It would be futile to attempt questioning here. I followed a group of prosperous-looking Mexicans outside, where the course opened up before me like a breath of clean air: rolling, strangely soft-looking green hills only slightly tainted by the omnipresent Tijuana brownness. The only thing to ruin it were the golf maniacs, dozens of them, milling around on a large patio, waiting to load their bags onto the scores of dilapidated golf carts parked in a blacktop loading area adjacent to the first tee. The whole scene had the air of an ancient ritual, completely American, prosaic and profound at the same time.

I walked over to a Mexican youth pulling beer bottles out of a large plastic trash can and handing them to golfers who grabbed them hungrily. When the trash can was empty, he took it back to a service shed to reload. I followed. "Habla Ingles?" I said, as he dipped his hands into a large ice machine.

"Yeah, I speak English," he replied, with a purely American-Chicano accent, "but it won't do you no good. You get one beer in the package deal and that's it. Two Margaritas and a golf cart. Todos. Comprende?"

"I dig you. What I'm looking for is the caddy master."

He stopped and stared at me as if I were an idiot child. "Caddy master? Are you jiving me? This dump don't have no caddies. Only class clubs have caddies."

"I should have known. Listen, I'm looking for a caddy. I know he's somewhere near Tijuana. He's hard to miss: an Anglo, about forty, short, sunburned, and very fat. He always wears dirty golf clothes. Have you seen him?"

"I ain't seen him. But we get lots of golf course bums around here. Ask Ernie in the pro shop." He pointed to a white one-man cubicle, where a fat Chicano was handing out golf balls. I walked over and got in line. All the golfers seemed to be high on some new drug I knew nothing about, chattering in English and Spanish about incomprehensible matters. I felt as out of place as Beethoven at a rock concert.

The tournament, or whatever it was, was starting and interest shifted to the first tee. The beer line had petered out and the golf ball line I was in had ended. Ernie gave me a harsh look that softened somewhat when he saw the twenty dollar bill I waved flag-like in front of him. "I don't want golf balls, I want information," I said, as he nodded, his eyes fixed on my money. I described Fat Dog.

Recognition flashed into Ernie's eyes. He grabbed for the twenty, but I pulled it away. "I seen that guy," he said. "He unloaded some balls on me a couple of days ago."

"Do you know where I can find him?"

"Naw, he's just a bum. A fly-by-night."

"Did you talk to him about anything other than golf balls?"

"Yeah. He told me he wanted to buy racing dogs. I told him to go to the dog track. I thought he was shitting me.

He didn't look like he had the money to buy no racing dogs. Then he flashes this roll on me. A couple of grand. Fuck me. A loco, you know? That kind of dinero and he's selling golf balls. Crazy."

"So you sent him to the dog track, right?"

"Hell no, man. I sent him to see my cousin Armando. He's got two litters of greyhound pups."

I gave Ernie the twenty and pulled another one out of my billfold. "Where can I find Armando?"

"Who are you, man?"

"I'm a nice guy. I want that bastard who sold you the golf balls." I pulled out another twenty.

"I'll take you to see my cousin," he said.

I followed Ernie's ancient Ford pickup. We drove east, through a maze of dirt roads, through shanty towns and hobo jungles of abandoned cars. Armando lived in an incongruous red-brick house on the edge of a giant culvert. The place was enclosed with accordion wire and as I pulled up behind Ernie I could see and hear children and greyhound puppies frolicking behind the fence.

Ernie told me to wait by my car, that he would get his cousin. I waited, restlessly. I felt I was getting close, that Fat Dog was nearby and at my mercy. I could hear arguing from within the house. A few minutes later Ernie came out followed by an older, even fatter Chicano.

Armando disdained my offer of a handshake. "My cousin says you want to find the fat gringo I sold two dogs to."

"That's right," I said.

"It will cost you fifty dollars," Ernie interjected.

"You've got it. Where is he?"

"First you give me the money," Armando said.

I was getting pissed, but reached for my billfold without hesitation. I handed Armando two twenties and a ten. He looked at me with contempt. "Where is he?" I asked angrily.

"You gonna fuck him up, gringo?"

"Maybe. Where is he?" I was ready to blow it all and trash the fat greasers right on the spot, but I held it in. I felt the blood start to pound in my head and the periphery of my vision blackened, but I said nothing, just let the two Mexicans play mind-fuck.

Finally Armando spoke: "That fat puto deserves what

he gets. I got a feeling about him. About you, too, gabacho, so I tell you. I rented him a shack I got. You take the Ensenada Toll Road, past the first toll booth, about forty miles from Tijuana, half mile from the sign that says 'Alisistos ½ mile.' Then you drive past the lakebed till you see a dirt road cut in toward the mountains on your left. You got to bang your car on the divider in the middle of the road to cross. Then you take the dirt road for three miles, to a fork. Then you go left for half a mile to the shack." I committed the information to memory while Armando and Ernie eyed me coldly. "Maybe you do me a favor, mano," Armando said. "Maybe you take care of the fat puto and I rent the shack to someone else. A shack like that, how do you say? In the middle of nowhere? Who knows what happens."

"Fuck yourself, greaseball."

"I forget you said that, man. This guy got two pups of mine. You bring them back, I give you twenty dollars." He spat in the dirt at my feet, an invitation for me to try something. I didn't. It was their country, their rules. I got in my car and drove away.

I headed for the Ensenada Toll Road, driving through Tijuana on my way. Just outside of T.J. I found a side road that dead-ended. I pulled off and got my shotgun out of the trunk, loaded it, and placed it beside me on the front seat, covered by a blanket.

The toll road southbound was wide open and beautiful, with the sea yawning wide and bright blue off to my right and the hillside shanty towns thinning out as I moved away from Tijuana. I was adrenalin-expectation high, but put all thoughts of the future out of my mind and concentrated on the moment: sunny, seaside uncharted territory, untainted by the grimness of my mission here.

I passed through the first toll booth and a few minutes later I spotted the "Alisistos ½ mile" sign, then the dry lakebed. I saw the dirt road immediately, so I slowed down and got ready to jump the concrete divider. I came to a complete halt and scraped over it with what seemed like a minimum of damage to my underbody.

The road led up into greenish-brown mesquite country, past several garbage dumps and a shanty town of adobe huts where several old women were tending a collection of chickens and pigs. Soon I caught sight of the fork. The road to the right led higher up into the hills; the left—the one I was to take—led downward, into what looked like a box canyon.

I turned off my engine and coasted in, keeping a foot on my brake. After one quarter mile by my speedometer, the road leveled out and turned one last time. I could see a beaten-up wooden shack in the distance, about three hundred yards away. I got out of the car and locked it, taking the shotgun with me. There was no one in sight.

As I drew closer, staying to the side of the road along a stretch of bushes, I could see that the shack was encompassed by a low fence of unevenly matched pickets driven into the ground at irregular intervals and linked together by heavy wire. About fifty yards behind the shack was a large wooded area. Nailed to the wall of the shack was a bus sign, depicting a greyhound in full stride.

When I drew up alongside the picket fence a putrid smell hit my nostrils. I saw a large swarm of flies buzzing about a foot above the ground and a half dozen rats scrambling beneath them. When I saw what they were interested in, my stomach turned. Two dead greyhound puppies lay in the sandy makeshift front yard, their stomachs open and spilling guts.

I pumped a shell into the chamber, stepped over the fence and approached the shack. I felt the hackles on my neck rise and my skin started to tingle. I could see that the flimsy wooden door was ajar, so I found a large rock and hurled it. The door flew inward, the wood splintering and giving off a ghostly echo. But no other sounds came at me and I could see no movement inside.

I approached cautiously, my shotgun held in front of me at body level. The same stench that pervaded the yard doubled as I walked through the doorway, so I knew there was something dead inside. It was Fat Dog. He was lying on the floor, nude, in a lake of dried blood. His throat had been slit and there were puncture wounds all over his torso and legs. A large rat was nibbling at one fleshy thigh. His mouth had been ripped open from ear to ear, exposing cartilage and rotten teeth. His nose had been smashed.

I picked up an empty tin can and threw it at the rat. It scurried out the door, flesh hanging from its teeth. I surveyed the room: walls of the cheapest grade building material, floors of rough wood, a formica coffee table with a case of dog food underneath it, a duffel bag containing golf balls and nothing else. No furnishings, plumbing, or lighting. Nothing but the corpse of Frederick "Fat Dog" Baker, caddy and arsonist, and my would-be gravy train.

I walked outside to the far corner of the pathetic little yard, away from the dead puppies, in order to get away from the smell of the dead looper and collect my thoughts. I felt composed and detached as I thought about the last stand of this psychotic dreamer. I felt absolute pity that anyone should have to live as Fat Dog did and die as terribly; tortured for hours or maybe longer. For his money? For the roll he may have been flashing in T.J.? I went back into the charnel house to look for clues. I was right the first time. There was nothing. When I walked back outside, my memory jogged: Fat Dog never lived indoors. He was a notorious hobo and pack rat. I charged into the wooded area behind the shack. It was about one hundred-fifty yards deep and thick with desert pines that allowed almost no light to enter.

It took me three hours of poking in bushes and checking out the bases of tree trunks to find what I was looking for. It was behind an uprooted scrub bush, nestled in a hollow tree trunk and wrapped in three giant plastic bags: a sleeping bag, two books on the care of greyhounds, a wallet containing $1,600 and no identification, the May issue of Penthouse, a 6-iron, and a pebble-grained leather ledger, almost identical to the ones Omar Gonzalez had found in Richard Ralston's house in Encino.

I opened the ledger, which was wrapped in its own smaller bag. It was set up in five columns, the first two containing lists of Latin and Anglo surnames followed by initials, the two columns separated by dashes in red ink. The third column held dates in no particular order. The fourth column listed amounts of money, ranging from $198.00 to $244.89. The fifth column was allotted the largest space: it held comments written in a minute hand in Spanish. The ledger had thirty-two pages set up this way and it spelled one thing: extortion, somehow featuring Richard Ralston.

I transferred the money from Fat Dog's wallet to my own and tucked the ledger under my arm. I walked back to my car, skirting the death house, feeling certain that Fat Dog had been attempting to blackmail Richard Ralston, or someone, and had paid for the crime with his life; that somehow Sol Kupferman and the Club Utopia firebombing were also connected. What nagged at me was the missing link: Omar Gonzalez's anonymous caller.

When I got back to the car I locked my shotgun and new evidence in the trunk and drove back to T.J. to find someone who could read Spanish.

It was almost six o'clock when I got back to Tijuana. The traffic was impossible, so I parked in the first space available in the downtown area. Street peddlers were out in force, hawking firecrackers and elaborate sets of fireworks: Roman candles, pinwheels, "atom bombs," and "houses on fire," selling them out of large open boxes leaned up against parked cars. T.J. was going to rock with the antics of swinging expatriates tonight.

My first stop was at an Army-Navy store, where I purchased a sturdy-looking shovel. Fat Dog deserved a decent burial and I was the only one to see that he got it. His golf balls would accompany him. I returned to the car and locked the grave-digging tool in the front seat, then went looking for an educated Mexican who looked like he could keep his mouth shut.

As I walked, I kept pushing thoughts of Jane out of my mind. I was likely to be down in Mexico longer than expected. Fat Dog had mentioned a "rich friend" with a "big castle." It would bear checking out. There was also the matter of Fat Dog's killer or killers—I might be able to dig up some leads on people who had been searching for the late unlamented looper.

I turned into an alley to avoid the sidewalk bustle, and heard footsteps crunching on gravel immediately behind me. I swung around, but it was too late. A fist crashed into my jaw. I tottered, but kept my balance, the ledger flying out of my hand. It was dark in the alley, but as I recovered from the blow and put up my arms to ward off others I recognized my assailant. It was Omar Gonzalez. That made me angry. As recognition and amazement lit up my face, Gonzalez followed with a left to my head and a right to my ribcage. He was fast and strong. The left caught me high on the cheekbone, the ring on his finger drawing blood; the right I deflected with an elbow. He was wide open and over-confident. I feinted with my left shoulder and as he drew away I slammed a right cross to the side of his nose. He went down, but came up fast, his knees wobbling. As he struggled to get up, wiping the blood from his eyes, I kneed him in the chin, full force. He went down again and was still.

I caught my breath and patted him down for weapons. Nothing. How had he gotten here so fast? And how had he known to come here? He would be rousing soon, so I picked up the dusty ledger, hoisted him onto my shoulder and carried him out to the busy sidewalk, where I sat him down beside a fire hydrant. Being T.J., this got only a few curious stares from passersby. Keeping a hand on his shoulder to keep him from tipping over, I applied pressure to the cut on my cheek. It was deep, but razor sharp and the blood was already starting to congeal.

Gonzalez came to with a start. He tried to stand up and start swinging, but was too woozy. He wiped blood from his nose. I kept a firm hand on his shoulder. "No go, Omar. Too many people around. The T.J. jail is a bitch. But I've got some very good news for you, if you'll listen . . ."

He didn't want to listen. The expletives began, first in Spanish, ending in English. ". . . Filthy scum-sucking fascist pig! Parasite! . . ." I let him go on and on.

When he ran out of epithets and breath, I spoke soothingly: "The man who was responsible for killing your brother is dead. Murdered. He's lying in an old shack outside of T.J. I'll show him to you, if you want. No tricks this time. I'll tell you the whole story of my involvement in this thing. The truth. You want to listen?"

"I'll listen, puto. I got nothing better to do."

"Good. It's a long story. Let's find a cantina."

I gave Gonzalez a handkerchief to wipe the blood from his battered nose. It wasn't broken, which made me feel good. After a block's walk, we found a combination restaurant-bar that looked clean and wasn't too crowded. From the window by our table we could see fireworks begin to light up the twilight sky. I told Omar everything— from the beginning, including the incredible coincidence of my recognizing Kupferman from a split-second meeting years before. The only thing I omitted was my involvement with Jane. Watching him as I recounted the tragedy that had been the central fact of his life for a decade I saw anger, grief, and fierce love light up his face. After I finished I sipped my coffee in silence and waited for his response. Finally it came, much more stoic than stunned. "Who do you think killed Fat Dog?" he asked.

"I'm not sure. He's tied in to Ralston from Hillcrest, ten years ago. They're connected by the similar ledgers they both had in their possession. It could well be that Fat Dog was trying to blackmail Ralston. I'm not sure. We'll know more when we decipher this ledger." I handed him the leather bound book. "You read Spanish, don't you?"

"Of course, yo soy Chicano." He said it with pride. We were moving toward becoming allies, but he was keeping his distance. I respected him for it.

"Read it," I said, "then we'll go and bury Fat Dog. Or I will, I should say. You can wait here."

"No, I'll go. I want to see this putrid piece of dog shit with its guts hanging out. I want to burn the sight into my brain."

"Then hurry up and read the ledger. It's getting dark. I want to be sure we can find the place."

Omar read fast, his eyes skimming the pages, showing no emotion. He read page by page for several minutes, then closed the book and stared at me. "It's not a bookie ledger like the ones I found at Ralston's house," he said. "The first four columns are the same thing. Names, some Latino, some Anglo, some that sound kind of black, followed by initials—R.R., that would have to be Ralston, J.L., H.H., D.D., G.V. Don't ask me what that means. The next column is odd amounts of money, with a dash, then a date, no particular order. The dates go back eight years to '72. After the dates, there's all these really odd amounts of dough—211.83, 367.00, 411.10. Like that. Funny. With no dollar signs, just the decimal points. Weird. In the next column there's another name, most of the time matching the one in the first column. Then, there's comments— spooky stuff. For instance—'Cousin, dead ten years,' 'Uncle, born here, valid D.O.B., died Mexico, '55,' 'Played ball with R.R., died 6–21–59.' Every line in this last column seems to refer to some dead person, or one of their relatives. Spooky. What do you think, repo?"

Another loose end seemed to be tying itself up. "I think maybe this ledger details some kind of Welfare scam. Remember those blank checks stuck in the ledgers you ripped off of Ralston? Everything in this new ledger seems to bear it out—the names, the amounts of money—all small and within the range of a monthly Welfare payment, and the comments in the last column—died such and such a date. I think that Ralston is working a Welfare ripoff, and that Fat Dog was involved somehow, or found out about it, and tried to blackmail Ralston, and was killed."

Omar was nodding his head, taking in the information and kicking it around. "What do we do now?" he said.

"Let's bury Fat Dog and head back to L.A. Ralston is the key to this case, I'm sure of that. When we get back I'm going to brace him."

We got up and left the cantina, my coffee and his beer practically untouched. We walked to the car, then headed for the Ensenada Toll Road.

It was almost dark and cooling off. We drove south on the toll road, skirting the ocean. As we pulled out of Tijuana I could see bonfires being lit in the shanty towns that filled the canyons on the land side of the road. The people who lived in the makeshift communities had no electricity, but their fires provided light and a glow that swept all the way across the highway to illuminate the Pacific with strands of gold. Given the corruption of Tijuana, where most of them probably worked, I wondered if they were jaded beyond redemption, as I was, or innocent enough to fill their lives with the simple beauty that surrounded them. Omar was evidently thinking along parallel lines.

"So much fucking beauty, and so much fucking poverty. But it's the poverty that finally gets you. So you come to America, meaning L.A., and you find some kind of chickenshit job and raise a big family, and stay poor. And you know what kills me, repo? There's not a goddamned thing I can do about it. Except to help the kids who rebel at the poverty and look for the answer in dope. You win one, and you lose twenty. But you know, it's worth the effort."

"Yeah. One thing you haven't mentioned: How the hell did you find me? How did you know to come to T.J.?"

"Easy. There was no place else to go. The only lead I had was those porno pictures, which spelled T.J. Also, you shanghaied me north, in the opposite direction. I cut through the rope about three in the morning and hitched into Santa Barbara. I caught the six o'clock bus to Dago and walked across the border. I been looking all over town for your car since eleven o'clock. Finally, I spotted it. Then I found you."

"You're a smart, resourceful guy, Omar. I have no doubt you'll go far in life, now that you're free of your obsession."

"But it's not over, repo. This puto Fat Dog is dead, but there's a lot more going on, you said so yourself. I want to know all of it."

"You will. But you're strictly a noncombatant. Remember that. When we get back to L.A., I'm going after Ralston alone. We're dealing with killers here, not Barrio punks with switchblades and a snootful of angel dust. So you take a good look at Fat Dog's corpse, and hold your nose while you're doing it. If you've got the stomach for it, I'll even let you desecrate it before the burial. He's the one who killed your brother, no one else. The rest is icing on the cake and that's *my* obsession. So when we get back to L.A., you keep out of it. You got shot once and survived. You were lucky. I'm going to find you a place with some friends of mine. You can stay there until this thing blows over."

"I'll think about it."

"You'll do it. I'll make sure you know what's happening. Just stay out of sight."

"All right. You know, this feels strange. I've been waiting for this moment for over ten years, but it feels like a big letdown. I wanted to kill the puto myself, slowly. And I would have done it. Scum like this Fat Dog don't deserve to live."

"You've got that all wrong, amigo. You might have killed Fat Dog—if the timing had been right and your conscience and conditioning shut off long enough for you to do it. I might have, too, if I hadn't been able to get him to confess and thought he might kill again. But he deserved to live. He just never had the chance. He had no choice in the matter. It was locked in, from the beginning. He was destined to become what he became. I'm no liberal, but I learned one thing from being a cop: that some people have to do what they are doing, that they can't help it. I tried to explain this to my fellow officers, but they laughed me off as a bleeding heart. I'm doing what I have to do, so are you, so was Fat Dog. The only difference between us and

Fat Dog is that our conditioning was tempered with some love and gentleness. His wasn't. All he knew was anger, hatred, and meanness. That's why I'm going back to bury him. He deserved better."

"I didn't think you were so soft-hearted. Do you consider what happens to the poor Chicano in El Barrio when you repo the car he needs to get to work in?"

"Yeah, I consider the consequences. And I come up with this: He knew what he was getting into when he signed the contract. All the repossessions I go out on are at least two months' delinquent. So tough shit."

"You're a tough nut to crack, repo."

"So are you."

We both got a laugh out of that one. For the second time that day I pulled my Camaro over the concrete divider, giving the undercarriage a good wracking. As I hit the dirt road, I turned on my high beams, throwing light on small hills of brown scrub, dust, and a rodent family on the move. I took it slowly, staying squarely on the road. This time I drove all the way up to the death shack, turning the car around so that I could drive straight out.

There was a large Coleman Lantern in my trunk. I lit it and mounted it on the hood of the car to provide light to work by. A slight breeze cut through the stench of the rotting greyhound pups in the front yard, leaving just a smell redolent of meat left out too long. I got the shovel and the large five-cell flashlight, which I handed to Omar.

"Dig this scene," I said, "you'll never see another one like it. The man who killed your brother is in the shack."

Omar followed my directions, playing his light over the dead puppies. He seemed to be hesitant about going into the shack, though, like a kid at the amusement park with a ticket for the haunted house, knowing it's the real thrill, yet afraid to go for it. "Go on, Omar. Get it over with. I want to get out of here."

He nodded and walked up the steps while I began to dig. I was at it for about three minutes when he came crashing out the door, bent over and holding his stomach. He went around to the side of the shack and vomited, then retched dry, his whole body shaking with each convulsion. Finally he finished and walked up to me. He was pale and the look in his eyes aged him by ten years. "Jesus," he said.

"Did you enjoy that?" I asked.

"No," he replied, "I wanted to look at his face, to try to read it, but there was no face to read. God. There were these bugs coming out of his nose and his guts hang . . . Jesus."

"He's been dead at least three days. Have you had enough?"

"Yes."

"Then you go and sit in the car. I'll bury him and we'll split."

I dug some Kleenex out of my back pocket, tore off a few small pieces and wadded them into my nostrils. Carrying the flashlight that Omar had left on the ground, I entered the shack. I was somewhat inured to violent death and stiffs, but Fat Dog's was too much: the stench crept through the wadded-up Kleenex and my eyes stung from the acidity of rotting flesh. I grabbed the corpse by both wrists and pulled. The left arm came loose at its socket, flying up in the air, spraying decomposing matter. I lost my balance and almost fell, letting out a strangled cry when a viscous glob of rented flesh flew up and hit me in the cheek. I brushed it off and took a moment to compose myself, then grabbed Fat Dog by the ankles and began pulling him toward the door.

I was about to begin my descent down the three shallow steps when I heard a gunshot ring out from the direction of my car. I dropped Fat Dog's ankles, grabbed my flashlight, and pulled my .38 from my waistband. Flattening myself up against the wall, I took frantic deep breaths to stifle my fear and allow my mind to operate. Some seconds passed, then I heard voices speaking in Spanish. Through the door crack I saw the shapes of two men approaching the shack. I waited. As they got closer, I could see that the man on the left was carrying a rifle, held in the crook of his arm, pointed downward.

When they were about two feet from the steps, I swung out and flashed my light dead in their faces and fired all six shots into them at chest level. They both went down and I hurled myself back against the inside wall and reloaded from the loose shells I kept in my back pocket. I heard moaning and in the next instant a volley of rifle shots tore into the shack, splintering the wood around me. I grabbed hold of a chunk of the splintered wood and yanked, cutting my hand in the process. I stuck my flashlight in the hole and surveyed the scene: one man lay in front of the steps; I couldn't see the other man, the one with the rifle, until an instant later when I heard a weak thumping and stifled moaning coming from the steps. He was trying to crawl into the shack, his rifle held out in front of him. I held my breath for a few seconds, then as I saw the rifle barrel make its way into the shack, I padded over and flattened it to the floor with my foot. The man who held it looked up at me from his place on the steps. I couldn't discern his features, but I could see a bright trickle of blood dripping from his mouth. It was over for him. I placed my gun up against his temple and squeezed off three shots. His head burst inward like a crushed eggshell. I walked over to where the other man lay. I was sure he was dead, but I emptied my remaining three rounds into the back of his neck anyway.

I walked back to my car, knowing what I would find. Omar Gonzalez lay dead, sprawled across the front seat, shot in the head. There was very little blood, the bullet obviously still embedded in his brain. I pulled him out by his arms and carried him gently to the incomplete grave I had intended for Fat Dog. If Fat Dog had deserved better, then Omar Gonzalez had deserved the best life had to offer. It took me half an hour to bury him. When I finished, I tried to bring to mind a Dylan Thomas poem about "Death having no dominion," but I couldn't recall the words.

I went over to the car and siphoned gas into a gallon can and carried it to the shack. I dragged the two killers inside to rest beside Fat Dog. After lifting their wallets, I doused the three bodies with gasoline and dropped a match on them. As they started to burn, I thought what a fitting end it was for Fat Dog.

By the time I got back to my car and pulled out, the shack was engulfed in flames. I headed straight for the toll road. Before I got there, I realized I was weeping for the first time since my early childhood discovery that tears did no good. Now they were streaming down my face and I was trembling like a child. For the third time in one day, I banged my car across the concrete divider. This time I was going south, toward Ensenada and an all-night liquor store.

## 9

I don't know how I made it into Ensenada or even why I fled south, deeper into a foreign country. When a body cries "alcohol," logic does not apply. Driving the winding coast road, I passed two toll booths and headed south. I shielded my dirt- and tearstained face from the toll takers, handing them a dollar bill and zooming past with what I hoped passed for a friendly wave. My body was functioning—the ritual of driving, of keeping all senses alert to the needs of the road, kept me from breaking down into total hysteria—but my mind wasn't. Fear, and the inchoate realization that my life had exploded into irreparable fragments kept my head slamming painfully, causing the windshield and highway to blur in front of me.

After a while, my panic became almost familiar, and the edge of it softened. I knew there was a panacea that would put everything in perspective: booze. And the only thing that mattered now was getting it.

Ensenada opened up below me in a scatter of light. Hugging the outside lane and concentrating on driving slowly, I saw the lights of ships illuminating the harbor. On the outskirts of town I found a road that led down to the beach. After about a mile I found what I was looking for: a beachside men's room. I sat on the toilet and let go of my bowels and bladder. Then I took deep breaths for one minute, gauging the time by the second hand of my watch. I washed my crusty face, first with warm water, then cool, and smeared some abrasive powdered soap under my arms in an attempt to eradicate the smell of fear. I combed my hair and started to feel a little bit better; my survival instincts were still intact. My tremors were all internal now, so I felt ready to face civilization.

I drove into town. Ensenada was a muted version of

T.J., less low-life, quieter, and featuring a sea breeze. The night was perfectly clear, and as I parked in front of the first liquor store I came to I glanced north, expecting to see the dusty brown Mexican Hills afire with my handiwork, but there was nothing.

The liquor store proprietor didn't give me a second glance when I purchased two fifths of Scotch, a bag of ice, and a quart of ginger ale. Now all I needed was a safe house, a place to hole up and drink. The sleazy downtown hotels would provide protective coloration for an outsized gringo, but they were too noisy, too close to the arena of tourism. So I drove south, feeling secure with my booze on the seat beside me.

On the south border of Ensenada, nestled on the edge of a housing development, I found my safe harbor: a two-story white stucco rooming house. The big sign out front said "cuartos"—rooms. I left my shotgun in the trunk and collected my suitcase and brown paper bag of booze. I rang the bell on the door lettered "managerio," and inquired in broken Spanish after a room for a week. The woman led me down the musty hallway to an open room with a bed, table, two chairs, a wash basin, and a huge lightbulb dangling on a cord from the ceiling, "Si," I told her. "Quantos?"

She replied "Fifteen dollar." I turned my back to her, not wanting her to see the size of my roll, then handed her the money. She reached into her housecoat and gave me a key. Then she looked me up and down sagely and turned and walked away.

I locked the door behind me and checked out my image in the cracked mirror above the basin. I looked gaunt and scared. I placed the two fifths of Scotch on the table and stared at them. They didn't go away, so I stared some more. I dumped my bag of ice in the sink, making sure the plug was securely in the drain. I put three ice cubes in one of the paper cups the previous tenant had kindly left behind. My mind was raging, but I felt perfectly calm. For one split second clarity hit and I knew what the consequences would be if I drank, but I shunted them aside. Pouring the cup full of Scotch, I drank it in one greedy gulp.

And I knew. The chickens had come back to roost. I had been saved again. I let the booze shake and warm my body. I sat down in one of the stiff wooden chairs, fondling my paper cup. My mind was just inches away from clicking into place, rushing forth with epigrams, pronouncements, and profundity.

I picked up the two wallets I had taken from the men I killed and placed them on a high shelf in the closet. *The men I killed*. That caused me to shake, so I had another drink. This time relief was instantaneous, my mind running with sentimental meanderings, fragments of my relationship with Walter and odd bits and pieces of symphonies and concertos. In stereo. I had been away a long time, and mother booze was being generous, throwing me a mellifluous parade as a welcome home present. I was with Beethoven at the first performance of the *Eroica*, with Bruckner as he sought God in the Tyrolean Alps, with Liszt as he seduced the most beautiful women of his day.

I went to the mirror and checked myself out: I looked normal again, even handsome. My normally ruddy face looked a little more florid than usual, but I attributed that to too much sun. I studied the planes and angles of my face, and decided that Fritz Brown, thirty-three-year-old ex-L.A.P.D. bimbo and repo king of the Greater L.A. area, would do. That caused me to smile and I amended my opinion slightly: my teeth were too small, and my eyes should be blue. Blue eyes were in. Women dug them. Even ghetto blacks were sporting blue contact lenses and getting laid as a result.

I looked around for a phone. Of course there wasn't one. I felt like calling Walter and telling him everything was okay. I thought of an old girlfriend named Charlotte who had been in love with the Chopin "Heroic Polonaise." She always wanted to listen to it before we went to bed. I always advanced the opinion, derived from Walter, that Chopin was a cornball and a sentimentalist. Now the "Polonaise" was banging through my brain like the repeated drone of an air raid siren.

My mind swung from Charlotte to women in general and from there to Jane. She was real, she was now. When I couldn't shake the image of our night together, I started to panic. I grabbed the bottle and drank until I passed out.

I awoke the next morning around nine without the shakes, not knowing where I was. When I saw the empty fifth of Scotch on the table, my memory kicked in and it all came back. I held my breath against a sudden burst of panic. It never arrived. That gave me heart. I was utterly dehydrated, so I dug the remnants of the bag of ice out of the sink and wolfed them down, sending chills throughout my body. As if in answer, a lightweight case of the shakes started, but I held them at bay while I shaved and walked down the hall for a quick shower. The hallway was dirty and the shower room even dirtier. The hall rug was threadbare and no thicker than a tortilla. The shower emitted a sluggish stream of brownish water and I had to tiptoe to avoid cutting my feet on the stucco chips that covered the floor.

Back in my room I counted the money in my bulging billfold—$3,123. As soon as I realized I had time and money on my hands, the shakes started again. It got bad fast this time. My ten months of sober living had not inured me to the payment that booze demanded. The case went through my mind. It was waiting for me, but for now it was out of my control. There was an easy remedy for the shakes: drink. So I did, this time sipping the Scotch slowly from the paper cup, mixed half and half with the lukewarm ginger ale.

I decided that if I could limit my plans to this single day, today, Monday, I would be all right. I could lie low for a few days, drink, then taper off and detox. Then back to L.A. But after a few drinks, my mind became mired in a welter of plans and conspiracies, always reaching toward the ultimate: the case and Jane. It was too much. I took a large slug, straight from the bottle, locked up the room and went outside. The "managerio" gave me a slight nod and a suspicious look as I walked down the hall.

At 10:45 A.M., it was already reaching one hundred degrees. There was a sea breeze that did its best to help, but failed. I decided to leave the car and walk into town—a 502 in a foreign country was all I needed. I walked through the streets of the housing development, a blatant ripoff of American values that nonetheless carried the essence of the Mexican ethos: women and toddlers sunning themselves on the steps of the plain one-story stucco dwellings, dogs cavorting happily and chickens squawking in their low, fenced enclosures. I waved to several groups of children and they waved back. I was never a child. I came out of my mother's womb full-grown, clutching a biography of Beethoven and an empty glass. My first words were "Where's the booze?"

I walked down to the road that paralleled the ocean. There were fewer turistas out now. Most of the people I saw driving were Mexicans with Baja license plates. The Coast Highway took me north into Ensenada proper, past scores of signs advertising fishing, lobster dinners, and Jai alai. I passed an impressive monument similar to the American one at Mount Rushmore, this one heralding three great Mexican patriots, their heads in striking bas relief.

I was drenched with sweat now, the alcohol spreading out through my pores. I found a bar that looked like a good place to replenish my liquid content and stepped inside, but the loud Mexican disco music that blared from the jukebox drove me straight back out the door. I tried a few other dives, but the "music" was the same. Finally, I found a quiet bar on a side street. I *needed* a drink now, and as I sat down at the bar I arranged a stack of one dollar bills in front of me. The bartender understood and when I said "Scotch" he brought it to me wordlessly, taking a single dollar bill as payment.

I was starting to feel nervous: Armando, who I was certain had nothing to do with Fat Dog's murder, might discover the destruction of his property and finger me to the cops. The fire I started might have spread. I was at a disadvantage not knowing Spanish—I could have checked the newspapers for mention of it. The tire marks I had left at the scene could be traced to my Camaro. My passage through the toll booths might have been noted. Fear breeds fear, and booze quells fear, temporarily.

I drank a toast to fear, draining my glass. The bar Scotch was good, so I set out on a regular procession of toasts: to Herbert Von Karajan and the Berlin Philharmonic, to Vladimir Horowitz, to Richard Wagner, and to the guy who designed the Hollywood Bowl. Since each of these toasts was a solid two ounces of juice, my fears were soon pretty well under wraps and I started feeling good, humming along with my fantasies again. I wasn't hungry, but I forced myself to eat a greasy plate of eggs and sausage that the barman's wife served me with a fetching smile.

After I had had about six drinks, a rational train of thought began to emerge, along with a syllogism: I am in a bad way. I am in a bad way because there are big pieces missing in the puzzle I am trying to solve. There are big pieces in the puzzle I am trying to solve because my mind is closed to new concepts in general, and new concepts in music in specific. Wino Walter Curran, my best friend, had been warning me for years of the danger of o.d.'ing on German Romanticism. Since music frees the mind, *new* music would free my old mind to fit together the big pieces in the puzzle I was trying to solve.

Brilliant. Booze does it again. It was time to hunt down some *new* music to play Greek chorus to the *new* mind of Fritz Brown. Beethoven, Brahms, Schubert, Haydn, et al. had had their day, and would have it again, in a better time, a time of reminiscence, shared with Jane. Now it was time for Bartok, Stravinsky, Debussy, and Ravel—all those dissonant guys Walter had been fruitlessly urging on me for so long—to come to my aid.

I left a three dollar tip on the bar and walked outside. The afternoon sun hit like a blow from a sledgehammer. I adjusted my cave dweller mentality to fit the needs of a Mexican seaside town, and went searching for music to think by. It seemed like an insurmountable task at first, given the cultural ambience of the city I was digging through, but soon I warmed to the job. The booze seemed to pop out of every cell of my body, yet I stayed pleasantly, floatingly high.

Ciudad D' Juarez, the main drag of Ensenada, was a miniature version of L.A.'s 2nd and Broadway: giant outlet stores featuring cheap clothing, cheap radios, cheap appliances, and an incredible selection of cheap watches. I tore through the record bins, past piles of Mexi-Rock, Mexi-Disco, Mexi-Folk, Punk Rock in English, and scores of old albums by such washed-up superstars as Perry Como, Tony Bennett and Nat "King" Cole. At my third outlet store, I hit my first jackpot—a battered copy of "The Planets" by Gustav Holst. Sir Adrian Boult conducting the BBC Philharmonic. It was a collector's item; it said so right there on the album cover. It set me back thirty-five cents. I inquired with the English-speaking salesgirl about record shops and she gave me detailed instructions to another one four blocks away. She repeated herself several times, no doubt on the valid assumption that drunks are bad listeners.

I really did smell like a still. I would have to clean up when I got back to my room with my booty. I found the record store. It was the most profound advertisement I had ever seen toward advancing the concept of the "ugly American." Every wall was festooned with bigger-than-life-size posters of current American rock and pop stars. The women looked vapid and challenging at the same time. They seemed to be challenging their male counterparts— equally vapid teenagers with tight pants, blow-dried hair, and pouts that looked like an incipient offer of a head job to an electronic thrill-out featuring seven amplifiers, eight biofeedback machines, thirty-seven dildos, cocaine, quaaludes, angel dust, and that porno guy with the fourteen-inch dick.

A hard rock record was playing at peak decibel. There was a strobe light flashing at two in the afternoon. I was behind the times; I thought strobe lights were out. A pretty, buxom Mexican girl wearing a T-shirt with Mick Jagger sticking his tongue out on it approached me like a long lost music lover. I couldn't think of anything to say, so I turned around and walked back out the door, not looking back. It was too much, too soon.

I persisted in my quest and was rewarded down the street: "La Mer" and "Prelude to the Afternoon of a Faun" by Debussy—Szell and the Cleveland. Also the "Petrouchka Suite" by Stravinsky—Ozawa and the Boston Symphony—and the grand prize: a boxed set of the Bartok "String Quartets" by the Guarneri Quartet. These cost me a fast three scoots. The Stravinsky was badly scratched, but the other records were in passable condition.

It was enough to begin my journey, but I wasn't satisfied. I hit a few more bargain bazaars and came up with "Kostelanetz Plays Gershwin," a disc of dubious merit. The only thing now missing was a stereo. I walked back to the first jumbo outlet store and for $149.63 bought a Panasonic "Zoom" Stereo System—two dinky three-inch speakers, a turntable with an automatic changer and a cheapshit, built-in amplifier. It hardly compared with my State-of-the-Arts System back in L.A., but it would be enough to rock my tiny fleabag room.

I hailed a taxi and loaded my merchandise in the back

seat. On the way out of town I had the cabbie stop at a liquor store where I loaded up on goodies: three half-gallons of Scotch, two six-packs of ginger ale, three bags of ice and a variety of canned meats and processed cheese food. I was storing up for what might be a long process of evolution.

My musical metamorphosis didn't happen. I listened and I drank for two solid days, fighting off anger, fear, and paranoia. I couldn't think of the case. When I tried to, my mind shut off and I reached for a drink or turned up the volume on the stereo in fatuous hope of speeding up my thought processes. The music didn't help at all. I didn't like it. It was great music that expressed profound thoughts, but it just plain didn't send me. I found the moderns and impressionists too abstract and dissonant. There was none of the heroism of Beethoven or the lyrical passion of Brahms. The Bartok "Quartets" made me think of Jane, so I couldn't listen to them at all.

I was getting a bad play from the manager, too: on the first day of my quest I ventured down the hall a half-dozen times to urinate, getting a contemptuous look each time. Somehow I got the feeling that she knew my history and regarded me as the precursor to bad times. So I didn't go out of my room again, electing instead to piss in the sink.

After two days I had had enough. I had tried eating the canned meat, but threw up immediately. Twice I had awakened dehydrated to the bone and had begun sobbing. I was afraid of the d.t.'s; they seemed imminent now. The room was stifling hot, even at night. On the third night I decided to go for a walk. I shaved and went down the hall and showered off the booze and sweat stink, this time avoiding the manager. The idea of movement and the performing of old rituals heartened me a little. Back in my room I filled a pint ginger ale bottle with Scotch and put on the last of my clean clothes.

I went out to the parking lot and checked my car. It was dusty, but unharmed; the shotgun and tape deck were still in the trunk. I patted them, for luck, and left them there. I got a box of bullets out of the glove compartment and loaded my .38, slipping a dozen extra into my pocket. I walked toward the beach, feeling less tired as the ocean breeze embraced me. After half a mile or so I reached the stone steps that led down to the water. Signs proclaimed "Estero Beach." I walked south, away from Ensenada; there would be less chance of running into people in that direction. Energy began to course through me, as I traversed the edge of the tide, the wet sand nestling my footsteps and propelling me forward.

I hadn't had a drink in over four hours, so technically I was sober. The booze that had permeated and putrified my system seemed to be lying in abeyance, waiting for me to make the first move. I secured my bottle in a mantle of sand, got down and cranked off twenty pushups. It wasn't too hard; the slight stiffness as I got to my feet felt good. Maybe it wasn't too bad, I thought. Maybe you can go back to L.A. as if none of this ever happened. Maybe it was time to get sober and stay sober.

The sound of muffled voices and the strumming of a guitar interrupted my thoughts. I was walking toward people, a late-night seaside gathering. As I crossed a rise in the sand, I saw a fire some hundred yards away and smelled roasting meat. The voices became louder and I could discern that the people were speaking in English. They were directly in my path, so I walked right up to them, feeling, strangely, only the slightest twinge of paranoia which I shrugged off—I was armed and they probably weren't. The aroma of the roasting meat was getting to me, as was, also strangely, the need to be with people. I reached into my chest and threw a big, booming "Hi!" at the people sitting in the sand—the first word I had spoken in days.

"Friend or foe?" a male voice returned.

"Friend," I said.

"Pull up a seat, friend," the voice answered.

I sat down in the sand. There were eight people—five men and three women. They were young—in their twenties, and seemed to be the counter-culture type at first glance. They were sitting on blankets and sleeping bags, knapsacks and backpacks piled in a heap behind them. The slightest trace of marijuana hung in the air.

I opened with what seemed like a warm remark: "You're the first Americans I've seen since I've been down here. That's a gas. My Spanish is lousy."

"National origin doesn't mean shit," a girl said coldly. "National origin is bourgeois pride. True friendship supersedes all that petty jive. True..."

"He doesn't mean racism," a bearded man interrupted. "He's just lonely. Right, man?"

"You could say that," I said. "I've been down here for a while and I don't know anybody."

"What's your name, man?" he asked.

"Fritz," said. "What's yours?"

"I'm Brother Lee. Going around to your left we have Brother Mark, Brother Randy, Sister Julie, Sister Carol, Brother Kevin, Sister Kallie, and Brother Bob. Sister Vicky is doing the cooking tonight." He pointed to a woman tending the fire a few yards away. I squinted to make her out. She was basting a carcass on a spit. I couldn't place the aroma.

"Are you people a commune?" I asked.

There was general laughter. One of the girls, I think it was Sister Julie, answered me. "Commune is a tired concept, Brother Fritz. We're together because we love each other and we care about the same things."

I forced a smile. "You band together to survive, camping out here on the beach, right? You share your food, your shelter, and your possessions, right?" Most of the group was nodding, and as I got accustomed to the orange light from the cooking fire, I could see that they were smiling. "Doesn't it get cold in the wintertime? What do you do then?"

"Then we move indoors man, what do you think?" This was from Brother Bob. He looked tougher than the rest, a white-trash, low-rider type. Maybe an ex-con. He was easily as big as I.

"Back off there, Brother Bob," I said. "I'm on your side and just making friendly overtures."

"You ask a lot of questions, man, and you look like the heat."

"I'm just curious, that's all. I'm a big city hick, tied down to a dull job that I have to go back to soon. You people have got a lot of freedom. I envy you." It was the right thing to say, a superb icebreaker. I proffered my ginger ale bottle. "Here," I said, "let's drink to friendship. It's good Scotch."

I took a long drink and passed it to Brother Mark, who passed it on to Brother Randy and the others. When it came back to me again it was almost empty. I didn't care. I had already decided this would be my last night of drinking. I ventured another question. "What's that you're cooking? I can't place the smell."

This got a big laugh all around. "It's a dog, Brother Fritz!" Sister Kallie called gleefully, "Come look."

I couldn't believe it. These gentle, if somewhat strident young souls looked like dog lovers, not dog eaters. I got up and walked the few yards to the fire. Sister Kallie followed me, presumably to dig the shocked look on the big square's face. When I checked out the barbecue close up, I started to laugh. I have never laughed as hard, before or since. The shape on the spit was unmistakably canine: a medium-sized, meaty tailwagger with gaping jaws, plucked out eyes and an amputated tail. He smelled delicious. I fell in the sand, convulsed with spasms of mad laughter.

Sister Kallie was jumping up and down, large breasts shaking beneath her peasant blouse, squealing: "He digs it! He digs it! He loves it!"

Finally I got to my feet, wiping tears from my eyes. Two of the men went to work carving up the beast as the rest of us looked on. I stroked the dog's head, petting it tenderly, as though it were still the loyal family pet. This caused another outbreak of laughter. Two cases of beer were dragged back from the surf in a net and we popped cans and dug into our feast.

I was ravenous. All eyes were on me as I poised my fork above a jumbo slice of dog meat. Finally, casting all trepidation and social conditioning aside, I dug in. It was salty, smoky and gamey, much like a venison steak I had once eaten. I choked on it a little at first, but gradually forced it down, followed by a huge gulp of beer. This brought a rousing cheer from my new found friends. After that it was easy and I scarfed the rest of my plate greedily. I forewent the bottle of soy sauce that was being passed around: I was a purist.

The city-bred protein entered my system, my first real food in several days, and a sublime elation came over me. It's going to be all right, I thought. This feeling was quickly engulfed by a wave of sweaty lust—directed at Sister Kallie and her big chi-chi's. Maybe dog meat was an aphrodisiac.

As I lay sated, staring up at the starry Mexican night, the girls cleaned up and Brother Bob expertly rolled joints.

It was party time. Soon the entire group was sitting around the fire, while I remained a few yards away, staring heavenward, wanting to be coaxed. I was. Sister Julie called to me. "Come on, Fritz, join us. It's sharing time." So I joined them.

I didn't want to destroy the moment, but there was a question I had to ask. "Where the hell did you get that delicious dog?" I said. "I want to thank his master."

Brother Lee answered me, lighting a joint and passing it. "We get our meat from two sources. There's a guy who runs a bait store down by the pier. He traps dogs and sells them to his cousin, who has a taco stand in T.J. The cheapest, juiciest, meatiest tacos in Baja. All perro meat. We trade him a bag of weed for two juicy hounds. Sometimes we find dead dogs south of here off a bend in the Coast Road. Cars squash them. Wham. Lots of times we have to ignore them, though. Their ribs get all smashed up and embedded in their skin. Too dangerous to eat."

"I toast all of you," I said. "Truly you are the survivors of both capitalism and the rapacious, fanatic counter-culture it spawned. When I said earlier that I envied you your freedom, I was bullshitting. I thought you were just another cadre of dumb hippies. But I was wrong to condescend. I apologize. In a small way, you have life by the ass and I salute you." They didn't quite know how to react. The joint was passed to me and I inhaled deeply. I was expecting more applause or laughter. Instead, through the blazing fire I got warm smiles and puzzled looks.

"What do you do back in L.A., man?" Brother Randy asked.

I gave it some thought. Another joint came my way and I hit again. This time even deeper. It was good shit. I hadn't been blown away on weed since my Hollywood Vice days, but I was getting there now; drifting into a shadow world of fantasy. I considered Brother Randy's question for a second, then answered: "I do my best to survive. Most of the time it's easy, but lately it's been tough. Mostly I repossess cars. I hope you people dig property rights enough to realize that repo men are necessary. We keep the credit racket in line, and keep America from going insane and bringing back the days of debtor's prison. People like you, the so-called counter-culture, can exist only in places where capitalism is strong. I used to be a cop, but I gave it up. I saw too much stuff I couldn't tolerate."

I stopped and took a blow off the pipe that was handed to me, became full-out zonked and surveyed my rapt audience. The women looked very beautiful. When I returned to my story, I took off on a rhapsody of poetic lies: "The corruption, the racism, the violence, I couldn't handle it. Dealing with so many lost people, most of whom were wearing blue uniforms, the young people trying to live differently, more honestly than their parents, and how the cops reviled them for their lifestyle. The blacks in the ghettos, the winos, the homeless derelicts of Skid Row. There was a gentle side to me I couldn't express, so in the end I quit. What I really wanted to do was learn to play the violin. But I didn't have the patience or the drive to pursue it." It had started out to be rhapsodic bullshit, but on finishing I felt that the whole fabric of lies contained some intrinsic truth that I couldn't put my finger on. I was floating so high on weed and dog meat that everything seemed within my reach, but this eluded me.

"So you came to Baja looking for something, right, Fritz?" This was from Sister Carol.

I laughed. "You could say that."

"Do you think you'll find it?"

"I'm not sure."

"How old are you?" my favorite, Sister Kallie, asked. Warm antennas or tendrils seemed to drift toward me from her direction. Her head seemed to be enclosed in a halo.

"Thirty-three."

"That's not too old to change your life," she said. "You've been through some heavy shit. Pain causes growth. You could still be a great violin player. I learned the guitar when I was twenty-four."

"Thanks. Maybe you're right."

The party started to break up. Everyone except the sullen Brother Bob wished me good night and invited me to return any evening to enjoy their hospitality. I told them I would take them up on it, only next time I would bring steaks and beer. They then wandered off, grabbing their bedrolls and heading for cozy sand drifts. Except for Kallie. She stayed behind, sitting cross-legged across from me by the remnants of the fire.

"Are you the odd woman out, Kallie?" I asked.

"Not really. Mark and I are together. I just felt like staying behind and rapping for a while."

"Thanks. I wasn't quite ready to walk back to my room yet."

"You know, I didn't believe most of what you told us. I believe you were a cop, all right. You look like one. But the rest of it was a con job, right? I mean about being sickened by the violence and racism and all that. Right?"

"I guess so."

"Why did you lie?"

"I'm not sure. I wanted you people to like me and I wanted to move you on a level you could appreciate, but I didn't want to give up too much of myself in the process, I guess."

"You're in trouble, aren't you?"

"Yes."

"Bad trouble?"

I nodded.

"I knew it. It's your eyes. They're scary. They're not normal, whatever that is."

"You're not afraid of me, are you?"

"No. You're scared enough for the both of us. I've got good antenna. I can tell when someone's hurting. You're hurting bad."

"I'll be all right, I think. There are some things I have to do down here, and a big mess waiting for me back in L.A. I've been drinking, but that's over, so I should be okay. I appreciate your concern, Kallie. You're a lovely young woman."

"Do you have a girlfriend?"

"I hope so. I got involved with a woman in L.A. just before I left, but I'm not sure what will happen when I return."

"I was just wondering."

"I've got some business to attend to that should keep me busy down here another few days. I'd like to see you again."

"I don't think that's possible. I want to give you something, but I don't want to get involved."

"I guess I was being forward. I'm sorry. I'm very stoned. It's a strange sensation."

"Don't be sorry, Fritz. I like you. I've got a thing for men who are hurting. It's kind of sick, I guess. If you want, you could stay with me tonight."

"I'd like that."

"Please don't misunderstand me. I don't want to get it on. I'm not promiscuous. I've got an aura. I can impart good feelings to people in trouble without sex. I'm a love carrier. I can help you. If you could see your own face, then you'd know how bad your vibes are."

"I'll do anything you like, sweetheart."

Kallie led me to a high sand drift away from the other brothers and sisters. We laid out a large double sleeping bag and got in with our clothes on. We held hands and cracked jokes for about an hour. After a while exhaustion caught up with me and I started to drift off. Kallie placed my head on her breasts and gently ran her fingers through my hair until I fell asleep. I awoke in that same position hours later, as dawn broke across the water. Kallie had bared her breasts during the night and they were flushed and sweaty from the weight of my head. As I came awake, she did too. I looked at her expectantly, hoping her nakedness meant that we could now make love, but Kallie shook her head. We stood up and embraced.

"Thank you," I said.

Kallie nodded and squeezed my hand. "Don't come back, Fritz. I know you. You'll do something to blow it here. I'll remember you in my meditations. Count on that." It was very final. I kissed her on the cheek and walked back to my life.

My room looked different when I returned to it. The squalor of peeling paint, the musty smell and the rusty furnishings caused me a long moment of self-revulsion. But that passed. The past was dead and there was a future to contend with. I started by pouring the remains of my Scotch down the sink. Then I carted my records up the fire escape to the roof of the building and sailed them off in the direction of the housing development. Most of them died abruptly, but some managed to land on the roofs and gravel front yards of the impoverished dwellings. It made me feel good, like a god sending culture to the culturally deprived.

Back in my room I hemmed and hawed, worried and fretted. It was time to shit or get off the pot. I opened the closet and reached up to the high shelf for the wallets of the two men I killed.

The first wallet belonged to one Reyes Sandoval. It contained a car registration, a baptism certificate dated 1941, scores of Catholic blessing cards, some Mexican currency, and a valid Baja California driver's license, sans photograph. He was born in Juarez October 1, 1940, making him thirty-nine at the time of his death. His height and weight were in kilos and meters, from which I figured him to be medium-sized. Neither man had weighed much as I dragged them into the hideous death shack. The important thing was his address, which was right here in Ensenada: 1179 Felicia Terraco. There was a photograph of a nice-looking, pleasantly overweight woman holding two cuddly children, a boy and a girl. Reyes Sandoval, Mexican gunsel, was a family man.

There was nothing else of any interest in the billfold—no notations or papers of any kind. I kept the driver's license and ripped the rest of the papers into tiny pieces and placed them in an ashtray.

The second wallet, a gaudy machine-tooled Tijuana souvenir job, yielded more: Henry Cruz, forty-two, was American born and possessed a California driver's license, issued to an address in Bell Gardens, a white-trash suburb of L.A. From the mug-shot-like photograph and my vague recollection of that horrible night, Cruz was the man who came into the shack after me, the one I killed at close range. There was forty dollars in American money in the billfold along with a piece of paper with a telephone number. I wrote it down and, except for his California license, burned the remains of both wallets, including the Mexican money. I took the ashtray full of charred paper down the hallway to the bathroom, dumped it into the toilet and flushed. I locked the room, got into my car, and headed for 1179 Felicia Terraco.

A friendly English-speaking news vendor in downtown Ensenada gave me directions, pointing north to a large scrub-covered hillside dotted with small houses. I drove up, taking a dirt trail that ran out of Ensenada proper straight through a large bean field. My trusty Camaro strained in low up steep, narrow streets lined with dwellings that ranged from "Tobacco Road" sharecropper shacks to proudly tended stucco four-flats with rock gardens. The street signs were hard to follow and inexplicably the numbers ran out of sequence. After backtracking repeatedly I found 1179, a cube-like, off-white hut of aluminum siding —the kind material trailers are made of. It was small, but looked comfortable. I could see airconditioning units attached to the side windows, denoting the Sandovals as members of the Ensenada middle-class. All I could do was wait.

I parked against a wooden railing that separated the road from the edge of the bluff. The view was spectacular: Ensenada to my left and directly below; to my right the crystal blue Pacific laced with darker seaweed beds and dotted with small boats.

After an hour or so I was rewarded. The Sandoval widow came out of the house, alone. She had lost weight since the picture in Sandoval's wallet had been taken and she looked troubled. She walked three houses down and got into an old Chevy and drove away, toward Ensenada. I let her go. What I wanted was probably in the house, whatever it was. I decided not to risk a daytime B&E. Too many prying eyes about. Since I would have to wait until nightfall, I drove down into Ensenada for a lobster dinner.

After the meal, I got a sudden urge to call Jane and tell her I was all right; I had been gone six days now. But I decided not to risk it. She would ask too many questions that as yet I couldn't answer. There was another call to be made, though. I dug out the number I had copied from the effects of Henry Cruz. He was an L.A. home boy, so Los Angeles was the obvious place to dial.

I found a bank of enclosed phone booths in a dark passageway at the back of the restaurant and shoved a handful of Mexican coins into the slot, first to reach the L.A. operator and then to get through to my number. No answer. After thirty rings the operator refunded my money, flooding the coin box like a Vegas payoff. I dialed again. This time the phone was answered on the third ring. A friendly sing-song voice called out "Hillcrest Country Club. May I help you?"

I almost died right there. Cruz. Ralston. Fat Dog. Kupferman. Hillcrest. The woman was cooing into the mouthpiece, her voice melding into my colossal adrenalin rush.

"May I help you? This is Hillcrest. May I help you?" I
hung up. There was nothing to say.

Henry Cruz, one of Fat Dog's killers, had been calling
someone—undoubtedly Richard Ralston—at Hillcrest. Fat
Dog was blackmailing Ralston and had been knocked off
for his perfidy. On impulse I called Hillcrest back. The
same operator answered. "Richard Ralston, please," I said.

"I'm sorry, sir," the voice returned, "the first tee is
closed for the day. Did you wish a starting time for mixed
foursomes tomorrow? . . . I . . ." She wanted to continue
her sing-song helpfulness, but I cut her off:

"Is Ralston the starter there? The caddy master?"

"Yes, sir, he is. If you'll . . ."

"Thank you," I said, and hung up.

I paid my check and cruised the Ensenada streets, killing
time before dark. The seaside town was coming alive with
the setting sun—servicemen in civvies beginning an evening of barhopping, Mexican Nationals out for a stroll en
familia, the curio shops jammed. As the sun dropped below
the ocean horizon, I headed toward the high bluff north of
town. This time it didn't take me long to find the place. I
parked in the same spot and walked across the dirt road to
the darkened house.

I had good cover; the night was dark and Mexi-rock was
blasting from the adjoining houses. I knocked on the front
door and then the back, getting no response. Looking both
ways for signs of trouble, I picked the back door lock with
a straight pin, sliding the bolt back with a jammed-in credit
card. I entered into a room that was part service porch,
part playroom. A beat-up washing machine and dryer
competed for space with a huge welter of dolls and broken
model airplanes.

Keeping my flashlight low to avoid creating glare, I
walked into the living room. I had to laugh. It was crammed
with T.V. sets and cheap stereo consoles, at least two dozen
of them, covering every bit of floor space. It was safe to
assume the late Reyes Sandoval was a burglar and/or a
fence. I flashed my light into corners. Nothing. No dressers, no tables, no shelves.

To the right of the living room was a kiddie-room—
sewing-room combo. More broken toys and an elaborate
loom of the kind that turns out Mexican souvenir blankets.
On the floor were a dozen Singer Sewing Machines. Reyes

was an inept killer, but a good thief. I checked the closet, tearing through racks of gaudy dresses and men's suits. Nothing. Nothing in the pockets except cleaning tags.

I saved the bedroom at the end of the narrow hall for last. It slept the whole family: there was a set of children's bunk beds against the wall and a jumbo canopied bed in the middle of the room. I closed the door and risked turning on the light. A score of cheap oil paintings of Jesus stared down at me from every wall. The artists had all portrayed Him as a Mexican. Above the bed a different, more somber holy man gave me the eye. I couldn't place him. He was a tough-looking Biblical Chicano with a shepherd's staff. Maybe he was the patron saint of low-lifers.

There were three sets of dresser drawers against one wall and a large walk-in closet. I dug into the dressers first and hit pay dirt. Pay stubs, a big pile of them, made out to Reyes Juan Sandoval and bearing the imprimatur of the Baja Nacional Cannerio de Pescado. Mrs. Galino's high school Spanish class finally did me some good: Reyes was a recent employee of the Baja Fish Cannery. I put one pay stub into my pocket. The job designation seemed to be "laborero," but the numerical computations were beyond my comprehension. The walk-in closet contained fishing gear: rods, poles, bait, and tackle boxes.

I was getting nervous and sweating in the sealed-up house, so I turned off the light and gave the kitchen a quick going-over—boxes of canned tuna fish, a refrigerator packed with leftovers, and a dirty sink. But I had a lead. I went out the way I came in, closing the door gently.

I consumed time on Sunday with swimming and aimless sightseeing. I located the fish cannery, a smelly factory on a low, flat wharf. I got up at four on Monday morning and drove there dressed for work.

It was lucky that I got there early. Some hippie types and destitute Mexican Nationals were milling outside the gate when I arrived, passing a bottle of Gallo White Port. From them I learned that there was a fleet of tuna boats coming in today and that a large number of swampers would be needed to unload them at eighteen dollars American or x number of pesos. I decided it was worth a try.

The crowd of work-hungry men swelled to about forty. At dawn a group of officious-looking Mexicans came down and began handing out "work cards" which we were exhorted to keep in our pockets, lest we lose them and forfeit our day's pay. Next we were formed into work crews of ten men each, and sent down to the dock to await the arrival of the tuna fleet. I was hoping they would never show, allowing me plenty of time to gently question my coworkers about Reyes Sandoval. But it was not to be— after a half hour's wait the ocean was churning and bubbling with scores of small fishing craft heading straight toward us.

It was the hardest day's work of my life. We formed a line at dockside and huge oilcloth bundles of smelly, greasy fish were passed to us from the ships. We passed them on up the line where pickup trucks waited to take them to the processing area. Soon I was drenched in sweat and my brand new work clothes were covered with fish oil. When one boat was unloaded, we took a two- or three-minute break while another one moored to the dock. There was little time for conversation. At eleven o'clock we took forty-five minutes for lunch. A vendor came by and dispensed chorizo, tacos, and burritos to the hungry slaves.

During our break I broached the subject of Reyes Sandoval to three gringos and three Chicanos. They didn't know who the hell I was talking about and couldn't have cared less. We resumed work and I vowed never to touch another tuna sandwich, ever again.

At long last the workday ended. I was beyond tired, the resident of a new realm of exhaustion. As the last tuna boat headed back to sea a beaming Mexican came down to the dock and distributed our pay envelopes.

As we filed out toward the gate in small talkative groups, I saw her. I knew I knew her, a severe, fiercely sexual woman in her mid-twenties with a red natural. A gringa.

I followed her. She was walking ahead of a crowd of women dressed in smocks—assembly line workers in the cannery, probably—but she was no factory peon. She walked ahead, aloof and proud, smartly dressed in a tailored pantsuit. I wondered what she would look like nude, then I remembered—she was the girl performing in the porno photos I had found in Fat Dog's arson shack! She was older now—a mature woman with the mien and sexual charisma of the very worldly. I remembered that she was the only girl in the pictures not performing with animals. It was too good, too *right* to pass up.

Keeping a safe distance behind, I followed her out the gate and down the broad boulevard that led into Ensenada. After a block she got into an old Mercedes. I dashed for my car, got in and jammed a U-turn up to the first parking space available behind her. Then I waited. She was still sitting at the wheel of her car, as if deciding on a course of action. Finally she pulled out, turning left into the middle of the Ensenada shopping district. I was right behind her. She turned left again on Ciudad D'Juarez and drove north, out of the city. Soon we were heading across the scrubland that fronted the bluff where the Sandoval family lived.

Keeping a car between us, I followed the old Mercedes up the bluff and around a mile or so of winding roads to Felicia Terraco. I wasn't surprised. Walter used to tell me that *everything* in life was connected. I didn't believe him. Now I did. It was eerie, almost like proof of the existence of God.

When she rounded the final turn before the Sandoval casa, I stayed behind. I waited five minutes, then left the car and walked around the corner. Sure enough, Red's Mercedes was pulled up in the Sandoval driveway. She had to return my way; Felicia Terraco dead-ended a quarter mile in the opposite direction. I waited nervously, discarding my fish-permeated shirt and tilting back the driver's seat so I could prop my feet on the dashboard.

Red skidded around the corner a few minutes later, narrowly missing the divider. I caught a glimpse of her fear-flushed face. She looked anguished and disoriented. I counted to ten and began pursuit. We were back in Ensenada in half the time it took us to make the trip up. Red Top was driving fast and erratically, sending up clouds of dust that kept me hidden behind her as she tore through the sandy area outside of town. I was getting frightened for her; she was distraught, self-destructive, and in imminent danger of totaling her car.

When she hit the busy Ensenada streets she cleaned up her act, slowing down and driving with restraint through town to a quiet residential block on its east side. This was a side of Ensenada I hadn't seen: tree-lined streets and up-to-date condo-convenience apartments that reminded me of L.A.'s better suburbs. She pulled up to the curb in front of an elegant, pseudo-French chateau apartment house, and I pulled up directly behind her. I was throwing caution to the winds, because there was no possible ploy I could use in confronting her. It would have to be direct, and that scared me. This was not my country.

She had not yet noticed me, I was sure of that. She was in some nether world of fear and self-obsession, staring up at the building as if debating the risk of entering. Then she bolted, slamming the car door and running into the large vestibule. I tucked my gun into my pocket and ran after her, entering the foyer just in time to catch sight of her going up a flight of carpeted stairs off to my left. I followed, taking the stairs three at a time. My rubber-soled work shoes made my approach soundless and I caught her in the fourth floor hallway, nervously unlocking an apartment door.

I waited until she was almost inside, then shoved the door open and grabbed her just as she began to scream, putting a hand over her mouth and wrestling her to a couch in the middle of the room. She was straining hard in my grip, with the unnatural strength of the very scared. As I sat her down, my hand still clamped over her mouth, I spoke as gently as I could: I'm not going to hurt you. Please believe me. I know you're in trouble. I'm going to mention some names. You nod if you believe I want to help you, okay? Then I'll let go of you and we can talk, okay?" She nodded, the terror in her eyes lessening slightly. "Fat Dog Baker, Richard Ralston, Omar Gonzalez, Reyes Sandoval, Henry Cruz." At the mention of the last two names she began nodding vigorously and squirming in my grasp. I let her go and sat back in the couch holding my breath.

She started to cry, and I made no effort to stop her. "Who are you?" she finally got out between sobs.

"My name is Brown. I'm a private investigator," I said. "The people I mentioned are all involved in a case I'm working on. I don't want to hurt you."

"Are Henry and Reyes all right?"

"I don't know. Is this your apartment?"

"Yes."

"I followed you here from the cannery. I could tell you were scared. What is it? What's frightening you?"

"Henry and Reyes are gone. They've been gone for a week. I know they're in trouble."

"How do you know?"

"I know. They were supposed to do this job for this rich man. This guy Henry used to play baseball with fixed it up. I knew it was wrong, I knew it was dangerous. I told Henry that, but he wouldn't believe me. He wanted the stuff too bad."

"What stuff?"

"You know. Stuff. Smack. This rich guy was going to give Henry a lifetime supply. Because the job was dangerous."

"Was Henry a dealer?"

"What do you mean 'was'? Is Henry all right? Tell me!"

I hesitated.

"He's all right as far as I know. Is he strung out?"

"Yeah. Bad."

"Was this guy Henry used to play baseball with named Richard Ralston?"

"Yeah."

"What kind of job was he supposed to do?"

"I don't know."

"Okay. Look, what's your name?"

"Dorcas. I mean Dori. Dorcas is a shitty name. It sounds like dork, so I use Dori."

"Dori, I know Reyes Sandoval is a burglar, and you tell me Henry is strung out. I don't care. I don't want to bust anyone. This case I'm involved in is too complicated to explain to you. I need the man who hired Henry to do this job. Then maybe I can find out if Henry is all right. We both know that this man wanted Henry to kill somebody, right? That's the only thing it could be."

Dori collapsed in sobs, her body quaking. "I know, I know, I know! Now this guy Ralston is after me. He says Henry is gone, Reyes is gone, and the dope is gone. He thinks I know where Henry is. I told him I know where the dope is—he can have it back—but Henry is gone and Reyes is gone and I just know they're dead!"

"Sssh. Maybe they're not. Ralston wouldn't be bothering you if he knew they were dead, right?"

"Maybe."

"Better than maybe. Probably. Can you tell me who hired Henry and Reyes to do this job?"

"I don't know his name. Ralston set it up. He's a rich American, I know that. He's got a huge house down the Coast. Henry told me about it, and I remembered passing by there once."

"Can you take me there?"

"I think so."

"Good. Has Ralston been hassling Sandoval's wife? I know you know her. I followed you there."

"Yes. Tina's scared, too. She sent her kids to T.J. to live with her parents."

"I think you and Tina should lay low for a while. I'll make you a deal. Show me this rich guy's place tonight, and I'll give you and Tina Sandoval some money to hide out on. I'll even drive you to the border."

"How much money?"

"A thousand dollars."

"Really?" Dori smiled for the first time.

"Really. I've got it right here." I patted my wallet.

"What about my things?"

"Forget them. You're probably in danger. Forget your job, too. You can always come back to it. If you can take me to this place, then I'll drop you with the Sandoval woman. We'll ditch Mexico tomorrow."

"But Tina's Mexican. She don't have a green card."

"Let me worry about that. Now pack a bag so we can split."

She went into the adjoining room and I surveyed the apartment: it was cheap plush, an unschooled person's idea of high class. Dori came back, suitcase in hand, surprisingly fast. She was pulling together nicely. The hardness I had discerned in her at the cannery was real. "One thing before we leave," I said, "where's this supply of dope Henry received?"

She nodded toward the bedroom. We walked in. She opened up a dresser. Hidden underneath some men's shirts were six plastic baggies of white powder. A fortune in heroin if the stuff was pure. I opened a baggie and tasted: the blood rushed to my head and my body shook for a brief instant. It was *very* pure. If I hadn't killed Henry

Cruz he would have died of an overdose before too long. I
looked at Dori.

"It's good stuff, isn't it?" she asked.

"Extremely," I said. "Stuff like this doesn't deserve to
live. We're going to hold a funeral service for it."

"But it's worth a lot of money."

"The money you'd get from selling it wouldn't deserve to
live, either. Where's the bathroom?" It was adjacent to the
kitchen. I carried the baggies in, and emptied them, one by
one, into the toilet. It made me feel pure and very moral.
When I flushed, it was almost like an act of penance for
my old sins. "Let's get out of here," I said.

We drove south in my car and we talked, or mostly Dori
did. She was nervous, worried, but excited over the prospect of my thousand dollars. She had had a long, hard
relationship with Henry Cruz. She was an L.A. girl, and
Cruz had taken her virginity when she was fifteen. They
had been together ever since. He had turned her on to sex,
which she loved, and to the L.A. doper ripoff underworld,
whose intrigue she found fascinating, and to drugs, which
she hated and never used more than nominally, to placate
Henry.

They had had their ups and downs. Henry had gone to
jail and she had hustled to keep him on dope while he was
inside. He had made her pose for specially photographed
"Deluxe Collectors Item" pornography books that he had
given his friends. He had fixed her up with the owner of
the cannery, where she worked as a combination typist-
party girl. The cannery mogul paid for her apartment and
gave her a grand a month in exchange for frequent nighttime visits.

Henry was a rat, she admitted, but she loved him, and
that was that. To my dismay, she was turning me on. My
mind was reverberating away from the case toward various
sleazy ploys to bed her. Her sexual power was overwhelming. To keep it at bay, I opened up a new line of questioning. "Tell me about Richard Ralston."

"What about him?"

"Everything. Think about it for a minute." While Dori
thought, I concentrated on my driving. The terrain was
unspectacular at night, dark hills on my left and the dark

Pacific on my right. I was concerned about Dori's reliability. Would she be able to find the place?

She read my mind: "Don't worry, I'm not conning you," she said. "Henry showed me the place. He was in fucking awe of it. It's some crib."

"You're a mind-reader, Dori. Tell me about Ralston."

"Ralston is kind of a low-level manipulator. A ladies' man, too. He's known as 'Hot Rod' because he's hung like a barracuda. I know, because Henry made me fuck him once. He and Henry used to play baseball together, minor league. Back in the fifties. He's into a lot of shit, gambling, bookmaking, all that. He's got this golf course job that's really a front, and he's got this hotel and bar that he owns. Really a sleazo racket. He's got all these poor old guys on pensions and Welfare living there, all booze-hounds. They live in his fleabag hotel and drink in his bar. It's their whole fucking life. Hot Rod collects their checks each month, subtracts their bar tab and rent, sells them cigarettes that he gets from a fence dirt cheap, and gives them a few bucks spending money. No shit! He told me about it once. Most of the old fuckers at the hotel are caddies too old to carry bags. Hot Rod says he's keeping them alive, if you can call it living. Personally, he's got a lot of style; you know, he's sexy and charming and all that. But basically he's a shit. That's okay, though. I like shits. I relate to them. Henry's a shit and we've been together a long time. You're a kind of a shit, too. I can tell."

"Thanks."

"No, really. I meant it as a compliment."

"Thanks."

We drove in silence, I was keyed up. My case was moving upward, in power, property and prestige from the depths of caddy despair to the seaside casas of the rich, and I was furiously anxious to unravel it, conclude it, mete out whatever justice I could, and return to Jane and Walter and some kind of peace. I checked my watch. We had been driving for fifty minutes. Dori started getting nervous, muttering to herself.

"Now?" I asked.

"Soon," she replied, sticking her head out the window to look for landmarks. "Okay, now," she said. "There's a road just beyond the next bend. Slow down and turn when I tell you."

I did and my headlights caught a wide, well-traveled dirt road leading straight up toward what looked like a pass between two large mountains. As we approached, the terrain flattened out and the mountains became hills. We passed between them, going inland toward a dark, cold, nothingness. It was very silent. Far in the distance coyotes bayed. The road meandered up and down among a series of small hills. It was utterly dark, my high beams the only light.

Gradually the road widened and off to my right a large white shape began to emerge and take form.

"There," Dori said, pointing toward it, "that's the place."

I pulled off the road. "You stay here," I said. "I'll be back within half an hour. Don't leave the car."

She nodded nervously. I took my shotgun and flashlight from the trunk and walked toward my objective. As I got within two hundred yards I realized I was looking at a rancho that would have made a Texas land baron proud. It was two stories high, of white stucco, and had three wings running in different directions. It was a stylistic mishmash, a cross between an American prison and a Turkish mosque. Lights burning in a huge picture window in the main front wing cast an orange glow over a carport that held three cars.

Surprisingly, there was no fence or surrounding wall. Whoever owned this palatial rancho evidently believed in the safety of the wide open spaces, so I walked right up to the cars and examined them: A '76 Ford Ranchero Wagon, a four-wheel drive Toyota Landcruiser, and a late model Volvo Sedan. All bore California plates, which I committed to memory.

I circled the house at a radius of fifty yards or so, to avoid being seen from the darkened rooms. The rancho was set on a foundation of concrete that extended out into the mesquite land that bordered it. By my watch it took me seven minutes to make a complete circuit of la casa grande. There was nothing out of the ordinary, only an eerie desert stillness. Suddenly music cut the night. It was unmistakable: the Schumann Fourth Symphony, the opening movement, the brass pounding up and down like a drum roll. My adversary was an aesthetic and he possessed a stereo system even better than my own, sending shock waves of German romanticism into mesquite land and canyons for miles around.

Dori was frightened, dropping her cigarette into her lap and burning herself as I opened my car door. I put the shotgun into the back seat and hit the ignition. "What's that creepy music?" she said. "It scared the shit out of me."

"That's the good stuff," I said, digging into the glove compartment and writing down the license numbers. "Learn to dig it, it'll set you free. The guy who owns that pad has taste."

"I think his taste sucks. Give me rock any day."

"Rock causes cancer, acne, and the creeping crud. Back to Ensenada. I'll help you move some more of your stuff up to the Sandoval place. Then I'm taking off."

"What about the money you promised?"

"You'll get it. A grand for you and a grand for Tina. I'm feeling magnanimous."

Dori grabbed me, hugged me fiercely and planted a big wet one on my cheek. "You're really a nice shit. You know that?"

"Thanks."

I pulled a U-turn and we began our return trip. Walter had indeed been right. Everything was connected. But was it decipherable? For the first time since Fat Dog knocked on my office door over two long weeks ago, I wondered if anything was.

When we got back to Dori's apartment, I gave her fifteen minutes to move as much of her stuff out as would fit into both our cars. She went about it hurriedly, hauling large armloads of clothes out the door and running down the stairs. I followed suit, not running. I noticed that she left untouched the men's clothing I had seen earlier. Within twenty minutes, both our cars were packed with feminine goodies and a lurid library of pop writers.

We then headed north, toward Sandoval Bluff. When we arrived at the Sandovals', I hurried to unload my car, stacking Dori's things neatly on the ground. No lights were on in the house. That was good; it would be easier to drop my bad news. I dug into my wallet, bloated with other men's money, pulled out two thousand in fifties and C-notes and placed them in Dori's hand. She just looked at me. A period in her life was over and she knew it. "Henry's dead, Dori," I said. "Reyes Sandoval, too. I saw their bodies. There's a big time bad scene going on and it's going to get worse. I'm not sure exactly what's happening, but you and Tina had better get the hell out of here and don't come back. Go to San Francisco, or Phoenix, or some place you've never seen before. Thanks for helping me."

She didn't say anything. When I kissed her cheek, I felt a slow trickle of tears. I got in my car and headed for the border, leaving behind in my room the cheap phonograph and an assortment of soiled clothes.

I pulled into T.J. at 2:00 A.M. I bought Jane a handbag made out of an armadillo's skin. I laughed when I paid for it. Its claws unlocked makeup compartments and it had beady rhinestone eyes. I fingered it for luck as I crossed the border back into California.

# IV

---

# SHOTGUN

## 10

I had changed during my stay South of the Border and expected to find L.A. changed when I returned. I was wrong. As I passed through the far-flung Southern suburbs of L.A. proper around dawn on the 405, it was as familiar as the sigh of an old lover: the same hazy sunshine, smog, billboards, blacktop, and boredom. Even the Santa Monica Freeway Eastbound, with its view of West L.A. as a green plateau and the Wilshire Boulevard skyscrapers and the Santa Monica Mountains in the distance, yielded nothing but a dull verisimilitude. But it was good to be back.

It was too early to call the DMV to check out the license numbers of the cars at La Casa Grande, so I took a shower and fell into bed to wait for nine o'clock. It was noon when I woke up, frightened. I didn't know where I was. I looked around for the wake-up bottle I kept by the bed when I was drinking, then realized I had been sober for four days. Then it hit me: I was back in L.A. and the case was active. But I hesitated in reaching for the phone. I thought of Jane and couldn't picture her face, just her body as it looked our one night together.

I went into the kitchen and made coffee. That helped. My head was clearing. Midway through my first cup, I dialed the DMV. I was reaching out to the top of my case and I was scared. For perhaps the fourth time since Fat Dog hired me, I impersonated a police officer. It worked again. I read the numbers off to an abrupt woman and she came back with the registration information after only a moment's wait.

When I got the news my head started to crackle and I began to laugh. It was too perfect; beyond poetic justice, beyond logic and reason. All three cars belonged to Haywood Cathcart, 11417 Saticoy Street, Van Nuys. Cathcart.

The L.A.P.D. lieutenant who "cracked" the Club Utopia firebombing case in record time in 1968. I felt calm, but my hands were shaking. I had to hold my coffee cup with both hands to take a sip.

I dug out my old Academy Yearbook from the bedroom and looked for mention of Cathcart. He was posed with several other officers listed as "guest lecturers," and his lecture was given as, Crowd Control—Techniques of Containment and Disbursement. I didn't recall the lecture. Cathcart was a tall, stern-looking, sandy-haired man of about forty-five.

I got on the phone again, this time to Parker Center. I wanted to find out if Cathcart was still with the department. I gave the information officer I spoke to a line of shit about media revival of the Utopia firebombing case, with emphasis on the fine work of Lieutenant Haywood Cathcart. Was Lieutenant Cathcart still with the department? The desk dummy bought it. Cops love to have their asses kissed in print.

"Yes," he said, "Lieutenant Cathcart is now Captain Cathcart, stationed right here at Parker Center with the Narcotics Division."

I thanked the cop and hung up. Cathcart. Cathcart. Haywood Cathcart. Captain Haywood Cathcart. I liked the euphonious ring of the name. It would look good in print when his world came tumbling down at his feet. Cathcart was not only veteran L.A.P.D. brass, but a murderer, heroin dealer, evidence suppressor, and—given the size of his pad in Baja—a tax-evader. He had to be the top man in this upward spiral of arson, murder, drugs, and dirty money.

I was right. One look at his cold face in the yearbook photograph taken a scant eight months before the Utopia blast told me that. Logic told me that the bombing was the genesis of his involvement. He was linked to Ralston, Ralston had set him up with Sandoval and Cruz; and the only possible motives that could tie this disparate, far-reaching case together were blackmail and money, something beyond the chickenshit bookie operations of Kupferman and Ralston.

As adrenalin and irony coursed through my bloodstream, I gloated on the moral perfection of a high-ranking L.A.P.D. bimbo being brought to justice by a former

L.A.P.D. minion out of moral limbo. I was getting restless. I dressed and got out the car. Driving would kill my vengeful fantasies and bring me back to earth. I headed west, toward Jane's.

She wasn't there. Neither Cadillac was in the driveway, but I knocked anyway. There was no answer, which was surprising. I had expected someone to answer, a maid, perhaps. I went back to the car to wait. I had a lot to tell her—mixed tidings about her brother's death and the other things that transpired in Mexico. She deserved to know the whole story, and be kept up to date on my progress.

And I wanted to be close to her gentleness and beauty. I decided to tell her about the two men I killed. She deserved to know that, too, and wouldn't condemn me for it. She was a clear-headed, practical woman. One night doesn't lay claim to a person's life, but our one night was a promise of a commitment and a future together in more stable times. And I wanted another loving night with her before the unpleasant, possibly violent job of bracing Hot Rod Ralston.

A car pulled into the circular driveway—a full pig Chrysler convertible—and a large, solidly built man in his middle forties got out and rang the bell. It was a quiet afternoon and I could hear the chimes from my post across the street. The man had a hard-edged look about him, like a cop or an insurance investigator. Maybe he was a business associate of Kupferman.

I was thunderstruck when Jane Baker opened the door and walked outside, carrying her cello case. She locked the door behind her, greeted the man with a warm smile and walked with him to his car. Whatever he was, he wasn't any cello teacher.

When they pulled out, I decided to follow. I found myself getting jealous. Jane knew my car, so I had to stay behind for at least a full minute, then head after them on the route they would most likely take—Beverly Drive South. I waited, trying to quash a feeling of dread in the pit of my stomach. Walter Curran: everything is connected. The man Jane drove off with had the mien of a cold, manipulative ex-athlete, like Richard Ralston. I didn't want it to be.

I picked up their trail on Beverly Drive and Burton

Way, inside the Beverly Hills shopping district. I came up right behind them, watching them huddle in conversation. The man pulled up to the curb on Beverly just south of Wilshire and Jane got out, lugging her cello. She didn't notice me as I drove by, continuing to follow the man in the Chrysler. He turned right on Pico, heading in the direction of Hillcrest Country Club. I started to pray for it not to be, but when we came up on Century City and Hillcrest and he flashed his left-hand directional, I knew, and was resigned.

There was a uniformed guard in the parking lot who admitted Ralston, so I had no chance of following him directly in. I turned right on the corner of Century Park East and parked in a No Parking Zone. I locked the car, placed a "Physician On Call" notice under my windshield wiper and ran across Pico toward a small gate off to the right of the parking entrance. A group of four scruffy-looking caddies were entering the gate, two of them sharing a pint of vodka. I walked in right behind them, staying a few yards back, hoping they would lead me to the caddy shack. They did. It was off to the left of a concrete walkway that bordered a large putting green.

There weren't too many golfers about; Tuesday afternoon was probably a dead time for golf. The shack was slightly below ground level, a white clapboard job with a green tar-papered roof, built on a slope that led downhill to what looked like an oil drilling site.

I walked inside and was greeted by a shrieking cacophony of noise: there were half-a-dozen card games going on at wooden picnic tables, and the players—for the most part poorly dressed, sunburned, middle-aged men— were gesturing frantically, throwing cards and shouting good-natured obscenities. The concrete floor was littered with trash, cigarette butts, and empty beer cans. Rows of lockers lined the walls; a T.V. blasting out a game show at full volume went unnoticed.

I walked through a smaller room that held nothing but lockers and dressing benches and found the can, passing along the way Scarecrow Augie Dougall, all six foot six of him, reading a comic book as intently as if his soul depended on it. The bathroom was filthy beyond description, with a row of showers that looked as if they hadn't been used in years. The floor was carpeted with urine-soaked copies of the Daily Racing Form and the walls were adorned with beaver photos of outrageously large breasted women.

I splashed some water on my face and recombed the part in my hair. I walked back through the shack and out onto a back service porch overlooking the oil digs. There was an old man sitting on an overturned trash can reading a Louis L'Amour novel and smoking a pipe. I walked to the railing of the porch and watched the oilmen working, checking out Pops out of the corner of my eye. He seemed to have trouble concentrating on his book. The noise of the card play distracted him. He looked like a lonely, opinionated old coot, so I asked: "Does that oil property belong to the club?"

He gave me a disgusted look. "Of course it does," he said, "providing more money for people who already got too much fucking money. They say it 'helps defer the cost of membership,' but shit, when you got the moolah these Hebes got, who gives a rat's ass for a few chickenshit million a year divided by five hundred fucking members? Can you tell me that?"

I said it was a mystery to me. I could see a windy monologue coming on, so I started popping questions, simple ones. "Do you loop here?"

Pops gave me another disgusted snort. "You could say that," he said, "but I'd rather not. I'm on Hot Rod's shit list, so I'm lucky to pick up a nine-hole single once in a while. Are *you* a caddy? You don't look like one. Too healthy."

"I'm a traveling caddy. They call me Coast-to-Coast Johnny. I'm in town checking out the accommodations of the various caddy shacks for an article I'm writing for Golf Digest. How come you're on Hot Rod's shit list?"

"I don't bet with the cocksucker. I don't drink at the cocksucker's bar, or live at his cocksucking fleabag hotel. Does that answer your question?"

"Vividly. I take it you don't like Hot Rod."

"You got that dead right. You oughta write an article on the caddy masters of America. They're all corrupt—bookies, pimps, and worse. They're all tyrants and shitheels and Hot Rod Ralston is the worst."

There was a general uproar inside the caddy shack, the sound of boxes being slammed down, followed by excited voices. Pops got up from his trash can and rushed into the fray. I joined him. Boxes full of clothes were laid out on the concrete floor, and dozens of old suits covered two of the picnic tables. A horde of loopers had descended on them like a pack of wolves, gathering them indiscriminately, irrespective of size. Pushing and shoving ensued, and the caddies' favorite verb, noun, adjective, and modifier, "cocksucker!" was heard many times with many different inflections. Within two minutes everything was snatched up and the loopers were proudly examining and displaying their booty.

Pops came back out on the porch gleefully bearing an old sharkskin suitcoat. He took off the ratty cardigan he was wearing, threw it out in the direction of the oil digs, and donned the suitcoat, strutting like a rooster. "Them Hebes is all right," he said. "They take care of us! This is a three-hundred-dollar coat. Look inside here, it says 'Made in U.S.A.'! This ain't no Taiwan piece of shit, this is the real goods! Goddamn," Pops went on, "now all I need me is a loop to make my day. Then I'll be hopping."

A loudspeaker crackled inside the caddy shack. "Augie Dougall, first tee, right away." That was interesting. There were dozens of hardier looking loopers around to pack bags. Pops thought it was interesting, too. "Cocksucking Hot Rod," he said. "I been here since six-thirty this morning. That beanpole gets here at noon, and he loops before me. Cocksucker."

I went back into the caddy shack in time to see Augie Dougall walking out the front door toward the first tee, stuffing his comic book in his pocket. I followed. The first tee was evidently a squat one-man cubicle where Hot Rod made his caddy assignments and sent players off. It was at the end of the large putting green I had passed by earlier. I stayed well behind, not wanting Ralston to see me. Dougall joined Ralston, and after a moment's conversation they walked together downhill past rows of parked golf carts to a large barnlike building. I followed again, slowly.

I could hear what had to be Ralston's voice as I came up on the side of the barn. It was slow, deep, and explaining patiently: "Trust me, Augie. I've always taken care of you, haven't I?" Dougall muttered something in answer that I couldn't quite hear.

I decided to risk a look inside. I flattened myself up

against the corrugated iron side of the barn and craned my head inside. The barn was for storing golf carts, and there were dozens of them neatly lined up, with long rubber cords attached to electrical chargers that were mounted on hangers suspended from the high ceiling. Ralston and Dougall were sitting together in a cart midway down the line, with their backs to me, too far away from me to hear. I hunkered down and crept into the barn, then squatted behind a cart several rows in back of the two men. From my vantage point it looked like a bizarre father-son relationship—Ralston the father speaking in placating tones to his outsized ungainly son, Dougall. Dougall's head was turned sideways to catch every well-measured word Ralston offered. I found myself reluctantly admiring Ralston. He was a formidable manipulator. I picked their conversation up in midsentence: "So . . . things are changing, Augie. It's nothing we can't handle, though. But Fat Dog got himself in some big trouble. He fucked with the wrong people and he got hurt. You're not going to see him again, Augie. Not ever."

"What did he do, Rod?"

"I can't tell you exactly. A long time ago he got away with a heavyweight scene. Some people got hurt. I took care of Fat Dog. A friend of mine got him out of some heavy shit. This was years ago when you and Fat Dog were tight. Heavy-duty shit, Augie. Heavy-duty. Did he tell you about it? He told someone, because it got back to the wrong people. And the only people who knew about it *before* were my friend and I and Fat Dog, of course. And he wouldn't tell the wrong people, Augie, because his ass would be up shit's creek if he did."

"He didn't tell me no heavy-duty shit, Rod. Just loopin' and racetrack stuff. Nothin' bad."

Ralston put an arm over Dougall's bony shoulders and squeezed tightly. "You're sure of that, Augie? You knew Fat Dog better than anyone. You were the closest thing he had to a friend."

"I'm sure, Rod. Honest."

"Because someone told a Mexican guy about what Fat Dog did. The Mexican guy hated Fat Dog. The Mexican guy went looking for Fat Dog and he got hurt, Augie. Hurt badly. Whoever told the Mexican about Fat Dog wanted to see Fat Dog hurt, Augie, and I've always thought you carried a lot of hatred around for him, even though you hung out together. Fat Dog made fun of you, Augie, I know that. You were his lackey, kind of. Did you want to hurt him, Augie?"

"I never wanted to hurt Fat Dog, Rod. He was my friend. Sometimes he was nasty, but I just got used to it. I never told no one nothin' about Fat Dog. You got to believe me, Rod." Dougall's voice was rising to a wail and his shoulders were shaking.

Ralston tightened his grip around them. "Because if you told anyone about Fat Dog, you could get hurt, too. You could get hurt as bad as Fat Dog or the Mexican guy. You read me, Augie?"

"Yes. I read you, Rod. I didn't tell nobody nothing."

"Okay Augie. Now, I happen to know that Fat Dog kept a scrapbook. A scrapbook that told about all the bad things he did in his life. He also ripped me off for a ledger, Augie, with writing in Spanish. I need that ledger. You know that Fat Dog was rich, don't you, Augie? Loaded. Heavy bread. And it's rightfully mine. I want that money. What do you know about that, Augie?"

"I know he used to have this scrapbook where he kept these clippings from all these tournaments he looped. Is that what you mean, Rod?"

"No, Augie, not that. You're sure you never saw any other scrapbook? A big thick one full of clippings and writing? Or a leather ledger book?"

"No, never."

"Okay, Augie. There may be some other guys Fat Dog hung out with who remember it. We'll let that one slide for now. One more thing, Augie, then I'll let you go. I've got a juicy nine-holer waiting for you. There's a detective nosing around. He's very interested in Fat Dog and his dealings. His name is Brown, do you know anything about that?"

"I seen him, Rod. I seen him. He was at the Tap and Cap askin' about Fat Dog. Said he was lookin' for him, that Fat Dog hired him. I . . ."

Ralston cut in sharply. "When was this, Augie?"

"Maybe two weeks ago."

"What did you tell him?"

"That Fat Dog's a tough man to find. That he sleeps outside. That's all, Rod, I swear."

"That's good, Augie."

"But I know more, Rod. Once me and Fat Dog was out on this loop at Lakeside and this car guy, the one who does them commercials on T.V. with the dog, was telling Fat Dog about this private eye he knew who was a real fuck up, who wasn't a real private eye, but was good for rippin' niggers off for their cars. That's what he said. He was real nasty about it, like the guy was workin' for him, but he was laughin' at the guy. You know what I mean? Anyways, later Fat Dog tells me, 'Someday I'm gonna have a use for that fuck up private eye, yes sir.' That's what he said, Rod. Honest."

"That's good, Augie, and very interesting. You keep quiet about that, and everything else we've talked about. You're a good man, Augie, and a good caddy. I've never regretted taking care of you. Don't do anything now to make me regret it. Keep your mouth shut and life will be smooth. A lot of people have gotten hurt recently by talking too much and fucking around with the wrong people. Don't let it happen to you, okay?"

"Okay, Rod."

Augie Dougall was practically blubbering and shaking with relief. He had escaped censure and punishment from the sternest and most menacing of fathers.

"Good," Ralston said. "Now go get Dr. Goldman and Sid Berman. They want to go a quick nine."

"'Berman and Goldman, wow! A twenty dollar nine-holer. Thanks, Rod." Augie Dougall ran off. Hot Rod Ralston waited a moment and walked out slowly. I squatted lower as he passed me. When I rose to my feet after a few minutes, my legs were stiff and I was very angry.

I drove to Beverly Drive just south of Wilshire and checked out the lobby directory of the building Jane had walked into. There was a simple listing for suite 463—R. Weiss, Stringed Instruments. I took the elevator to the fourth floor and walked down the hall to 463. Through the oak door I could hear cello chords followed by a patient European voice offering criticism. It was enough. I went back down to the lobby to wait.

I waited half an hour, until Jane came out of the elevator followed by an ascetic looking oldster with a cane who was gesturing as though he longed for a baton and a podium. Jane had her back turned to me and was eating up everything the oldster had to say. I wanted to run to her, but stayed seated. The old man concluded his lengthy farewell and retreated back into the elevator. Jane was just about out the door when she turned in my direction and saw me. I stood up and smiled. "Hello, dear," I said.

She placed her cello gently on the floor. "Fritz, I . . ."

I walked to her and took her hands. "I'm back," I said, "belatedly."

She looked shocked, but finally managed a smile. "How did you know I'd be here?"

"I followed you."

"You—"

"I followed you here. I rang your doorbell and when no one answered, I decided to wait. When Ralston picked you up, I tailed you here."

"Am I a suspect in this thing you're investigating?"

She was pulling away, so I let go of her hands. "Of course not. Don't be angry. We have a lot to talk about. My car's outside."

We walked to the car. Jane was scrutinizing me the whole time, quite directly. I couldn't understand her resentment. It went beyond my invading her privacy. When we settled into my car, she placed a tentative hand on my arm. "You look different," she said. "It's hard to place, but your features have changed. What happened in Mexico?"

"I killed two men. And I got drunk."

"Oh, God!"

"Yeah. Where do you know Ralston from?"

"Richard? What does he have to do with this?"

"A lot. Will you answer my question?"

"From Hillcrest. We've known each other for years."

"What's the basis of your relationship?"

"What do you mean?"

"I mean have you slept with him?"

"How dare you ask me that! One night doesn't give you a claim on me. I've had enough. I'm going to leave."

"No. Not yet. Please. I'm sorry. I'm pissed off because this reunion isn't coming off the way I expected, and Ralston is in this thing up to his ears."

"You didn't have to cross-examine me the way you did."

"I was hurt, jealous. Ralston is a notorious well-endowed cunthound and he's had years to work on you."

"What an ugly thing to call someone. For your information, Richard is a business associate of Sol's and a very decent person and yes, we did have an affair, briefly, several years ago."

"That's all you had to say."

"You've changed, Fritz. You've gotten harder. Did you really kill two men?"

"Yeah. They were trying to kill me. Brace yourself: they killed your brother."

"What did you . . ."

"I found his body outside Tijuana. In a scuzzy little shack that's going to give me nightmares for the rest of my life. The killers came back for something and I killed them."

Jane looked out the window, watching the passing parade on Beverly Drive. When she spoke again it was very softly. "I don't feel anything. He got what he paid for. Don't tell me the details, I don't want to give form to the thing. But it was terrible, wasn't it?"

"Beyond words."

"Is it why you got drunk?"

"Yes."

"But you're sober again, right?"

"Right."

"Good. I'm sorry for the way I've acted today, Fritz, but what you told me about Richard Ralston upset me. He's been very supportive of Sol since the warehouse fire."

"In what way?"

"He's been conferring with Sol a lot, driving him places, cheering him up."

"You don't believe me about Ralston, do you? Would you believe me if I told you he was responsible for your brother's death?"

"No, I don't, and no I wouldn't! Look, you admitted you were a lousy cop and maybe you're a lousy detective. Richard is a good man. He loves Sol. If they were both involved in bookmaking, I don't care. It doesn't hurt anyone. And listen to me, Fritz: If you hurt Richard in any way, I will never speak to you, ever again. Do you understand?"

"Yeah, I understand. I understand that you aren't capable of accepting reality. Richard Ralston is a thieving, fucking, low-life predator. Your brother was just murdered, your former lover is responsible, your best friend is probably being blackmailed and all you can think about is your fucking insulated Beverly Hills lifestyle."

Jane turned red and swung at me clumsily with her closed fist. I let her hit me. "Do it again," I screamed. She hit me again and again, each time harder, then collapsed into tears. I pulled her to me and stroked her head. "Good, darling, good. Get it out. I understand, really. Just try to understand me. I've been waiting for this thing for a long time. It's *mine* and I'm not going to blow it. But it's no good without you. Ten people have been killed since this thing started and I'm the only one who can end it. But there's got to be some kind of decency and kindness waiting for me when it's over."

Jane looked up at me. Her tears had stopped and she looked strangely composed. "What do you mean?" she asked.

"I mean that I love you. We can have a good life together when this is over."

"But I don't know you."

"Do you care about me?"

"I don't *know* you!"

"Ssshh. We'll have time to court properly when all this is over."

"Oh, God, don't you . . ." Jane started to sob again, and again I held her, very gently. We stayed that way for a minute, then I tucked a hand under her chin and lifted her head toward me. Her face was mottled and her eye makeup was streaked. I pulled out a handkerchief and wiped it off.

"Will you do a few things for me, sweetheart?" I asked.

"I guess so."

"Good. One: stay away from Ralston, and two: tell Kupferman I'll be calling him, probably tomorrow. Tell him who I am and what I've been doing. Tell him it's very important."

"All right."

"Good. Will you have dinner with me tonight? At my place?"

"I can't. I have to study and practice. And I want to be near Sol and have time to think."

"All right. I'll drive you home."

"No. I want to be alone. A walk home carrying my cello will clear my head. You understand, don't you?"

"Of course. I'll call you soon."

I leaned over and we kissed. Jane's lips brushed distractedly against mine. She maneuvered her cello out the car door. "Be careful," she said.

I nodded and watched through the rear-view mirror as she lugged her cello up Beverly Drive and out of sight. When she was gone I realized I had forgotten to give her the armadillo purse I had bought in Tijuana.

I was tired. My encounter with Jane had diffused my anger into a vague hope that was enervating in itself. Sleep was what I needed, but I was too tired for that. My only recourse was the tried-and-true run to Walter's place. I wanted to commit an act of symbolic liberation and his back yard was the place for it.

It was sweltering when I pulled into his driveway. His mother's Mustang was gone, thank God, and I found Walter sitting on a lawn chair in his back yard, his feet immersed in a kiddies' wading pool. He was reading a science fiction novel and sucking on a short dog. Several more short dogs were cooling in the pool. He looked about half-bombed. "Moon to earth, moon to earth," he said as he saw me coming. "The noble private eye returneth from his search for the Holy Grail in Mexico. Chastened, methinks." Leave it to Walter to throw in one solid perception in his line of horseshit. "Was it fruitful, Fritz? Did you see the mule act? Did you 'eat out' at the Blue Fox? Did you score me some dope so I can get off the sauce?"

"Negative to all that rebop. I did learn one interesting thing, though. I found out who killed The Black Dahlia."

"Oh, yeah? Who was it? The Ayatollah? It has to be him. That clown looks exactly like a fag who tried to grab my dick in the swimming pool at the Hollywood Y when I was twelve. It has to be him."

"Wrong. It's you, you bastard, because all that mystical Buddhist shit you've been whipping on me for all these years about everything being connected is true. I congratulate you. The twenty-five or thirty I.Q. points you have on me has never been more evident. Since everything is connected, the concept of karma must be valid, too. Ergo, it's time to clean up my act and get out of the repo racket. After I clean up a big mess I'm involved in. I haven't decided what I'm going to do yet. Maybe get Cal to set me up in my own classical record store, something like that. There's a woman in my life now that I have to consider. And since karma is a valid concept there's probably some nigger who's looking for me right now with a Saturday Night Special for ripping off his Cadillac. I can't risk that. Jane needs me. So you were right. I salute you, reluctantly.

"But there's no victory without pain. You have to pay the price. The one thing that I resent most about you, as much as I love you, is your insane addiction to television. The booze, the music, the sci-fi are all understandable. But the T.V. shit is beneath you. It's even beneath me. So your T.V. set has to die. Today. Right here in your back yard. I will perform the execution. You will be compensated. I have over six hundred dollars in dirty money that I have to get rid of before I begin my new life. So we do it. Now."

I had expected high-flying resistance from Walter, but he just smiled. He fished out a short dog from the pool and drained it in one gulp. He shuddered and smiled again. "Let's do it," he said. "I'm resigned. Six hundred scoots will get me a half-pound of Columbian and that hooker you told me about. It's time I got back into the mainstream myself. Let's do it."

We went into the house and lugged the old G.E. console back out into the yard. We placed it in a preeminent spot next to old lady Curran's rose garden. Then I got the Browning pump and a box of shells out of my trunk. Walter was practically jumping up and down in anticipation. "Three shots," I said, "then we get the hell out of here before the fuzz shows up. Stand in back of me. Glass is going to fly." I paced off twenty yards from the T.V. to Walter's back porch. Walter sat on the steps behind me, sipping T-Bird in silent glee. I slipped a shell into the breach and pumped it into the chamber, took aim, and fired. The T.V. screen imploded with a huge, reverberating *kawhoosh!* Glass, wood, and metal fragments flew out the back and filled the air before coming to rest in the smoke-filled back yard. The air smelled like burning technology. I squeezed off another shot at the wooden carcass and blew it in half.

People were coming to their windows now in the apartment building across the alley and Walter was whooping and yelling like some new alcoholic species of loon. I pumped another shell into the chamber and handed it to him. "Your turn," I said, "anywhere but in my direction."

He nodded and tore throughout the yard, searching for a target. He ended up settling for the garage wall and blew a hole in it the size of a Volkswagen, the recoil knocking him to the ground. I helped him up and we tore for my car, through a driveway littered with T.V. detritus and smelling of cordite.

When we got to my place I made espresso and sent out for a giant anchovy pizza and a fifth of vodka and mixer for Walter. When it arrived we scarfed the pizza in two minutes flat and sat back and talked, and it was the best, the sanest talk we had had in a long time.

Around midnight I gave Walter his six hundred clams and sent him off in a cab. He was going to get a motel room on the Strip until his mother cooled off and I concluded my case. Then it would be sobriety. I believed him this time. There were distinct flashes of the old Walter and flashes of remorse for what he had become.

Before I went to bed a dire thought crossed my mind. Ralston knew about me and probably wanted to silence me. He knew where I lived and had the wherewithal to have me killed. But I quashed the thought. I knew now: I was going to do more than hold in life. I was going to win.

## 11

I woke up the next morning feeling hung over. Drifting in and out of sleep, I felt a dull persistent banging somewhere, like blows muffled by acoustical padding. I tried to think of Jane's face. Forming the image was easy this time. Gradually, I realized that the banging wasn't inside my own head, but was a loud rapping at my front door. I threw on a T-shirt and a pair of Levis and went to greet my caller.

When I opened the door I knew immediately that they were cops: their size, stern demeanor, and eighty-dollar suits were as good as a neon sign proclaiming "officious city flunkies on a power trip." I greeted them warmly. "Good morning," I said. "What can I do for you?"

"Are you Fritz Brown?" the taller and more forceful-looking of the two asked.

"Yes."

"I'm Sergeant Larkin, Riverside County Sheriff's Department. This is Sergeant Cavanaugh, L.A.P.D." They both flashed badges at me. "Could we talk to you? Inside?"

"Sure. Come in."

They entered and gave my living room a quick perusing. Cavanaugh's eyes fell on my holstered .28 lying on a lamp table. "Do you have a permit for that weapon, Mr. Brown?" he asked.

"Yes, I do. And I have a permit to carry it concealed. I'm a licensed private investigator."

"I see," Larkin said, as they both sat down on my couch, uninvited. "Do you own any other weapons?"

So that was it. Old lady Curran had blown the whistle on me. But why was a Riverside County dick involved? "Yes, I own a Browning 12-gauge pump shotgun."

"Could we see it?" Cavanaugh asked.

"Sure. One minute." I walked into my bedroom. Maybe the jig was up, and I was going to get popped for discharging a firearm within the city limits. But I didn't think so. These guys were too reserved and ominous. I brought the shotgun into the living room and handed it, butt first, to Larkin.

He slid open the breech and chamber and took a healthy sniff. "This gun has been fired recently," he said.

"Last night," I answered. "I assassinated a T.V. set. With the owner's permission. If you want to bust me for shooting off a gun in the city, let's do it now so I can bail out."

"That's not what we're here for, Brown," Cavanaugh said.

"I didn't think so. Riverside County doesn't give a rat's ass what I do with my shotgun in L.A. What is it then?" I sat down in my easy chair across from them.

"Where were you last night between 10:00 P.M. and 2:00 A.M.?" Larkin asked. He was wearing an offensive and shiny yellow dress shirt that must have set him back all of $2.98. It was giving me a headache.

"I was here. In bed. Why?"

Cavanaugh took over. "Were you ever a police officer, Mr. Brown?"

"Yes, I was. I was with the L.A.P.D. for six years."

Cavanaugh gave me a wide smile. Its phoniness told me he already knew the answer to his question. "So we were old colleagues," he said. "What divisions did you work?"

"Wilshire Patrol, Hollywood Patrol, and Hollywood Vice."

Cavanaugh and Larkin gave me identical half-smiles and nods of the head. They were a smooth pair, like Abbott and Costello. Larkin leaned forward confidingly. "Do you know a man named Stanley Gaither? AKA 'Stan The Man?'" he asked.

"I met him once, briefly, a short while ago. Why?"

"We found your business card on his body."

"Jesus Fucking Christ. Was he murdered?"

"Yes, last night in Palm Springs. Along with two other men. Caddies. They were found shot to death under a freeway overpass."

"Oh, shit. Shotgun?"

"Yes. Six expended shells from a 10-gauge were found.

The three guys were blown to shit. How did you meet Gaither? What was the basis of your relationship with him?"

"What 'relationship'? I met him in a bar. He bought me a drink and told me about himself, how he was a compulsive car thief, and how he was in therapy to learn to control his compulsion. I told him I was in the repo business and I might be able to help him get started ripping off cars legally. He took my card. I haven't seen him since."

Larkin and Cavanaugh stared at me impassively. I couldn't tell if they believed me. "Have you ever met a George Hansen, AKA 'Hamburger' or a Robert 'Bobby' Marchion?" Larkin asked.

"No. Are they the other two stiffs?"

"That's right. Do you know any other caddies?"

"No, I don't play golf. It's not my idea of kicks."

"What is your idea of kicks?"

"Great music and beautiful women. What's yours?"

"Have you got a problem, Brown?" Cavanaugh interjected. "Normal people don't go around shooting T.V. sets."

"What's normal? I have an aesthetic soul. I'm the hit man for an international cartel of aesthetic souls who hate T.V. I get paid ten thou a hit. That's how I'm able to live in luxury in the Hollywood Hills."

"Don't fuck with us, Brown," Cavanaugh said. "I checked your personnel file this morning. You were a fuck-up and a disgrace to the department. We're investigating a multiple homicide and we don't have to take shit from some repo asshole. You watch yourself. The State Board of Vocational Standards doesn't like P.I.'s to go around shooting off shotguns. You could lose your license."

"If that's all you have to say to me, why don't you leave?"

Cavanaugh couldn't resist a parting shot. "You watch your step, Brown. We'll probably check you out again."

"I wait with bated breath," I said as they walked out the door.

Ralston. Cathcart. Fat Dog. Augie Dougall. Now three dead loopers in Palm Springs. There are no coincidences.

Caddies do not get knocked off Mafia-style. Augie Dougall was the place to start.

When I arrived at Hillcrest, Augie Dougall was not in the caddy shack. The fry cook at the lunch counter told me he hadn't shown up today. Try the Tap & Cap, he said. I took him up on it and split. As I walked out of the shack, the place was afire with talk about the looper killings, which had made the morning papers.

I drove west toward the Tap & Cap, stopping first on Pico and Veteran to buy the L.A. *Times.* It was on the second page:

## THREE DEAD IN PALM SPRINGS SHOTGUN KILLINGS

(A.P., U.P.I.) July 16—Palm Springs Police and Riverside County Sheriff's spokesmen announced today that there are no clues in last night's brutal slaying of three men, found shotgunned to death under a freeway embankment on Interstate 6 near the Palm Springs-Cathedral City border. Sheriff's Department spokesman Sgt. A.D. Larkin said that the three men, all of whom were employed as caddies, were drinking and taking drugs at their campsite under the embankment.

"We found several empty whisky bottles and a cache of quaalude capsules," Larkin said. "Right now we're thinking that the killings are tied in to a drug rip off. The killer came back for the drugs and panicked after he did the killing. We're checking out all known intimates of the deceased and expect a break at any time."

The dead men are Stanley Gaither, 41, of West Los Angeles, Robert Marchion, a transient, and George Hansen of the Desert Flower Trailer Park, Palm Springs. The bodies were discovered by a group of Boy Scouts and their leader returning to Cathedral City from an overnight camping trip.

Not much. But the address of one George Hansen might be worth something. I ripped the article out of the paper and put it in my shirt pocket.

The Tap & Cap was almost deserted when I got there. The bartender and a crippled old black news vendor were reading the *Times* article aloud at the bar as I walked in. "Po' motherfuckas," the old newsy was saying, "po' fuckin' 'Burger' Hansen. Hungriest fuckin' goat I ever did see. I remember when . . ."

I interrupted him with a stern look and an abrupt gesture. "Excuse me, gentlemen," I said, "I'm with Amalgamated Insurance and I'm looking for a Mr. Augie Dougall on a matter of urgent importance. I was told he frequents your establishment."

The old news vendor started to say something, but the barman cut him off. "You got that all wrong, mister. Augie Dougall lives here. He gets a free room for cleaning the place up."

"Excellent. Is Mr. Dougall here now?"

"No. He left early this morning. He said he was going up to Palm Springs on the bus. He got real shook up about those three caddies who got killed up there. He knew 'em. He said he's gonna crack the case. He's cracked *himself*. He ain't gonna crack nothin'."

"I see. How terrible. I have a sizeable check from a dead uncle for Mr. Dougall. *Very* sizeable. Do you know where Mr. Dougall will be staying in Palm Springs?"

"I don't know, but he's got a cousin up there, in Cat City. In fact, Augie's got a letter from him that he forgot to pick up this morning, he was in such a hurry." The barman rummaged beneath the bar and came up with an envelope.

I grabbed it out of his hand and tore out the door, adding theft of government property to my list of crimes. A moment later I saw the crippled newsy hobbling after me. He didn't have a chance. When I got to my car, I tore open the envelope and read:

Dear Augie,

I hope you are doing good. I am, but it is too dam hot in Cat City. My air conditioner went on the bum and now I am roasting. Is it hot in L.A.? I bet it is. No releef for the wicked, ha! ha! Hows caddying? Do people play golf in hot weather? You wouldn't catch me on a golf course without a six pak of cold ones and a fan. Ha! Ha! Listen. Something funny happened yesterday. This guy came by the house and said he was looking for some things that crazy fat buddy of yours might of left here. Fat Dog, the guy who wouldn't use the spare room, who slept in the yard? The guy offered me 50 clams to let him look for the stuff. He said Fat Dog stole some valuable stuff with sentimental value from him and he wanted it back. I told him forget it!!!!! Fat Dog didn't leave nothing here. It was real suspicious. He told me he used to caddy with you and Fat Dog, but he wouldn't tell me his name. I went out later and when I got back, my house had been gone through. It wasn't tore up, but I could tell that someone had searched the place. But it ain't going to happen again!!!!! Jerry Plunkett is going out of town, and I'm going to borrow his mean old doberman!!!! Anyone tries to mess with my house and Rudolf will chew his ass off!!!!! Ha! Ha! What kind of crazy people are you hanging out with anyway? What was this joker looking for? Solid gold golf balls!!!! Ha! Ha! Next time you go on a toot come on up. I know a barmaid who likes tall guys. She's about 6'2" herself. Ha! Ha!

Your cousin and buddy<br>Charlie.

Charlie, my friend, if you knew the kind of people your erstwhile cousin hung out with, you wouldn't be Ha! Ha!'ing quite so much. Bad-ass dobermans are not much use against shotguns, arsonists, and crooked cops.

I tossed the letter into the glove compartment. Augie Dougall was headed to Cathedral City now, running from the frying pan into fire. If he traveled by bus his most logical point of departure would be Santa Monica Greyhound on 5th and Broadway. I drove there, fast.

The woman at the counter told me an extremely tall funny-looking man aged about fifty had purchased a ticket for the 7:15 bus for Palm Springs. That was enough for me. I hit the Santa Monica Freeway to the Harbor, to the Pomona. Soon I was passing through the depressing Eastern suburbs of L.A. with my top up, airconditioner on full and cassette player blasting Wagner. I was filled with expectancy and the calm certainty that whatever awaited me in the desert would not be dull.

I stopped in Riverside for gas, then switched on the radio for the rest of my journey. I found a Palm Springs station and lucked into a news report on the caddy killings. It was obvious they had taken the desert resort community by storm. The newscaster went on dramatically: there were no clues, the motive was still "up in the air," Gaither and Marchion had no known next of kin, while George Hansen's wife had been informed of his death. Another newscaster took over and announced that he had a Special Report on the world of caddies. I turned the volume up.

The newsman, his voice dripping with sentiment, began:

"I've known a lot of caddies in my time. A lot. They're a strange, adventurous lot. A group of men for whom freedom and love of golf reign supreme. Many of them have given up on the idea of family life and a nine-to-five job just to be where the golf action is. Caddies love golf and they know the courses where they work like the backs of their hands. And what golf stories they have to tell!!

"When I was broadcasting at KMPC in Los Angeles, it was my pleasure to play golf with Dick Whittinghill at picturesque Lakeside Country Club in North Hollywood. I remember one caddy we had, a scruffy character named Leo. Leo was a golf authority who compared certain aspects of Dick's swing to that of the great Jimmy Demarit. Dick used to keep a bottle of vodka in his bag and he often invited Leo to join him in a drink. It was Leo's custom to walk ahead of his players to identify their balls. Dick would always yell to him 'Have I got a shot, Leo?' and Leo would drop the bags and do a little jig right there on the golf course! It was wonderful to see! One day Dick hit his ball right up behind a tree. It was a crucial shot. Dick and I were playing a five dollar Nassau and he needed to win this hole. Leo wasn't dancing any jigs when he walked to Dick's ball. When Dick called out 'Have I got a shot to the green, Leo?' Leo called back, 'You have several shots to the green, Mr. Whittinghill!' Spoken like a true caddy!

"Caddies are being phased out, sadly, in favor of golf carts. What a shame. A caddy can take ten shots off a high handicappers game. The pro's couldn't do without their caddies. I've known a lot of caddies, yes sir. Some drank too much, some talked too much, and some were too opinionated. But I have never met a stupid caddy or one who didn't love the game of golf and the club where he worked.

"Now this tragedy. Right here in Palm Springs, the golf capital of the world. The authorities tell us there were drugs involved! I say 'Baloney.' I have known many caddies who imbibed a bit too much, but never have I known a caddy to take drugs! Never have I known a caddy who would knowingly disgrace the game of golf!

"Robert Marchion, George Hansen, Stanley Gaither, the heart of every golfer in America mourns for you and prays for a swift, merciless justice for your killer. We thank you from the bottom of our collective heart for your service—greens read well, good yardage calls, traps raked and heavy bags cheerfully toted. God bless you in your final resting place. This is Don Castleberry, signing off with Special Report. Have a good day."

I couldn't think for my sudden anger. My mind was seized with a boundless hatred for America. America, with its optimism, boosterism, and yahooism that opted for sentiment over truth every time. America, that would turn the truth of the lives and deaths of three men into a cheap advertisement for an infantile game.

After a few moments my anger subsided. I was in the desert now, the smog was behind me. It was sweltering outside, but the arid landscape was beautiful. I was snug in my air-conditioned cocoon, and in the matter of the people versus Haywood Cathcart, Richard Ralston, and Fat Dog Baker, I was the arbiter of justice, not America.

Palm Springs shot up in the distance, a green shimmering oasis in my tinted windshield. Cathedral City, if my memory served me, was to the southeast of the Springs, a working-class community on the edge of the desert mountain range. I got Augie Dougall's letter out of the glove compartment and checked the return address: Charles Dougall, 18319 Eucalyptus Road, Cathedral City.

I passed through Palm Springs on Palm Canyon Drive, the ritzy main drag. The expensive boutiques and gift shops that lined its immaculate sidewalks were closed for the summer. Only a few restaurants, coffee shops, and gas stations seemed to be open. The few people about seemed in a hurry, rushing toward some air-conditioned sanctuary. I took Palm Canyon out of town to where it turned into a desert highway, winding around to Cathedral City and Indio.

Cathedral City was as I remembered it—dusty residential streets crowded with old wood frame and faded stucco houses reaching up toward some scrub-covered mountain too insignificant to name. I bumbled on to Eucalyptus Road, almost missing it, jamming right at the last second. I put my car in low and climbed up slowly, scanning the house numbers.

18319 was midway between highway and mountainside. It was white with aluminum siding, the dream house of a modest dreamer. There were small statues of forest animals guarding both sides of the narrow walkway. They had been pink once, but were now faded almost white by the sun. I parked and alighted from my car, shedding my suitcoat as the sun hit me like a blast furnace. I rang the doorbell and was answered by a dog's furious barking. Old bad-ass Rudolf, no doubt. I rang again. There was no one but Rudolf at home.

I drove to a gas station, and asked the attendant if he knew where the freeway embankment was where the three guys got shot. I gave him a big ghoulish smile. He returned it and we related, one ghoul to another. Before giving me detailed instructions on how to find it, he elaborated his theory of the killings: the "Mafia" was responsible. The three dead caddies wouldn't cut them in on their golf course dope action, so they had to be "snuffed."

I thanked him for his help and took off for the scene of the crime. I was there within five minutes. It was just an innocuous freeway offramp, the wide overpass providing shelter from the sun. It looked like a good place to get drunk and shoot the shit. Only today the sand flats on both sides of the roadway were jammed with cars, working-class men in Bermuda shorts, housewives with children in tow and low-rider types in tank tops and cut-offs spilling forward to see the place where death and drama happened. I joined them and right away found my prey in the middle of the crowd, standing a head taller than everyone else.

I walked up behind him and tapped his shoulder. He turned around. I could tell he recognized me immediately. "Hi, Augie," I said, "remember me?" He looked around for a means of escape. I glimpsed an eerie intelligence in his eyes.

"I remember you," he said, "from the Tap and Cap. You were looking for Fat Dog. What do you want?"

"I want to make sure the thing that happened to Fat Dog doesn't happen to you."

"What happened to Fat Dog?"

"He's dead." I grabbed my necktie, twisted it up to form a hangman's noose and contorted my face. Augie grimaced. He was very scared. "A lot of people have been dying, Augie. Thanks to your old buddy, Hot Rod Ralston. You're next unless you talk to me."

"Hot Rod said that Fat Dog just got hurt."

"The big hurt, the final one. Talk to me."

Augie gulped and moved his feet in a little dance of fear. He was sweating now, but not from the heat, and I sensed that he wanted to talk. I went on. "I talked to the barman at the Tap and Cap this morning. He said you came up here to help the cops find out who killed those three caddies. The barman thought you were crazy, acting like a kid. But I don't. I think you're a good man and you've got a lot of guts. If we work together we can crack this thing. What do you say?"

"I say right on! I say Augie Dougall's taken enough shit in his life. I say fuck 'em all and save six for the pallbearers."

"Good man. Let's get out of this heat. I've got a car with airconditioning."

We walked to the car. I locked us in and put the air on full. Augie fiddled with the seat release, finally pushing it all the way back to provide adequate leg room. He had at least three inches on me.

"A lot of people think you're nothing but a big dummy, don't they, Augie? But I know different. I'm a trained observer and I can tell intelligence when I see it, I'll tell you what I'm interested in: Fat Dog, Ralston, some sort of Welfare scam and how it all ties in to Sol Kupferman. Be honest, Augie. I heard that conversation you had with Ralston yesterday. He means to hurt you, he thinks you've been lying to him. We can't let that happen. I'll start by laying my cards on the table. Fat Dog Baker firebombed the Club Utopia back in '68. Let's go from there."

Augie went ashen faced. He started to cough and lit a cigarette. When he spoke his voice was breaking. "Jesus God. You know. And Hot Rod knows and God knows who else. Jesus."

"How did you find out, Augie?"

"Fat Dog told me, when he was drunk. I believed him. He hated Kupferman because Kupferman was taking care of his sister. He used to get his rocks off by starting fires. I believed him."

"Did you put Omar Gonzalez onto Ralston?"

"Yeah. I knew something funny was going on between Fat Dog and Hot Rod. Fat Dog gave Hot Rod a lot of shit, and Hot Rod's a bad man to fuck with. Once they was having an argument at the first tee and Hot Rod says 'Don't forget what I know about you, you bastard.' So I figured he *knew*. I figured if he *knew*, he might have written it down somewhere. That's why I called Gonzalez. I remembered him from the *Joe Pyne Show*. I figured maybe I could get at Fat Dog and Hot Rod through him."

"Why did you want to get back at them?"

"For treating me like a slave! Like a retardo! Always laughing at me for being so tall! Augie, the stick! But I'll show them! I'll get the scrapbook and name names! I'll go to the police and be a hero! I'll . . ."

I placed a gentle hand on his arm. "What do you know about this scrapbook, Augie? The first I heard about it was yesterday."

"I don't know nothing about it, except Burger Hansen and Bobby Marchion was killed for it. They was both old running partners with Fat Dog. Burger used to be in the golf ball business with him. That's why they was killed. It's got to be. They was just drunks and loopers. Nobody murders people like that. They used to get drunk and smoke dope under that embankment. They never hurt nobody. Now they're dead. That's wrong! It's evil!"

"I agree. And the evil is about to stop." I tried a stab in the dark: "Tell me about Ralston's Welfare scam, Augie."

Augie's face went blank. "What Welfare scam?"

"You tell me."

"I don't know nothin' about no Welfare scam. Hot Rod's got this hotel he owns where all these bums on Welfare live. Winos. He collects their checks each month and takes out for their rent and bar tab. Is that what you mean?"

"No, Augie. I was just thinking out loud."

"Hot Rod's evil. You got to be evil to do something like that. Hot Rod don't care about nothin' but money and fucking women. Once he showed me these naked pictures he took of Fat Dog's sister with her legs open. He told me he fucked her. I knew her. She was a sweet young girl. She used to cook really good spaghetti at the caddy lunchstand. And Hot Rod talked about her like she was scum."

"You mark my words, Augie, within one week Hot Rod Ralston is not going to have a pot to piss in. Four people that I know of are dead because of him and he's going to pay for it." Augie looked at me with unabashed hero worship. "One last thing," I said, "you told Ralston yesterday that Cal Myers told Fat Dog about me on the golf course. Exactly what did he say?"

Augie screwed his face in a memory search: "That you was a private eye in name only. That you was on the sauce. That you weren't as smart as you thought you was. That you liked to give people shit."

"That's all?"

"That's all I can remember."

"And Fat Dog said he was going to 'use' me for something, right?"

"Right. But he didn't tell me what it was."

"You sure?"

"Yeah. I remember I asked him, but he said never mind. Fat Dog could be real silent and crafty like. What are you gonna do now?"

"Talk to Burger Hansen's widow, look for the scrapbook. What about you?"

"Hide out with my cousin. When you go to the cops, will you tell them I helped you?"

"In spades, Augie. But you can't stay here in Cat City. Someone was looking for the scrapbook at your cousin's place. You've both got to blow town. You got bread?"

"Not much."

I checked my wallet and laughed. Forty-three dollars. In the course of the last three weeks I had dished out more money to informers and victims and to assuage my guilty German soul than I had earned in my first year as a cop. "I'm Tap City, Augie," I said, "but I'll tell you what to do. Cal Myers owes me one—you get back to L.A. and call him. Tell him Fritz Brown said for him to lay a grand on you. Don't mention this case or what it's for. If he won't give you the bread, say this: January 29, 1971. That will pry it out of him."

"Ain't that like blackmail? I know Cal Myers. He's a hard case and a cheap loop. Catbox Cal they call him, 'cause he's always in the sand trap."

"Don't worry. He'll kick loose. I'll take you back to your cousin's pad. When he gets back, tell him you've both got to split for a few weeks. Has he got a car?"

"Yeah."

"Good. Get in it and take off." I started up my own battered chariot, pulled it off the shoulder and pointed it towards Charlie Dougall's house. "Do you know Hansen's wife, Augie?" I asked.

"Well enough," he said. "She's a good old girl. Loopers who get hitched up have a knack for picking loyal women. She put up with a lot of shit from old Burger. She didn't like his drinking, though. She's in A.A. herself, that's why Burger used to get bombed under the freeway. Marguerita wouldn't let him drink at home. You know, Fritz, I feel good. It's real funny. I don't know what's going to happen, where I'm going to, but I feel like I've done something. Something real. For the first time."

"You have, Augie. You've done something very few people could have done."

"You really think so, Fritz?"

"I know so, Augie." I pulled up in front of his cousin's house and handed him one of my business cards. "Here's my card, Augie. Call me in two weeks and I'll tell you how this thing came out. In the meantime, get out of town and be careful."

We shook hands solemnly, then Augie broke into a big loving grin and extricated his Abraham Lincoln frame from my Camaro. I waited until he was safely inside the house, then split.

The Desert Flower Trailer Park was in Section 14, Palm Springs' poverty pocket. I had been hearing about Section

14 for years. Middle-class elitist cops, connoisseurs of low-life, spoke with awe of the tawdry, unpaved collection of tarpaper shacks, trailer parks, and abandoned cars that existed just half a mile off of Palm Canyon Drive. Every commercial center has to have a slum to house its destitute, and Palm Springs was no exception. Only here the dichotomy was more obvious and the center of desolation more isolated: two minutes from downtown Palm Springs in the middle of a gigantic sand flat, Section 14 stood, not quite visible from the broad streets that formed its perimeter, lest it ruin some tourist's vacation with intimations of reality. Dog packs were rumored to roam through it at night, searching out cats and desert rodents for food. Most of its population—drunks, Welfare recipients, car washers and restaurant workers at two dollars an hour—sought air-conditioned refuge during the summer days and returned to swelter at night.

As I pulled off Ramon Road and drove north on Section 14's garbage-strewn dirt access road, I felt timeless, like a Steinbeckian capitalist exploiter. The Desert Flower Trailer Park was on the south border of Section 14, saving me a trip into its dark inner sanctum. There were no flowers to be seen, desert or otherwise; only a permanently-grounded fleet of beatup, tarnished, small trailers, most of them sans cars. I looked at my watch. It was 7:04 and getting dark. There was no one around. I parked my car and locked it, surveying it in the process. It was nine model years old and dusty. It blended right in. If I was lucky no one would deface it out of envy or resentment.

At the head of the two long lines of trailers was a shack marked "Office." I banged on the door. An elderly woman in a robe answered, smelling of gin. I inquired after Marguerita Hansen. The old woman perused me from head to toe. "Cop?" she said. I nodded affirmatively. "At the very end on the left, number twenty-three." She slammed her door, blowing dust on my trouser leg.

Marguerita Hansen's trailer was one of the nicer ones, a chromium "air-stream" of the type popular in the early 50's. It looked well kept-up, the chrome carrying a minimum of dust. It had an electric buzzer next to the door that went off resoundingly when I pushed it. A woman of about fifty came to the door a minute later.

My first thought upon seeing her was that twenty years

ago she must have been a real beauty. She was a honey blonde, tall and plump. Her face was blotched from crying. She held on to the door for support and looked down at me. "Yes?" she said. "Are you from the police? They said I could wait for a few days before making my statement."

"I'm not with the police, Mrs. Hansen," I said. "My name is Brown, I'm a private investigator. I'm investigating the murders here in Palm Springs and some other things that may be related. Could I speak to you for a minute?"

When she hesitated, I handed her my billfold, open to the photostat of my license. She took it, checked it briefly, and handed it back. "All right," she said, "come in."

The interior of the trailer was spotlessly clean. There was a couch, a coffee table, and two chairs arranged neatly. Up against one wall were boxes full of men's clothes. Standing next to them were three golf bags, filled with clubs. Marguerita Hansen caught my gaze. "Those were George's things," she said. "I don't want them around anymore."

I nodded as I took a seat on the couch. "I'll try to make this brief. First, I don't think the deaths of your husband, Marchion and Gaither had anything to do with drugs, as the police have been suggesting." She sat down in a chair across from me. I continued: "I think their deaths can be traced directly to two men—Richard Ralston and Frederick 'Fat Dog' Baker. I . . ." I stopped. Marguerita Hansen came alive at the mention of the two names. "Do you know these two men, Mrs. Hansen?"

"Yes. Yes, I do. George and I have known Dick Ralston for years. He and George used to play minor league baseball together when they were teenagers. He got George his start as a caddy. And George and I were foster parents to Freddy Baker and his sister when they were little children."

"What?" Suddenly I was shaking.

"I said Dick Ralston and George were old friends and that we were foster parents to Freddy Baker and his sister. My God, why are you staring at me that way?!" She began to sob. I let her cry while I tried to clear the gathering storm clouds in my own mind. After a minute she controlled herself. She looked at me guiltily, as if ashamed for her show of emotion.

"Mrs. Hansen," I said, "I understand your connection to Richard Ralston. But you tell me that you and your husband were foster parents to Fat Dog Baker and his sister?"

"Yes, that's right."

"His sister, Jane Baker?"

"Yes."

"Who's about twenty-eight years old now?"

"Yes, that's about right."

"My God. When was this?"

"In 1955. Freddy was twelve and Jane was three."

"How did this come about?"

"A man I knew arranged it. Why I'll never know. He was a wonderful man, an old friend, and he knew George and I wanted children, but couldn't have any. He paid us very well to take care of them. We loved them so much. They were orphans. We were their second foster parents. Their first died in a fire the year before." A fire. Jesus God.

"What was this man's name, Mrs. Hansen? It's very important."

She hesitated. "Sol Kupferman," she said.

Oh, God. Oh, shit. "And this was in 1955?" I almost screamed it.

"Yes. Why are you getting so upset?"

"I'm sorry, but what you've told me—and I believe you —contradicts most of the evidence I've gathered so far. How did you know Kupferman?"

"My brother introduced us. Sol was a very rich, glamorous, considerate man. He was supposed to be in the rackets, but I didn't care. He had just lost the woman he had been living with for years. She committed suicide. He was heartbroken. We comforted each other. Why he was interested in the Baker kids, I'll never know. He was always doing nice things for people. Anonymously. He told George and I that we must never mention him to the children."

"And he arranged the adoption through an adoption agency?"

"Yes. The County Agency."

"And what happened? Finally you gave up the children?"

"We had to. George was drinking heavily and Freddy became a wild, terrible boy. The adoption people took them away from us."

"And that was the last you saw of the children? Or of Kupferman?"

"No. Sol and Dick Ralston fixed George up with a job

caddying at Hillcrest. He sent us money at Christmas time. He still does. But I haven't seen him for over ten years."

"And Freddy and Jane were sent to other foster homes?"

"Yes."

"Have you seen them since?"

"Not Jane. Freddy once in a while throughout the years. Not recently. He turned into a terrible, vicious-minded man, and I wanted nothing to do with him. He and George used to caddy at the same tournaments and sometimes he brought Freddy home, but I told him not to. Freddy scares me."

"So you haven't seen him recently?"

"No, but I knew he and George still saw each other. They even did 'business' together, if you can call it that. About ten days ago Bobby Marchion came by. He dropped off some keys for George from Freddy to his golf ball business. Freddy had sold George thousands of golf balls for four hundred dollars. They were in this cheap hotel room in L.A."

"Do you still have the keys?"

"Yes."

"Could I have them? I'll gladly pay for them."

"You can have them for free. I've had enough of golf bums, golf, and golf balls. I've been sober for three years in A.A.; I've got a Higher Power in my life, and George, as much as I loved him, was a terrible burden. It's God's will now that I move away from my old acquaintances. With George gone, I can do that. So you take the keys, with my best wishes." She went to a drawer and handed them to me, three of them on a rabbit's foot chain.

"What's the name of the hotel?" I asked.

"It's the Westwood Hotel in West L.A. The room number is on the big key."

I thanked her and pocketed my prize. "One thing before I go," I said. "Do you know of a scrapbook that Freddy Baker had?"

"No, I'm sorry."

"Don't be sorry. You've been a tremendous help." We shook hands. I walked out the trailer door.

"God bless you," she called out after me.

I didn't take the blessing to heart. I couldn't. I was flying high on my own omnipotence. I got a cheap motel room in Indio. It was dirty, but air-conditioned, and in the morning I got up and drove back to L.A.

# V

---

# CONCERTO FOR ORCHESTRA

## 12

Back in L.A., my first stop was the Hall of Records on North Broadway. I was armed with two dates of birth and was hunting for big game: birth certificates to prove a theory that was forming in a dark corner of my brain. I explained to the harried, underpaid black woman working the records counter that I was Frederick Baker, born in L.A. on 7–14–43 and I needed my birth certificate because all my I.D. had been ripped off. While I was here, I said, I wanted to get a copy of my sister's birth certificate also. She was going to Europe soon and needed the copy to get a passport. Would it be possible? I asked. It would be.

I gave the girl Jane Baker's D.O.B., 3–11–52, and sat down to wait. The expected results came fifteen minutes later. No Frederick Bakers or Jane Bakers were born in Los Angeles on the dates I had given. So far, my theory was bearing out. I trusted that the birthdates given to me by Jensen at L.A.P.D. R. & I. were accurate. If my next gambit didn't pay off I would have to make a computer check of all births on those dates, which might prove difficult and futile; for if Jane and Fat Dog were born outside L.A. County, I was screwed.

I pulled off my next ploy. I found another busy clerk and told him the same story, this time substituting the name Kupferman for Baker. I hung out nervously for twenty minutes in the crowded waiting room until the clerk called out "Kupferman!" Though I was expecting it, I nearly jumped out of my skin. I paid the man his Xeroxing fee with shaking hands, then took the copies to a corner of the room and read them, suppressing shivers all the while.

Frederick Richard Kupferman was born in Cedars of Lebanon Hospital on July 14, 1943. He weighed nine pounds six ounces. A Fat Dog from the start. His parents were listed as Solomon Kupferman of Los Angeles and Louisa Jane Hall of Pasadena. Jane Elizabeth Kupferman was born in the same hospital, of the same parents, on March 11, 1952. Everything is connected. The anti-Semite is a Jew. The beloved cellist is a daughter. Which explained Kupferman's interest from the start in the Baker siblings, which explained his overpowering fatherly love for Jane and his reluctance to deal with Fat Dog's psychoses. And they were born out of wedlock, by the same woman, nine years apart. Unmarried parents were frowned upon in those days. Why no marriage? And the nine-year gap between births. Who did little Freddy live with during those years?

Marguerita Hansen had said that Sol Kupferman's longtime paramour had committed suicide. Why? She had also told me the first foster parents were killed in a fire. Started by Freddy? Was he psychotic that young? Only Kupferman could answer those questions, and I wasn't ready to talk to him yet.

I found a pay phone down the corridor from the records storage room and called the Los Angeles County Bureau of Adoptions. Impersonating a police officer—again—I demanded information on Frederick and Jane Kupferman. It was going well until I told the clerk their dates of birth. "I'm sorry, officer," I was told, "our records only go back to 1956." I hung up, stuffed the two birth certificates into my pocket, retrieved my car from the lot on Temple and headed for the Harbor Freeway and the Hotel Westwood.

The Westwood was a solidly built, tan concrete building on Westwood Boulevard about a mile south of the Village. It was a one-story walk up, L-shaped, situated above a dry cleaner's and photography shop.

There was a small parking lot in back of the building. I ditched the car and walked up the rickety back steps. Walking into the hotel was like walking into another era. The flat finished white stucco walls, ratty Persian carpets in the hallway and mahogany doors almost had me convinced it was 1938 and that my fictional predecessor Philip Marlowe was about to confront me with a wisecrack.

I found room 12 at the far end of the tail of the "L." There was no one in the hallway, but from within the rooms I could hear T.V.'s and radios blaring. I unlocked the door and walked into golf ball heaven. There were crates of golf balls on the floor and shopping bags of golf balls on top of them, piled up to eye level.

There were no furnishings in the room except an old mahogany dresser with three boxes of golf balls on top, and when I opened the four drawers, they were, naturally, filled with golf balls. There was a sink next to a window looking out on the parking lot. It was filled with golf balls. There was a metal trash can below the sink. It, too, was filled with golf balls. Against one wall was a closet door that I could barely glimpse through the maze of golf ball crates. I looked at it with trepidation. There was probably a golf ball junkie sleeping inside who would kill me on the off-chance that my pockets might yield a few golf balls.

I risked it anyway, clearing away a half-dozen crates of the pebbled sporting eggs. They were heavy little fuckers. The closet contained jumbo plastic laundry bags full of golf balls, piled up to a top shelf. I couldn't see anything on the shelf, but swept my hand across it impulsively and came away with a key ring. There were two keys on it and they were labeled, in the tiniest of print, with the names of country clubs in the L.A. area, followed by numbers: Wilshire 71 and Lakeside 16.

I stopped and thought. Fat Dog's access to the country club milieu of Los Angeles was profound, but only on the level of caddy. Caddy shacks contained lockers that were probably numbered and these keys were locker size. I could tear this room up looking for the scrapbook and come up with nothing but golf ball jaundice, so I split, locking the door behind me.

Only one thing troubled me. Marguerita Hansen had given me three keys. Keys to what? Then I flashed. The community shower and toilet might require a key to enter. I tried them both and they fit. I felt like a third grade kid who had solved a difficult puzzle.

Wilshire Country Club, located midway between downtown and Hollywood, yielded nothing but hostile looks from a particularly motley group of loopers who watched suspiciously as I strode purposefully into their caddy shack, unlocked locker number 71, came up with nothing but more golf balls and promptly split, happy that my theory had been validated.

I drove out to Lakeside, taking the Cahuenga Pass past the Hollywood Bowl and over the hill. I parked my car on a side street leading up to the Lakeside Clubhouse entranceway. The clubhouse was old Spanish, with a low red-tiled roof that seemed to promise warm good times. It was 2:00 P.M., a Thursday, and the clubhouse was nearly deserted. I walked right through. Being reasonably Anglo-Saxon and tastefully dressed, no one stopped me. I could hear pieces of golf anecdotes as I walked through the dining room and out onto a patio with a great view of the flat golf course.

It didn't take me long to spot the caddy shack; it was the only piece of run-down property on this otherwise splendid preserve, and the carelessly dressed men coming out of it were a dead giveaway. So I strolled over and entered Caddyland once again, my hands stuck in my trouser pockets, my fingers crossed for luck. This caddy shack was relatively clean and the card games that were going on were relatively sedate.

I extracted the key for locker number 16 from the key ring and walked into the locker room in back of the card room. Aside from two loopers asleep on wooden benches I had the dusty room to myself. I stuck the key into the lock, turned it, and stepped back, expecting an onslaught of golf balls that never came. The locker was empty except for one large, double-strength supermarket bag. When I looked inside I knew I was home. There was one large yellow plastic notebook binder and several dozen bankbooks and savings and loan passbooks. My heart made a brief, joyous "Ka-thud" and I slammed the locker door shut and walked into the caddy day room.

I couldn't resist a parting salute to the assembled loopers, so I yelled, "Loop on, you heroic motherfuckers! You have achieved a place in my heart rivaled only by the Berlin Philharmonic Orchestra! Long live the fine amenities of a well-hit chip shot! Long live Stan The Man, Burger Hansen, and Bobby Marchion! Let the bummer roll! Looping U.S.A.!" I didn't wait around for their response. I tore out of the caddy shack, my arms tightly encircling what I knew would be a priceless piece of L.A. history.

I couldn't go home to read it. I couldn't go home at all, not with Ralston and Cathcart knowing what they did about me, so I drove back over the Cahuenga Pass to the little park across Highland from the Bowl. I found a place on the grass in the shade, took a deep breath, and dug in. The notebook seemed to be in three orderly sections. I could tell even before I opened it: there were three colors of paper—white, yellow, and blue. The white section was in the style of a ledger and I immediately recognized the printing as Fat Dog's; much neater than in his letter to Jane. The ledger obviously noted racetrack winnings: the first column contained dates going back to '62, the second the names of the horses, the third the odds, and the fourth the amount of money won. It had to be money won, since each amount was followed by several happy-looking exclamation marks. I drew in a sharp breath as I riffled through the white pages: Fat Dog had won a fortune in the past seventeen years.

I dropped the notebook, reached in the bag, pulled out a handful of bankbooks and gasped: $11,000 in deposits in one bank, $9,600 in another, $8,000 in another, $12,300 in another, $6,000, $14,000, $8,000, $9,900, $13,000, $4,500, $17,000, $11,250 and on and on and on. There were thirty-four bankbooks in all, all to branches in the Greater L.A. area. I did some quick figuring and came up with a rough total of at least three hundred grand. Over a quarter of a million dollars. I checked the signature on each passbook: Frederick R. Baker. But the words were too well-formed to have been written by Fat Dog. Someone else had made the deposits. But who?

I wiped sweat from my face, rolled up my sleeves and went back to the notebook. I felt suddenly nauseated, but I clenched my teeth and started on the second section, which contained newspaper clippings of fires in the Los Angeles area followed by humorous comments in Fat Dog's inimitable printing. It was the most ghastly reading I have ever done. The clippings were carefully taped to the yellow paper, which was encased in thin plastic to protect it from aging. It took me only a few minutes to conclude that Fat Dog was a lifelong arsonist and a mass murderer unparalleled in modern times:

From the Los Angeles *Mirror*, April 2, 1961:

## FAMILY OF THREE DIES
## IN GARAGE BLAZE

A family of three met a blazing death yesterday when their garage-playroom burst into flames. Los Angeles Fire Department spokesman Capt. C.D. Finan said that Howard Rosenthal, 37, his wife Mona, 34, and their daughter Eleanor, 11, of 9683 Sandhaven, Westchester were playing ping-pong when their playroom caught fire. They suffocated almost instantly. The cause of the fire was traced to internal combustion, a deadly combination of heat and gas-soaked rags found in the garage. Funeral services for the Rosenthal family are pending at Malinow Silverman Mortuary, Hollywood.

From the *Herald Express*, September 10, 1963:

## SUPERMARKET FIRE CLAIMS
## LIVES OF TWO

Two heroic supermarket cashiers died last night as they went back into the blazing inferno that was Ralph's Market on Third and San Vincente in West Los Angeles. The two men, Donald Bedell, 26, and William Jones, 31, were trying to rescue the market's payroll and were consumed by flames. Cause of the blaze is as yet undetermined and property damage is estimated at close to a half million dollars. There were several shoppers inside the store when the fire broke out, and Bedell and Jones moved them to safety before returning to open the safe. Bedell is survived by his wife Donna. Jones by his parents, Mr. & Mrs. Robert Jones of Long Beach.

From the *Times,* January 29, 1964:

## TWO DIE AS CAR
## EXPLODES ON FREEWAY

A young married couple met their death on the San Bernardino Freeway yesterday in a freak accident when a leaky gas tank and sparks from an overheated engine combined to send the car exploding into flames near an offramp in Arcadia. The couple, recently married, were Mr. and Mrs. Willard D. Jamison of Santa Monica. A passing motorist saw the blazing car and flagged down a nearby Highway Patrolman, but by then it was too late. Fire engines arrived on the scene minutes later and put out the fire. Funeral services for the Jamisons will be held at Gates, Kingsley and Gates Mortuary, Forest Lawn on February 2.

Below were Fat Dog's comments: "The Fat Dog is everywhere! I can see everywhere!!! I roast 'em, toast 'em and make the most of 'em!!!!!"

On and on it went. The scrapbook contained clippings in chronological order of fires up until last year. Fires that took lives, fires that destroyed homes, cars, industrial property. All flawlessly executed. Sol Kupferman and Louisa Jane Hall had spawned a genius: malignant, clever beyond belief, and evil beyond comprehension.

I had reached the year 1972, and had counted 16 deaths, when I couldn't go on. I was as still as a leaf, but inside I was screaming. Tears of anger and disbelief began to stain the yellow pages. The evil was staggering, the brilliance behind it unfathomable. Given enough time, Fat Dog Baker would have burned Los Angeles County to the ground. And he had chosen *me*, Fritz Brown, "detective in name only," to help implement his plan of revenge, blackmail, and God knows what else, directed at Kupferman, Ralston, and God knows who else. God. That was funny. There was no God. But for the first time I found myself wishing there were. I took deep breaths for a minute or so. They actually helped; I felt slightly calmed as I went on to the blue pages.

The first several were devoted to newspaper clippings of the Club Utopia firebombing. I pored over them, looking for something I didn't already know. There was nothing, just the initial accounts of the tragedy, the apprehension of the bombers, their "fourth man" story, their trial, appeals, and eventual execution. Lt. Haywood Cathcart was highly praised for "almost singlehandedly bringing the culprits to justice"—Mayor Sam Yorty. Cathcart called the "fourth man" story "pure hogwash. A cheap ploy to avoid the green room at San Quentin that isn't going to work."

Cathcart's involvement in the Baker-Ralston-Kupferman mess had to date from the bombing; it was only logical. He had to be the lever, the buffer, the balance between Fat Dog and Solly K. I turned the page and found out just how monstrous his culpability was. Following the Utopia clippings were notes on Cathcart:

"Something bad happened, but it's going to be okay. Cop—H.C., hassled me today. Says he thinks he can pin me to 4th man in Utopia torch. Says he remembers seeing me in area. Said I'm hard to forget. True—there is only one Fat Dog!!!! Says he don't care—guys who threw bomb will fry. Asks me—You know about book at Utopia? All caddies bet the horses. I tell him I don't book action with no Jews. Says he don't like Jews, either. Why? Why, why, why, did you torch the joint? he says. So I figure it out. He wants something. He's got something in mind. He hates Jews (big blond German-looking guy!!!) and he knows about Solly Kike being in mob. So I tell him about Solly Kike. I hate him!!!! He smiles. You going to be my watchdog, he says. We'll do real good together. Then he says—you firebug? I try to say no, but he hits me. I can read your mind, he says. Don't fuck with me and you'll be able to do whatever you want in peace. Just keep your mouth shut and you'll make money!!!! He scares me. He can read my mind. He knows. After I did toy store in Valley, he gives Hot Rod letter to give me: 'You got a thing about toy stores, Fat Dog?' it says. 'Remember, I know you. Your buddy.' He does know me."

I waded through twenty-five pages of anti-Semitic and racist drivel before there was more mention of Cathcart:

"The Big Man is everywhere. He knows my M.O.!!!! He sends me notes after my jobs, calls me his genius little boy. Good watchdog! He says! He's everywhere. A tree on Bel-Air front nine. A big dog on L.A. South. An evil squirrel on Wilshire 8th. Won't let me have Jane! Lots of money. But no Jane. Money don't mean shit with no family. H.C. has X-ray eyes, like Superman. He can see at night, too. Like a cat. A big mean cat."

The rest of the blue pages contained more anti-Semitism. I turned back to the yellow section to look for mention of a toy store fire. I found it. It occurred on October 14, 1973 in Sherman Oaks. Cause of blaze undetermined. The proprietor and his son were seriously burned. That was the final indicator.

I drove to my bank on Hollywood and LaBrea and withdrew $500 in twenties from my safety deposit box, then drove to a storage garage on Melrose and paid to have my Camaro stored for two weeks. I got my expensive reel-to-reel tape machine out of the trunk before I left, then took a cab to a car rental agency on Wilshire and Normandie, where I rented a two-year-old Ford L.T.D.

Next I went looking for interim housing. Feeling the need for an injection of beauty, I opted for the beach and found a quiet court-style motel on Pacific Coast Highway, north of Sunset. My room was clean and afforded a view of the ocean. I paid for a week in advance.

Then I dictated into my never-before-used tape deck for three hours, using up four reels of tape. I spoke of the case, starting at the beginning, running in chronological order, with frequent digressions. I covered everything, including my killing of Henry Cruz and Reyes Sandoval. When I finished I sat back and thought of Haywood Cathcart, and of myself. Both cops. Both cops gone bad, to different degrees. I wondered at his motives for joining the police department, then examined my own.

I had wanted a way to express my sense of fair play and my love of beauty. I had wanted to crack wise and kick ass on those who deserved it. I had wanted to express a cynical, world-weary ethos tempered with compassion that women would eat up. I wanted low-level, uncomplicated power over other people's lives. To be 6'3", 200 pounds, with a blue uniform, a badge, and a gun seemed like a wonderful ego boost. The streets by day; Beethoven, booze, Walter, and women by night.

But I was a terrible policeman and an abuser of power. My dispensing of justice was arbitrary and dictated by mood. I ripped off dope dealers for their weed, smoked it myself, and congratulated myself on my enlightened stance in not busting them. I shook down prostitutes for quicky blow jobs in the back seats of squad cars. Whatever I touched in my search to assert, to be, turned bad.

But Cathcart, assuming he became a cop for similar reasons, went beyond me in his desire for power. Real power. Money power. He was obviously the Big Man in the Welfare ripoff, holding Sol Kupferman moral hostage in the process—first through Fat Dog, now through God knows what lever. And he remained anonymous, like a Republican fund raiser, savoring the real influence of power. No need to grandstand in a blue suit for Haywood Cathcart, he knew where the real goodies lay. And his complicity by silence was overpowering: he let Fat Dog burn and kill and sent him notes calling him my "genius little boy." I thought my capacity for moral outrage was long dead, but it was attacking me now like a jungle carnivore. No, no, no, no, I said. Yes, yes, I said a dozen times in succession.

I walked down to a liquor store on Sunset and P.C.H., bought a fifth of Scotch and returned to my room. I put it up on the bookcase and stared at it. I said no a dozen more times. Then yes a dozen more. Then it rose up from the bottom of my soul with a screaming finality. Yes. Yes. I couldn't run from it. I took the fifth of Scotch outside and smashed it to pieces on the pavement of Pacific Coast Highway. Yes. Yes. Yes. It was locked in a moral imperative: Cathcart had to die.

I rose the next morning from a troubled sleep populated by my old patrol partner Deverson, a mad collector of Fab 40 records and women's pubic hair. The songs were all there in my dreams: "Runaway" by Del Shannon, "Chanson D'Amour" by Art and Doddie Todd, "Blue Moon" by the Marcells. I took three Excedrin to knock them out, and drove to a clothing store on Santa Monica Mall and bought four changes of clothing—short-sleeved shirts, pants and socks, and shaving gear. At a phone booth I dialed In-

formation and got Richard Ralston's address: 8173 Hildebrand Street, Encino.

Then I thought: brace him at his pad? Too risky. At
Hillcrest? Too many people around. Surveillance—wait
and pick my shot? Also too risky. Ralston was on edge and
would spot me sooner or later. I needed an "in," someone
who knew Ralston and his modus operandi. After a moment I remembered the resentful old looper I had talked to
at the Hillcrest caddy shack two days ago.

I placed another phone call, this time to Hillcrest, and
learned that Ralston would not be in today, that Friday
was his day off, and that his assistant, Rudy, would be
acting as starter. Divine providence. I drove to Hillcrest,
parking on a side street off Pico.

Pops was easy to find—he was the only caddy left in the
shack, an indication of his low status. He saw me approach
and grimaced. "Hi, Pops. Remember me?"

"I remember you," he said, "I'm not senile. And don't
call me Pops or I'll call you Sonny Boy."

I laughed. "Fair enough. What should I call you?"

"Call me Alex."

"Okay, Alex, call me Jack. What's the matter? No loop
today?"

"Fuck no. That punk Rudy puts all the duck loopers out
before me. He wouldn't know a good caddy from a rhi-
noceros. Dirty cocksucker."

"You hurting for cash?"

"I'm always hurting for cash."

"Want to make a quick loop with me? The fastest loop
of your life? Maybe ten minutes for twenty-five scoots?"

"You're talking my language, Jackie-Boy. What do I got
to do?"

"Just talk to me. Let's go out on the porch." Alex followed me, licking his lips. "You hate Ralston, don't you,
Alex?" I said.

"I hate the cocksucker's guts. Why?"

"I don't like him myself. He ripped me off on a bet. I
want to get even. I've got to get him alone to do this. I
need to find out something about his routine, so I'll know
when to make my move."

Alex looked at me fearfully, nodding his head slowly.
"And you'll pay me for providing you with this info?"

"Right."

"And Hot Rod ain't gonna find out about me tellin' you this?"

"You have my word."

"You got anything against trespassin' late at night?"

"No."

"Then I'll tell you. I know the time and I know the place. But I need thirty-five clams. My rent's due."

"You've got it. Talk to me."

"Tonight's the night, big fella. Hot Rod plays poker every Friday night, here in the shack with all his pet goats. The game usually lasts until about two in the morning. The loopers go home and Hot Rod stays here 'cause he lives way out in the Valley and he's gotta be on the first tee at six-thirty Saturday morning for all the heavy play. So he sleeps in the maintenance shed off of the eighth hole. He's got a little room there with a cot. There's no one around. No one shows up until six in the morning. You can have him all to yourself."

It sounded good, so Alex took me on a little tour. When we were about two hundred yards from what I assumed was our destination, Alex halted and grabbed my arm. "That's it," he said, "that's the maintenance shed. Hot Rod's gotta come this way. You see that first little door? That's where he craps out. I don't wanna go no further. I don't want nobody to see me showing you around. Okay?"

"Okay." I got out my wallet and handed Alex two twenties. "Thanks, you've been a big help. Take care."

Alex grinned toothlessly. "You too, big fella, and if you've gotta get rough, kick him once in the balls for me, only don't tell him where it came from." He smiled again and took off running in the direction of the caddy shack.

I stayed behind and watched a twosome of women play the first hole. It seemed timeless, yet completely foreign to me. There was one caddy in the group, a tall blond kid in his early twenties. I wondered if he would wind up as a career looper. I hoped not. If looping was sadness, it was also the line of least resistance to many things—from income tax to the credit society. But the balance was unequal. In the end, looping was more what you ran from than the small freedoms it allowed you.

I drove to an electronics store in Century City and purchased three hours worth of blank tape, then drove to my motel. I dug through the shopping bag that contained Fat

Dog's horror journal and bankbooks, then burned the contents of the journal in the bathroom sink, watching a history of unsung malfeasance go up, appropriately, in flames. When the evil words were obliterated, I doused the pages with water and carried the sodden mess outside to a dumpster. I put two of the bankbooks in my pocket and stashed the rest under the mattress.

I called the manager and told him to buzz my room at ten that evening. Then I lay down and slept dreamlessly.

At eleven-thirty that night I was sitting on the cool grass of the first hole at Hillcrest Country Club, waiting for Hot Rod Ralston and armed for bear. The night was warm, but the wet grass brought the temperature down a good ten degrees. I felt solidly good, confident that my case was winding down, armed now with facts as well as weaponry. And my motives had changed. What had begun as self-aggrandizement would have to end as anonymous moral victory, for I had no intention of publicizing my involvement in the case, or paying for the killing of Cathcart.

I waited over three hours. At two-forty by the dial on my watch I heard a man coughing, coming toward me from the direction of the caddy shack. He was whistling and turning toward my resting place in the trees. It was obvious he couldn't see or hear me, but I backed into the woods, giving him a wide berth, then swooped silently up on him as he entered the ninth fairway, jamming my gun into his back and reaching a containing arm across his chest. He bolted reflexively, but stopped when he realized it was hardware digging into his backside. He said "What the fu . . ." then stopped.

We stood still a moment, him bewildered, but catching on and me high on adrenalin. "That's right, Ralston," I said, "It's a gun. It's loaded, but I'm not. We're going to do some walking and talking. Next stop the maintenance shack. Move." I grabbed his belt with my left hand, keeping my gun in my right, pointed at spine level. We walked.

"I want you to know that I only have sixty-five dollars on me," Ralston said. "I lost tonight. You would have done better to catch some of the other guys in the parking lot. I'm almost flat, buddy."

I didn't like the remark. It was condescending and indicated a lack of respect for my intelligence. I didn't answer him until we were on the paved roadway leading to the shed. Then I yanked his belt back hard, sending him down to the concrete head first. While he was down, stunned and squirming to get up, I kicked him in the head, back, and ribs. He stifled his cries. He was trying very hard to maintain his composure. I squatted next to him, the barrel of my gun resting on his now bloody nose. "Resign yourself to two things, Ralston. One, that tonight you are going to pay for some past sins, and two, that you are going to tell me everything you know about Haywood Cathcart, Fat Dog Baker, Omar Gonzalez, Sol Kupferman, Welfare rip-offs, and arson. And Ralston—if you don't talk, you die. Now let's have a seat in your little room. Get up."

He got to his feet. I grabbed his belt again and he moved forward, then fumbled in his pockets as we reached the door. As his key entered the lock and the door opened, I released his belt and kicked him full-force in the small of the back with the flat of my foot, thrusting him airborne into the dark room. He crashed into something wooden. This time he screamed. I found a light switch and flicked it on. I looked at Ralston's handsome, bloodied face. He was scared, huddled on the floor next to an overturned nightstand.

The room was dank and sparsely furnished: a cot, a water cooler, the nightstand, and a deck chair. I told Ralston to get up and sit on the edge of the cot. He did, slowly. I shut the door behind me and drew a paper cup of water from the dispenser. I handed it to Ralston, who gulped it down. I removed my tape deck from where it was jammed into my pants, located an outlet next to the nightstand and plugged it in. I took a seat in the deck chair and eyed Ralston. I hardly knew where to begin. There was so much I needed to know.

Ralston broke the silence. "Look," he said, his voice under control, "Hurting me won't help you. Fat Dog is dead. The men who killed him are dead. He was an arsonist. He started a lot of fires. He burned down Kupferman's warehouse. I know that Fat Dog hired you, why I don't know, but all this trouble began about that time. Sol Kupferman is a generous man. He'd be grateful to you. I could put in a word for you."

It was the wrong thing to say. I dug brass knuckles out of my pocket as Ralston maintained eye contact with me and rambled on with his plea bargaining. "Solly K has been known to set people up in business, the whole shot," he was saying as I leaped on top of him and slammed my iron clad fist twice into the fleshy part of his back. He started to scream, then thought better of it and began to whimper.

He was shivering, and I placed an arm on his shoulder and spoke softly: "Ralston, I know most of it. But you can put together some of the pieces. I need to see how it all works. If you don't talk to me, now, I'm going to go internal. I'm going to bang your kidneys until it's all over. If you don't talk to me, I'll maim you, *then* I'll kill you. Tonight. Is it Cathcart that's worrying you? Are you afraid he'll get at you for talking to me? Nod if that's true." Ralston nodded, vigorously. "Good, that's what I figured. I've got a handle on Cathcart. I know he's cold, utterly ruthless, and a killer. But I'm worse. Cathcart might kill you for talking to me, but that's an unknown factor. If you don't talk to me, you die. That's absolute. And Cathcart's finished. I've got Fat Dog's scrapbook, I've checked out Cathcart's palace in Baja, I know he's got to be the big man in this Welfare scam. He can't do you any good now. But if you help me you'll survive. You gonna talk?" Ralston nodded again.

I gave him a minute to compose himself, while I loaded the tape deck with a spool of blank tape. I attached the condenser mike and held it a foot or so from Ralston's face. He flinched as he saw it, but cleared his throat as if preparing to speak. He was utterly demoralized and hurting. I took a voice reading, and played it back. The reception was good. Ralston fidgeted on the cot as I introduced myself to the machine and said that this was the companion interview to my previously recorded notes. I held the mike in my left hand and kept the brass knuckles coiled into my right fist, which I waved in front of Ralston. "The truth, Ralston," I said. "Get ready. What is your name?" I said into the mike.

"Richard Ralston."

"Your age?"

"Forty-seven."

"Where are you employed?"

"At the Hillcrest Country Club."

"In what capacity are you employed?"

"As the starter and caddy master."

"How long have you had this job?"

"Since 1958."

"How did you get the job?"

"Through Sol Kupferman."

"How did you know Kupferman?"

"Through baseball. We got friendly at the old Gilmore Field games. I was a shortstop for the Hollywood Stars. Kupferman was a big fan."

"Did you help Kupferman run his bookmaking operation at the Club Utopia?"

Ralston squirmed and ran a sleeve over his sweaty face. "Yes. I collected the bets, sent guys to the track to place them, that kind of thing. It was penny ante, but Solly paid me well."

"Are you still involved in bookmaking?"

"Yes. Still small time."

"When did you meet Frederick 'Fat Dog' Baker?"

Ralston started to open his mouth, then changed his mind. He seemed to be gathering his mental resources. I raised my right hand, metal encased, to within an inch of his face. "The truth, Ralston," I said, "I know everything about Fat Dog and Solly."

Ralston nodded, resigned. "Sol Kupferman told me to bring Fat Dog out to Hillcrest. This was when he was about fourteen or so. For some reason he wanted Fat Dog around. I got him started caddying. There was another caddy, George Hansen, that Solly felt sorry for, and fixed up with a job at Hillcrest. He used to be Fat Dog's foster father. Solly fixed that up, too. Later I figured out that Fat Dog was really Solly's son, born out of wedlock."

"Who firebombed the Club Utopia in December 1968?" I asked.

Ralston shuddered, and trembled when he said it: "Well, Fat Dog Baker planned it, and used the three guys who were caught for it, I forget their names, to do the actual job."

"Did Kupferman know his son did the bombing?"

"He found out later. Cathcart told him. That was Cathcart's lever on Solly. He popped Fat Dog for the bombing, but let him slide, because he wanted to squeeze Solly. Cathcart came to me and made me talk. I knew him from 77th Street Vice. He rousted me a few times, when he was on the Vice Squad. I told him Fat Dog was really Solly's son. He told me not to let Fat Dog know, ever. He told me he had big plans for Solly and that he could use me to help him out."

"What kind of plans did he have for Kupferman?"

"The Welfare gig. He was planning it then. He needed a penman. Solly was the master penman of the West Coast. He made a fortune counterfeiting and signing stock certificates for the mob. Cathcart wanted him to sign the checks, to get payment."

"Do you mean the Welfare checks that people receive fraudulently?"

"Yeah. The signatures all had to be different."

This was puzzling. "But don't these checks have to be signed in front of the person who pays out the money?"

"Yeah, but Solly's got over two dozen liquor stores that he owns and partnerships in a couple dozen others. All the checks get cashed there."

"How does this scam work, exactly?"

"Cathcart's got eight or nine caseworkers working for him. Investigators, too. Solly forges the applications, the caseworkers submit them for approval, the investigators, who are really just pencil pushers, pass them, and supervisors working for Cathcart authorize payment. He's even got a guy in Sacramento monitoring the computer checks. It's foolproof."

"Where do you get the names of the phony applicants? Are they documented?"

"All the way. Solly does the printing and all the signatures, phony Social Security cards, birth certificates, the whole shot. He's a genius."

I kicked this around in my head. "Does the ledger that Fat Dog stole from you contain notes on the documentation?"

"Yes. How did you know about that?"

"Never mind. You did the writing in that ledger, right?"

"Right."

"Why in Spanish?"

"No real reason. Just a fail-safe."

"How long has this scheme been in operation?"

"Eight years. Since '72."

"How much money does it bring in a month?"

"I don't know. Thousands. Cathcart is filthy rich."

"Who killed Fat Dog Baker?"

"Two Mexican guys. Cathcart ordered it."

"Why?"

"Fat Dog was going insane. He was making insane demands on Cathcart. He told Cathcart to make Solly give up Jane. They live together, you know. She's his daughter, only she doesn't know it. He kept telling Cathcart he would blow the whole thing sky-high if he didn't order Solly to cut Jane loose. When Fat Dog torched Solly's warehouse, it was the last straw. Cathcart had him killed."

"Exactly what 'lever' has Cathcart been holding over Kupferman?"

"Jane. He knows she's Solly's daughter. He'll spill the whole sordid story to her, if Solly ever balks at cooperating. She knows a little about Solly's past, the grand jury investigations, that he was a mob moneyman and all that. But it would kill her if she knew Solly was really her father. Also, Jane's mother was a dope addict, a crazy woman. She committed suicide right after Jane was born. Solly worships the ground Jane walks on. He'd never blow it with Cathcart and risk Jane finding all those things out."

Thoughts of Jane cut through me like a knife. "Cathcart's a nice guy, isn't he?"

"Cathcart is a fucking iceberg. He knows it, too. He told me once, 'I'm like an iceberg—cold and seven-tenths below the surface.' "

"Have you ever heard of Omar Gonzalez?"

"Yeah."

"He burglarized your pad. Someone tried to kill him here in L.A. Who was it?"

"Cathcart. I told him my house had been burglarized and my ledgers swiped. He dusted the place for prints and came up with Omar Gonzalez's. He knew Omar from the Utopia investigation. He had some guy go after him with a shotgun, but the guy blew it."

"How did Fat Dog steal your ledger in Spanish?"

"I don't fucking know! Fat Dog could do things you wouldn't believe!"

"Who killed the three caddies in Palm Springs?"

"Cathcart had some professionals do it. He knew Fat Dog had the scrapbook. I was sure Fat Dog would never entrust it to Augie Dougall and I had had his cousin's place in Cathedral City checked out. Cathcart figured Hansen or Marchion had it. I checked out Hansen's trailer myself. It wasn't there. His old lady wasn't the type to get involved and Marchion was a transient. I told Cathcart all this, but he still ordered the hit."

Warily, I asked my next question: "Who told you I was involved in this case?"

"Jane Baker. We've been friends for years. She's not involved in any of this. She calls me up when she gets worried about things. She . . ."

I arced my right hand and slammed Ralston hard in the neck. The teeth of the brass knuckles made small puncture wounds that shot little streams of blood. Ralston screamed. I shut off the tape machine. "You *never* mention her to me, scumbag," I said, "not ever. You understand?" Ralston nodded, cowering against another blow. "Now tell me this," I demanded, "does Cathcart know me?"

"Yes," he whimpered.

"Does he plan on having me hit?"

"Yes. He's got a guy out looking for you. Staking out your place."

"Has he checked out my record with the police department?"

"Yeah," Ralston said, rubbing his bloody neck. "He thinks you're holed up somewhere drunk. And afraid."

"You and Cathcart are good buddies, aren't you?"

"He trusts me. He knows I'm afraid of him."

"Right now your survival depends on two things: doing what I tell you and maintaining Cathcart's trust. This case is never going to go before the cops or the law. This is my case. Cathcart is mine. This tape is going somewhere safe. If I don't check in at regular intervals at certain places, the media gets my whole file, which includes a complete report of your complicity in the Welfare scam, your accessory to murder, your knowledge of the Utopia fire and your bookmaking racket. If I stay healthy, you stay safe. I want you to call Cathcart and tell him that someone called you and told you I was seen asking questions in Palm Springs. Drunk." Ralston nodded, almost eagerly.

"Now. I have a load of bankbooks with Fat Dog's name on them," I said, "but the signatures aren't his. Do you know anything about them?" When he shook his head, I knew he was lying. "That's a pity," I said, "because there's a fortune in cash waiting to be had. Just for the hell of it, why don't you sign 'Frederick R. Baker' a few times for me."

I dug a notepad and pen out of my pocket and handed them to Ralston. He wrote the name three times, then backed off, fearing a blow. I took out one of the bank-books and compared the signature to Ralston's; a perfect match. "Don't worry, Hot Rod," I said, "I won't hit you again. You managed Fat Dog's money for him, is that it?" He nodded. "Where did he get the money?" I asked.

"He played the horses. He was a good handicapper. He got money from Cathcart. He looped. He never spent a dime. He was a cheap, stingy fuck."

"I believe it. On Monday we're going to withdraw the bulk of the money. I'm going to keep most of it, but I'll lay a substantial sum on you. I'll be at your pad at ten Monday morning. Right now I'll drive you to that little hospital down the street. They'll fix you up real nice. You might have to call in sick, but what the hell, you've been on the job twenty-two years, you can afford to take a day off now and then."

I found a towel on the nightstand and handed it to Ralston, who wiped his face. I gathered up my tape deck, turned off the light in the little room and we left, walking all the way to my car on Century Park East. I dropped Ralston at the L.A. New Hospital on Pico and Beverly Drive. He didn't say a word the whole time. I didn't blame him. He was in the deadliest of limbos.

As I pulled up at the emergency entrance, I said: "You call Cathcart tomorrow. Tell him what I told you to. Make it convincing. I'll be by your place at ten Monday. Be ready."

He just nodded as he got out of the car. He was very pale.

## 13

I spent the next morning engaged in some soul searching. I did it during a long walk on the beach, the ideal, most cinematic locale for soul searchers. The beast kept rearing its ugly head, but I fought it off. I was entirely justified in what I did to Ralston; he wouldn't have broken otherwise and I needed him to get at Cathcart. Still, it was my most vicious episode of violence since breaking Blow Job Anderson's legs, and unsettling because Richard Ralston would never be the same. The hard-voiced manipulator who had seemed so formidable during his interrogation of Augie Dougall had broken fast under physical duress. If he had a well-developed image of himself as a stoic pragmatist, it was now leaking water.

But these things were secondary to the crucial point: in order to survive, Richard Ralston was now going to be my ally, not Haywood Cathcart's. He would help me bring down Cathcart's well-constructed house of Welfare checks forgery, extortion, and murder, and that was all that mattered.

While on my journey of soul searching, I decided to quit working for Cal Myers. I bore him no rancor for his low opinion of me, which, expressed to Fat Dog, had set the incredible events of the past month into motion. In a strange sense, I was grateful: he had been the catalyst that put Jane Baker in my life and awakened in me a power to deal with horrendous happenings that I didn't know I possessed. The knowledge of that power and the viability of the moral decisions I had recently been forced to make convinced me of one thing: I was too good to be a repo rip-off man. Besides, I would soon be rich from Fat Dog's ill-gotten gains, which I deserved as a tribute to my good work that would regretfully have to remain anonymous.

So I dug the loaner out of the motel lot, found a pay phone on P.C.H. and gave old Cal a buzz. His secretary told me he was out on the lot and had him paged. He was very anxious and bluff-hearty when he picked up the phone. He always expected in the back of his mind a blackmail attempt by me, based on the events I witnessed in January of '71. That was when I was working Hollywood Vice, drinking heavily, and taking uppers to cut the edge off the booze. A call came in to the desk one night from an outraged landlady who was convinced that an "evil man" was using an apartment he had recently rented, but didn't live in, as a love nest to seduce little girls. She wanted us to check it out.

It was a typical, busy Hollywood Saturday night, so the desk officer routed the call to Vice, rather than to patrol, who normally would have handled it; and the Vice Sergeant, who thought the call was a waste of time, and who thought I was a shithead, handed it to his most expendable officer: Officer Brown. I thought it sounded like a fluke, too, so I checked out an unmarked car, drove to the apartment of an informant and got blown away on hash before driving to the address on Sycamore near Fountain.

The landlady was suspicious of me at first, since I wasn't in uniform and was slightly tottering from the dope I had smoked, but the sight of my badge calmed her down. She told me the "evil man" was in apartment 12, with two young girls. I told her to go back to the Lawrence Welk Show, that I would take care of it.

As I approached the door of number 12, I heard the giggling of a young girl and a man's sexual grunting. The door looked flimsy, so I drew my gun and kicked it in. I recognized him immediately: Cal Myers of Cal Myers Pontiac, Ford, etc. He was on the floor, nude, being fellated by a pre-pubescent chubby blonde girl, who promptly stopped blowing him and started to scream. There was another girl, about the same age, brunette, also nude, holding a camera. She started to scream, too. I started to get an erection and she dropped the camera while Cal Myers reached for his pants. After a few minutes I got them calmed down. The girls put on robes. My erection continued, unabated in the least by all the tension. I checked the apartment out and came up with dozens of snapshots of

Myers and the two girls fucking and sucking. It was a heavy bust for Myers, but I didn't want to do it. I *couldn't* do it; it went against the aesthetics of my lifetime of horniness.

I took Myers into the kitchen and read him off. When he realized I wasn't going to bust him he genuflected wildly before me. I told him *never, ever*, to fuck around on my beat again. I collected the snapshots and put them in my pocket. This scared him, but he was so relieved at being spared the law that anything short of castration would have seemed merciful. He asked me my name several times and I told him. Dimly, my reptile mind was beginning to perceive that he might want to show his gratitude for my mercy. So I told him: Officer Fritz Brown, L.A.P.D., Hollywood Division, Badge number 1193. He committed it to memory and rushed out the door.

I dropped the two girls off on the Boulevard, near The Gold Cup. The evening was young and they had plenty of time to look for other action.

I got a call at the station about a month later. An unidentified caller had left his number. I called it and it was Cal Myers. He suggested we get together. We did. He wanted to give me a car. I said forget it, I didn't begrudge or condemn him for his interest in young girls. He insisted. I relented, but I told him I would rather have a good stereo system. I also told him that I had ripped up the photos and had no intention of ever blackmailing him, but if he wanted to lay some goodies on me out of gratitude, then, what the hell, I would be gracious and accept. He smiled, but I could tell he didn't believe me.

A week later he called me at home and told me I had carte blanche at a prestigious stereo equipment store in the Valley. I went there with Walter and ordered my dream system, which arrived at my pad two days later, along with a technician to set it up.

I called Cal to thank him and assure him that his secret was safe with me. I could tell he still didn't believe me. I desperately wanted him to, and thereafter I would call him up, drunk, and offer my assurances, which were never really accepted. Gradually, we became friends, although I knew he harbored a deep fear of me, and we met every few weeks or so and got drunk together. Our relationship was

a strange mixture of mutual respect and attributing qualities to each other that we didn't possess: Cal thought I was
cold, hard, intelligent, and impenetrable, which was horseshit. I convinced myself that he was deeply sensitive beneath his businessman's exterior and a potential aesthete,
which was also pure horseshit. All we both wanted to do
was get by, which meant markedly different things to each
of us.

When I got kicked off the police department in '75, there
was never any question what I would do for a living. As
soon as I was out of work, Cal's paranoia regarding me
was given full rein. I went to work repossessing for him to
assuage that fear, as well as for the money.

It had been a good relationship in some respects, but
now it was dead. And Cal had been mistaken from the
beginning. I *had* destroyed the snapshots, almost immediately.

When Cal came to the phone bluff-hearty, I knew he
was upset. Augie Dougall and the thousand dollar kick-
out, perhaps. "Well, well," he said. "Man about town Fritz
Brown. Where the hell have you been?"

"Around," I said. "Has Augie Dougall been in touch
with you?"

"He sure has. Fucking beanpole Abraham Lincoln. That
was dirty pool, Fritz, mentioning that thing to him. Fucking unworthy of you."

"I'm sorry, Cal, really. But all I told him was the date.
Did you give him the money?"

"Reluctantly. I figured he had to know you. What was it
all about?"

"I can't tell you. But thanks. If it's any consolation, you
helped Augie out of a lot of trouble."

"Some consolation. You know, I think I've seen him
before. Is he a caddy? I think he packed my bag at Lakeside."

"He's a caddy. How's business? How's Irwin doing?"

"Business is dandy. Irwin is doing a good job. He's a
nice guy, for a Jew. That nephew of his is a natural repo-
man. He don't take shit from nobody. When are you coming back to work?"

"I'm not, Cal. Consider that grand you gave Augie as
my severance pay."

"You can't do that, Fritz! You're my man! We've been together for a long time. Look . . ."

I broke in on his sudden panic, trying to sound firm: "Yes, I can, Cal. I have to. The last time you saw me I had a different life. It's changed now, and I've changed. I don't want to do repos anymore. I'm going to get married. I've come into some money. I want a new life. I've got to cut our ties or my new life won't work. Keep Irwin and his nephew. They'll do you proud. And Cal? I've never told anyone about you and those two girls. I burned those photographs the night it happened. All your fears all these years have been groundless. I would never fuck you over, for anything. I appreciate everything you've done for me. You've been a good friend, but it's time to move on, and ripping off used cars isn't part of the kind of life I want to live. Can you accept that?"

"I don't know, Fritz, I . . ." his voice was very soft.

"You'll have to, Cal. Goodbye and thanks." I hung up, closing a long chapter of my life.

When I walked out of the phone booth I realized for the first time that maybe Cal, in his own fashion, loved me and liked having me around for reasons totally unrelated to fear. When things change, everything changes. It's a new game entirely and suddenly you know what you had all along.

I drove into downtown L.A., taking the Santa Monica Freeway, to Mark Swirkal's office. I left him the master tape containing my complete verbal record of the Baker-Cathcart case and the tape with Richard Ralston's confession and told him what I wanted: storage of the tapes in his safe deposit box at the bank, in perpetuity or until I told him otherwise. Should I fail to contact his answering service once during every twenty-four hour period with the message "Crazy, Daddy-O!" he should immediately retape three copies and have them delivered by hand to the office of the L.A. District Attorney, the Crime Desk of the L.A. *Times*, Internal Affairs Division of the L.A.P.D., and the news desk of KNXT T.V. His fee for this would be one hundred and fifty dollars a month, hopefully for life. He agreed readily, fascinated by the mystery. I told him under no condition was he to play the tapes. He nodded, gravely. I trusted him. He was a solid, good man.

I called Sol Kupferman from Mark's office. His maid

answered and told me she would get him. He answered a second later. He had a soft, New Yorkish voice. "Hello?" he said.

"Mr. Kupferman, this is Fritz Brown. Has Jane Baker told you about me?"

"Yes, she has."

"Good. I need to see you. Today. It's very important. Can you meet me this afternoon?"

"I think so. Where?" His voice sounded distant and worried.

"In Griffith Park, in the parking lot by the observatory at two o'clock."

"Why there, Mr. Brown? Why not my home or your office?"

"Mr. Kupferman, to be frank, because Haywood Cathcart may be having you followed, and I can't afford a run-in with old Haywood just yet."

"I see you know quite a bit about my life, don't you?"

"I know everything about what's transpired in the past ten years. Will you meet me?"

"Yes. How will I know you?"

"I've seen you before. I'll meet you at the observatory at two o'clock."

"Yes. I'll be there."

"Good. Come alone."

"I will. Goodbye, Mr. Brown."

"Goodbye." I hung up and checked my watch. Ten forty-five. I said goodbye to a mystified Mark Swirkal and drove to Griffith Park. I wanted to get there early to check out the scene. If Kupferman's phone was tapped and there was some kind of relay to Cathcart, he would be sending someone after me. Also, I didn't think it was too likely, but if Kupferman was so used to being under Cathcart's thumb that he panicked at the prospect of my upsetting the apple-cart, he might tell Cathcart himself, dooming me.

The parking lot of the observatory was filling up when I got there: buses filled with kiddie groups, sight-seeing families with small children in tow, bored high school loafers looking for an afternoon's diversion. But nothing suspicious-looking. Los Angeles looked otherworldly from my mountaintop vantage point: a hot, shimmering valley shrouded in smog.

I took a bench seat near a drinking fountain and waited. At exactly 2:03, Kupferman's white Cadillac pulled into view. There were no cars following him. I watched him park, lock his car, and get out and walk around. While he was doing this, I surveyed the crowded parking lot for telltale signs of surveillance. Nothing. I got up and walked toward him. He was craning his neck in every direction. He nearly jumped out of his skin when I spoke softly to him. "Mr. Kupferman? I'm Fritz Brown."

He recovered fast, looked up at me and gave me a firm handshake. "Mr. Brown," was all he said. I searched his face for signs of familial resemblance to Jane and Fat Dog. There was nothing but the pale blue eyes, but it was enough. In that respect, the three Kupfermans were all of a kind.

"Let's take a walk, Mr. Kupferman," I said. "We need some privacy."

He just nodded, gravely, and let me lead the way. We walked north toward a hiking trail leading up into the Griffith Park Hills. Kupferman was immaculately dressed in a pale olive gabardine suit, linen shirt, and wide tie. He was the very picture of stoic dignity. Even his two-hundred-dollar alligator shoes did nothing to detract from this image. His face, sunlamp-tanned and Semitic, was a history of patience in the face of adversity, and the brilliant blue eyes spoke of a refined intelligence. I knew I was going to like him. We walked uphill on the dirt path. Kupferman was starting to pant and strain a little, so I slowed my pace. When we reached a plateau about one hundred yards up from the parking lot, with a view in all directions, I stopped. By way of introduction, I said: "We've met before, Mr. Kupferman. At the Club Utopia, about two weeks before it was bombed. You were sitting at the bar and spilled a drink on me. I've got exceptional recall. If it weren't for that recollection, I wouldn't have become involved in this affair to the extent that I am."

Kupferman nodded. He didn't seem shocked by my reference to the Utopia. "I see," he said. "That is extraordinary. Of course, I don't recall it. Exactly what do you know about this 'affair,' as you call it, Mr. Brown?"

"Call me Fritz," I said. "I know everything, except for a few gaps I hope you'll fill in for me. I know everything about the Utopia bombing, the Welfare scam, Haywood, Ralston, and the fact that Freddy and Jane Baker are really your children."

Sol Kupferman went pale and for a second started to reel. I put a firm restraining hand on his shoulder. Gradually he calmed himself, the sunlamp tan returning. "And what do you intend to do with this information?" he asked.

"Nothing," I said. "It dies with me. Jane will never know. You don't have to worry about Freddy. He's dead."

"I know. Jane told me."

"Cathcart had him murdered."

"I figured as much."

"How do you feel about that?"

"Relieved, somehow. Freddy was my son, but he was an animal, and it was all my fault. I gave him up as a child. I'm the guilty one. Freddy just followed his instincts, which were insane."

"Tell me about that, Mr. Kupferman. There's one gap in my investigation: you said you gave Freddy up as a child. Why? Who were his first foster parents? There was almost a nine year gap between the birth of your two children. What happened during that time?"

"What will you do if I don't tell you?"

"Nothing. You've been pushed, bled, and tortured enough. I just want to close this thing out in my mind so I can do what I have to do and get it over with."

Sol sized me up with shrewd blue eyes.

"And Jane will never know?"

"Never."

I watched Sol weigh the pro's and con's of confession. Finally he sighed, and said: "All right. Freddy and Jane's mother, Louisa Hall, was the love of my life. The most beautiful woman that God ever created. But very disturbed. Suicidal. She loved me, but was abnormally attached to her father, who hated me because I was Jewish. He knew of our liaison and mentally tortured her for it. And Louisa took it, withstood it out of love. She couldn't give up her father and she couldn't give up me. But she wouldn't marry me; she knew that it would drive her father away for good. When Freddy was born, something in her snapped. She wanted a baby, desperately; we planned it, I figured that marriage would have to follow, it being 1943. But when Freddy was born, she snapped. She hated him.

He repulsed her. She wanted to be rid of him. She wouldn't nurse him. I had to hire a wet nurse. She gave me an ultimatum: 'Put him up for adoption or I will leave you forever.' I couldn't face that prospect, so I did it. But not through an agency, not formal adoption. I gave him to an old business associate and his wife. They lived near Monterey. They were Russian Jews, immigrants. They Americanized their name to Baker. They gave it to Freddy, even legally adopted him. I got regular reports from Baker, over the years. Freddy was a wild sadistic boy. He killed little animals. I felt guilty, but I put it out of my mind. I was making a lot of money, illegally. I won't go into it. Things were going well with Louisa. She was getting better, less depressed. In 1951, she told me she wanted another child. After the birth she would marry me. I believed her. We had the baby. Jane was born in March of '52. Things were good for about a month. We were making wedding plans. I was pulling out of the rackets. Then Louisa's father committed suicide. Louisa went mad. One evening I caught her trying to strangle Jane in her crib. The look in her eyes, my God!!"

Sol hesitated, faltering, then mustered new resources of candor and went on: "I hired a male nurse to look after Jane. I sent Louisa to the best psychiatrist on the West Coast. He diagnosed her as schizophrenic. I put her into a private sanitarium. When she came out on a visit one day, when Jane was one and a half, we took a drive to the beach and went for a walk on the Palisades. A young couple came by, pushing a baby in a stroller. Louisa saw them and started to scream. She ran to the cliffs, climbed the barrier, and threw herself off. She fell all the way to the Pacific Coast Highway. She died instantly, of course. I was in grief, terrible grief. I blamed myself and I blamed little Jane. I couldn't live with her. I took her up to the Bakers in Monterey to be with her brother. I told Stas Baker to somehow convince Freddy that Jane was his sister, even though Freddy was old enough to know that Baker's wife wasn't pregnant with her. Somehow he did convince Freddy. Maybe just psychically, Freddy knew Jane was his blood.

"The following year, 1954, I got a telegram from Baker's brother. There had been a fire at the Baker house. Baker and his wife were dead, but Freddy and Jane had survived.

I flew up there. I stayed away from the children, I was too ashamed to see them, but I bribed the child-care officers into placing Freddy and Jane with friends of mine in Los Angeles. I knew the woman, we had had an affair, and her husband was a decent sort, so I knew the children would have a good home. After I had arranged that, I asked around Monterey about Baker and his wife. Somehow I felt guilty about them, too. Then I found out the truth about Stas Baker: that he was a sadist, a bully who tortured his wife mentally and Freddy physically. When I knew him in the 30's, he was just another mob stooge—a courier runner/sometime accountant. A quiet, decent sort. A man who seemed grieved by the fact that he and his wife couldn't have children. But I was wrong. He was a monster and he begat another monster. My son."

Kupferman's voice during his monologue had taken on qualities of feeling and resonance I had never before heard. The deeper he reached into his past, the deeper his voice became, until it had subsided into a hoarse whisper that was more grieving than any amount of sobbing or wailing could ever be. I could tell that he didn't want to continue his story. He sat down on the dirt path, depleted in every way, unmindful of his expensive suit. I sat down beside him. He stared at the ground, lost in his own guilty history.

"Let me finish for you," I said, placing an arm around his shoulders. "Freddy and Jane went to live with the Hansens. Freddy grew up crazy, Jane grew up to be the Jane we both love. You wanted to be close to your children, without breaking your own anonymity, so you had Richard Ralston bring Freddy out to Hillcrest. Jane followed. Freddy was unreachable, but you became Jane's mentor and dear friend. Freddy bombed the Club Utopia. Cathcart knew of your link to Freddy, through Ralston, and instigated an extortion scheme. He's been sucking you dry ever since. Is that right?"

Sol Kupferman shrugged free of my protective arm. "Yes, you've got it all," he said.

I decided to spare him the knowledge of his son's extended career of arson and murder.

"Have you been sending money to the relatives of the Utopia victims?" I asked.

"Yes," he answered softly.

"Does Jane deliver the money?"

"Yes."

"Do you have much personal contact with Cathcart?"

"Hardly any. Ralston is his liaison man."

"How so?"

"How much do you know about the Welfare operation?"

"I know that you sign all the phony documents, including the checks themselves, and that they're cashed at your liquor stores, and that Cathcart has the thing monitored from inside the Department of Public Social Services from every angle."

"That's about it. But Ralston is the liaison on every level involving me and the inside people. Cathcart just pulls the strings, holding the fear over everyone."

"So Ralston would have all the records on the inside people?"

"Yes."

"Good. That fits. Ralston and I recently became acquainted. I got a confession out of him. He's more afraid of me than he is of Cathcart."

Sol gave me a strange, inquisitive look, tinged with awe. "What exactly do you want out of this? I don't understand your motives at all," he said. "Jane told me Freddy hired you in the first place, but that doesn't fit. What do you want?"

I stood up. Sol did, too, brushing dirt from his pants. I pointed south toward the smoggy L.A. Basin. "I want a little piece of that, a little piece of the mystery, the insanity, the life. I want revenge, for you. I want to see Cathcart fall. And I want your daughter. I want to marry her. I love her. I think she's in the process of learning to love me. Has she told you how she feels about me?"

Sol smiled, for the first time in our brief acquaintance. "She told me she feels very drawn to you emotionally, but is slightly afraid of you. She called you 'walking ambivalence.'"

I smiled back at Sol and laughed. "An astute remark. She's a very intelligent woman. I understand this ambivalence she sees in me. She caught me at the tail end of my old life and the beginning of my new one. This case is the dividing point. But very shortly it'll be over and we can court in earnest. Then she'll see the more stable, beauty-loving side of me."

"This case will never be over, Fritz."

"What do you mean?"

"Cathcart has me. I have to serve him. If I don't, Jane will learn everything, and I'll be ruined. With Freddy dead, no one else will foul things up or get hurt. The violence is over, thank God. But Cathcart is too protected, too insulated. He's beyond the law. He *is* the law."

I looked out over my city. All I could see were the tops of buildings jutting out of a brown haze. I looked back at Sol. "I'm going to kill him," I said.

I waited a long moment for his response. He was staring at the ground as if he were trying to dig a way out of his life with his eyes. "Don't do it, Fritz," he said. "Cathcart deserves it, but it's wrong. I killed men, forty years ago, and I've had to live a terrible guilt-ridden life. If you kill Cathcart, even if you get away with it, you'll never stop paying the price. Just let it go. If you care about Jane, don't do it. She deserves better than a killer." Sol's eyes, face, and whole soul were imploring me with the force of his experience.

I believed what he said, absolutely, but he was morally wrong. Cathcart's death was the only right denouement to this tragedy. "No, Sol," I said finally, surveying the city again, "he dies. And a lot of people will live free as a result. That's undeniable."

Sol was shaking his head frantically, denying the truth. He looked like an Old Testament sage rebuking a young zealot. "No, no, no," he said, "it's wrong. Can't you see that? How in the world do you expect to get away with it? Cathcart's a shark and you're a minnow. It won't work."

Suddenly I was angry. I grabbed both his trembling shoulders and pulled him toward me. "Don't fuck with me, Sol! I can be just as bad as Cathcart. He dies. Maybe you've been on such a guilt trip for so long that you need Cathcart to punish you for your sins. That phony karma shit won't wash. He dies, and if you try to warn him or fuck with me in any way, I'll go public. I'll blow the whole thing to the media, including the facts of your children's births. I mean that. I've got a fail-safe operation going. If I don't survive this case then it all goes public!" I released him, giving his shoulder a gentle squeeze in the process. I felt guilty myself, now. Sol Kupferman was an almost saintly man, but he carried guilt around with him like a contagion. He was very pale again.

I tried to lighten things up. "A couple of years from now, we'll be laughing about this. Jane will wonder at our secret rapport, but she'll never know. I'll be your unannounced goy son-in-law."

Sol didn't even hear me. "I have to go," he said, moving toward the downhill path.

We walked down to the parking lot in silence. When we got there, I said, "Tell Jane I'll call her after this is all over, which should be soon. Tell her we spoke on the phone. I don't want anyone to know I'm in L.A. And of course don't tell her what we discussed." Sol nodded, funereally pale. "Cheer up," I continued, "soon this thing will be nothing but a giant evil memory, like a cancer successfully removed. Try to think of it that way."

Sol said, "I will" and forced the beginning of a weak smile, but I didn't believe him. He got into his Cadillac and drove away, his whole spirit conveying centuries of Jewish pessimism.

I drove back to my seaside motel and checked out, taking my traveling roadshow—tape deck, bankbooks, clothes, and hardware—north to Ventura, where I found another beachfront hideaway, a slightly nicer, more modern motel room.

I called Ralston at his house in Encino and told him our plans had been changed: he was to meet me at the Bank of America branch on Van Nuys and Tujunga in North Hollywood at ten o'clock Monday morning, and was to bring a list of all his D.P.S.S. contacts. I asked him if Cathcart had been in touch with him, and he said yes, that he had told Cathcart I was spotted, drunk, asking questions in Palm Springs. Cathcart had seemed to like that. Ralston was being a good scout, so I threw him a bone of encouragement, saying that he'd be in for a nice financial surprise on Monday, then hung up.

I killed the rest of the weekend fantasizing myself as a rich man. A quarter of a million in cold cash, carefully invested, would keep me off the streets for the rest of my life. I thought of possible investments, creative ones, and came up with a great idea: a classical music store. Records and tapes from the most prosaic to the most esoteric. A music book store second to none: biographies of composers, pictorial histories and sheet music. A Hollywood

Boulevard cultural oasis. Rock and roll morons would be politely but firmly sent away. I would manage the store and Walter would be my aide-de-camp. I would retain my P.I.'s license and the office as a tax dodge. I would search out moderately good string players to join Jane in playing chamber pieces. Jamming with musicians of similar ability would have a salutary effect on her . . .

I would buy a big rambling house in the hills and several friendly dogs. Jane and I would have our separate lives, each revolving around music—Jane's cello lessons and constant practice, my taking care of the store. At night we would sit in our living room and listen to music, then go upstairs and make love. Eventually, we would have children, preferably daughters. It would be a good life. It was possible now.

I left Ventura at seven-thirty Monday morning. Nine forty-five found me stationed across the street from the B. of A. at Van Nuys and Tujunga in North Hollywood. I was nervous, but felt safe: there was nothing transpiring outside the bank that resembled a setup. Ralston was securely under my thumb.

He showed up a few minutes later. He pulled into the bank parking lot, got out, and stood nervously by his car. He was wearing sunglasses, presumably to hide his battered face. I walked across the street and joined him. He didn't say anything, just stared at me through his dark glasses. "Good morning, Ralston," I said.

He cocked his head. "Good morning," he replied.

"Are you feeling all right?" I asked. He nodded again. "Good," I said. "Take off your glasses. We're going to be making some heavy withdrawals and I don't want you looking like a gangster about to split the country."

He did it and I was amazed: his nose was hardly swollen, although it was purple-tinged, and his eyes were barely blackened.

"Let me outline my plan," I said. "I want you to drive your car. We will hit every bank I have passbooks to. You will withdraw all but five hundred dollars from each account. In hundreds and fifties. Twenties are okay, too, if it's all they have. Try to be inconspicuous. Tellers are required to report large deposits, but not withdrawals. You deposited the money, right?"

"Right."

"Good. Then some of the tellers will remember you. I've got our itinerary all mapped out. We've got a long day ahead. Did you bring the information I asked for?"

"Yes." Ralston fished in his coat pocket and handed me a neatly printed list of names. I winked at him and gave him a blue cardboard passbook, pointing to the front door of the bank.

"Do your stuff, Daddy-O," I said.

While he took care of business, I scanned the list of names, which were set up in columns, as in the manner of bookie ledgers I had seen. The names, all men's, in one column followed by phone numbers in the other. Since several of the numbers were identical, I concluded they were office phones.

Ralston returned after a few minutes and motioned nervously for me to get into the car. Once inside, he reached into his pocket and handed me a roll of crisp new bills. I counted them, then broke out laughing: ninety-three C-notes. He started up the car. "Onward, Hot Rod," I said.

We drove from one end of the Valley to the other, then over Coldwater Canyon to Beverly Hills and from there to the Miracle Mile, becoming richer and richer in the process. Before we left the Valley, I stopped at a supermarket and grabbed a large brown shopping bag. Soon it was jammed with cash.

While Hot Rod was making a withdrawal on Wilshire in Beverly Hills, I stashed the bag under my suitcoat and walked across the street to the Mark Cross Leather Goods Shop and bought a huge leather suitcase, paying for it with four crisp, brand-new C-notes. Back in the car, I lovingly transferred the bills from paper bag to suitcase. I felt very high, much like I did the first few times I got drunk.

Hot Rod returned, dumped $7,400 in centuries and fifties in my lap and gave me a pained look. We had been conversing very little. He had confirmed what I thought about the phone numbers—miracle of brevity, they were the actual *at work* phone numbers of the Welfare contacts—but all my other attempts at conversation went sullenly ignored. I had emasculated this man and he would not kiss my ass or give me the satisfaction of compounding his capitulation.

It gave me pause. I would *need* him to get at Cathcart. If

he fingered me to old Haywood, it would be ink on my death warrant.

I checked my watch and counted the remaining bankbooks. It was 2:10 P.M. and there were nine remaining, containing a total of over $70,000. I estimated we had at least $265,000 in my suitcase. I looked at Ralston and slapped his shoulder, then tossed the passbooks into his lap. "For you, Hot Rod," I said. "Over seventy thou. Spend it in good health."

Ralston smiled briefly, then shook his head. "You're out of your fucking mind to think you can get away with this," he said. "You don't know Cathcart. He's out of his mind, too, but in a different way. You better blow the country now, while you've got a chance, because sooner or later he'll find you. Then it's all over."

"No, you've got that wrong. Let's reverse it. Sooner or later I'll find him. *Then* it'll be all over."

"You're crazy, Brown."

"Not really. Tell me about Cathcart. I know he's brilliant and I know he's an iceberg. Big fucking deal. But I'm curious about one thing: with all his money, why does he continue to be a cop?"

Ralston didn't even have to ponder this question. "Because he loves it. All the good guys versus the bad guys shit. He eats it up. He hates niggers. He's always talking about keeping the niggers under control so they won't revolt. He says he loves doing his part to keep the Welfare State solvent, that it's a counter-revolutionary broadside. He says sooner or later the niggers will breed to the point that they'll have to be dealt with violently, but in the meantime they provide a scapegoat for the poor white moron to hate, and it's important to keep them strung out on dope, in jail, and on Welfare. It's spooky. I don't particularly like niggers, but I don't want to hurt them. Cathcart's cuckoo on the subject."

"Did he supply Henry Cruz and Reyes Sandoval with heroin as payment for killing Fat Dog?"

"How did you know about that? They're dead."

"I know. I killed them."

Ralston reacted with a contorting of his whole face. "Are you going to hit Cathcart?" he asked incredulously.

"Hit Cathcart? Hit?" I answered, equally incredulous.

"Who do you think I am? Marlon Brando in *The God-father*? I don't want to hit Cathcart, I want to become his buddy. I'm a nigger trainee with aspirations. All I want is a million-dollar Welfare check and a lifetime supply of soul food. Then I'll convert to Judaism and join Hillcrest. You can fix me up with a good caddy when I learn to play golf."

"You are crazy."

"Shut up. Tell me more about Cathcart. What does he do for kicks?"

"He goes marlin fishing in Baja. He listens to this really serious music. He talks about the cops being the front line of containment against the niggers. That's about it. He's got no family. He doesn't go for women, so far as I know."

"Where does he live?"

"He's got an apartment in Van Nuys. He tries to live cheap so that it looks like all he's got is his cop's salary."

"How often does he go down to Baja?"

"Every few weeks, I think."

"How does he get down there?"

"He drives. He's got kind of a cover-up going. He owns a little house outside of Del Mar. He tells the people he works with he's going there. He says it's part of the picture he's painting: he makes good dough as a Captain and he can afford a small place down there."

"Does he spend any time at the place in Del Mar?"

"I think he stops overnight, to make it look good. Then he drives to Baja. The guys he works with know he's a fishing fanatic. He's got it all figured out."

"He sure talks a lot, for a careful man."

"He trusts me. He knows I'm scared shitless of him."

I let the remark hang in the air, dead weight between us. Then I harpooned Ralston with my coldest hardest look. When he started to avert my gaze, I said: "Stay scared of me and you'll survive. You'll have your hotel, your bar, your job, your health, seventy grand plus whatever else you've got going. Now drive me back to my car."

We drove silently back over Coldwater to the Valley, a fortune wedged between us on the front seat. When we pulled up to the bank in North Hollywood, I said: "Stay loose, Hot Rod. I'm blowing town for a while. I'll call you when I get back."

He stuck out his hand, which surprised me, and we shook. "I still think you're crazy," he said.

I laughed. "Sometimes I wonder myself."

I disengaged my hand, grabbed my suitcase and Ralston took off.

I left that night, leaving my loaner car in the lot at L.A.X. and catching the 8:00 P.S.A. flight to San Francisco. I insisted on taking my Mark Cross suitcase on the plane with me. The baggage people and the stewardess on board told me they understood. It was a work of art and too beautiful to be buffeted around in the plane's luggage compartment. If only they knew.

The coffee the stewardess brought me was good and strong, but I felt vaguely uneasy. I was unarmed for the first time in years. I had had to check my gun into a locker in the terminal, since pre-flight metal detectors would have given its presence away. But the uneasiness left as I sipped the coffee and enjoyed the lights of Los Angeles from my window seat.

When the plane landed at San Francisco International some ninety minutes later, I was on pins and needles of anticipation. It never failed: the San Francisco Rush. Just approaching my favorite adopted city was cutting through all the trauma and fatigue of the past month. Frisco! Only this time the Frisco of my new life: sober, rich, and possessed of a mission.

Getting into a cab outside the airport felt like four martinis kicking in while listening to Beethoven's Fifth, only this time it was Brown's Fifth. The Fifth "B"—Bach, Beethoven, Brahms, Bruckner, and Brown—all Germanic, all possessed of a mission, theirs musical, mine the destruction of evil. Suddenly I wanted a woman, and voiced this almost immediately to the cabbie. A last fling before a life of blissful fidelity. He understood. I even described what I wanted. Three hundred and fifty scoots for an all-nighter, I volunteered, plus a C-note for the person who set it up.

The cabbie, who was old and probably Greek or Italian, turned around to face me in the back seat, practically salivating. Where are you staying? he asked. I told him the Mark Hopkins. I told him to send the girl to Mr. Bruckner's suite. He knew just the one. She would be knocking on my door within the hour. The cabbie almost fainted when I handed him a crisp C-note upon leaving.

I booked a suite for one week, at ninety-seven dollars a night, paying cash, of course. A bellboy appeared out of nowhere to grab my suitcase. I kept a close eye on him as we took the elevator up to my suite on the eleventh floor, a spacious, old-fashioned, two-room job with expensive pseudo-antique furniture and large French windows opening on an incredible view of Nob Hill.

I whipped a fifty on the bellboy and he almost fainted. I told him to let the bummer roll and buy himself a bag of good shit, that for the next few days I could afford to be generous. I also told him to send up champagne for one and a pot of coffee. After thanking me effusively, he ran out the door, still scrutinizing the bill to see if it was real.

The hooker was a disappointment. Not tall, not particularly large breasted, with rather muscular legs and sort of a cheap face. We talked for the better part of a half hour as I savored the prelude to sex. With me, part of the thrill with prostitutes is the certainty of fucking, followed by the anticipation, followed by the ultimate thrill: watching them undress. So when Danielle (obviously a business alias) did a slow, seductive strip, I was more than ready. But it was a quick, violent, disappointing coupling, tinged with guilt and a rambling mind: I thought of Jane and Cathcart throughout. When I finished, I paid her and told her to take off. She was thrilled with a three-hundred-dollar quickie and kissed me and skipped out the door.

After she left I couldn't sleep, so I buzzed Walter in L.A. He answered on the first ring, dead drunk. I could hear the blasting away of a T.V. crime program through his slurred voice. I tried for twenty minutes to engage him in conversation, but it was no use, he wanted to talk about Jimmy Carter and the anti-matter credit card. Finally I despaired, told him I loved him, and gently hung up.

Next I called Mark Swirkal's exchange and gave the password, then laid down on the bed and passed out.

During my sleep that night, a strange dream sequence began. It was Fat Dog and me, in a complete reversal of roles: Fat Dog, wearing a blue uniform and a gun stopping jaywalkers on Hollywood Boulevard, and me carrying golf bags that seemed to tear at my muscles through my sleep. Just before I awoke, a poem, or fragment of one, ripped through my dream:

There's an electric calm at the
   heart of the storm,
Transcendentally alive and safe and warm.
So get out now
And search the muse,
The blight is real,
You have to choose,
The choice is yours,
Your mind demurs,
It's yours, it's his, it's ours, it's hers.
Moral stands will save us yet,
The alternative is certain death.

My dream world went up in an inferno of fire and screaming: a 1957 Chevy had just exploded on the freeway. The tall spire of the Los Angeles City Hall collapsed in a heap of rubble and severed limbs flew toward me. I woke up drenched in sweat, straining to remember the words of the poem. I found a pen and some hotel stationery in the nightstand. Gradually the words came back and I wrote them down. Obviously, they were a resurgence of some long-buried, long-forgotten poem discovered during my high school poetry reading days. But who was the author? A memory as fine as mine should be able to recall that, too.

I stared at the words on the paper: storms, muses, and moral stands. The very history of my thirty-third summer.

I showered, put on clean clothes, and went looking for a safe place to put my new fortune. I selected a somber, formidable old B. of A. on Market and Kearney, walked in and inquired about safe deposit boxes. The branch manager was most helpful, took my payment for a five-year rental fee on three boxes, handed me my keys and left me in privacy to stuff the square metal boxes full of money. I retained ten thousand dollars for operating expenses, which left me with an incredibly stuffed wallet and billfold.

Next I went looking for the U.S. Passport Office. I found it on Montgomery Street, within walking distance. The clerk took my application and told me that normally a birth certificate was required as I.D., but since I was a licensed private investigator he could overlook it. He kept glancing furtively at my left armpit, no doubt trying to determine whether or not I was carrying a heater. He referred me to a photographer down the street and told me to bring a photograph back later today. My passport should be ready in ten days.

I made a fast circuit: photographer's shop, quick photo session, back to the Passport office with the photo, all within one hour. Which left me at a strange juncture: alone in San Francisco with ten thousand dollars in my pocket, an empty Mark Cross suitcase, no desire to get drunk or laid and suddenly bored with my beloved city.

Not knowing what to do, I walked northwest. When I passed the Main Branch of the San Francisco Public Library on Larkin and McAllister, I knew I had found my destination. I headed straight for the poetry section on the second floor. For the next six hours I pored through hundreds of volumes, looking for my dream poem. It was nowhere, either as a complete poem or as a fragment of one. I gave up when nervous hunger and eyestrain combined to give me a colossal headache.

A gourmet meal in Chinatown and a walk back to the hotel in the brisk night air put me in better spirits. But with sleep came more nightmares—without poetry this time, but just as vividly violent: monsters wielding golf clubs rising out of sand traps to attack me. On waking the next morning I hoped for a failure of memory, for if the dreams continued after the killing of Cathcart, I would surely go insane.

I had three things left to accomplish in San Francisco: scoring some dope, preferably heroin, acquiring a handgun, illegally, and formulating a plan for eliminating Cathcart. I started by buying some used counter-culture garb at a second-hand store in the Haight-Ashbury. Bell-bottom pants, sandals, a tank top bearing the likeness of a rock and roller named Neil Young, and an Army fatigue jacket. When I changed into my outfit back at the hotel, I knew it would never work. It was impossible. I had that outsized, moustached, arrogant-elitist look indigenous only to cops. Nobody on the street would sell me a firecracker, let alone a large quantity of heroin.

I approached the bellboy I had tipped so generously. The best he could come up with was cocaine or quaaludes. I decided to forego second-class drugs and to try instead to cop some smack in L.A., where I knew the territory and could probably shake down some connections.

Late in the afternoon I called Ralston at Hillcrest. The switchboard girl put me through to him at the first tee. When he said, "First tee, may I help you?" his voice sounded strained.

"This is Brown," I said. "Are you busy?"

"Not really," he replied.

"Good. How's our buddy? Have you talked to him?"

"Yeah, today in fact. He thinks you're in Mexico. He got word somehow that Cruz and Sandoval are dead. He thinks you did the job. He's pissed and maybe even scared. He's going down there himself this weekend to look for you." It was almost too good to be true, but I believed him. My mind ran around in circles for long moments. Finally, Ralston broke in: "Brown? Are you still there?"

"Yeah. Look, when do you think he'll split for Baja?"

"I don't know. He usually leaves Friday nights, after he gets off duty. But maybe it's different this time, because the trip is strictly business. Why?"

"Do you know his address in Del Mar?"

"No, I've never been down there. And I won't ask him, in case you're thinking of asking me to. I'm not fucking with you, I just don't want to do anything suspicious. I've been staying away from him. When he called me today he said he wanted to see me, but I begged off. If he sees I've been beat up, he'll know something's wrong."

"Listen, Daddy-O, don't mess with the big fella. Are you afraid for your ass, Hot Rod?"

"Yeah, I am. Because I'm sane. Are you?"

"Yeah, but it's almost over. I'll call you when it is."

Before he hung up, Ralston told me to be careful at least half a dozen times. In a cursory way I took each admonition to heart, but the wheels in my brain were already grinding out a plan.

I enlisted my bellboy buddy and we made a little recording on tape. My plan was starting to jell. I took a 7:15 flight from San Francisco International to San Diego Airport and rented a car from the Hertz office at the terminal. The rest was simple. I called Del Mar Information and asked for the address and phone number of Haywood Cathcart. It took all of three seconds for them to give it to me: 8169 Camino De La Costa, 651-8291. Cathcart's policeman-criminal mentality and sense of normalcy had dictated a phone listing ("I'm a police officer of high rank, and a solid American citizen. What have I got to hide?").

I drove up the Coast Highway to Del Mar. Del Mar is a rich town, built upwards on rolling hills from the sea, but it does have a middle-class beach front enclave and that's where I found 8169 Camino De La Costa. It was so perfect that I almost collapsed in gratitude. *Maybe* there was a God.

A twisting road led me down to a giant parking lot. I parked and walked along the sand, checking out the house numbers. The houses, large bungalows really, were identical: white wood frame, obviously built as part of a development fifty or sixty years ago, and were spaced a solid fifty yards apart, separated by sand drifts. I found 8169. It was the most immaculately kept place on the beach front. I walked around the back. There was a chain-linked barbed-wire fence around a small back yard of some kind of synthetic grass. Old Haywood. Keep the property value up, and the niggers out. Through the fence I could see that the back door entered into some kind of service porch. It was a good setup and my mind clicked methodically with embellishments on my plan.

I drove back to San Diego and spent the night in a Hyatt Motel. The next morning, Thursday, I returned the car to the airport and flew to L.A., where my other loaner was waiting in the parking lot.

It took me all day to accomplish what I had to, but I was satisfied with the results. A shakedown at gunpoint of Larry Willis and two black drag queens had provided me with three ounces of heroin, a small bag of coke, and some assorted uppers and downers. A seven-hundred-fifty-dollar payoff to an old informant from my Wilshire Patrol days had got me a cold Iver-Johnson .38 revolver with a silencer.

After I had everything I needed, I started to get scared: there was nothing left to do but the act itself.

I dropped off the overdue loan car at the agency. They were pissed and about to call the fuzz. I gladly paid the extra money they wanted, took a cab to L.A.X. and hopped a plane for San Diego.

Once ensconced in a motel in nearby Escondido, I started to get scared for real. I wanted to drink, but didn't dare. If I did I would die. Throughout the night I tried to sleep and comforted myself with the poem I seemed to have composed myself:

There's an electric calm at the
   heart of the storm,
Transcendentally alive and safe and warm.
So get out now
And search the muse,
The blight is real,
You have to choose.
The choice is yours,
Your mind demurs,
It's yours, it's his, it's ours, it's hers.
Moral stands will save us yet,
The alternative is certain death.

It helped. I slept. But the nightmares came again, all run together: Fat Dog in his patrolman's uniform, exploding Chevys, golf course monsters. I woke up finally at two in the afternoon of the Big Day. I had been asleep for nine hours.

I spent the rest of the afternoon trying to calm the screaming in my mind. The poem helped some more. Gradually, tenuously, a semblance of electric calm emerged, and I ran with it.

## 14

The practicalities of my prelude to assassination came first, and taking care of them intensified my calm. I ditched the loaner car, bought a pair of surgical-thin rubber gloves at a hardware store, and changed into a T.V. repair jumpsuit I had bought on impulse at the thrift store in San Francisco. I took a commuter bus into Del Mar, where I killed time walking along the streets trying not to think. But at this I failed. I thought, frantically searching out my plan for hidden flaws and pumping myself up with logic. I was in danger of losing my electric calm.

Besides the basic assumption that Cathcart would spend the night at his house, I was counting on one other thing: that his intelligence, monomania and justified paranoia would preclude the keeping of any records detailing his malfeasance over the last ten years. Ralston and Kupferman were his executives, bonded to him by extortion and fear. Solly signed the documents, Hot Rod took care of his books. But now they were walking a duplicitous tightrope of which Cathcart knew nothing. They were my allies, victims of my own benign extortion.

Around dark I got rid of my jumpsuit, which made me feel better. It had been good cover—I looked the part of an outsized T.V. repairman—but the clothes I was wearing underneath were better for night work: Levi cords, desert boots, and a cotton sportshirt with the tail out. My .38 was well hidden. The battery operated tape machine I was carrying looked normal. I was white and all right.

I found a pay phone near the beach and delivered the password to Mark Swirkal's service. At eight o'clock precisely, heart thumping, skidding, and lurching, I walked to my destiny. There was a cool breeze and a very dark sky that outlined the stars brilliantly. I made my way down to the beach-front parking lot. There was a Landcruiser parked there, identical to the one I had seen outside Cathcart's pad in Baja. I squatted down, lit a match, and examined the license plate. It was Cathcart's.

I walked along the sand, carefully counting the number of houses from the parking lot. Cathcart's was the sixth, and his lights were on. I hunkered down and walked around to his back yard, then hopped the fence. I tore my shirt and cut my hands on the barbed-wire, but my tension overrode the pain.

There was absolute silence in the little yard. I got out my gun and switched off the safety. I counted to one hundred, then placed the tape deck on the ground in the middle of the yard and pushed the "play" button. During the six second pause before the action started I ducked up against the wall next to the back door. Then it started. First the loud noise of glass breaking, then the bellboy's voice screaming, "I told you to have my dinner ready, you stupid bitch! How many times have I told you that?!" More breaking glass—my falsetto screams—more breaking glass—the bellboy again—"Cook my dinner now, you fucking bitch! Or I'll kill you."

The back door slammed open. Cathcart was there, peering out into the night. I crouched and fired into his chest. The gun jammed with a loud click. Cathcart swiveled toward me and pointed his arm in my direction. I tried to move, but it was too late. There was a burst of noise, a flash of red and a slamming into my upper chest. I fell over and began to roll, still clutching my gun. Cathcart stood on his porch, turning his head, trying to adjust his eyes to the dark. I aimed and fired. This time it worked. Cathcart ducked, but not in time. I caught him somewhere in the torso, for he grabbed his chest as he flew backward into the service porch.

I got up and ran toward him, heedless of the possible consequences. As I got to him, he was lying on the floor. I was a perfect target framed in the doorway. Cathcart raised his arm to fire, but I threw myself on top of him before he could squeeze the trigger. I pinned his arm down with both my hands and brought my right knee into his groin, full force. Once. Then twice. Then again. Finally, he went limp and relinquished the grip on his weapon.

Panting, sweating, bleeding, and hysterical, I flung his

gun back into the darkness of the house. Outside it was quiet. The tape had run out. In the darkness I started to babble. It was all over. I had blown it. I had won, and lost. There was just too much noise. The fuzz would come. So I waited, on the bloody floor, my body strewn across Cathcart's.

I listened to his breathing through the overflow of my own. I tried to recite my poem, but I couldn't remember the words. Once I thought I heard Cathcart stirring, so I clubbed him in the head with my gun butt. I started to shiver, drenched in sweat. Suddenly, I remembered my wound. It wasn't sweat I was bathed in, it was blood. I felt for the wound. It was next to my shoulder blade, above my heart. Above my heart. Something dim resounded in my mind. I tore open my shirt and ran a hand over my back. When I found it I started to laugh. It was funnier than Walter at his best or the roasted dog. It was an exit wound and the blood that covered it was starting to congeal. I laughed until I passed out from shock.

When I awoke I checked the luminous dial on my watch. It was ten-fourteen. I flashed and did a double-take, then started to blubber. I had entered Cathcart's driveway at nine-twenty. It was almost an hour later and no cops were on the scene. I listened to Cathcart's uneven breathing for a second, recited jumbled fragments of my poem to myself, then gathered my strength and stood up. I staggered, my head reeled but I remained upright. I took a deep breath and it gave me confidence. I was certain none of my vital organs had been hit.

With a gigantic effort, I grabbed Cathcart's arms and pulled him back into his house. It was slow going; he was a large man. I dragged him through the kitchen into a large carpeted area. I risked switching on a light. A modest living room, couch, coffee table, and chairs were illuminated. I walked back and collected both our guns. Cathcart's was a snub-nosed detective's special.

I sat in a chair and stared at his inert body. He was a formidable-looking man. Iron gray-blond hair, sharp features. The body of an athlete at fifty-five. I knelt over him and opened his shirt. I had hit him in the left side of the chest. Almost as if in answer to my probings, Cathcart awakened and spat out a stream of blood. He looked at me. I looked back. I discerned immediately that he knew who I was. That was good. I wanted him to be lucid when I killed him. "Hi, Haywood," I said in a hoarse voice, "you want some water?"

He stared some more, then finally nodded. I brought him two glasses of sink water. The first I threw in his face. It served its purpose. He yelled, spit out some more blood, and raised himself to his elbows, gritting his teeth against the pain. Crouching beside him, I placed a hand in back of his head and raised the glass to his lips. He took a tentative sip, then spit the water out, with a blood chaser, and gulped the rest of it down, regaining a degree of what I took to be his former malevolence. When he spoke the voice was rich, cold, and almost stentorian: "You realize that you are in way above your head, don't you, Brown?"

"No, Captain, I don't. I'd say you are."

"I checked your personnel file, Brown. You were the worst scumbag ever to con his way into the department."

"I'd say that's relative, Captain. I'd say I was a bush league pinch hitter compared to you."

"Comparing low-life scumbags doesn't concern me. What exactly do you want?"

"You mean as the price for my silence?"

"Yes."

"A million-dollar Welfare check. To be presented to me by you on national T.V. After the ceremony, you can make a little speech on your theory of nigger containment. You can retire from the department and begin a new career in politics."

"Brown, literal-minded people like you often make good policemen, but you weren't even that. How does it feel to know that what you've done with me will ultimately be judged as the biggest fuck-up of your fucked-up life?"

"I'd say that's relative too, Captain. I'd say what I've done with you is the one saving grace of my fucked-up life. I'd say I've fucked over a lot of people in my life. Hurt a lot of people. Caused a lot of pain. But compared to you? Unleashing Fat Dog Baker on the world? That you can even compare the two of us is beyond comprehension. Can't you see what you are?"

Cathcart smiled and spit out some more blood. "We all have saving graces, Fritz," he said, "even you. I was struck by one of your fitness reports. One of your superiors wrote: 'This officer seems to be interested in only two things: getting drunk and listening to classical music.' I felt a strange affection for you when I read that. I love great music, too."

"So did Hitler," I said.

Cathcart nodded. "What exactly do you want, Brown? Revenge for your life?"

"I want to wipe you off the face of the earth."

"I see. Will you take me into my den? There's something I want to show you."

I considered it for a second, then decided to do it. One final act of mercy. I helped him to his feet, my gun in his side. He reeled, but managed to limp the twenty feet or so to the den. I went in first, keeping him covered, and flicked on the light. It was a wood-paneled room, with an ornate walnut desk and two overstuffed leather chairs. I shoved Cathcart into one of them. He winced. I looked around the room. The walls were covered with framed photographs of police groups: groups of smiling patrolmen in uniform standing next to early 50's vintage black-and-whites, groups of stern-looking plain-clothesmen in front of station houses, candid shots of cops at their desks writing reports. A wave of nostalgia hit me. This had been my life once. I pointed to the walls. "Is this what you wanted to show me?" I asked.

"No," Cathcart said.

"That's good," I said, "because I've been there. Although there is one photograph I'd love to see."

"What's that?"

"You and Fat Dog with your arms around each other outside of a burning house. You and your 'genius little boy.' Tell me one thing: how did you nail him for the Utopia torch?"

"Very easy. I am a good police officer, unlike you. I had been seeing Freddy in the neighborhood for weeks. From his garb I knew he had to be a caddy. When the three men I caught described the 'fourth man,' I knew immediately who it had to be. I hung out at the various country clubs in L.A. until I found him. Then I extricated a confession, and that got me to thinking."

"You filthy cocksucker," I said.

Cathcart smiled. "Open the top drawer of my desk, will you, Brown?"

I opened it gingerly and found a velveteen book-style photo holder, the kind that wedding pictures are kept in. I opened it and gasped. Inside were two lovingly mounted likenesses of Anton Bruckner. "Do you know who that man is?" Cathcart asked.

"Yeah," I said. "He's a friend of mine."

"And of mine. But he's more than that. Do you like his music?"

"I love it."

"Good. You love Bruckner. But you don't understand him. What his music meant. It's about containment. Refined emotions. Sacrifice. Purity. Control. Duty. The muted melancholy throughout his symphonies! A call to arms. A policeman who loves Bruckner and you can't feel his essence. He never wed, Brown. He never fucked women. He wouldn't expend one ounce of his creative energy on anything but his vision. *I have been Anton Bruckner*, Brown. You can be, too. You come from good stock, you're a big strong man. You can be of service, it's just a question of re-education. I'll tell you what I'll do. I'll . . ."

I had had enough. The blood was pounding in my head so hard that I felt about to explode. I aimed my gun at Cathcart and shot him four times in the face.

I went into the living room and lay down on the couch. I fell asleep. I woke up four hours later, feeling hallucinogenic. A shower helped. I put on a pair of Cathcart's pants and one of his shirts. I combed my hair. I collected my tape deck from the back yard and put it in a paper bag I found in the kitchen, along with my silencer fitted .38. I dumped the dope I had ripped off of Larry Willis all over Cathcart's living room. I found the keys to the Landcruiser on the coffee table. I put them in my pocket. My hands were going numb from hours of wearing rubber gloves, but I kept them on.

I gave Cathcart one last look before I left. His face was obliterated, a gaping hole on top of his neck. Skull and brain fragments were stuck to the wall. His body and the chair he was sprawled in were a mass of drying blood. Rigor mortis was setting in and his arms were stuck in their last pose of reaching out to me.

I took the pictures of lonely Anton and put them in my paper bag, too. I left the death house, locking the door behind me, then drove to the motel and got my suitcase.

It was dawn when I got back to L.A. I was woozy from shock and lack of blood. I left Cathcart's car on a side street in Santa Monica, then took a bus all the way out Wilshire to the Ambassador Hotel, which was within walking distance of Walter's. My shoulder was numb, but aside from that and shock-induced fatigue, I felt all right.

After I ditched the rubber gloves, circulation slowly returned to my hands. It was a symbolic, life-enhancing feeling. Five seconds after croaking "Crazy, Daddy-O" to the girl at Mark Swirkal's service I passed out on my freshly made-up hotel bed.

The next several days run together in my mind. I know that when I woke up at the Ambassador, I was in great pain from my shoulder wound and knew I had to do something about it. I remember taking a taxi to Irwin's apartment off Melrose and Fairfax. He had a doctor brother I had been hearing about for years and now was the time to summon him. I remember that he came, along with Irwin's nephew Uri, and that he immediately gave me a shot of something that sent me into the Twilight Zone. I remember Uri embracing me, delighted with his new position as Cal Myers's repo man, waving his master keys in front of my face and calling me the "only good German in history."

"I'm an American, you stupid fuck," I retorted. "Brown is an American name."

Irwin's brother poked around and cleansed my wound, bandaged it and gave me some pain pills. They had a subtle effect. I thought my continued disorientation was due to shock and the trauma of murder, but I was wrong. It was due to a system full of codeine. I discontinued their use after two days. I couldn't afford to be zoned out. I still had things to do before I could officially say "it's over."

Feeling returned to my shoulder. By Monday I could move it without too much pain. That morning I started to sweat out news of Cathcart's death, buying all the local papers and hanging out in front of Walter's newly-purchased T.V. set. There was nothing, just the usual rebop—Jimmy Carter had announced that he planned to campaign on "his record," Reagan announced that he would run on "the issues," and Walter offered a running commentary that kept me laughing until my shoulder ached.

I called Ralston Tuesday morning and gave him the good news. "Cathcart's dead," I said into the phone, "it's over."

Ralston just said, "Thank God." And let the line go dead.

On Tuesday night I dumped all the evidence of the killing into the Pacific Ocean: the gun, my bloody clothes, Cathcart's clothes I had stolen, the tape deck, and the portraits of Anton Bruckner. I felt an impulse to keep the likenesses of lonely Anton, to give them a good, sane home, but they had become ghastly objects. I tore them into small pieces and fed them to the sea.

The next day, armed with a pocketful of dimes, I called the Welfare contacts on the list Ralston had given me. At the first sound of a voice on the other end of the line, I said "Cathcart is dead. The scam is dead. I have evidence linking you to fraud and extortion. Stop all payments now." Before the listener could respond, I hung up. I connected with all but three of the people on the list. It was good enough. Ralston would take the brunt of their fear and grief, as well he should. He had gotten off easy.

News of Cathcart's death hit the media Wednesday night. It was attributed to suicide. I was watching T.V. with Walter when I got the word: Haywood Cathcart, 56, Captain, Los Angeles Police Department had died of a self-inflicted gunshot wound sometime over the weekend at his "fishing retreat" in Del Mar. He had been a twenty-eight-year veteran of the L.A.P.D., was considered an exemplary officer, and was famous for "single-handedly cracking the famous Club Utopia firebombing case in 1968 that sent the slayers of six bar patrons to the gas chamber." His superiors said that he had left no suicide note, but had been distraught recently over family matters.

As the somber-voiced newsman concluded his report, I started to weep. The fix was in. The L.A.P.D. had some inkling of what was up and had stonewalled it. If Cathcart had left no records, I was free.

Walter was dumbfounded at my tears. He had never seen me cry and had no idea of their origin. But he did his best to comfort me, embracing me and clumsily pawing my head. "What is it, Fritz?" he asked. "Did you know that cop who shot himself? Was he your buddy?"

I didn't answer him, I just let myself be comforted. It was over. That night I went home to my pad, expecting to find it ransacked. It wasn't. It was intact, waiting for me like an old friend. I looked at the calendar above my desk. On the space for June 30, I had marked, "Fred Baker— one week at one hundred twenty-five dollars per day." It was now August 1. I had been in limbo for five weeks, had killed three men, had learned truths that few would know. I had been correct on the morning it all started. My life *had* been about to change, irrevocably.

The next morning I took a cab to the storage garage and got my old Camaro. I was reunited with another old friend, who had been washed and polished during my absence.

I called the Kupferman residence. It was time for the only reunion that mattered. The maid answered, distraught. "Mr. Kupferman had a heart attack last night. He's in the hospital. He be real sick maybe gonna die."

She started to ramble, but I cut her off: "What hospital?" I yelled.

"Cedars Sinai," she said.

I hung up and tore out. The hospital was in West Hollywood, on Beverly near La Cienega, and by running lights and taking side streets I was there in fifteen minutes. I parked illegally and ran inside, flashing some absurd piece of fake I.D. at the reception lady and demanding to know where Sol Kupferman was. Cowed, she told me room 583, West Wing.

I jammed for an elevator and ran wildly down the corridors until I saw Jane sitting on a chair outside the room that had to be Sol's. "Darling," I called as I ran toward her, "is Sol all right?!"

Jane rushed toward me, screaming "Killer, killer, rapist, dissension center! Murderer, killer!"

We collided and she flung her fists and arms out at me with hysterical fury, scratching, clawing at my face, her eyes full of tears. I tried to control her, but it was no use. I had no will to be assertive, so I just let myself be pummelled. But she didn't stop, and her screaming "killer, killer, killer!" was drawing a crowd of hospital people.

"I hate you, I hate the day I let you fuck me!" she screamed, then lunged inside my sportcoat and grabbed my gun out of its holster and leveled it at me. We both froze, and for long seconds there was silence in the corridor. Then she screamed "Murderer!" one last time, threw my gun against the corridor wall and ran away from me.

I retrieved the gun and made for the elevator, thinking— Oh God, oh God, oh God, was it all for nothing? Was Sol dead?

A large young doctor caught up with me outside the elevator. He was scared, but he wanted to know what was going on. I showed him my P.I.'s photostat and told him I was on a case and was licensed to carry a gun. He seemed satisfied. Then I asked him, "Is Sol Kupferman dead?"

"No," he said, "he's going to make it."

I don't remember what I felt as I left the hospital, except that there was nothing left for me in Los Angeles. Even though Sol was going to live, Jane's hatred of me held a brutal finality. Our last moments together had been so ugly that I could never surmount them. I got in my car and drove to San Francisco.

## 15

I spent a week in San Francisco, waiting for my passport to come through, getting immunized and buying clothes and other provisions for a trip to Europe. I left the night of August 10, flying to New York with two suitcases and twenty-five thousand dollars in cash and traveler's checks. Before I left, I sent Mark Swirkal five thousand dollars in traveler's checks and told him to destroy the tapes.

I got moderately drunk on the plane and full-out drunk in my hotel room near Kennedy International.

The following day I caught a Lufthansa flight to Munich. I was in Germany for two months, drunk and sober. I took a steamer up the Rhine. I caught the Berlin Philharmonic under Karajan. They were magnificent, but only part of me was there for the performance. I visited Beethoven House in Bonn and Beethoven's grave. I didn't feel what I thought I would. I made love to a lot of very beautiful, high-priced German prostitutes. At the Wagner Festival in Bayreuth I got drunk and beat up two British students who seemed to be bothering a young Fraulein. In Stuttgart I broke down sobbing in a beer garden and was hospitalized with incipient d.t.'s.

At the end of October I flew back to America and settled in San Francisco. I rented an apartment in Pacific Heights and looked around for investments, something creative. I couldn't find anything, and Frisco began to pall. It was too beautiful, too ethnic, too counter-culture. The people I passed on the street seemed to be congratulating themselves on their good taste in living there.

In May of the following year I returned to L.A. Repatriated to my smogbound home town, I started to get on with the business of my life. I bought a house in the Hollywood Hills, near the Yamashiro Skyroom. I invested badly. First

I set myself up as a sandwich entrepreneur with a small restaurant near the Music Center. It was a lunch and after-concert place that featured jumbo sandwiches named after composers. I was hoping the place would turn into a hang-out for musicians from the Philharmonic, but it never happened. Finally, after an investment of eleven months and eighty grand, the joint folded. My next investment was safer and turned into a resounding success: I bought a liquor store on 3rd and Western in the heart of the old neighborhood. I've got a smart black guy who runs it for a grand a month and ten percent of the action, and a smart tax lawyer to help me hold onto my money. All I do is sit back and rake it in. As of this writing, I am worth seven hundred fifty six thousand.

Shortly after returning to Los Angeles, I got a letter, postmarked New York from Jane Baker:

Dear Fritz:

It has taken me a long time getting around to writing this letter, because it has taken me a long time to resolve my feelings about you. I apologize for my actions on the day of August 2. It was absurd to call you a killer. At the time I blamed you for Sol's heart attack, which was ridiculous, but understandable. To me you were the catalyst of all those terrible events that awful summer. Later I learned that they had been set in motion many years before, and all you did was stumble into them and try to help the victims as best you could. Thank you for that. Sol has told me that you acted courageously and were responsible for lifting a terrible yoke off his back.

Sol is doing very well, by the way, and so am I. I am attending Juilliard and getting good! Some day I will be a good cellist, worthy of the Strad I play with and the love Sol has given me. Sol is here in New York, too, and is enjoying his retirement and nurturing a new fondness for modern art.

I feel strange about you, Fritz, and somehow guilty that I couldn't love you. I know you had put great hopes on our being together. I sensed in you a desperate loneliness and a great thwarted love of beauty that contradicted the violence that seemed to define your character. Try to pursue that love of beauty, Fritz, try.

Maybe if you listened to less violent music, it would help. Beethoven and the romantics sometimes tend to create violent emotions in people already prone to violence. Listen to some baroque, enjoy the delicacy of it. Listen to the impressionists, they have a great statement to make, one I know you could appreciate.

I have to go now. Thank you for all the help you gave Sol and me. Sol won't tell me the whole story, but I know you acted bravely, and with great concern for us. Try to love. I will always remember you fondly.

Sincerely,
Jane Baker

I do try to love. Sometimes it's easy, sometimes it's hard. Sometimes I'm drunk, sometimes I'm sober. Sometimes I think of Fat Dog and his "plan" for me and wake up shaking. Sometimes I forget completely about his malevolent genius. Why me? Since that summer I have interviewed at least a hundred people who knew Fat Dog, and I still have no inkling.

Walter died last year of cirrhosis of the liver. He was thirty-four. His mother had him buried with a Christian Science service. I got drunk and disrupted it. The fuzz came and busted me, but all it cost me was a hundred dollar fine. I miss him terribly. Some night I'm going to steal his coffin and transport it to the beach, where a big raft will be waiting. I'll put Walter on the raft, ignite it, and send it out to sea. I'll have speakers hooked up all along the beach to blast out Wagner as my beloved comrade floats to a fiery Valhalla.

I get restless sometimes at night and go for long walks on golf courses. While walking the fairways I feel very much in touch with some kind of transient spirit world, a world in constant ellipsis.

When I think of what happened that summer I think not of myself, but of the other people involved. Nothing that went before or will happen after can touch that summer when I was part of the insane, tragic music of so many people's lives. That summer was my concerto for orchestra

—each instrument in the orchestra having a voice equal, yet distinct from all the others.

So I go on, heeding Jane's advice. I have not performed violence on a human being since hurting the two boys in Bayreuth. I try to appreciate beauty. Most of the time I'm equal to the task, but sometimes my mind turns to wild flights of fantasy, envisioning other electric calms and moral stands that might bring me permanent salvation. When I think of these things, my reason and love of beauty desert me and I hang suspended like a bizarre hovercraft in a holding pattern over Los Angeles. But I hold.

I listen to a lot of music.